The King

was in his

Counting House

I0628300

Daniel McCoy

Racing House

ISBN 978-1-84327-937-2

The Racing House Press
20 Cambridge Drive
London SE12 8AJ, UK

1

The big problem with being dead is that there's fuck all you can do about it. I told Tony this but he wasn't having it. Only gone and got married, hadn't he. Three months later I finally get him out to the pub again and what happens? Come nine o'clock he tells me he has to go home. I ask him why and he says his beloved's Granny had just snuffed it and she's all upset and wants him back home. They was going to have some sort of session with a weegee board or something to try and get in touch and see if the old bird is all right up there. I had to laugh. I could see from his face that even he didn't really believe what he was saying but he couldn't admit to himself the real reason he had to go was that the wife didn't like him being out late and coming home pissed.

How the mighty was fallen. I mean, we are talking about a man who used to think nothing of sinking ten pints a night and then going out and having the biggest doner kebab you have ever seen in your life. All the trimmings—tomatoes, onions lettuce and a pile of meat the size of the Mount Everest. Like as not, he'd splatter it across the pavement outside the shop. But if that happened he would be straight back in to have another— and another, if he'd had a real skinfull. He must have been the biggest customer of every kebab shop in this part of South London. I ain't never seen a live kebab. Must be funny-looking creatures, judging by what you see turning on them spindles, but I tell you this. They was in serious danger of going extinct when Tone was in his prime. The boy could scoff for England.

Now I was looking at a broken man. "You don't understand, Spence," he says. "We all have to grow up sometime. I can't be going out boozing every night. Me and Prunella wants to settle down and have kids." (Prunella? I ask you, Prunella!!) I understood only too fucking well. Time to get serious. "Well if you feel like that Tone you can fuck off." He looked at me, shook his head sadly, and then off he fucked. He'll be back when he's been Prunella'd up to his eyeballs. They always come back.

Meanwhile what was I going to do for the rest of the evening? Looking round the boozer, it didn't look too promising. There was only a handful of people in. Hardly surprising. Place was a tip. Only reason we come in was that it was about fifty yards from Tone's love nest. Ain't nobody going to make a pilgrimage to the place. All the paint was peeling. The carpet hadn't never been cleaned; it practically crawled along the floor. The decoration was some London Palladium posters from the fifties—MCs in dickie bows with mouths like the Blackwall tunnel and chorus girls kicking their legs up and waving their fannies in the air. Judging by the dust they hadn't never been touched since they was put up.

And the beer was total piss. Not that the punters seemed to give a toss. In one corner there was a pair of shaven-headed, tattooed bozos, shouting at each other and playing pool. In the other corner was a couple who sat there not moving, not saying nothing. He had a beer belly so big it must have been years since he seen his feet and she had hair that stuck out like candy floss, so white she must have washed it in Domestos. You practically needed shades to look at it. Sitting all by himself in the middle was an old geezer—Scotch, they're always fucking Scotch—whose marbles had long gone. He just sat there, his pint in front of him, swearing to himself with the spit dribbling down his chin.

"Fuckinbastardenglishcuntinwhatdysayjimmy ...."

So I got talking to the barmaid, Maureen. Not exactly beautiful but—how should I put it?—perky. Plenty out front and plenty behind, lacy top and a skirt just above the knee, tight enough to see the cheeks of her arse and a little bulge of suspender. She sprayed on so much *O de Comeandgivemeone* you got a blast of it from 20 feet away. I wasn't that interested really, but anything was better than watching old Jock McFuckbrain drooling into his beer. We got chatting and she kept giving me drinks on the house. Said the manager wouldn't even notice. The bastard was his own best customer apparently. He was lying upstairs on the bed in his underpants, pissed out of his head, watching dirty videos and tossing himself off. She told me he never even bothered to come down to lock up these days. She reckoned the landlords was already on to him. Chance was he would be out before Christmas and like as not behind bars. "Only bars he's ever likely to be behind."

I was well bladdered by closing time, but I had to show a little gratitude and give her a hand clearing up the tables. Then, it was "could she share my cab?" Her place was on my way home. Then, "would I take her to her door?" The stairs were dark and there could be muggers and God knows what about. Then, "just come in for a moment while I turn on the light". It was then I find out her old man is out on his Territorial Army exercises and she had exercises of a different sort in mind. Before I could say a word she had her tongue so far down my throat it was practically wiping my arse. I was gasping for breath, going down for the third time, when there was a loud ring at the door. It was the cabbie wanting to know where his fare was. "Yes." I was thinking to myself, "Saved by the bell!" But she was up, across the room, knickers round her knees, had the door open, bunged the cabbie his fare and was back on top before I could make a move.

I heard somewhere it was treason to prong a soldier's moll and you could still get topped for treason. I was past caring. Whatever they give you for it, I already done worse. I was hung, drawn and fucking quartered. She had thighs that could crack a cannonball. And talk about a gobble. I had to have a good look afterwards to make sure it was still there. It was, but only just. It weren't coming out to play for a good while, that's for sure.

I did get breakfast in the morning, though. Full English, including the banger. Not bad really. Least I deserved, in my humble opinion. Perked me up a bit but, what with the booze and the rest, I still felt like I'd been dragged backwards through an elephant's arsehole. Then she was off to the day job; something in the Council so she said. I thought I'd better give the office a try. Bound to be something to do there and if I still felt like living death I could try a session at the Belleville Massage Parlour. They do you very nicely there.

Didn't have long to wait for the bus. Not like the old days when they hunted in packs. You waited ages for one and then half a dozen turn up at once. Somebody must be doing something right. Fuck knows how that happened. The bus takes the tour of our beautiful borough, past all the sights. Past the old Odeon, was a cinema, closed; was a bingo hall, closed; was a snooker hall, closed; now just closed. On past the dump, calls itself a "Recycling Centre" now. Still a dump. Past plenty of churches—the Redeemed Christian Church of God, black, packed on Sundays; the Everlasting Light of Our Saviour, black, packed on Sundays; the Good Shepherd, white, few old women on Sundays; the Christadelphians, ain't never seen anyone go in there; and lots more. Then it goes past the dog track, or what's left of it. They don't want the working man to enjoy himself no more. It's being knocked down and they're building flats for prices you wouldn't fucking believe. They reckon the yuppies are going to come to Dogswell because everywhere else in London is too expensive. If they do they're in for a shock.

Finally we get into Dogswell High Street, the biggest collection of pound shops, fast food joints, pawnbrokers and bookies parlours in the entire Universe. "Nothing wrong with Dogswell High Street that a couple of bulldozers couldn't put right." as my mate Tony used to say, before he caught a dose of the Prunellas that was. Hitler could have done the place a favour if he'd flattened it, but even he couldn't be arsed. His boys just flew right over and done the East End instead. Says it all, don't it?

The bus stops right outside the office. There's a brass plate on the door, which in my state I could just about read if I screwed my eyes up: The Weintraub Location Agency. That's me. The office is above the Oh Calcutta Tandoori. Can be a bit of a whiff of Chicken Vindaloo at times, but the rent is cheap. You can't have everything. I was just about to go in when there was a sudden rumpus from the corner shop next door. A couple of the usual Dogswell tearaways rushed out followed by two brown boys and a little brown lady. I asked her what happened.

"They are always trying to steal things from the shop. Beer, food, cigarettes, anything. Then they yell insults at us. Call us Pakis. Why do they say things like that?"

"Don't take no notice of them luv. They're just scum. Nothing wrong with being from Pakistan, is there?"

"But we are not from Pakistan, we are from Bangladesh."

"Bangladesh? What's that?"

She give me a bit of a look. "Bangladesh is a country. It is near India, like Pakistan."

You learn something every day. I went up the stairs and opened the door. The nail-filing, gum-chewing, phone-yapping hoorie that calls itself a receptionist—aka Fanackapan—was looking straight at me.

"Someone to see you in your office."

I looked at my watch just to check. It was just after half past nine.

"Who comes to see me at this time of the morning? What do they want?"

Fanackapan gave her usual imitation of a corpse trying hard not to laugh.

"Dunno. She wouldn't say. Said she wanted to see you personal."

That was all I needed, the way I was feeling. Women wanting to see me "personal" always meant some bird in floods of tears because her old man had run off, leaving her with the kids, the bills, the HP payments and probably the payday lender to keep sweet. Like as not he'd gone off with her best friend, or her sister, or even her mother—you'd be surprised how many women round here can't keep their hands off their daughter's boyfriends. I even had one who run off with a vicar, a woman vicar as it happened, though I don't think he was that fussy anyway. He used to bang her on the altar. May God have mercy on their souls. And like as not our wronged woman wouldn't be mad at him, she "just wanted him back". I give up. Some of us can spot a scumbag at a hundred yards but there's plenty that never learn. Roll on brain transplants I say.

I opened the door to my office and got a very big surprise.

2

What was sitting there was the most expensive woman I had ever seen in my life. Expensive clothes, expensive face, expensive way of sitting and a very expensive whiff of perfume. Don't ask me what it was but it must have been worth at least a pony a sniff. You don't expect much change out of a million for one of her sort. She looked up as I came in.

"Mr Weintraub?"

"Yes. What can I do for you?"

She held out her hand. "My name is Rachel Silver. I was hoping you might be able to help me."

The handshake was soft but firm if you know what I mean, like she was used to dealing with loads of servants or whatever. I sat down and looked her from across my desk. Blond, one of those haircuts that turn up round the ears. Thirties, I would guess, though these types spend so much on themselves you never can tell. I don't mind admitting I'm partial to posh totty and normally I might have felt a knob-throb or two. But on this occasion it could have been Marilyn Monroe draped starkers across a four-poster and I wouldn't have wanted to know. Besides, I couldn't work out why she would come to see me. Maybe she found the only cabbie in London that would come south of the River and he dumped her in Dogswell when he realised he hadn't a fucking clue where he was. Anyway, I thought we had better start with the usual.

"Would you like some tea or coffee?"

"Tea would be very nice."

I gave Fanackapan a shout. About time it did something.

"Could you do some tea for us please Miss Simmonds."

Fanackapan came in; it was wearing a skirt that couldn't have been much more than six inches long. I've seen wider tape-measures. She stood there, chewing gum like she hadn't a care in the world. No question; she has definitely got to go.

"How do you like it? Milk? Sugar?" she asked.

"Is it China or India?"

"Must be India. Comes from Patels on the corner."

"I'll just have it without anything then, thank you."

"And I'll have the usual, Miss Simmonds."

She looked at me with a 'is that the usual pint and whisky chaser, or is it the usual double brandy or do you just want a cup of tea?' stare and then went off to do the necessary.

I thought I had better find out what this was all about.

"How exactly can I help?"

She breathed in, then sighed, then it came out. "It's my husband."

What a surprise. It always is, unless of course you're a man and then it's the wife. Husbands and wives are what keeps yours truly in business. Three cheers for the great institution of marriage say I.

"What's he done?"

She wasn't having that. She shook her head.

"Oh no. He hasn't done anything. It's what has been done to him. I think he may have been kidnapped."

"Ah. Stop right there." said I, "That's criminal. We don't do criminal. We're finders. If your husband runs off with his secretary or whatever, we can find him, wherever he was hiding. But if it's a crime you have to go to the Police. More than our licence is worth for us to get involved."

I always put that bit in about the licence to impress. As the chairman and founder of the National Association of Location Agencies, I awarded the licence to myself. The real reason I don't do criminal is because I don't want to get my head bashed in. There are some right animals in our part of the world. I should have told her not to bother with Dogswell cop shop neither. They wouldn't have the foggiest about kidnapping. Murder, rape, GBH, taking and driving away, all the usual—yes. Bang you up as soon as look at you, guilty or not. But kidnapping? You must be joking. How do you spell that madam? Try West End Central. More their sort of crime.

She looked a bit agitated.

"Well, it's a bit more complicated than that. Actually, I think he may have kidnapped himself."

I began to think somebody was having a laugh. Two could play at that game.

"Well, in that case he can pay himself a ransom and we can all live happy ever after."

Now she was getting flustered. I even thought I saw the eyes begin to get a bit wet.

"I don't think you are taking this seriously Mr Weintraub."

"Look," I nearly said "Darling". My usual style is to call all female clients Darling. Saves any embarrassment about forgetting their names. On the other hand, you can be a bit previous with the darlings with some birds. She definitely looked like one of that sort.

"Look Mrs Silver. I don't mean no disrespect, but you're obviously a long way from home. Why would you come all this way with a story that is a bit unusual, to put it mildly? If you just want to find your husband, there are big name private investigators you could use. I hear Hercule Poirot's available right now. You look as if you could afford his fee."

She didn't like that.

"Look, Mr Weintraub, I came because my husband grew up round here. I had an idea that he might be tempted to return to his roots."

"He wouldn't get killed in the rush. Those that can get out of here stay out. Anyway, why pick me to come and see?"

She started blinking.

"Because ..."

"Because what?"

"Because I thought you were, eh, Jewish."

For once in my life I was fucking speechless. Where did that one come from?

"Pardon?"

"I assumed from your name that you were Jewish?"

"What, Spencer?"

"No, Weintraub. That is your real name isn't it?"

"Real as any other. One name don't last long in this game?"

"You mean that it isn't the name you were born with?"

"Certainly not."

"So what was that?"

"You really want to know?"

"Yes."

"Reginald Nutbeam."

"Why did you change it?"

I've heard some fucking stupid questions in my time. Where do you start? I thought I'd spin her a story.

"Well, as it happens there's another Finder called Reg Nutbeam. Operates up North, Luton or somewhere. It's one of the rules of the National Association of Location Agencies—I'm the chairman as it happens—that no two Finders can have the same name. Bit like actors. That outfit of theirs, Equity, says that, if two actors have the same name, one of them has to change it. Same with Finders. It wouldn't do if you looked Reg Nutbeam up in the book and there were two of them. You wouldn't know which was which. You would say that's no good. They can't even sort themselves out. How do they expect to find the person I'm looking for? The other Reg was older than me so I had to change my name. Simple as that."

She gave me a funny look. Not sure she believed me.

"So why did you choose your present name?"

"Ah well, family reasons really."

My Granddad, as it happens, was a big fan of Spencer Tracy. He loved that film *Bells of St Trinians*, where Spencer Tracy played that vicar who looked after all those boys. Wouldn't be allowed now of course. He'd be banged up straight away for kiddie fiddling. But that was then, and anyway I don't think Granddad would have minded a bit of that Kathryn Hepburn neither. He was a dirty old dog.

She perked up at that.

"You mean there *is* a Jewish connection. Is Weintraub a family name?"

Not exactly. Not at all, if I'm honest. Fact is, I was looking for a bit of distinction. I wanted a name that nobody else round here had. I got Weintraub off the back of an American bubblegum packet. "Manufactured by the Weintraub Bubblegum Corp." So, truth to tell, Spencer is a bit short on the kosher credentials. On the other hand I do like a pretty face. If the lady wanted Jewish, the lady could have Jewish. Then I remembered my Granddad was always talking about someone called Holy Moses. Actually it was Holy Fucking Moses. That sounded a bit Jewish. He got the expression off a mate of his in the War, Izzy. They was in the ARP together. Now Izzy *was* Jewish, from the East End. And suddenly I had a brainwave—Jack Charlton.

Jack, as every aficionado of that great year 1966 remembers, was a stalwart of the glorious World Cup team, along with his brother Bobby, now Sir Bobby of course. When Jack hung up his boots, he was looking around for a job and someone suggested managing the Irish football team. Well, Old Jack was always one for a challenge but when he got to Dublin he took a quick look at the bunch of one-legged spud-bashers they had in the Irish team at the time and said to himself, "Sod this for a game of soldiers. I'm going to have to get myself some proper footballers." So he scratched his head for a while and then it come to him. He announced that if your Granny even had a budgerigar called Shamus you was qualified to play for Ireland. Talk about a result! In a couple of weeks he had half the footballers in England banging on his door, begging to get a game for Ireland. So I thought where Jack goes Spencer will follow: if your Granddad had an ARP mate called Izzy, you was entitled to call yourself Jewish. Stands to reason.

"I'ain't sure about Weintraub, but my Granddad was always talking about someone called Holy Moses. He was Jewish, wasn't he?"

She didn't seem that impressed.

"Next you'll be telling me there were rabbis in your family?"

She was trying to be a bit sarky, so I was a bit sarky back.

"Not recently. That's what they got that quaringteen for. Keeps all them mad dogs out the country. But I've been having a think and I'm fairly sure I'm definitely part Jewish on my Granddad's side of the family."

She give a bit of a smile. The old Weintraub patter was doing the business as usual.

"Actually Jewishness descends from the female line, but never mind. You must think this is all a little odd. My husband and I *are* Jewish, but we're reform. We're not what you would call devout. It's just that coming down here and not knowing anyone—it was a hunch really. I just didn't know what to do—I just thought it might be easier to talk to someone who, well, shared a sensibility, if you know what I mean."

"Oh, course. Sensible's my middle name. So what exactly is this all about?"

Right on cue Fanackapan barged in without a by your leave. She stopped chewing for a second as she put down the tray.

"D'you want biscuits? We got digestives and them ones with chocolate and jam in."

"No thank you."

Fanackapan gave her best "suit yourself" look and tottered off. If them heels were any higher they'd be stilts.

Rachel Silver leaned back and—what's the word?—pursed her lips. Pursed is the right word. Purses are for money and you don't get teeth like that for free. Not with the NHS these days. It's a second mortgage job to get a filling. Fucking disgrace. It's a wonder there's any teeth left in England.

"My husband is an investment banker. He's a director of Goldbury & Newman; you may have heard of them. Last week, Tuesday, he was supposed to go to Geneva for a couple of days. He's often away on business. Later that day I received a call from one of the other directors asking if Reuben—that's my husband—was at home. I was very surprised. I said, 'No, he's in Geneva. Didn't you know?' There was silence and then he asked if he could come and see me at my home that evening. Naturally I was a bit worried and tried to ring Reuben but his mobile was switched off. That wasn't unusual. He always switched it off during meetings and he could be in a meeting at any hour of the day or night so I left a message asking him to ring.

"That evening one of the Bank's directors, Bernard Cadogan, the Deputy Chairman, arrived. He said that Reuben had been due in Geneva but hadn't caught his flight and hadn't contacted either the Bank or the people he was due to see. And then he looked rather embarrassed and said there was another matter. Had Reuben mentioned anything about an account at the Bank? I said that Reuben didn't often discuss his work with me. The Bank frowned on it and he certainly hadn't said anything about any particular account. Why did he ask? At that he looked even more embarrassed. He said this account was of a particularly sensitive nature. It was probably nothing but, what with Reuben being out of contact, I would understand that they had to make a few enquiries. When I did hear from Reuben I must tell him to contact the Bank immediately so that it could all be sorted out. I can tell you Mr Weintraub, I didn't know what to do. I told him that I was thinking of contacting the police to report him missing but I asked if I did would that mean he would be in any sort of trouble? He asked me to wait until the next day to see if he got in touch."

She stopped for a bit and looked at me. I looked back. I had to admit it made a change from the usual "My husband's run off with Doreen from next door and he's taken all the housekeeping too." On the other hand, what was all that shit about kidnapping?

"So what you're saying is that there wasn't no kidnapping at all. Your old man—Reuben—has just done a runner with whatever there was in that account."

The head shaking started again.

"The next morning the same director called. He sounded, how shall I say, distant. No, they hadn't heard from Reuben but the good news was that the problems with the account had been cleared up. So why, I asked him, had Reuben gone missing? He felt Reuben had been under a lot of strain lately, a lot of very important projects, and he probably just wanted to get away to clear his head. He was bound to get in contact soon."

"Did you believe him?"

"I wanted to, desperately. I wanted to believe that it must have all been a mistake. On the other hand, I had this nagging doubt. Reuben was a director. The Bank would have been terrified about news of a director being involved in impropriety getting out. Their clients would have left in droves. They would certainly have made up any deficit and no one but a very few directors would have known. And if Reuben hadn't done anything wrong, why had he disappeared? I didn't buy the strain theory. Reuben just wasn't like that. I don't mind telling you I was frantic. I kept calling Reuben's mobile but it was always switched off. I spent a sleepless night, worrying about it all, and I decided to go to the Police."

"So, what did they say?"

"I didn't go. Yesterday morning I got a call to say if I wanted to see my husband again I was to follow instructions that I would receive and on no account to contact the Police."

"Who was it?"

"I don't know. I didn't recognise the voice. It sounded funny—metallic, maybe even artificial. A bit like that scientist, what's his name? Stephen Hawking. He said that I was to prepare to transfer £2 million to an account and that they would give me details of the account very soon. If I didn't do so I would never see my husband again. As you can imagine, Mr Weintraub, this was the most enormous shock. I had to sit down and try to get a grip of my emotions. I just didn't know what to think. It was then that I had this awful suspicion that perhaps Reuben had arranged the whole thing, that he had withdrawn the money from his account, stolen from the bank and was now trying to get his hands on more by faking his kidnapping."

By this time I was saying to myself, "Spencer, old son, this is a wind up." A mental deficient baboon wouldn't believe half of it. Nobody comes down here talking of kidnaps, two million quid and the rest. Take a look. Beautiful downtown Dogswell it is not. Besides, I may be the dog's bollocks finder-wise, but even I don't flatter myself that I'm Finder of choice to the Quality. And as for me being Jewish and all, it just didn't make sense. On the other hand, the motto of our profession is "The client is

King"—or Queen in this case—and this particular client looked like it was good for a bob or two, while, as it happened, at that moment in time, yours truly was more than a bit short in the spondulicks department. Two can play the wind up game, Spencer, I said to myself, keep turning the handle. Softly, softly, catchee money.

"Very interesting story, Mrs Silver. Not the sort of tale we usually hear round here. What exactly would you like us to do for you?"

"I would like you to find my husband, of course."

Where did I start?

"Without wishing to state the bleeding obvious, if you'll pardon the expression, if he really has kidnapped himself, why don't you just pay the £2 million he's asking for? After all, it's his own money."

She didn't like that.

"No, no. I had better explain further. Not all Jews are rich, whatever you may think. Reuben came from a poor family. His father came over here just before the war a child refugee. He ran a cobblers shop near here for many years. I understand it was demolished a few years ago."

Funny enough, that rang a bell.

"Was it in Hope Street, just up there on the right, off the High Street? Got knocked down for Council offices."

"Yes, I think it may have been."

"I remember the old boy. Spoke with a funny accent. My Mum used to take the shoes there to be mended when we was kids. There you are. Small world, innit?"

"Yes, I suppose it is. What I'm trying to say is Reuben doesn't have that sort of money. He has only recently been made a Director of the Bank and, while he could be described as very comfortably off by most standards, he doesn't have millions, yet."

"So why would he be asking for it?"

"Because I do. My father left me a great deal of money, but he left it in trust for my use only. It's not that he didn't trust Reuben—he liked him really—it's just that he was very cautious with money. That's why he made so much of it."

"What's stopping you paying it?"

"Because I haven't the faintest idea what has happened to him. If it were just a question of paying £2 million to have my husband back safe and sound, I would write a cheque this minute. But has he been kidnapped or not? Is he in financial trouble or not? I just don't know …"

I spotted tears. Blubbing birds are a bit of an occupational hazard in this line of work. I always have a special box of tissues handy just for the occasion—pale lavender with smell to match. Very soothing, so I'm told.

"So why ask us to find him. Why not get yourself a big-time private firm?"

"Because he once told me—it was on our honeymoon actually and we were talking about where we would go to hide away from the world—he said that if he wanted to disappear he would come here. Much easier to hide in the anonymity of a place like this, where half the people are immigrants anyway, than on some Spanish Costa, where he would stand out like a sore thumb. If I was going to find him I had to start somewhere, so I thought of here. And then I thought it would be better to use someone who knew the area, so I looked in the Yellow Pages and saw your name. Your ad said you found people. How do you do it?"

Now there's a question.

"We have our methods, but you wouldn't expect me to divulge all the tricks of the trade, would you. Commercial confidentiality and all that. And since you brought up the subject, there is the little matter of the fee."

"Yes, of course. How much do you charge."

Paydays have been a bit thin lately so I thought I'd whack on a surcharge and see how it went down.

"We charge £350 a day for my services and £250 a day for my associates, plus VAT and expenses of course."

"Your associates?"

"Yes, they're specialists in this sort of work. Top boys. Essential if we're to get a result."

"And how long do you think it will take?"

"How long's a piece of string? But we've got to get something to you by the end of the week, don't we, so you can decide whether you're going to pay this ransom or not. "

That brought on the tears again. Another hanky.

"That's fine, that's fine. Whatever it takes. Just be as quick as you can."

I called Fanackapan in.

"Miss Simmonds, will you draw up our standard contract for Mrs Silver. Our usual rates, £350 a day for me and £250 a day for the associates."

She looked like she'd been smacked round the gob by a wet haddock. She don't do discreet that girl. I definitely feel a P45 coming on.

"No time to lose. Let's get down to business. We got two possibilities. One, that your husband really has been kidnapped, in which case he could be anywhere, and two, that he's done a runner and he could be around here somewhere. Not a lot to go on, either way, is it? Let's start with what we have got. This phone call. Do you know the number?"

"Yes, it came up on my phone. I wrote it down, here."

"OK, that's a start. You were told that you had to pay money into an account. Do you know who owns the account?"

"No. I don't even have the account details. He said he would be in touch again with them but I haven't heard anything more. I know people who could do a search for me if I had those details but I'm willing to bet it would turn out to be a nominee account?"

She had me there.

"A what?"

"An account in the name of a company, which will be owned by another company or a number of companies all of which will be registered somewhere where they don't have to disclose the names of directors or anybody connected with them. And once the money is in the account it will be spirited off somewhere else, to banks all round the globe, so that it will be untraceable, even by expert accountants."

As a lead that didn't sound too promising. Even going to my local bank does my head in.

"Do you have a picture of your husband?"

She fished inside her bag and took out a small leather picture frame. He looked like your standard issue banker wanker to me. Clean-shaven, sharp suit and tie, with that look that says we have all the money you need but it will cost you a packet.

"This'll have to do for the moment. Now we need to know who he's been contacting. What about his phone and computer?"

"His only phone—the only one that I know of anyway—is a Blackberry that he uses for work. He probably has it with him, but it always goes to voicemail when I try it. He did have a computer but it broke a couple of years ago. He uses an iPad now."

"What, all that important bank work on an iPad?"

"Oh no, they're not allowed to do any bank work on computer outside the office. Security you see. These devices are easily hacked so I'm told. Reuben just uses it for web browsing and personal emails."

"Is he on Facebook or Twitter or anything like that?"

Facebook and Twitter and all that social media bollocks are the location agent's dream. You wouldn't believe the number of dozos who scarper but still say what they've been up to and post pictures of themselves on the Internet, usually with a hand on the tits of their latest squeeze. Like as not they'll say they've been up at such and such a club or pub or else there's something there that will tell us where they are. Easiest money I ever make.

"No, the Bank frowns on that sort of thing. They feel it might lead to compromising situations."

"Well what about the personal stuff—letters, bills and all that?"

"My personal assistant and I handle all those things. I know this is going to sound funny to you, but for a banker he really isn't very good with money. I have a degree in anthropology from Oxford and an MBA from Harvard. I think I can manage the Council Tax."

"Is there anything else that might help—notes, letters that sort of thing?"

"Nothing. Believe me I searched high and low when this thing happened to see if there was anything that might give me a clue as to where he had gone."

"Would you mind if I took a look? Could be something you missed. And I'd like to take a look at the iPad too, if possible."

She seemed a bit hesitant. Probably didn't want me bringing down the tone of her place.

"I suppose you must. Is there anything else you need to know?"

"Yes, we need details of all his credit cards and bank accounts. Sooner or later he's got to want a bit of cash or use a card and then we should know where he's been. And is there somewhere he likes to go—club, music, theatre, that sort of thing? Does he play golf or tennis or anything?"

She shook her head.

"He's not much of a joiner, I'm afraid. He leaves all social matters to me and he's not very sporty either. But bank accounts and credit cards, I don't understand. Aren't they all confidential? How can you possibly find out if money is being taken out?"

I put on my most professional expression—a bit smile, a bit wise nod, a bit don't you worry your pretty little head. I've been perfecting it for a long time. It don't often fail.

"That's what you pay us for Mrs Silver. We have our methods. Nothing illegal of course, but we like to keep it in the profession. It's not something that you need to know or should want to know."

"Yes of course, I quite understand. Is there anything else you need from me?"

Certainly was. The time was right to ask for a bit of cash upfront.

"There is one thing. We normally require a deposit for a job like this. Two days fees for myself and one associate. Fully refundable of course if not entirely satisfied."

I always throw that "fully refundable" bit in. Sounds good but the chances of anyone getting anything back is zero. The shyster that done the small print in our contract was an evil genius.

"No problem. Will you take a cheque?"

Actually there was a problem. The bank just changed our overdraft limit, "because of your past credit history" Fucking cheek, after all them banksters done! We was already way over the new limit. Any cheque would just be snaffled by the bank.

"Well we *can* take a cheque but our financial advisors won't let us start work on a job until the cheque has cleared, which as you know can take a good few days. No disrespect but we've had some problems with rubber cheques in the past so our financial advisors make 'no start until cheque cleared' an iron rule. You know what financial advisors are like."

"I take your point. Would a credit card be acceptable?"

"That would be much better. We could start straight away then. Ah, here's Miss Simmonds with the contract."

Fanackapan put the papers down and her mouth did a big silent Oooh.

"If you would just sign there and there Mrs Silver, we can then get to work."

"I would like to read it first."

"Naturally. Please do. It's the standard contract you will see with any member of our association. There's a little bit of legal jargon here and there but that's lawyers for you. Protects you as well as us of course."

She started reading and I could see her eyes beginning to look a bit glassy.

"Oh I suppose it's all straightforward. Where did you say I signed?"

She took a gold pen out of her handbag and put her monicker, all girlie swirls, on the contract. Now I just had to sort out the card.

"I'll just go and get the terminal for your card. Won't be a minute."

We can't actually do the card ourselves. The bank would charge an arm and a leg for the privilege, even if they would let us do it—which they wouldn't. I do it for cash with Ali who runs the Oh Calcutta Tandoori downstairs. Actually it's a nice little system. There's no Vat on restaurant food so I stick the Vat on my bill, run it though him and, hey presto, twenty percent extra for free. When we first started he wanted the whole of the Vat bit for himself. I wasn't having none of that and I eventually beat him down to twelve and a half percent—still criminal if you ask me but what can you do?

Ali was in his usual place in his little cupboard of an office behind a mountain of paper. "You must have won the lottery Mr Spencer." he said when I told him what to put through his till.

"Big client Ali. Important job."

I took the terminal back upstairs and she put her card in. You have to hold it a certain way otherwise it don't pick up the signal so I held it for her and shut my eyes as she put her pin number in. I pressed the button, the terminal said "card accepted" and out came the receipt. I handed it to her and she started reading.

"What's this? 26 poppadoms, 12 Tandoori Specials, 32 bottles of Cobra beer (600cl)—and I see there's a lot more."

"Ah, apologies, I should have mentioned it before. That's our special client confidentiality system. We do a lot of domestics and some men round here can turn very nasty if they think their wife or girlfriend is spying on them—which they might do if they caught sight of a mention of the Weintraub Location Agency. So we always put though our bills as meals in an Indian restaurant. Nothing to get suspicious about then."

"Very thoughtful." she said as if she didn't really mean it. "Are we done now?"

"Yes, I think everything is satisfactory. You can rest assured that if your husband can be found we will find him."

She said she didn't need a cab so I showed her downstairs and into the street. I came back upstairs and parked my carcase in the office chair. "Spencer, old son," I said to myself, "this looks like it's your lucky day. Maybe you should feel like shit more often."

3

I went round to see her a bit later. She was at her "town house", a nice little pad in the better end of Chelsea, Baring Square, just off Sloane Square. I was let in by the home help. Something foreign. Couldn't understand a word she was saying. Rachel Silver was lounging on one of them sofas without a back. She was dressed even more expensive that when I first saw her—mostly cream, silk or cashmere or something. I ain't too good on that sort of thing. The way she was sitting her skirt came just above her knee and this time I noticed her legs, the sort I would pay serious money to get acquainted with any other time. The room we was in was not quite as big as the Albert Hall and had a grand piano in the corner. The floor was very fancy wood with a few even fancier rugs strewn around and there was some big pictures on the walls. Very modern. Something told me they wasn't prints.

She wasn't exactly unfriendly but she didn't seem too keen to have me around. I get that sort of attitude sometimes and my way round it is to try a bit of chat about themselves. Nothing too personal just something to oil the wheels so to speak. She told me about her Daddy, who was dead now, but had been the Big Cheese at the Bank. She was definitely Daddy's girl. Everything he did was wonderful. They had a "country estate" apparently. Something Daddy give them as a wedding present. I got the impression that he wasn't that keen on her husband to start with but had come round eventually. Nothing new there.

Once she'd told me a bit about herself she wanted to know a bit about me.

"'Location Agent', that's a rather unusual, ah, profession, isn't it? How did you come to be doing that?"

"Long story. I'm not sure you would really be interested."

"No really, I am interested. A Location Agent is not something I had ever heard of before."

"That's because we like to keep it low profile so to speak, so nobody knows we're after them. I got into it a bit by accident. I left school at sixteen. I was in the duffers class. No point in hanging around. Only got one exam, Woodwork. I can still do a mean tenon joint, though I say so myself. Anyway, I did a load of jobs, a bit of everything—labouring, car mechanic, bookies runner, a bit of plumbing—you name it I probably done it. Ended up working for a firm of debt-collectors. It was run by a bloke called Steptoe. He was a right bastard, if you'll excuse my language, made Scrooge look like Father Christmas."

She gave a laugh at that.

"I seem to remember Scrooge did turn into Father Christmas."

"Yeah, I seen the film too, but you know what I mean. Steptoe would take the last penny out of a starving widow's purse and he wasn't too fussy how he done it, neither. Anyway, there's always plenty who owe money around here but a lot of them aren't too keen to pay it back and they do a runner. So Steptoe had me try to track them down. Turned out that I was good at it. I often knew where they was going before they even got there. After a while the word got about and I was asked to do a bit of finding on the side—husbands what had skipped off, tenants that had done a moonlight, all that sort of thing. It started to pay and in the end I told Steptoe to stick his job. I'd had enough of the grief and earache it give me. You should have heard all the yelling and crying when we used to come for the money. So I set myself up in business, as you see."

She looked a bit surprised.

"You can make a living at it?"

"No shortage of people needing to be found round here. I've got a few regular clients, like the local letting agents and betting shops. I do a bit of work for the Council sometimes when one of their tenants goes awol. Then there's the single jobs, like yours."

"So you're willing to look for anybody, whether they want to be found or not?"

"Yeah, mostly, though I do turn a job down sometimes."

"Really, why?"

"If there's kids involved. Fathers or mothers running off with the kids and not letting the other know where they are. Things get very messy then. Clients don't always tell the truth, no disrespect, but there's ordinary lies and there's lies when kids is involved. You wouldn't believe the stories some people make up. I don't usually want to know."

"I gather from that that you do sometimes take them on."

"Sometimes. I ain't exactly soft-hearted but sometimes you hear stories that bring tears to your eyes. I help them out but after that I let the others—lawyers, social workers and the rest—sort things out. I don't want to get involved."

"Very commendable, I'm sure. So all you do is find people?"

"Not all. I do a few other things, like private security—bit of personal protection, bodyguards, and bouncers for night clubs. The local coppers are always looking to earn a bit extra."

From the way she was looking I was talking about a world that she didn't know existed. So I thought best to move on and get down to the business in hand.

She said her husband had a little office and we went to look though any papers. There was nothing much there. I had a suspicion that it had been cleared out. She gave me bank details for their joint account and one she said her husband used for things he bought himself. Then we had a look at his iPad. I checked the browsing history. That usually gives a clue to what someone has been up to but there was nothing. Then we look at the email program. It could still be opened but everything before he disappeared was wiped. There was a few later ones, mostly the usual spam. There was just one that was different:

Dear Mr Silver,

Thank you very much for the lovely flowers. I much appreciated talking to you and I am sure my husband would have been very happy to share ideas with you. It was his life's work, after all.

Good luck with your researches.

Best wishes

Marilyn Haigh

I asked her what it was about. She was a bit vague.

"I'm not sure. Reuben told me he was thinking of writing a book on European history. I know he talked to some people about it, mainly academics I think. This woman mentions his researches so I suppose it was something to do with that."

"Did he ever mention this Marilyn Haigh? "

"Not that I remember. He sent her flowers so I assume she had been helpful to him. Reuben always liked to repay kindnesses."

I took a note of her email address. Worth a follow up. Probably nothing to it but it always looks good to look busy.

...

I went back to the office. Fanackpan gave me the usual cheery look, like I'd brought in a dog turd and plonked it in her lap. She needed something to do.

"Get Dany B to come round."

"I thought you said he was on your mobile."

Talk about buying a dog and barking yourself. Sometimes I think she forgets what she's there for. She finally got her finger working. I heard her talking and then she looks at me.

"When do you want him?"

"ASAP."

She went on talking and then put the phone down.

"Well?"

"Well what?"

"When's he coming round then?"

"Oh, he's down the King William. Says he'll be round soon as he's finished his drink."

That could have been any time that year, knowing Dany B, but as it happened it was less than half an hour before he poked his head round the door.

"Spencer, my man, your summons is answered. Danilbert Bullimore is at your service."

He always talked like that when he'd had at least half a dozen of his specials—rum and Christ knows what. Only time he used his real name. What is it about blacks that they give their kids such dipstick names? Close to child abuse if you ask me.

I wasn't feeling like taking much shit that day.

"Look Dany, if you're bladdered you can fuck off now.

He put on his sorry-for-himself face.

"Sorry Spence. Hard night last night. Needed a little pick-me-up."

I let it go. Dany was a hair of the dog man. Pissed or sober, at least he knew where his arse was, well most of the time anyway, which is more that could be said for most of the bastards round here. He used to be a DS; first black CID Dogswell ever had. Got a lot of stick for it. Served him right. Being a black copper was asking for it from both sides. Toss up who hated you most, the villains or the other coppers. Anyway, he could give as good as he got. Besides, you could do very nicely down Dogswell nick back then if you played your cards right—talk about the Land of Opportunity—but he let it go to his head. Took a very silly drink off a couple of lags who was looking to do the Abbey National on Attlee Grove and wanted to know if any Plod would be around when they was on the job. They was from the Bermondsey Irish mafia and what Dany didn't know was that they was being trailed everywhere by a Scotland Yard undercover squad with some hot shot in charge who thought that bagging a few bent bluebottles—Dany wasn't the only one—would do wonders for his chances of promotion. Four of them went down. Dany got four years, along with a P45 up the arse. Chief Inspector Hot Shot who done him is now in charge of traffic cones in some God-forsaken shithole up North, I am sorry to say. He's been told by his old mates in the Met that if he's ever seen south of Watford he'll be nailed by the bollocks to the middle lane of the M1.

I looked him straight in the eyes. They was both almost looking in the same direction.

"Got a little job for you. You up for it?"

"What's it worth?"

"Hundred and fifty a day."

"Cash in hand?"

Dany didn't like to trouble the taxman, or the vatman.

"OK."

"Expenses?"

"Bus fares."

"Cabs?"

"Only if you have to."

Cab fares. Do not get me on cab fares in this great city of ours. It's a second mortgage job to step in a black cab these days. The Great Train Robbers had nothing on cabbies. You practically have to make an appointment even to speak to them. "Excuse me Sir Cabbie, would you care to enlighten us with a few of your thoughts on the current political situation?" Worse than royalty. Come to think of it, I did hear of a cabbie marrying a commoner the other day.

"You're not giving anything away, as usual Spence. All right, I'm interested. What's it about."

I gave him a bit of the picture.

"Dunno. Could be something, could be nothing. Rich bird turns up this morning—a definite looker as it happens, but that needn't bother you—and says her old man's disappeared. Maybe he's been kidnapped, or maybe he kidnapped himself, so she thinks. From what I can see, he's done a runner. Probably shacked up with some trollop. Shouldn't be too difficult to find him but let's take our time about it. She's obviously got more money than sense, so we can string her along a bit, milk the old expenses."

"Sounds like a few cab rides to me Spence. We got anything to go on?"

"Only his phone number and this other one. She says some- one called her on it saying she won't never see her husband again."

Dany looked at the number and sniffed.

"It's a mobile. They didn't bother to hide it, so a hundred to one on it's nicked or a pay as you go. Probably thrown away by now."

"Probably. Look, we've got to put something in our report, so see if you can find out anything about it."

Dany nodded. Then he looked up and made a puzzled face. He was sobering up.

"You say she's a rich bird. So why'd she come to you?"

I didn't need the third degree.

"My reputation. She's heard of me. I'm well known in rich bird circles."

He guffawed.

"Come off it Spence."

"Well, if you really want to know, it's because she thinks I'm Jewish."

That really set him off.

"Ho, ho ho. So, if she sees me she'll probably think I'm the King of the Zulus."

"Just go and find out where that fucking phone call came from!"

....

He come back late that afternoon.

"Billy the Bone says your credit's no good any more. I had to slip him a score to get the info so I want it back. No joy on Silver's phone. It's been off for days. The other one was a pay as you go, as I thought The only thing he could find out was where it was bought. And guess where? That phone shop, next to Boots on Dogswell High Street."

That was a turn up. So there was a local connection, after all.

"So I thought I'd pay them a visit, turn on a bit of the Met how's-yer-father; see if I could get anything else. At first the bloke behind the counter said he couldn't tell me anything. It was a phone shop; they sold loads of phones. That's what they did. What did I expect? How could he remember any particular one? Anyway, he gets the sales book out and looks up the number. It was sold a couple of months ago and whoever bought it paid cash, so that was no go, but then he says he does remember something. It was the last of that particular model, they were offering them at twenty percent off, and he remembers the bloke who bought it because he saw him again only a couple of days later. There was a march a couple of months ago by the English National Front."

"What, those blockheads always going about waving flags and fighting at football matches?"

"Got it in one. Anyway, there was a bit of a ruck right outside the shop, police and all, and he saw the bloke who bought the phone holding up the ENF banner at the front of the march."

"I remember it now. Any description?"

"White, of course, quite tall—he thought about six feet—thin. Short dark hair, not a baldie like most them, and a scar on his left cheek."

Well, that wasn't bad. Something to go on.

"A nice juicy bit to put in our report, Dany, and from that description we might even be able to find out who this scumbag was. What we need is a bit of gobby Plod who was at this ruck and who'll talk to us. Any ideas?"

"You're spoiled for choice there Spence. Is Jimmy Dalrymple still around? He always had time for a chat."

Jimmy Dalrymple, of course; Mr Gobshite. The laziest bastard in Dogswell nick, which is saying something. Should have thought of him myself. He was on our books. He does a few spots for us as a bouncer at a couple of the local night clubs on his nights off.

"Just the boy. Must have his mobile number here somewhere."

Fanackapan had sodded off; gone to have her face fixed or her nails painted or something. I had to scratch around for the phone book. Anyway, we found it, put the phone on speaker and Dany dialled the number and put the phone on speaker.

"Hello?"

It sounded like someone had just woken up.

"Jimmy, it's Dany Bullimore here."

"Dany. Long time no see. I heard you was out. How's things?"

"Getting by, Jimmy, getting by. Whatya doing at the moment."

"I am on duty my son, preserving the peace of the London Borough of Dogswell, as you would expect. At this very moment in time I am in Dogswell Manor Park. I have taken up my position on a bench in front of the duck pond so I can keep an eye on things. Got to be sure there's no major criminal activity, like dropping litter or dogs shitting on the grass, or ducks shagging in public in front of the kiddies. Wouldn't want any of that. And you should see the skirts on some of these young girls. Shouldn't be allowed. I might have to give some of them a talking to."

"Dogswell sleeps all the sounder for your efforts Jimmy. I'm here with Spencer. He wants to have a word."

"Whatya Spence. I was just about to give you a bell. I think I could manage a few evenings the next couple of weeks."

Jimmy has more brass than a trumpet factory. He is always after something. You've got to keep him in his place.

"Listen Jimmy I got a right earful after you was last on. They said you was titting up all the girls, pretending you was looking for drugs."

"Nah, it was nothing Spence. They love it. Gets them in the mood."

"No it don't Jimmy. They don't want some fat, greasy copper putting his paws all over their tits. Leave it to their fat, greasy boyfriends. Any more of that and you're off the books. Got it?"

"OK Spence, I promise I'll be good."

"You'd better be. Now the reason I was ringing was to find out if you was in that rumpus a couple of months back on the High Street, the one with the English National Front."

"I certainly was my son. I was there with Dogswell's finest. What a day! Them English Fronters was marching about something—immigration or white power or fuck knows what. I don't think they had a fucking clue themselves. They only go for the bother anyway. Of course the other side had to have their own demo, didn't they. There was a load of Pakis jumping up and down yelling Alleyoop the Casbah and something called the Socialist Workers Party waving posters about. Workers my arse! By the look of them none of them had ever done a day's work in their lives. We even had a bunch of Rastas with a steel band. I think they was looking for someone's bonce to play a tune on. Then the rumpus started. It was handbags really, but we couldn't have a riot on the streets of Dogswell, could we? So we waded in and knocked seven shades of shit out of both sides. Haven't had so much fun in years. The papers all ran with it. The *Sun* done us proud. Called us 'The Thin Blue Line'. You must have seen it. I got all the cuttings if you haven't. And the best bit was we had to make sure it didn't happen again, didn't we, so we was all on call for the next six weekends—on over-time. Made a packet! Just bought myself one of them new tellies out of it—fifty two-inch plasma screen, surround sound. It's like going to the pictures ..."

I decided to step in.

"Yeah, yeah Jimmy. I think we get it. I'm asking because I was wondering if you remember a bloke in the ENF—thin, dark hair, about six feet, with a scar on his cheek? He was probably holding the banner."

There was a bit of a pause. He sounded suspicious.

"What d'you want to know for Spence?"

"I'm just doing a bit of work Jimmy, for a client. Got to keep body and soul together. Nothing illegal, nothing to worry about. I just need an identification."

There was another bit of a pause.

"His name's Curting, Steve Curting. He's got a bit of form, GBH, the usual, but long time ago. I did hear he was dealing but we ain't caught him at it yet. He's too fly for that. Gets those hoodie wankers to run around for him... I shouldn't really be telling you this ... you're not recording this are you?"

"No, course not Jimmy."

"You sure Spence? You sound funny. Bit tinny."

"I swear on my mother's grave Jimmy."

"Sorry to hear your mother's dead, Spence."

"She's not Jimmy, but you know what I mean. I am definitely not recording this."

"Well, the thing is, I think he may be a snout as well. He was picked up during the ruck and taken down the nick. I know he was questioned by one of our DS's, Tugwell, because I seen them talking, but that was the last I saw of him. He definitely wasn't charged or nothing. I thought that was a bit funny. They did charge a couple of skinheads, as well as the few Pakis they could catch and a couple of dog-faced slappers from the Socialist Worker's Party. What a pair! Wouldn't stop yelling about 'police brutality' and 'imperialism', whatever the fuck that might be. Mean anything to you?"

"Not a bean, Jimmy."

"Thought not. Should have charged them with brutality to my fucking ears. Maybe I will. I think I might be coming down with something they give me. What's that thing squaddies get when they go off to the wars?"

"Clap."

"Nah, you know what I mean Spence, the thing that fucks up their minds. Makes them go all doolally."

Dany piped up. "You're thinking of PTSD, Post Traumatic Stress Disorder, Jimmy."

"That's the one Dany. I think I'll have some of that. Should be good for a couple of weeks off at least. I've been looking to get a bit of fishing in. My brother's got a new boat. Ooh, I think I spot something a bit tasty. Look at the skirt on that! Sorry Spence, have to go. Have to do a bit of liaisonning with the public, if you know what I mean. See y'around."

With that he was gone. And he gets paid for it. Now that *is* a crime. On the other hand Jimmy D had told us something, though what exactly, fuck only knew. What had we got? I could do a good write up for the report, talk about our "extensive investigations" with our "extremely well placed sources", maybe hint at a conspiracy, suggest more enquiries. I'm pretty good at the old report writing, though I say so myself; worth £350 a day of anybody's money. But I would have to be going some to make a connection between a hot-shot banker and a drug-dealing low-life with a bunch of shaven-head scumbags for mates. The only reason any of those bastards go to a bank is to hang around outside and mug old ladies who'd gone in for a bit of cash. I asked Dany if he had any ideas.

"Reuben Silver was Jewish wasn't he. The ENF don't like Jews."

I rolled my eyes to heaven.

"Dany, the ENF don't like *nobody*. The list of who they don't like covers most of the human fucking race. They don't even like the BNP, and they're another bunch of flag-waving dickheads."

"They specially don't like the BNP. So where do you suggest we go from here?"

Good question.

"Maybe we should try and have a word with this Curting."

Having a "word" could mean one of two things. It could mean just a quiet chat; maybe he wouldn't even know what we was on about. Or it could mean taking along a couple of heavies, hanging him upside down and threatening to pull his tongue out his arsehole if he didn't start singing. The main problem with the second is that you have to be sure there wasn't nothing bigger and heavier on the other side and, on this particular occasion, we wasn't. So that was out.

You could almost hear Dany trying to think.

"Maybe we could ask around, find someone who knows Curting, what he's up to. Maybe there's someone in the ENF."

"Like who?"

"I dunno. What about Gazzer Biggs?"

I couldn't think of nothing to say. Dany had finally lost it. That spell inside had done his head in. If Curting was low life, Gazzer Biggs was sub-fucking-terranean. He was a snarling, scrapping, spitting turd-ball that hardly ever got off its knuckles. He made Guy the Gorilla look like Prince fucking Charles.

Dany just looked back at me.

"You got any better ideas?"

4

Gazzer Biggs lived on the Brackford Estate. It weren't so much a sink estate as sunk without trace. It had less chance than a used johnny in a cesspit of floating back up. It was down the scrag end of Linfield Road, which itself ain't exactly Bond Street. You go through fancy iron gates to get in—or rather gate. One had gone missing. Ten to one it was in a scrap dealer's yard round the back of the station. Naturally the spray boys had been at work all over the place. Looking at what they done I had to admit some of those little bastards got talent. Christ knows where they get it from. On the wall by the gate someone had done a big head of a devil or something, with his tongue hanging out. When I got up closer I saw its mouth was a round blue plate that read, "Winner of the 1972 Architectural Design Award for Modern Living." Yeah, well.

There's two types of cars on these estates. There's the burned out ones. The kiddies like to have one last bit of fun after they get tired of joy-riding around in them so they torch them. Then there's the ones being "mended". There's always half a dozen blokes on the estate that fancy themselves as mechanics. They have these old bangers up on bricks and all you see of them are their bums sticking up in the air as they poke around inside with a spanner. You hardly ever see the cars actually going though.

I managed to dodge between the cars and the dog shit, rubbish and the oil pools—and the kids. If it's been raining their favourite trick is to ride their bikes through puddles as you walk past, trying to spray you. I caught one of the little bastards doing it once. Saw him coming, picked up a stick and stuck it in his wheel as he went past. He went arse over tit right into the puddle. Revenge is sweet.

Gazzer lived in a high-rise round the back, Councillor Albert Jerrold House. I don't think old Councillor Bert would be too pleased if he saw it now. There's two knocking shops and the biggest crack den in Dogswell in there to my certain knowledge—and God know what else. Gazzer's place was on about the eighth floor. Lift? Don't make me laugh. Most of it was in the scrap yard about a week after they opened the block. So you have to go up the stairs and get a real conkfull of piss and puke. I mean, they must know people are going to piss on the stairs so why don't they put bogs on them, or at least drains. That would win my Architectural Design Award for Modern Living. I don't know what they pay architects for, I really don't.

I went along to his door, number 87, and knocked. It opened and there stood Eth. Eth, or Ethniope I think her name is, is Gazzer's moll. Eth does ugly big time. An eyeful of her would put the shits up the Brigade of Guards. Still, she was friendly enough to me, even had something that you could call a smile, if the light weren't too good,.

" I'm looking for Gazzer, Eth. He around?"

"Sorry, Spence. He ain't here. He's up the park, taking the dog for a walk."

I supposed that meant he was out for a spot of Paki-bashing or queer-rolling. I knew he liked to keep his hand in.

"That's a new one on me Eth. What's he up to now?"

She shook her head.

"No, no, he really has bought himself a dog. He's taking it for a walk in the park."

What, you mean one of those things that wags its tail and goes woof?"

She gave me a funny look.

"Sort of."

. . .

If you ain't never been up Dogswell Manor Park, I could say you'd missed a treat. It ain't Hyde Park, but it ain't that bad neither. Actually, the Council keep it quite nice. They even manage to keep kids and dogs from ripping up the flowers and grass, most of the time. You've got to be a bit careful where you go though. It's on a slope. The higher you go, the dodgier it gets. At the top there's a lot of trees and bushes. One bit is the Shirtlifter's Corral. You should hear it at night. Sounds like the cat's chorus. The other is where all the druggies go. You have to watch your step there. I knew one bloke, Barry something— forget his last name—who took some slag up there and gave her a right seeing to. Her arse was like a pin-cushion by the time he'd finished. Lucky she didn't catch nothing. He weren't so lucky though. Caught the biggest dose of clap this side of the Black Death. He was still bent double when I saw him a couple of months later in a pub, still cursing "that bitch" and saying what he'd do to her if he ever saw her again.

"There's only one thing for it Baz my son." I said to him, "You'll have to have it off. But don't worry. Science can work wonders these days. They'll give you a new one, twice as big as that little dangler you got now. The ladies'll love it. You can have go-faster stripes and lights on it. It'll even play music while you're on the job. She'll be coming round the mountain when she comes . . ."

He didn't like it. Didn't see the funny side at all. Called me all sorts of names. I'm blushing even now. So I told him he was a cunt-struck wanker with turds for brains. He didn't like that neither.

I was almost down by the pond when I spotted Gazzer about a hundred yards away on the grass. Even at that distance you could always tell one of the ENF brigade by the tattoos. They've got tattoos everywhere, even on their heads. Most of them have their heads shaved, whether they got hair or not. Gazzer had a big red circle on the top of his head with an H in the middle. Don't ask. He's also got IN on one ear and OUT on the other. I sometimes wondered whether he had "Shake it all about" on his todger, but that wasn't the sort of question you asked Gazzer. Not if you wanted to live. The tattoo that all the ENF lot really want though is the Full Adolph. That's a whole SS division— guns, tanks, planes, the lot—goose-stepping right down the back and up the arsehole. There's only one bloke in London that can do it apparently but he wouldn't let you have it unless you was a big knob in the ENF.

Gazzer was being dragged along by the biggest, ugliest dog you ever saw. It was one of them Pit Rotwhilers, about as wide as it was long, with legs that I swear had no joints in them. It sort of pronked along by waggling its arse, a load of slobber dripping from its mouth, so you could see where it had been all over the park. It had teeth like one of them dinosaur things you see on telly, Tyrannosorearses. I reckon if they still had Tyrannosorearses the ENF would put a rope round one's neck and take it up the park to scare the old ladies shitless and send the kiddies screaming for their mums. They might be pug-ugly pinheads who couldn't get a shag in a million years but everyone likes a giggle now and then.

You got to be a bit careful talking to Gazzer. He could be a bit touchy sometimes. I thought I'd try the cheery greeting.

"Hiya Gazzer. Got a new dog then?"

He had one of those faces with a nose like a squashed potato, ears like cabbages and eyes that you couldn't actually see—as they say, pissholes in the snow. He didn't say nothing for a couple of seconds.

"Nah, I'm taking me fucking Granny for a walk. What's it fucking look like, you blind cunt!"

He fancied himself as a bit of comedian, did Gazzer. He even tried a walk-on at our local comedy club, the UpYourious. Calls itself "Dogswell's answer to Les Jongleurs" though who Les Jongleurs is when he's not at home playing with himself I've no idea. He ain't never been on when I've been up there, that's for sure. Anyway, Gazzer thought he would give it a go in the open mic session. What a fucking disaster that was. The punters was pissed out of their tiny brains as usual and started booing before he'd even opened his mouth. He only got a few seconds into telling his favourite joke—the one about two Pakis, a ten-pound note and a steamroller—when the MC gonged him off.

They found the MC about half an hour later in the khazi. He'd had his head rammed down the bowl and a bog brush up his arse. Last we saw of him. Mind you, he wasn't no loss. In fact he was pretty useless as an MC if you ask me. I was up there the other night and they got a new MC now. Much better.

I thought I'd treat myself to a slash and had a quick look round the bogs. Didn't see no brushes though. Funny that.

Gazzer was still giving me the look so I thought I'd try another tack.

"Nice looking dog Gazzer. So what's its name?"

This time his face sort of creased up.

"Fifi."

"Fifi? Fifi??? Nobody calls a dog like that fucking Fifi. They're all called Rambo or Gnasher or Tyson or Asbo or something. Not—most definitely not—Fifi. Besides it wasn't no girlie. I was looking at a pair of bollocks the size of tennis balls and a dong that swung about like one of them cranes they use for building skyscrapers, only bigger. That mutt could've shagged everything in the Crufts Dog Show and still had half a tankfull left.

"Unusual name for a dog like that Gazzer. Besides, from where I'm standing it don't look like no lady."

His face creased up even more.

"You heard that song 'A Boy Called Sue'?"

Yeah, I'd heard it. Johnny Cash. Streak of Yank piss. He only had one note—"My-name- is-Sue-How-do-you-do?" You'd have thought his Mum and Dad or someone would have felt sorry for him and bought him another note for Christmas or something, but no such luck. He'd still be singing that same note now if only he weren't so fucking dead. What the fuck was Gazzer on about? He wasn't exactly the brightest button in the box. His skull must have been at least six inches thick, judging by all the times he'd been hit on it, and, if there was more than one brain cell rattling around in there, they hadn't never been introduced. But I was beginning to think he was trying to be funny.

"Yeah, I heard it. So what?"

"It's about a cowboy who called his son Sue. Everybody laughed at him so he had to give them a spanking. Toughened him up a treat."

"And, your point is, as they say?"

"Calling him Fifi does the same for the dog."

You had to laugh. That dog needed toughening up like I needed a pneumatic drill up my arse.

"Did it work?"

By this time his face was so puckered up you couldn't see where his eyes was and his mouth was so open you could see every one of the half-dozen teeth he still has left.

"Try calling him Fifi and he'll bite your fucking bollocks off!"

I gave his Fifiness the eye. I thought I might try my Conan the Barbarian look. Show it who's master. But then I looked at all them teeth and the slobber and the fucking size of it and thought maybe not this time. Try another tack.

"I thought you had to have a muzzle on that sort of dog?"

He cackled.

"You want to put a muzzle on him? Who'll I send the bits to?"

Enough of this. I hadn't come to talk about dogs.

"OK Gazzer. Delighted as I always am to chew the fat about man's best friend, I wanted to have a chat with you about something else. Was you on that rumpus on the High Street a couple of months ago, you know, the one that got in all the papers."

He shook his head.

"Nah, fucking missed it, didn't I. Got absolutely rat-arsed the night before. We was singing *Rule Britannia* in the Pirates till half past fucking four in the morning and I woke up late. It was all over by the time I got there. I was absolutely fucking gutted, I don't mind telling you."

If I hadn't known better, I'd have thought he was going to cry.

"The reason I ask is that I've got a job on. It's just a little domestic, nothing serious, but I've been told that Steve Curting might be able to help me out. He's one of yours, isn't he? I heard he was in that ruck. I thought maybe you could let me know where to find him."

He pulled another face.

"If he don't want to be found, you won't fucking find him. He's like the Scarlet fucking Pumpernickel. They seek him here, they seek him there, but they can't fucking find him anywhere. Can't stand the cunt. He's always handing out the orders but he's never around when the trouble starts. Besides, there's got to be more than a touch of the Dago about him. You only have to look at him. I don't think they should have let him in the ENF at all."

"I didn't know the ENF was that fussy Gazzer. Besides, you can talk. What about Eth? I thought shagging blacks was off-limits for all you ENF lot."

He wagged his finger at me.

"That's where everybody gets it wrong. We're the *English* National Front. We're an *English* party. We hate Pakis, we hate Micks, we hate Jocks, we hate Taffs, we hate Yids, we hate Yanks, we hate Krauts, we hate Frogs, we hate Dagos, we hate Wops, we hate Japs, we hate Spics, we hate Chinks. We hate anyone that's not English. But if you was born and bred in England and stand up for your country you can join."

I'll say this for the ENF, they was equal opportunity haters. The Race Board, or whatever it's called these days, would be proud of them.

"I think I get the picture Gazzer, but you let blacks in do you?"

"We got a few. Not many, 'cos not many of them was real patriots, but we have some. 'Coons for Queen and Country', that's what we call 'em."

"And what do you have to do to show that you're a 'real patriot'?"

"The usual. Fly the flag—the proper English flag, not that mongrel Union Jack thing. That's for the fucking BNP. Stand up for the National Anthem, fight for your country."

"What, you mean bash a few Pakis, Micks, Jocks, Yids or whatever?"

"Yeah, 'course. Then you got to support the right football team."

"And that is?"

"There's only two—Bow United and Dogswell."

Why those two, fuck only knows. It's not as if we haven't got football teams coming out our ears in London.

"And how do you choose?"

"Depends what side of the river you come from."

"So you're a Dogswell man are you? I heard they was rubbish, bottom of the Tutti-Frutti Paraplegics League or something."

He didn't like that.

"The manager's a fucking Dago arsehole. He ain't gonna be around long. We'll get a proper English manager and then you'll see. Anyway, who gives a shit about the football? Half the time we don't even go in. We hang around the car park for the other team's supporters. We like to give them a whacking when they go in and another one when they come out. But if we do go in we have to take their end, don't we. Then we sing 'No one loves us. No one loves us. No one loves us. We don't care.' Fucking great! You should try it sometime, Spence."

Can't wait. My idea of Heaven. Besides, I hate fucking football. A lot over-paid ponces chasing a ball round a park while lot of boneheaded arseholes yell their heads off.

"I'll have to take a rain check on that one Gaz. Very busy. Lot of domestics on Saturdays."

But there wasn't no stopping him. He was off down memory lane.

"'Course it ain't the same since they moved to the New Doghouse. You had much more fun at the old Doghouse. We used to get really tanked up and get on the roof and piss on their supporters. 'We're singing in the rain, just singing in the rain. It's a wonderful feeling, to piss on you again.' In those days Dogswell FC was a name that you walked in fucking fear and trembling of. We had a copper from Dogswell nick, old Ted Broadstairs, who used to go in to the other team's dressing room and say 'Listen lads, if you get injured, best not to come off the pitch, else you might get another kicking from the spectators.' He wasn't kidding, neither. And just to make sure, Harry Bloggsworth, the manager—best manager Dogswell ever had; we're collecting for a statue to him—had his biggest reserves running up and down the touchline and they'd give anyone what took a throw in or a corner or whatever a right tonking. Worth a least a goal a game, that was. And you could get in for five bob. Now it costs you an arm and a leg. It's getting so that the working man can't afford to go to football no more. That is a fucking disgrace! When the ENF get in we're gonna shake things up. Cheap football tickets for everyone English—free for pensioners and kids!"

Maybe he had a point. He sometimes did. Anyway, I had to humour him.

"Bound to sweep the country with that one, Gaz. But look, any idea where I could find this bloke Curting? I'm trying to track down some scumbag who's done a runner and Curting might know where he is. I had the little woman in my office yesterday—floods of tears, kiddies crying for their Dad, the fucking lot. You know how it is."

You have to lay it on with a trowel for the likes of Gazzer. He was practically in tears himself.

"There's some real shitbags around, Spence. I don't know how anyone can do it, leaving little kiddies like that"

Yeah, yeah. I know for sure that Gazzer has a couple of kids he ain't seen for years. Whose fault? Who knows? But put it this way: if I was a kid the last thing I would want to see every morning at breakfast would be Gazzer. But he did seem to be thinking. You could see it coming out all over his face, like a big dose of senna pods had been stuffed up his brains.

"I tell you what I'll do, Spence. Seeing as kiddies is involved, I'll ring up our central office and see if they know where he is."

"Can't you give me the number and I'll call them?"

He put on a real no-can-tell face.

"That number's secret. We don't give it to no one, else every Paki, wog, coon and Christ know what would be yelling down the line. "

He reached into his shirt pocket and pulled out a very top-of-the-range mobile. Where the fuck had he got that?

"Another secret, Spence. Can't tell you where. This phone's got the lot—camera, internet, email, GPS…"

"What's GPS?"

"GPS is GPS. It tells you where you are."

"But you know where you are. You're in Dogswell Manor Park."

"Yeah, but if I didn't know it'd tell me."

"I see. It's a phone for twats who don't know where the fuck they are. What about email? Sent any yet?"

"Nah, not yet. Tell the truth, I ain't quite worked out how. I get loads coming in but they're all about making my plonker bigger. Fucking cheek. I bet mine's bigger than anything they got. Soon as I get the hang of email, I'll tell them that if they don't stop sending that shit I'll go round there and sort them out."

"You do that Gazzer. And maybe you could also call your office, like you said."

He started pressing buttons. After a few shits, fucks and bastards and looking at the phone like he was about to throttle it, he managed to make it work.

"Gazzer Biggs here, Dogswell branch ... Biggs !.. Dogswell branch! ... yeah that's right, Biggs .. I'm trying to get hold of Steve Curting. Any idea where he is? ... Who wants to know? A friend of mine who's trying to track down some scumbag that's run off and left his wife and kiddies in the shit. He thinks Steve might know where he is ... I know you're not a fucking lost property office!... All right, all right, I'll tell him."

After another bit of button pressing and cursing he managed to turn it off.

"They say they don't know where he is, but if you want to see him he's probably going to be at the next Branch meeting."

"When's that?"

"It's at the Pirates, this Thursday. Usually starts about eight."

Just then Fifi decided it wanted walkies. Probably spied another mutt and fancied lunch. When Fifi wanted walkies, Fifi got walkies. Off it went at about a hundred miles an hour with Gazzer on the other end of the lead, yelling and swearing and digging his heels in behind. Last I saw, both of them was disappearing through the park gates into Dogswell Park Lane.

5

Why the Pirates Arms? You may well ask. The pub was put up before the War—you can tell from all the whitewash and wooden beams—about two hundred years after they hanged the last pirate. And besides, Dogswell ain't exactly a seafaring town. The nearest thing to a salty sea dog we got is the Chinaman in the Yingyang Fish Bar and, looking at his fish, fuck only knows what they was swimming in when they was caught.

I got there a bit early. Thought I'd have a look around. It was one of those big old pubs, massive in fact, five or six different bars, half of them shut. Its glory days was long gone. My old Mum told me there used to be a boating pond opposite. Peter Pan's Pond they called it. Just after the war all the families used to come down and have a paddle and row a boat—"Come in number 5, your time's up!"—all that sort of thing. Then they would go across to the pub and the kiddies could sit outside and have lemonade and crisps while the grown-ups went inside and sank a few. "Used to be lovely!" she'd say, "A real treat." Nothing like that now. There's a supermarket where the pond used to be. Well actually, there is a pond still there but you could practically spit across it. Room for a couple of ducks from my bath but that's about it.

I bought myself a pint and took a few sips and then suddenly I spotted something I hadn't seen for years. In a dark corner, lonely and clearly unloved, was a bar billiards table.

Do not get me on the demise of bar billiards in this fair country of ours. Time was when you could go into a pub round here and there was an even chance of finding a table. No longer. They ripped them all out and put pool in instead. Once again, England bends over and gets reamed by the Yankee dollar. I ask you, what is pool? Just a load of balls practically covering the table and a couple of brain-dead yobboes whacking them as hard as possible till they're all gone. Where's the skill in that? I mean, how hard can it be? With bar billiards on the other hand you have to put a bit of slowth on the ball, knocking it gently off the other ball against the cushion and into the hole, missing the mushrooms, Hit the 200 mushroom and you're out. It's a game for subtle and devious bastards, not for slam-bang merchants like pool.

I had to have a go. I had to get a token from the bar to play. Turned out to be an old shilling. I ain't seen one of those since I was a little kid. Shows how long it had been in. The barman tried to charge me a quid for it till I told him it was only worth 5p. Then he let me have it for free. No one to play with of course. I doubt if anyone in the pub knew what the table was for, let alone knew the rules. So I knocked a few balls about. Rusty, very rusty, but I fancied I could feel the old form coming back. A couple of hours, and someone to play, and I could be bang on.

The pub started filling up, mostly with the biggest load of pug-uglies I'd ever seen in my life. These guys made Shrek look like Laurence Olivier. There was a few others different. You couldn't exactly call them smart, although they obviously fancied themselves. They had hair for a start and they was in suits too tight for them. Half of them had dark glasses too. Talk about acting the baddie. You couldn't make it up.

Some of the uglies was well-oiled already and started singing—*Rule* fucking *Britannia*—who'd have guessed? There was other songs I'd never heard before, mostly about whacking fuzzy-wuzzies over the head in far and distant lands. There was a bunch making a real racket just next to the table, starting to put me off my game. I recognised a couple of them as the scumbags who tried to rob the Bangladesh shop. They was talking about it, only what they was saying weren't what I saw. They way they was telling it, they was practically planting the Union Jack in the ruins of Crackers, or whatever the capital of Pakistan is called, and taking it back for the Empire. I thought I'd put them straight.

"It's Bangladesh."

One of them looked at me like I just laid a cow turd.

"What you on about?"

"Their country ain't Pakistan, it's Bangladesh. They wasn't Pakis, they was Bangles."

That was too much for what little brain he had left.

"Listen, I know a fucking Paki when I see one and they was fucking Pakis. Besides, whoever heard of a country called Bangladesh?"

I had to admit he had a point there. "Have it your own way" and went back to playing the game.

I saw Gazzer come through the bar door and then one of the suits stood up and yelled,

"The meeting starts in five minutes. Everybody upstairs."

We went up, about thirty of us, into this huge great room, big enough for ten times as many, easy. It was like an old time music hall. Lost of gold paint and pictures of men and women dressed up to the nines, and dancing about. And a couple of massive chandeliers hanging from the ceiling. Mind you, it had seen better days. There was dust everywhere. Most of the paint was peeling and most of the pictures had bits missing, but it must have been a real sight in its glory days. Didn't know there was anything like it in Dogswell.

I grabbed a chair and sat at the back. At the front, three of them sat behind a table. One I thought must be Curting; he was thin with a small scar on his cheek. In the middle was the chairman, an oily-looking type, always pushing his hair back off his forehead. The third was a cut above the others, judging by his suit, which was definitely expensive, and his tie, silk if I weren't mistaken.

The chairman stood up and said the minutes of the last meeting was "taken as read". You had to laugh. How many in that room could read? Then he had a go at what he called "the Media". I weren't really listening but I know the BBC was in there somewhere, along with the local rag. Apparently they all overlooked the fine charity work the ENF done—keeping Moslems off our streets, giving the gays a bashing, cracking a few black skulls, that sort of thing—and called them a bunch of fascist thugs instead. I could have told them there's no gratitude. Turn the other cheek, like Jesus. Your reward will come—if not in this world then in the next.

Then he introduced sharp suit as Dr Jasper Dimmuck, "the ENF's leading intellectual thinker." Must be a lot of competition there I thought, but if he knew enough to get a suit like that he must know something, so I settled back to listen. Dimmuck looked around and started:

"Gentlemen."

That got them sitting up. I doubt any of them ever been called a gentlemen before, except when they go for a slash in a pub, which don't count. He was about 40 I guess, not very tall, a bit stout, with brownish hair going backwards and quite a posh voice, but it wasn't really kosher, like he'd bought it with speech lessons rather than having it rammed up his arse from when he was born like all them public schoolboys.

"Gentlemen, we are here to discuss a conspiracy—but a conspiracy of a most peculiar kind, where conspirator and victim are one and the same. We, the people of England, have become willing agents of our own destruction. What do I mean by that? Take a step back. I know how well aware you all are of the ebb and flow of history—how empires come and go, how kings and emperors, generals and conquerors, blaze across the world stage and then disappear, remembered, if at all, in a footnote in some dusty tome.

"But does it have to be like that? Is there some iron law of historical gravity that says what goes up must always come down? I say to you that there is not; that sooner or later one people—and the ideas that embody the essence of that people—will break out of this historic cycle and achieve a lasting, permanent ascendancy. That people could—indeed should—have been the English, but just as the prize was within our grasp we began wantonly to throw it away. It may indeed be too late. Englishness and the English may soon be at one with the pharaohs, the Roman emperors and the cities of the plain. If it is not too late then we are all that is left to prevent that fate. You gentlemen are the last, best hope of England.

"Look around you at the rest of the world. What do you see? What language do people aspire to speak? English. What political system do they aspire to live under? Democracy. The two in my view are coterminous. No dictator could spout his poison in English and expect to be taken seriously. The history of Europe over the last centuries is the history of despotic nations bidding for world ascendancy at the point of a gun and being broken on the rock that is England. Who now bothers to learn their language? Who cares about their culture?

"Yet at the very moment of triumph we shrink from seizing the fruits of victory. Who can deny that England's voice is weaker now than for two hundred years? Why? Because we no longer believe in who and what we are. Instead we have become infected with self-doubt. We allow other cultures to demand equality with our own in our own land, parading and preening themselves as if they were at home while we are forced to sit silent in the shadows. England, which once presided over an empire on which the sun never set, is now being colonised by those it once ruled.

"Do not get me wrong. I am not nostalgic for Empire. That game is no longer worth the candle—too expensive, too much trouble. But what the Empire did was spread the seed of Englishness. They imbibed our culture, they learn our language, they speak it, they think it. Do not let anyone fool you that language is neutral in the ideas it conveys. That notion is for the birds and the cultural relativists. To speak a language is to become enmeshed in its ideas, in its essence. And if you own the language then you own the ideas.

"That is why we, the ENF, the *English* National Front, are *cultural* nationalists. We have no time for the blood and soil fantasies of the BNP and the myriad other so-called "patriots" from all over Europe, most of whom have long since been consigned to the dustbin of history. That way lies the madness of calibrating skin pigmentation, measuring skulls and deciding whether an eighth or a sixteenth of the wrong sort of blood disqualifies you from membership of the master race. Our single most important demand is that to live in England you must be—or become—English. Yes, you can *become* English but it is a hard and unremitting process. Integrate or emigrate, that is our message. What is not acceptable is to live here as if you were still in a peasant village.

"But our ambitions go far beyond the narrow boundaries of England. Our model is the Roman Empire. What was the proudest boast of its inhabitants? *Civis Romanus sum*—I am a Roman citizen. You were no longer a nobody in some God-forsaken province but a citizen of an empire that ruled the known world. So those who share our language, our culture, our ideas will become in a real sense English, part of an ever-spreading multitude that will enable us, the fount of this culture, to make our great, everlasting mark upon the world.

"You gentlemen are the new English vanguard. You will go forward and carry the message to the masses. You will liberate them from their shackles, nurture their pride in country and culture, lead them towards greatness and be there with them when they scale the mountain peak. Soon we will be able to say with pride, like the Romans, *Civis Anglicanus sum*, I am an English citizen, and the world will bow in respect. This is your moment. I know you will not fail."

I was quite impressed. You don't often get that class of bollocks down here. I'm not sure the "vanguard," whatever the fuck that might be, quite got the message though. They was back on the same old, same old.

"What I want to know," piped up a bloke with tattoos and a squashed nose. Mind you, most of them looked like that; you couldn't hardly tell the difference between them. "What I want to know is what is you going to do about the bunch of nig-nogs what moved into the maisonette downstairs from me, making a right racket all hours of the day and night and cooking stuff that smells to high heaven. Put my cat right off his food."

"Was they Pakis?" asked another squash nose.

"No they wasn't fucking Pakis." said squash-nose number one, "They was nig-nogs, you know, the black ones with fuzzy hair. They got funny caps and long dresses right down to the ground—the men as well—and they prance about and sing and stuff."

There was a lot of shaking of heads. Black men in dresses, prancing about and singing. That was definitely out of order. Something had got to be done.

Dimmuck didn't look too happy. I don't think he thought he was there to discuss the ins and outs of prancing nig-nogs.

"Gentlemen, I realise that you all have your individual problems in the multicultural hell that is modern Britain but you should take them up with the relevant authorities—the police, the council, social services—or start campaigning at a local level. We are here to discuss the bigger picture—the future of this once great country of ours and how we can shape it."

This time the heads nodded. They was definitely up for shaping the future—with fists, baseball bats, pickaxe handles, anything they could lay hands on. Be in great shape after they'd finished with it. Just then the chairman said that Dimmuck had to go to another meeting and "discussion" could continue in the bar."

We all trooped downstairs. Time to talk to Curting. I collared him just as he was about to buy a drink, so he couldn't get away.

"Steve Curting?"

"Who wants to know?"

I gave him my card. Cards are always good for that sort of thing. If you got a card you got a bit of status.

"Spencer Weintraub, Personal Location Agent." You could see his lips move as he read it. "What's that mean?"

"It means I'm looking for someone and I'm hoping you might help me find him."

He was even more suspicious.

"Weintraub don't sound English to me. Is it a Yid name or something?"

"It's my professional name. You've got to have one in my line of work."

He put on a bit of a smirk.

"What was you called when you was an amateur then?"

"Reggie Nutbeam."

Now the one thing you can say about Reginald Nutbeam as a name is that it is definitely English. No question. Curting couldn't say nothing.

"Who was you looking for then?"

"Bloke called Reuben Silver. Looks like he's done a runner. His wife's all upset and wants to know where he is."

"Never heard of him."

That was a bit too quick. Even if you can't remember a name you rack your brain for a couple of seconds at least.

"The thing is, his wife says she got a call from your phone after he disappeared from someone she didn't know and wouldn't give his name wanting to get in touch with him."

"Who says it was my phone?"

"When we checked the number it turns out that it was bought from that phone shop on Dogswell High Street and the bloke in the shop recognised you because he saw you a couple of days later in that ruck your lot had, outside the shop. What did you call it? March for Freedom?"

He didn't seem too concerned.

"I might have bought a phone there but so what? He must be mixing me up with someone else. What's the number?"

I showed it to him.

"Nah, not mine. Have a look."

He pulled out a phone. I waved it away.

"That's OK. I believe you. Just doing my job. You have to follow up these leads. Shame to see a fine lady in such a state and the kiddies all crying for their Daddy."

He gave me a sharp look. That was the giveaway. He knew there wasn't no kiddies.

6

"When you have eliminated the impossible, whatever remains, however improbable, must be the truth."

"You've been at the dictionary again, Dany."

"Nah, Spence, it's Sherlock Holmes, innit. I'm just trying to get my head around things. Have a look at this. It's cctv from Ali downstairs."

"Ali's got cctv?"

"Yeah, for when someone does a runner. Shows it to the Plod. They never catch them but it makes Ali feel better. I wanted to get a look at this bird you think is so hot but the pictures are shit. This bit is interesting though."

He was watching her as she walked about fifty yards down the street and got into a car. The car pulled out and came back towards the shop.

"What's interesting about it?"

"The car."

"It's probably the cab she came in that waited for her."

"How many cab firms do you know that use top of the range Mercs?"

"Not round here obviously but up West—different class of cab firm so I'm told."

"Maybe but you say this bird's a real looker *and* she's loaded. So, number one, why does he do a runner and, number two, why come to these parts? It doesn't make sense."

"Well Sherlock, maybe his thing is fat, ugly, skint birds, of which, I don't need to remind you, we have our fair share around here. Maybe he likes doing it doggie style, so he don't care what they look like so long as they howl like a baboon on heat while he's giving it to them."

"He could buy every slag in Dogswell with the money he's got, if that's all he wanted. That can't be the reason. There's got to be more to it than that."

"Who knows, Dany my son, who knows? The heart has its reasons, not to mention the cock. In my experience people do the stupidest things for the weirdest reasons. There's no accounting for taste. But on the other hand, we have a lead. The lady said he might be round here. I don't buy it but what do I know? And Curting definitely knows something. So, we can legitimately go on with our investigations. The clock is ticking and the lady is paying. Let's go to it."

"Go to what?"

"What do you think? A bit of legwork. Spin it out. If he's around here then he's got to be staying somewhere. We check out the hotels and the estate agents in case he's renting or bought somewhere. If he is on the pull round here, then maybe he's going to some pubs or clubs. Let's do a quick tour this afternoon and see if we can pick up something. Looks good on the report. Very professional. We'll split it. You take north of the High Street up to Dogswell Cross and I'll take south to the Park."

"Taxis?"

"Don't take the Mickey. I'm going to start checking out the banks now."

. . .

You can't get away for long in this wicked world without having to pay for something. That means sooner or later your bank is going to hear from you. Banks, as everyone knows, are criminal conspiracies against the public and like all criminals they don't want no one to know what they're up to. Which means that they try to make it difficult for us honest hard-working finders to find out what what's happening to their accounts, like any change of address or where someone's taking money out. However yours truly has a way of beating them at their little game—black girls.

Go to any bank round here and I guarantee you that almost everyone behind the counter is a black girl—well-turned out, quick, on the ball. Sometimes they do stick a white girl at the end, but only after she's had the operation to get the fag out of her mouth.

Believe it or not, a lot of the black girls round here want to make something of theirselves, which is more than can be said for a lot of the blokes. And, being used to a bit of class, they're not exactly interested in having a boyfriend who's a wannabe rapper or drug dealer with his underpants hanging over his trousers. This is where yours truly makes his move. There's a couple of bars where most of them hang out and I make it my business to get to know at least one girl from every bank in Dogswell. There's a bit of a technique to it—the chat of course, the rep-part-tee as we say. A lot of them are pretty good at that. I often have to work hard to keep up. You buy them a few drinks, take them out for a meal and maybe the theatre. A lot of them like musicals. I never try to go for an early shag. That's always a bad move. Actually a lot of the time I don't even bother. I find it's better to do them a favour—like finding their dads. Most of their dads have long since buggered off with a new woman and now that they're full of themselves they want to find him and tell him what a complete arsehole he is. I do them a favour; they do me a favour.

Goldbury & Newman, as I found out after a bit of internetting, is a very posh peoples bank. It's a subsidiary of one of them too-big-to-jail, give-us-squillions-or-we-pull-the-plug-and-you're-all-in-the-shit, banks, the Royal London & Provincial. My girl in the RL&P is Berneece.

Berneece is a very sharp cookie indeed but nice with it. Doing well for herself in the bank and on a decent screw. She and I go back a good few years, though I ain't never had a shag there, mainly because she's never interested. Surprise, but there you go. She was getting married to some tosser who was poncing off her while he said he was "developing projects". Naturally she was paying for everything, including the wedding, but then he done the usual—ran off with a white bint. If that weren't bad enough he ran off with her money as well, because she was stupid enough to have a joint account—to help him with his "projects". That's where I came in. She asked me to find him. Wasn't difficult. He hadn't gone far, so she wanted an extra service that I sometimes offer—getting the money back.

You have to do these things right if you want to get a result. I like to have a heavy on either side—one white, one black. They have to look the part—dark suits, thin ties and shades. I go dressed smart casual. The best black guy I use, Obadiah, is a pastor at our local holy-roller church, the Redeemed Christian Church of God. He says it's his Christian duty to restore goods to their rightful owner. I don't argue. My usual white bloke is Mick. He's a plumber in the day job. I ain't never asked him whether he had any religious opinions about this line of work though he did once say he could do me a very good price on a bathroom suite if I ever needed one.

You have to get the verbals right too. I like that bit in the James Bond movie where the villain strokes the white cat and says, "Personally Mr Bond I abhor violence but some of my associates are less fastidious." They're slow learners round here so you have to pep it up a bit. The line I usually take is, "Listen sunshine, as you can see I am a reasonable man. I'm giving you one minute to cough up, otherwise I walk out and leave you with these two. No knowing what they might do when I'm not there to hold them back." That usually does the trick. If I need to put a bit more pressure on I threaten to cut their bollocks off with a rusty knife. Never fails.

Berneece's tosser was real wimp. I had hardly opened my mouth and he was practically blubbing. He hadn't had time to spend much of her money so we got most of it back. I heard that a couple of her cousins went round later and gave him a good spanking, which more or less made up for the rest. Berneece has naturally been grateful to me ever since and will always help out if I need info about a scumbag and his money. I have a little bit of code I use when I ring, just in case anyone is listening.

"Hello Berneece my angel, it's your favourite cousin Reggie here. I've got some interesting news for you. How about a drink this evening."

"I'm busy at the moment."

She's always busy that girl. Whatever time you phone her, day or night, she's busy, busy, busy.

"It's very interesting news. You definitely want to hear it."

That's my code for things are a bit urgent.

"OK where?"

"See you in the KB, six o'clock."

There's a lot of pubs in Dogswell. Used to be a lot more of course. When I was a kid, the road I lived in had eight and that was nothing special. On the next crossroads up there was one at each corner. All closed and knocked down now. You might have thought the locals must have been out their skulls every night to keep them in business, though funnily enough I don't remember people being more pissed then than now. If anything less. Mind you, then it was men that got plastered and women only got tiddly on Babycham or port and lemon or whatever. You didn't get none of this yoof stuff—girls honking in the street, legs in the air and knickers all over the place.

As is well known, there are pubs and there are boozers. There's actually a couple of very nice pubs in Dogswell, up near the park. One, the Crown, calls itself a "gastro pub", serves fancy food at even fancier prices. Go in there and ask for a pint of brown and mild and they wouldn't know what you was on about. The other, the Old Grey Goose, has a fantastic display of flowers outside. Wins prizes every year. A real credit to the governor, Dermot, an Irishman as it happens.

I didn't think there was much point in looking for our Mr Silver in the boozers. Not his sort of places at all. Most of them can't be long for this world. Dismal, dirty, depressing and dear. Three pounds fifty or more for a pint of kangaroo piss—do me a favour! Only the Wetherspoons pubs have a decent pint for a decent price and they're all converted supermarkets and the like, so the atmosphere can be a bit off. I blame these pub companies. They bought up thousands of pubs, probably paid over the odds, and are now trying to get their money back by fleecing the punters. The poor old licensees have to work all hours for sweet FA and can't do nothing about it. The sooner they go bust the better. The only decent pubs are the ones where the tenants have a bit of control or, better still, where the landlord owns his own gaff, but they are few and far between these days.

It took me most of the afternoon to check out the bars, restaurants and pubs that I thought he might have been in. I wasn't expecting to find out nothing and, as they say, I wasn't disappointed. Nobody had seen nothing, nobody knew nothing. Our Mr Silver didn't seem to be much of a one for the going out. After that I did a ring round of the estate agents and letting companies. I'm the goto guy when they want to track down any tenants who done a midnight flit, so they all owe me. None of them had seen sight nor sound of Silver or anyone that might look like him. By that time it was getting on for six so I headed for the KB.

The KB is a proper local. Its real name is the King William the Fourth. There's picture of His Royalness on the board outside—a fat bloke on a horse. What he done to deserve a pub named after him I've no idea. Maybe he was William the Conqueror, although looking at him he'd have had a hard time even conquering Dogswell.

Jim the landlord was a copper in the days when coppering meant something round here. Used to take a nice steady little drink off a printers who was doing stuff for some porn merchants in Soho, the ones what had the Flying Squad on the payroll at the time. Went on for years. Did it proper. Never got greedy and bunged a bit to his sergeant to keep him sweet. He made enough out of it that when he retired from coppering he bought himself a pub. That's the way it should be done. Nothing fancy, nothing greedy, just steady. Nobody gets hurt, everyone's happy.

Jim runs his pub like a pub should be run. It's well used most nights except Mondays—as he says, there's fuck all to be done about Mondays except abolish them—and there's a darts team, two football teams and they're even talking about a girls football team. On top of that he organises coach trips to the coast in summer and Christmas parties for OAPs and kids. He's a one man Social Services department is Jim.

Berneece was already there when I turned up, although the way she gave me a peck on the cheek I could tell she hadn't quite come down from all the busyness. I got the drinks in, white wine for her and I took a pint of my usual, Old Speckled Hen, proper cask-conditioned ale, not some kangaroo piss out of a keg that most of the pubs round here serve up.

"So what's all this about Spencer?"

I don't like to give too much away. I did tell her this case was a bit different from the usual but when I mentioned Goldbury & Newman she put up her hands.

"Stop there Spencer. There's no way. We don't have access. It's all top people that have accounts there, even royalty so they say."

"Look Berneece, all I need to know is if he's got a new address or if he's taken anything out of an ATM or whatever. That can't be too much of a secret."

"Spencer I've told you. Goldbury & Newman is not on our system. If I wanted to know anything about an account there I would have to go to our manager and the first thing he would ask is why I wanted the information. It's more than my job is worth."

Another fucking dead end I thought. Might as well just enjoy the company.

"How's work going Berneece? Been promoted yet?"

"As a matter of fact I have Spencer. I've been appointed head of my section. Start next week. How about you?"

"This new bit of work which should be worth a few bob. Fanackapan's giving me grief again though. She has to go."

"What are you talking about Spencer? Sharon is the only thing that keeps your office going and you know it. You would be out of business without her. You're the most disorganised person I've ever met and I doubt if anyone else would put up with you."

Everyone tells me that but I don't see it. There has to be someone else that could run my office and not give me a grade one pain in the arse.

"Cobblers to that. Anyway, let's change the subject. How's your love life?"

"Need you ask? I've even tried this dating app on my phone. I've been out with a couple of real no-hopers. God how people lie about themselves. How about you?"

"Can't complain. The ladies still love me."

"God Spencer, much as I love you, you're a real sexist pig. Most of the time you come across as a boorish, chauvinist, dickled doofer who's only interested in one thing. How you get away with treating women like you do beats me. They must be gluttons for punishment."

"What do you mean? I always treat them nice."

"Don't make me laugh. Fuck 'em and forget 'em, that's your motto."

"No, no. I'm not like that. I haven't forgotten you have I?"

"You haven't fucked me either, though it's not for want of trying."

Time for another drink. Jim himself was behind the bar; unusual, he don't normally come on till about eight but some lazy bit of a barmaid hadn't turned up, so we got chatting.

"Ain't seen you for a while Spence; how's business?"

"Hasn't been too clever lately Jim, but as it happens I've just picked up a nice little job. While I'm here I might as well combine business with pleasure. Don't suppose you've ever seen this bloke?"

I pushed the picture of Silver across the bar. He picked it up, looked at it, and kept looking.

"I think I have. In fact I'm sure I have. He was in here last Friday. I remember him because he had a very expensive suit on and a Rolex on his wrist—worth a couple of grand and the rest—and he was with this woman Spence, I tell you, she was that gorgeous she could have been a model and she was dressed up to the nines as well. We don't often get that sort in here. They was here till about ten, then went off in a cab."

Gobsmacked don't even come into it. I only showed him the picture because I wanted to give the impression that I was working on something important.

"Any idea where the cab went?"

"No. I didn't call it. Donny did, I think. He ain't on tonight but the cab company would probably know."

"What cab company?"

"Doggiecabs, round the corner. Dot's in charge. She'll know if anyone will."

I took the drinks back feeling like I'd won the pools.

"Berneece, my angel, you have done the business without realising it. We must meet more often."

I told her what Jim had said. What a turn up. I could have saved a lot of shoe-leather by popping round for a pint at my local, but never mind. We had nearly tracked the bastard down. Then the question was what we were going to do when we found him? We could just tell his wife and let them sort it out. On the other hand, he must have had a good reason for skipping the love nest and, more to the point, he might be willing to reward those who keep shtum about where he was. Now I know that there is such a thing as duty to the client, but I can tell you for nothing that things marital are always a lot more complicated than they look. You don't always do right by the client by giving them what they say they want, even though they are paying. I think we needed to box clever. I gave Dany a ring.

"Dany boy, have I got news for you. I think it's jackpot time. I'm in the KB with the lovely Berneece. I've been talking to Jim and guess what? Reuben Silver was in here last Friday, believe it or not, with some bird. They left in a cab. I'm just off to the cab firm to find out where they went."

There was a bit of a pause.

"Funnily enough Spence I was just about to ring you. Did you hear there was a shooting in Dogswell Park last night?"

"I heard something on the radio this morning. So what?"

"I've just been talking to Jimmy Dalrymple. He's down there now. They haven't released the victim's name yet but he's given it to me."

"And?"

"And the victim is one Reuben Silver, late, it seems, of this parish."

7

"I just don't understand. Why would anyone want to kill him?"

She looked like she'd done her bit of crying but she'd had a week to get over the shock—if there was a shock. You can't always tell with her sort. There wasn't nothing much I could say.

"I don't know any more than you do. We'll just have to wait till the police catch someone, if they do. Can't always depend on it."

We had to go round to see her and tell her what we had come up with. She was stretched out on a sofa in some full-length slinky number. I suppose that's how they do the grieving widow up West. It ain't like that in Dogswell. They'd be in T-shirt and leggings, either rolling around screaming and bawling their eyes out, or else laughing their heads off.

"Oh God, the police. Aren't they dreadful! They were here this morning asking me all sorts of questions. Was Reuben having an affair? Did he have money troubles? Did he have any enemies? Who were his friends? It just went on and one. Hardly a word of sympathy. You would think they would show some consideration. This last week has been dreadful. The police, the press—my God, the press. I never realised how intrusive they could be. The so-called qualities were the worst. My maid tells me someone from the *Telegraph* repeatedly banged on my front door."

"That's what they do. It's a big story, top banker getting shot. Sells a lot of papers."

"Using the dead to sell papers. That's disgusting! Thank God for the Bank. They protected me from the worst, but the autopsy, then the funeral. I don't know how I got through it."

Yeah, well. I was sorry about her old man but look at it from the coppers' point of view. Rich banker with even richer wife does a runner and ends up in Dogswell with a bullet in the back of his head. Don't exactly look like a straightforward domestic, do it? Sympathy ain't exactly the first thing on their minds. Suspicion is what they do and suspicious is what they very obviously was.

"Someone gets killed and more often than not it's their nearest and dearest that done it. Sad but true. That's our modern world for you."

"Oh God. They couldn't possibly suspect me, could they? Don't you think they will catch whoever did it? That would be awful. I couldn't live with it. What can we do? Do you think you could catch his killer?"

Sometimes you don't know whether to laugh or cry.

"No, murder's a job for the police. We're finders. We find people. Alive people. We almost found your husband, only someone got to him first. We don't do none of that private eye stuff. You only get that in books. If you really want to hire a private detective there are plenty in the phone book, but believe me they don't do Sherlock Holmes any more than we do."

She weren't going to be put off.

"Yes of course, I understand. I know about private detectives. A couple of my friends have used them to check up on their husbands. Dreadful people; real creeps. I wouldn't dream of using them, but you're different. You know Dogswell; you might be able to find out something. The police are telling me nothing. I need to know what happened. Couldn't you just make some enquiries. Maybe find out what he was doing, who he was seeing. Anything would help. It's not knowing that is so awful. Look, I appreciate that this sort of thing is expensive. I'll pay you fifty per cent more than your normal rate."

Call me a pushover but I can't resist a woman when she talks like that. Since Dany was with me I didn't want her to mention any actual sums in case he got ideas, so I thought I'd better give in.

"OK, we'll use our contacts, ask around, but I can't guarantee we'll come up with something. People tend to clam up with this sort of thing. Nobody knows nothing if you know what I mean."

"Yes of course. Anything, anything at all, would help."

Now if there's one thing I pride myself on it's professional-ism. If you take on a job you have to do it proper. I had told her straight I thought our chances of finding out much was zilch but that didn't mean we wasn't going to try. We would spend the next week or so asking every low-life, scumbag and chancer in Dogswell if they knew something and like as not come back at the end of it with sweet FA. I would be paid handsomely for my efforts and Dany would get a very nice bung as well. Fair or what?

"Well if we're going to get anywhere, the first thing we have to do is ask you a few questions, get a bit more background. What you tell us will be for our ears only. We are discretion personified, if I say so myself, but you've got to be absolutely straight with us, else we can't do the job properly. Understand?"

That was another bit of professional business. It may look like you're putting a bit of pressure on the client but that's what they like. You give them the no-nonsense, hard-boiled ap-proach, make them feel that you're the one to get to the bottom of things. They get that little frizz down the spine. They feel that this boy don't take too many prisoners. It's all part of the pack-age. It's what they pay for.

"I think so. What did you want to ask me?"

"Well, for a start, there's this woman he was with. Any idea who she is? Did you know that Reuben was playing away, par-don the expression.?"

She went a bit red.

"I have no idea who she is. I've always trusted Reuben abso-lutely. How do you know they were having an affair? She might be a business associate."

And I might be the King of Siam. It's well known that most of the world's banking business gets done in Dogswell pubs.

"We don't know if police know about her yet, but chances are they soon will. If we could get to her first she might tell us something. On the other hand, she might be the one that done it. Maybe it was a lover's tiff. Are you absolutely sure you have no idea who she might be? The description we have is blond, looks like a model, expensively dressed."

She put on her haughty face.

"In our circles, blond and expensively dressed is more or less par for the course. Model looks, I grant you, is rather more subjective, but I dare say a number of my acquaintances could answer to the description. Money has a way of compensating for any number of original flaws. However, I really don't think she is anyone I know. Reuben simply wasn't attracted to that sort. If anything he preferred them blowsy and frowsy. He had a bit of a thing for barmaids, so he told me. Not that I think he did anything about it. I would have known. Reuben was a terrible liar."

Or a very good one. He may like barmaids but he managed to marry a gorgeous bit of stuff with zillions attached. It didn't add up but there was no point in pushing it. She wasn't going to tell me nothing even if she knew. Try something else. Maybe the Old Bill knew something.

"What exactly did the police want to know?"

She sighed and rolled her eyes.

"I told you, they asked if either of us had had affairs."

"And you said?"

"I've told you that too: of course not!"

"You just told us about Reuben. What about you?"

"How dare you! What is this, the Inquisition? No, absolutely not!"

"OK, OK, I have to ask. Just doing the job. What else did they want to know?"

"They kept asking me if I knew why Reuben had, what can I say, left, disappeared? I said I had no idea. It was a complete mystery to me.."

"Did you tell them you thought he might have kidnapped himself?"

"Of course not! He's been killed. It's obvious that whatever happened it was done to him, not by him."

That had to be true. He couldn't have shot himself and then hid the gun after he done it. It looked like a professional job according to my snout, Jimmy D. One shot to the back of the head and nothing left for the forensic boys to chew on.

"What about work? They must have asked about that."

"They did. They asked if he had any money worries. I said no, he's a banker. That made them smile."

"Ten to one they're already sniffing around at the bank, talking to the top brass. What do you think they might be saying?"

"I really don't know. They certainly will not be free with information. The bank places enormous emphasis on discretion. They have a lot of very distinguished clients. There's a strict rule that bank business is not even to be discussed with spouses. My feeling is that, even if there were problems with any of Reuben's dealings, the first instinct of the bank would be to cover things up."

Why wasn't I not surprised. Normally I don't get too worked up about someone trying to pull a fast one on the boys in blue but when it comes to a question of who is the biggest villains, coppers or banksters, it's no fucking contest. Hanging is definitely too good for them banksters. I think we should throw them one by one off that big tower block in Canary Wharf, and see if they bounce—like most of their fucking cheques.

"What, you mean they would have checked out his office and computer and stuff before the police arrived?"

"I think that's entirely likely. Anything remotely sensitive would have been removed."

"What have they done with his stuff then? Thrown it out?"

"Oh no, that would be far too insecure. Reuben once told me that all documents have either to go into secure storage or be securely shredded and old computers have to have their hard disks permanently wiped before they are let out of the building. I understand that they have to call in outside computer experts to do it."

"So maybe Reuben's computer hasn't been wiped yet. It would be very handy if we could get a peek at it. It might give us an idea of what he's been up to."

"I don't see how that would be possible. I very much doubt that they would even let you in the building and they certainly wouldn't allow you, or anyone else, to touch his computer."

She was probably right. I told her that the first thing to do was the basics. We needed to find out where her husband had

been staying and see if we could find out what he had been doing there.

...

It didn't take long to find where Silver had been hanging out.
Jimmy D gave us the SP. He had rented a flat in one of the big
old blocks along the Peckham Road. Used to be Council, now
it's run by the Pegasus Housing Association. He'd done it over
the Internet, which is why I hadn't picked it up from the agents.
It was the usual deal, cash. The bloke doing the renting wasn't
supposed to let it out to no one else, so, with the coppers all
over it, he was now in shit with Pegasus. Jimmy D reckoned
he'd be thrown out.

I had a look round. The place was what you used to call respectable working class. It was kept quite decent. Not too much
rubbish about and the paintwork was good. It looked like the
residents was mainly older. I didn't see many kids around. Silver's flat was three floors up. I couldn't get in because it was all
locked up with police notices on it, so I tried the flats on the
same landing. A couple of them was out but the one next door
was opened by a little old coloured lady, West Indian I guessed
from the accent. She said her name was Cynthia and she was all
smiles when she saw me, insisted I come in and have a cup of
tea. Her place was a little palace. Lots of nick-nacks everywhere
you looked, pictures all over the sideboard and frilly cushions
on all the seats. I couldn't sit down without squashing something. While she made the tea she gave me a bit of her life history.

"I don't see many people now. I have two sons but they
don't come to see me. One is in jail, so I suppose he has an excuse. The other one works for a big supermarket. He married a
girl from Barbados; very snooty Bajans are in my experience. I
say to him, 'Royston why you don't marry a nice Jamaican girl,
or even a white girl? They are not so high and mighty.' But he
wouldn't listen. They never do, children, do they?"

I wouldn't know. I asked her about Silver and she said she met him a couple of times when she was putting out the rubbish.

"A very nice man. Such a gentleman. I was so sad when I heard what happened him. I told him all about me operations— both hips. Everyone tell me you would never guess. Mr Akrobartty at Dogswell General is the man to go to if you ever need a hip I told him."

She did a little jig to show me. Medical tips was not what I was there for. Did Silver say what he was doing there?

"Now that is a funny thing that you should ask because I ask him the exact same thing. He spoke so nice, not like the riff-raff you get round here. Most of them never heard of the Queen's English. Who let them in I don't know. And his clothes were very nice, very expensive. What, I said to him, was someone like you doing here? Do you know what he said? He said that he had lived in Dogswell when he was a young boy and he had come back for a holiday. How we laughed! Who would come to Dogswell for a holiday?"

Now that *was* funny. I asked her if she ever saw anyone else come to the flat.

"Only the caretaker. I keep my eye open for any strangers on this landing. They could be burglars or God knows what. I see the caretaker come with two of his men and they went into the flat when Mr Silver wasn't there. "

"Did you tell Mr Silver?"

"Oh no. It was just a couple of days before you know what and I didn't see him. I told the Police though. I saw his picture on the television and I phoned them up straight away saying that is my next door neighbour that has been murdered. Ten minutes later they come knocking at my door. That is the fastest they have ever been. We are always phoning them about things on this estate and they can take hours to come. Sometimes they don't come at all."

"Where does this caretaker live?"

"On the ground floor of this block. You ring the bell if you want to see him."

I thanked her for what was a very good cup of tea and went down to see the caretaker. I had to ring the bell a few times before he showed up. He looked a bit annoyed.

"What do you want? You're not a resident are you?"

I softened him up with my usual spiel about me being a private investigator in very important case and just looking for a bit of information. I told him what Cynthia had said about going to Silver's flat.

"Yeah, I thought it was a bit funny. They wasn't our lot. They said they was from the Gas Board investigating a leak but I told them that the gas in that flat had been turned off because the resident hadn't paid his bill. They said they wanted to look round just in case. You can't be too careful with gas. A leak could blow this block apart."

"How did they get in?"

"I've got the old Council keys. A lot of them haven't bothered to change the locks so they still work."

"What did they do?"

"I didn't see. I just stayed by the door like they asked. Health and safety they said. They went in and had a good look round for ten minutes or so and then came out. They said everything was OK; it was a false alarm. Then they left. I told all this to the coppers."

"Did they seem interested?"

"Not really. What's interesting about a couple of gasmen?"

"Did Silver know they had been in?"

"I never saw him. He wasn't supposed to be there, was he? Tenants aren't allowed to sub-let. I didn't know he'd been there until after, you know, he got done."

I asked for descriptions but he wasn't exactly the observant sort. White, not much of an accent, medium height, medium build, brown hair, wearing suits, that was both of them. He said he would recognise them if he saw them again but my guess is that they won't be showing their noses round here for a while. Fuck knows who they was.

8

"I found it. Knew it would come in handy some day."

Dany slapped the picture down on my desk. What did we see? Chief Inspector, as was, Jack Dapper, the pride of the Metropolitan Police, wearing only a big hat and a pair of socks, riding cowboy-style on a strapping black girl, who was wearing only a big smile.

Jack was a bit of a star in the old days, often in the papers for collaring some villain or other, but like most of us he needed a bit extra to keep body and soul together, especially given the pittance they paid coppers in them days. Different now of course. Constables are up there with cabbies in the gold-plated stakes. He didn't do nothing too serious. He was in with some big-shots who ran night clubs and strip joints in Soho. He used to tip them off if the coppers was planning a raid, things like that. They used to bung him a few bob and invite him to their parties, which must have been fun judging by the picture we was looking at.

Jack come a cropper though when he rubbed them up the wrong way. His boys arrested one of the sons of a big shot who was trying to muscle in on some clip joint run by another outfit. There was a bit of a barney and everyone got banged up and charged before Jack realised who one of them was. It was too late then; nothing could be done about it. The big shots wasn't too pleased, so they sent pictures of Jack enjoying their hospitality to his bosses at Scotland Yard. They wasn't too pleased neither.

Dany had the picture because he was on Jack's team at the time, before he come to Dogswell. You can't keep a secret at Scotland Yard. The place is like a sieve, so pretty soon they was all over the shop. Everyone thought they was a hoot. Dany liked one so much he kept it as a souvenir.

Jack had to take the usual rat run. He discovered he had some dreaded lurgy that meant he couldn't do police work no more. He had to retire on medical grounds—on full pension of course. Naturally, once he retired he made a miraculous recovery and started looking round for a nice little earner to boost his pension. The job he landed was Director of Security at Goldbury & Newman.

Director of Security sound important but from what I hear it ain't that big a deal. These big banks have ex-coppers on their payroll because it looks good, looks like they take security seriously. They don't actually get told anything of what the banks are up to. There's no way banks are going to let some toerag copper poke his nose into the business of top people. They're there just there for show. Anyway, Dany says he heard that Jack's usually pissed by lunchtime and spends most of his time clipping post-boys' ears and titting up any secretary silly enough or desperate enough to let him.

"I think you should give Jack a ring Dany, for old time's sake. Let him know you still remember him. Tell him how pleased you and I would be to call on him at the bank."

"Why don't I do that Spence. If we're going to get a look at this computer maybe we need someone with us who knows about them."

"Good thinking Dany. Sounds like a job for Deepak."

Deepak is my goto bloke for computers. He's a bit of what they call a hacker. He says he's a member of the "Revolutionary Cyberworkers Collective." Fuck knows what that's all about. I had to get him to write it down just so I could try and get my head round it. Complete mystery to me—all geeky and left-wing—but he is absolute mustard when it comes to computers. I get him in when mine goes wrong—funny things happening all over the screen or the emails don't work. He just presses a couple of keys and everything's up and running, sweet as a nut. He said to me once, "Computers are like dogs Spencer. They smell fear. If they think you're scared of them they'll crash all over the place. You need to give them a look that says, 'Don't even think about it Sunshine.' and they'll be as good as gold." I don't think I've got that look quite right yet.

Dany rang the bank and got the switchboard to put us through to Dapper. I listened on the extension.

"Hello Jack. This is a bit of a blast from the past. It's Dany Bullimore. Do you remember me from the old days at the Yard?"

He didn't answer for a couple of seconds.

"Yeah, I remember. I heard you got done for taking a drink off some bone-headed bogtrotter. I always knew you was a stupid cunt."

"Thanks for the reference Jack. I must remember to ask you next time I'm looking for a job. The reason I rang is because I just found something that reminded me of those old days and I thought to myself, 'I must give Jack a call.' I'd put it away and forgot all about it but I just found it again today. It's a picture of you, believe it or not. You're looking very happy. You're not wearing much though—and she's wearing even less."

I could hear him choking and spitting. Pissed or not, he knew he was in trouble.

"You bastard! What do you want?"

"Oh come on Jack. That's no way to talk to an old mate. We just want to come along and have a chat about old times. Chew the fat and all that."

"We? Who's we?"

"Me and my associate Mr Spencer Weintraub. He's a location agent. And our IT director Mr Deepak Nandy."

"What the fuck is a location agent?"

"He finds people Jack."

"And who's he looking for?"

"That's what we want to talk to you about Jack. Don't worry, we're not after money or nothing. It's just a friendly chat. You might be able to help us with a bit of information."

He was still humphing and grumphing.

"Where do you want to meet?"

"At the bank Jack."

"The bank! I can't just let anyone in here."

"You can let us in Jack. Say we're consultants, helping you keep Goldbury & Newman bank ever more secure."

He had to think for a few more seconds.

"When do you want to come?"

Dany looked at me and I mouthed "tomorrow".

"Tomorrow Jack."

"Tomorrow! Fuck me. You're in a hurry."

...

"Well, what do you fuckers fucking want?"

Jack's mood hadn't exactly improved since yesterday. Shame, because he seemed to be very nicely set up. You'd have thought it would have give him a nice warm glow inside. Nice office in a fine old City building, big desk, comfy sofa and pictures on the walls of him shaking hands with various bigwigs, usually with a bunch of Met top brass in full getup—the ones that look like they had scrambled egg poured all over them. I thought I had better try to smooth things a bit.

"Look Jack, we ain't here to do you over or nothing. We thought maybe you could help us. We're looking in to the death of Reuben Silver. His wife says she's not been told nothing and wants us to help her keep track of what's going on."

He started doing an impression of a volcano.

"What the ... We got a murder enquiry on our hands and what happens? A bent copper, a tosspot what calls himself a 'Location Agent' and some hairy hippy say they're helping the murdered man's wife and come here asking questions. You must be joking. Fuck off out of it now!"

Dany just smiled sweetly.

"Calm down Jack, calm down. We've all got a job to do. I don't need to remind you that whatever these nice pictures on the wall say, you ain't always been whiter than white. We all have our little failings and it's best if we keep these things to ourselves, which we will do if you give us a little help."

His shaking got a bit less.

"What sort of help?"

"Well, for a start, what about the gossip? Big shot director of posh peoples bank found dead in Dogswell with a bullet in his head. That don't happen every day of the week. Bound to set a few tongues wagging. Anyone around here know something? Did he run off with the money? Was he playing away? Anything like that."

"Nah. You got to realise what sort of bank this is. They don't talk about nothing. The directors sent a memo round. The usual stuff—great sadness, deepest sympathy, all that shit—and told everyone to button their lip and don't talk to no one. The bank's reputation was on the line."

"What about you Jack? You're Director of Security. You must be kept in the loop, as they say."

The muscles on his jaw stood out and his teeth grinded together.

"I don't do directors' security. Not that sort anyway. They do their own."

So the bank buys a dog and barks itself. Well, it can afford it.

"OK Jack, what about the coppers? They must have been sniffing around."

"Couple of City of London woodentops. Those wankers are about as likely to catch whoever done it as I am of nabbing Jack the Ripper."

"What did they do?"

"Mostly they hob-nobbed with the directors. They must have been in with them for a couple of hours. Came out absolutely pie-eyed."

"And you wasn't in with them Jack, as Director of Security?"

"No, I already told you that."

"So you did Jack. Wrong sort of Security. Did they have a chat with you?"

"Sort of. Asked me the usual—when he'd last been in, who he'd seen and whether he had behaved any different recently—but to be honest they didn't seem that interested."

"What about his office? They must have searched that."

"Yeah. They went in, fished around a bit and took away a few things."

"But you'd already tidied it up."

He did a bit of a double-take.

"Who said that?"

"His wife said that's what the bank would do. They wouldn't want nothing embarrassing to come out."

He gave us a look for a couple of seconds and then nodded.

"Too fucking right. If those bastards found something juicy it would be in the papers the next day. The tabloids have bought them lock stock and barrel. The Bank couldn't have that."

"They certainly couldn't Jack. That's what they employ a Director of Security for. Job well done. So what happened to the stuff you took from his office?"

"The directors took the papers away. Dunno where they are. They'll be locked away somewhere secure. You won't be able to see them."

"What about his computer?"

"It'll be going for scrap."

"Is it still here?"

"I've no fucking idea! I don't do computers."

"If it is still here Jack, where would it be?"

"There's a storage room where all that stuff is kept. Probably there."

"Could you take us down there Jack. We'd like to take a look."

...

The room was in the basement. It had no windows and when Jack turned on the light all you could see was rows of metal racking stuffed with computers and screens and all sorts of electronic stuff.

"How do we know which one was Silver's, Jack?"

"It should have his room number on it; 121 I think."

It took us about ten minutes to find it. It seemed to be all there. We found a socket on the wall, plugged it in and switched it on. "OK Deepak," I said, "do your stuff."

After a bit up came the screen asking for a password. I thought that would stymie us.

"How do you get the password?"

"No need." Deepak was fishing in a bag he's bought with him and pulled out one of them little pen drives. "There's a few ways to get in. Let's start with this."

He switched the computer off, put the pen drive in, switched it on again and pressed a key. A load of text came up on the screen. He hit a few more keys. This time the screen came up with little pictures on it.

"What's happening now Deepak?"

"This is Linux, the peoples' operating system Spencer. They didn't block booting from a USB drive. Tut, tut, tut. Very careless. Let's have a look and see what we've got." Deepak started looking at the files. "There's his emails. Quite a few of them. And there's his Documents folder. Mostly Word and Excel files and a few PDFs. Now what's this? This folder's encrypted."

"What does that mean?"

"It means we need a password to open it."

"Can't you do what you did just now and get round it?"

"No, this time we really do need the password."

"So what do we do, try and guess it?"

"No, that's a mug's game. We could be here all year. We'll have to take the hard disk with us. I've got some software that will sort it out back at my place."

I looked at Jack who just shrugged. Deepak took out a screwdriver and in about twenty seconds had the disk out and in his bag.

"That's about it Jack. Thanks for the help. We're all done."

He didn't look too happy.

"I'll have to see you out, otherwise someone will start asking questions, but I'm going back to my office first. I need a drink."

....

Jack opened his office sideboard and I could see a good few bottles of Scotland's finest export staring back at me. He seemed to be treating himself very nice.

"I suppose I should offer you bastards something now you're here."

"Put like that Jack, how could we refuse? Deepak don't drink though. You got anything for him?"

He pulled out a can of Coke, then poured out two very decent tots of scotch for Dany and me and an even bigger one for himself. He swigged down half of it in one gulp and slumped back in his chair, shaking his head.

"I hate this fucking job. I only do it for the money. The people here treat you like shit. They got so much money they don't know what to do with it. They got houses and cars and yachts. They got the wife in the country estate and the mistress in a flat in town and it's Ascot and Henley and champagne and caviar and opera and fuck knows what. And how do they get it? They're fucking bean counters, that's all. Because they count it they think they make it. They take the punter's money, stick it on the stock market or whatever and take the winnings for themselves. Do it anywhere else and they'd be locked up."

He knocked back the rest of his drink and poured himself another glassful.

"All I ever wanted to be was a copper. Best fucking job I ever had. What a time we had then. You must remember Dany, what a time, eh? The public'll never know what we had to do to keep them safe. Wish I was back there now. Back in the real Force though, not with that bunch of pen-pushing jobsworths they got at Scotland fucking Yard now. They wouldn't know how to catch a thief if one was plonked gift-wrapped on their desk and tied up with ribbons. It ain't the Force no more Dany. They've ruined it. They've fucking ruined it."

I thought he was going to start crying but he just took another couple of swigs.

"Back in the day we had to get out to get our collars. Now they just sit at desks looking at screens. Call that coppering! How do they catch a villain these days? Fuck knows. Probably just stick 'thief' into Google and email whatever comes up saying 'You're nicked.' Job done. And it all goes into the crime statistics automatic like, because it's on the computer.

"We had to learn the job the hard way; didn't we Dany, the best way. If you was a young copper you had to do your apprenticeship on the beat. You might get a cup of tea or a free meal off a café owner so you would look out for his place. Maybe you took a few bob off a publican when he wanted a lock in. Where's the harm in that? You had to get to know the magistrates so they wouldn't give you no grief when you was up in court. They call it 'networking' now but we was at it before anyone even thought of the word.

"Did you ever meet Dickie Elton Dany? No? Probably before your time. He was a DS in Hackney and he was the magistrates' darling. He had one particular favourite, a little old Irish woman. She liked a drop and Dickie used to go round to her place with a bottle, pretending he had a warrant for her to sign. He would leave the bottle and tear up the warrant afterwards. She always done him proud when he turned up in her court. Anybody he charged was lucky to escape with his life. It come in very handy in one particular case. Old Dickie was throwing the book at a villain he had been after for years. He was doing him for burglary, receiving, pimping, GBH—everything but actually having his hands on the crown jewels. He had all his verbals in line—'Yes I done it; bang to rights Governor; fair cop'—all that cobblers. Good verbals was a matter of pride in them days. It was icing on the cake and Dickie was one of the best. I once heard someone say he was the Shakespeare of verbals. Only when it come to court the scumbag produces a letter from the Governor of the Scrubs saying that he was in jail when all the offences was supposed to have taken place. His brief come over all pompous and suggested the magistrate might like to refer the matter to the Director of Public Prosecutions. She wasn't having none of it. She said his client had obviously misled an honest copper, Dickie, with his cock and bull confessions and sent him down for six months for perverting the course of justice and wasting police time."

By now he was well away, dreaming of the glory, glory days.

"Great times, great times Every Saturday night we had the race down to Southend. Last one there had to buy a round for the whole squad. When we got there we used to have a few jars and then we'd burn up the town. Got right up the noses of the local woodentops. You wouldn't remember Eric Rambler Dany. He was only a DC then but he always won. He was quicker than Stirling Moss. Should have been in them grand prixes. We was in Rover three point fives in them days. Fucking shit off a shovel they was! Nought to sixty in about half a second. The locals was in Morris fucking Minors. Can you believe it! Eric's party piece was to creep up behind them and then give them a right blast on the siren and the old two fingers as he whizzed past. He'd be out of sight before they got over the fright. Their Chief Con was always complaining but nobody ever got more than a little slap on the wrist. Couldn't have country bumpkins coming it over the boys from the Met could we?"

He filled his glass again and took another big swig.

"Nobody knows what proper coppering is these days. Now it's keep your nose clean and tick all the boxes and you're a DCI before you're out of short trousers. You don't catch nobody that way. We had to get down and dirty. OK, we bent the rules a few times, but so what? Who got hurt? I remember once when a big men's outfitters off Oxford Street got done. Suits and shirts and socks all over the place when we got there. We just tidied up and helped ourselves to a few things. One of our sergeants had a daughter that was getting married so he got the full outfit, including the top hat. I got a very nice suit; lasted me years. It was all on the insurance so who gave a shit? It wasn't like we was the Flying Squad. They used to get their hands on hundreds of grand after catching some big bank robbers. Did they give it all back? Did they fuck. But they was angels compared to these bankers. They've swindled the whole country out of billions and what do they get for it? Billions more. And what's our precious Scotland Yard doing about it? Sweet FA. I'd like to see a few of us old guard get our hands on them bankers. They'd soon wish they was never born."

The thought of banging up a few bankers seem to perk him up a bit but then he was off again.

"Mind you, you can't nick everyone all the time. You'd have to lock up half London if you did. You had to keep a lid on things, make sure things don't get out of hand. You had to get to know the villains so you could get to know what was going on. We used to go down to boozers like the Prince of Wales, near the Elephant. Been pulled down a long time now, but in them days you would have a right load of villains using it. Lot of boxers too, British champions some of them, and all the big gang bosses and their hangers on, wives and girlfriends all sitting along the wall drinking their port and lemons. You could learn a lot there if you played your cards right, but it was give and take. You might have to slip someone a pony—or even a ton—to get the SP on a job. Then all you had to do was wait around the joint till the bastards turned up and nick 'em. Better than working. On the other hand, fair's fair, you might take a few bob to look the other way when one of your snouts wanted to do a little job for hisself. As I said, give and take."

He was clutching his glass tighter and tighter and I swear a tear was rolling down his cheek.

"At the end of the day we caught the ones that mattered, didn't we Dany. We was thief-takers Dany, proper thief-takers. You only have to ask yourself, was you safer then or now? Answers itself, don't it?"

9

Deepak's place is an old bakery in a street off the back of Dogswell Town Hall. It has still got the baker's name painted over the door. Inside it's just a big room with half a dozen desks with big screens on them and a bunch of geeky types, who look as if they haven't seen daylight for a few years, staring at them. Fuck knows what they do. I wouldn't know how to ask. Deepak was sitting by his screen, swigging a cup of something.

"OK Deepak, what've we got? You cracked it yet?"

He gave me the sort of look that was half way between a smile and a "Fuck off. Who do you think you're talking to?"

"We're getting there."

"What does that mean?"

"It means that he's used the standard Windows EFS—Encrypted File System to you Spence—but there are a number of encrypted folders with different passwords so we're going to have to crack more than one. After that we decrypt the certificates and then we're cooking with the proverbial. I've got a very nice piece of Russian software that does the biz. They must have developed it to stick it to the Yanks."

"Glad to hear it Deepak, but are you telling me that you ain't got nothing yet?"

"Yeah, we have. We've decrypted one folder. Turns out he used his wife's name as the password—Rachel. He may have used something similar for the others—mother's name, dog's name, postcode, football team, date of birth, that sort of thing. I've got a password cracker working on it but it could be slow. Any of that sort of info you could get me would help."

"I'll have a word with the widow woman. You said you've got one folder open. What's it all about?"

"It's called Georgev."

"Georgev?"

"Yeah. George with a 'v' on the end."

"Don't mean nothing to me. What's in it?"
We went over to the computer and he clicked on the folder.

Did His Majesty, I then asked, realize the dangers of the situation, and was he aware that revolutionary language was being held, not only in Petrograd, but throughout Russia? On the Emperor saying that he was quite aware that people were indulging in such talk, but that I made a mistake in taking it too seriously, I told him that a week before Rasputin's assassination I had heard that an attempt was about to be made on his life. I had treated this report as idle gossip, but it had, after all, proved true. I could not, therefore, now turn a deaf ear to the reports which had reached me of assassinations, said to be contemplated of certain exalted personages....An Ambassador, I am well aware, has no right to hold the language which I have held to Your Majesty, and I had to take my courage in both hands before speaking as I have done. I can but plead as my excuse the fact that I have throughout been inspired by my feelings of devotion for Your Majesty and the Empress...You have, sir, come to the parting of the ways, and you have now to choose between two paths. The one will lead you to victory and a glorious peace—the other to revolution and disaster. [17 January 1917]
Sir George Buchanan, *My Mission to Russia*, p 48-9

Bad news from Russia, practically a revolution has broken out in Petrograd and some of the Guards regiments have mutinied and killed their officers. This rising is against the Govt. not against the war
George V *Diary* 13 March 1917

I fear Alicky is the cause of it all and Nicky has been weak... I am in despair.
George V, *Diary,* 15 March

"'Bad news from Russia'. What's that got to do with the price of bananas Deepak and who are these characters?

"Well at least we know now what "georgev" is."

"We do?"

"Yeah. Isn't it obvious? It's George V, George the Fifth."

"George the fifth what?"

"*King* George the Fifth!"

"OK, OK, I get it. King George the Fifth. Was he before or after Henry the Eighth?"

Deepak looked at me as if I'd just dropped in from Mars.

"You really are ignorant about your country's history, aren't you Spencer. Henry the Eighth was around over four hundred years ago. George the Fifth was only a couple back from the old bird we've got now. He was her grandfather."

"OK, *that* George the Fifth. So who's this Nicky and Alicky?"

"Ah, that's Nicholas the Second, the last Tsar of Russia and his wife Alexandra. He was deposed by revolution in 1917 That's what George was talking about. He seems to be saying that a lot of it was his wife's fault. Sir George Buchanan, who was the British Ambassador to Russia at the time, seems to be saying if Nicholas didn't do something things could go very badly. He was right."

"Wasn't that the revolution that let the Commies in?"

"No. This is the first Russian revolution, in March 1917, although it's called the February revolution because the Russians were still using the old calendar which was a couple of weeks behind ours and it was still February according to them. The second Russian revolution was in November 1917, or October if you were a Russian, when the Bolsheviks under Lenin and Trotsky seized state power and founded the Soviet Union."

You learn something every day.

"Bit like the old buses eh Deepak? You wait ages for a revolution and then two come along at once. How do you know all this?"

"I'm a revolutionary socialist Spencer. We go big on the Russian revolution."

"My fault for asking. OK, let's have a look at some more."

It is with the sentiments of the most profound satisfaction that the peoples of Great Britain and the British Dominions across the seas have learned that their great ally Russia now stands with the nations which base their institutions upon responsible government.

Much as we appreciate the loyal and steadfast cooperation received from the late Emperor and the armies of Russia during the past two and a half years, yet I believe that the revolution whereby the Russian people have based their destinies on the sure foundation of freedom is the greatest service which they have yet made to the cause for which the Allied peoples have been fighting since August 1914.

Lloyd George, *Telegram to the Provisional Government of Russia,* 20 March 1917

Stamfordham instructed to complain telegram "a little strong" coming from a monarchical government.

George V, *Diary,* 20 March 1917

"Lloyd George, wasn't he a bit of a ladies man? What's he doing sending telegrams to Russia?"

"I give up on you Spencer. Lloyd George was the British prime minister at the time. He was congratulating the Russians for overthrowing a despot and instituting democracy. Lord Stamfordham was George's private secretary. Evidently George wasn't too keen on monarchs being deposed. Shall we read on?"

Events of the last week have deeply distressed me. My thoughts are constantly with you and I shall always remain your true and devoted friend, as you know I have been in the past.

George V, Telegram to Nicholas, 21 March 1917

On March 21, while His Majesty, was still at the Stavka, I asked Miliukoff whether it was true, as had been stated in the Press, that the Emperor had been arrested. He replied that this was not quite correct. His Majesty had been deprived of his liberty—a pretty euphemism—and would be brought to Tsarskoe under an escort furnished by General Alexeieff ... he should remain at Tsarskoe till his children had sufficiently recovered from the measles for the Imperial family to travel to England.

He was most anxious that the Emperor should leave Russia at once. He would, therefore, be grateful if His Majesty's Government would offer him an asylum in England ... I at once telegraphed to the Foreign Office for the necessary authorization.

Buchanan *op cit* p104

The King and His Majesty's Government readily offer asylum to the Emperor and Empress in England which, it is hoped, they will take advantage of during the war. You should, at the same time, impress upon the Russian Government the necessity for making suitable provision for their maintenance in this country.

British Foreign Office. *Telegram to Sir George Buchanan* 22 March 1917

"So when he got kicked out of Russia we was supposed to take him. How come and what happened when he did get here?"

"It's a bit more complicated than that Spencer. Read on."

Minutes of the Petrograd Soviet Executive Committee Session of March 9 Concerning the Disposition of the Imperial Family

1. ON THE ARREST OF NICHOLAS ROMANOV.

In view of the information that the Provisional Government has decided to permit Nicholas Romanov to depart for England, and that he is at present on his way to

Petrograd, the Executive Committee has decided to adopt extraordinary measures, immediately, for his detention and arrest. An order has been issued for occupying all the railway stations by our troops, and commissars [vested] with extraordinary powers have been dispatched to the stations of Tsarskoe Selo, Tosno. and Zvanka. In addition, it was decided to send radiotelegrams to all towns with instructions to arrest Nicholas Romanov and, in general, to adopt a series of extraordinary measures. At the same time, it was decided to inform the Provisional Government at once of the unswerving determination of the Executive Committee not to permit the departure of Nicholas Romanov for England, and to arrest him. The Trubetskoi Bastion of the Peter and Paul Fortress was decided upon as the place of confinement for Nicholas Romanov, and its commanding personnel was changed for this purpose. It was decided to carry out the arrest of Nicholas Romanov al all costs, even if severance of relations with the Provisional Government is threatened.

That sounds like the Commies to me Deepak. Looks like they wasn't too keen on Nicholas coming here."

"They weren't the only ones. Keep going."

The King has been thinking much about the Government's proposal that the Emperor Nicholas and his family should come to England. As you are doubtless aware, the King has a strong friendship for the Emperor and therefore would be glad to do anything to help him in this crisis. But His Majesty cannot help doubting, not only on account of the dangers of the voyage, but on general grounds of expediency, whether it is advisable that the Imperial Family should take up residence in this country.

Lord Stamfordham, to Arthur Balfour, Foreign Secretary, 30 March 1917

"What's this? Is George changing his mind about Nicky coming here?"

"He certainly is Spencer, but as Balfour, who was the British Foreign Secretary, pointed out, it was a bit late to be having second thoughts. They were clearly very embarrassed and wanted to keep the offer open.

> ... while His Majesty's ministers quite realize the difficulties to which you refer in your letter ... they do not think that, unless the position changes, it is now possible to withdraw the invitation which has been sent and they therefore trust that the King will consent to adhere to the original invitation which was sent on the advice of His Majesty's Ministers.
>
> Balfour to Stamfordham 30 March 1917

"So did George take any notice?"

He doesn't seem to have done. If anything he becomes more insistent."

> Every day the king is becoming more concerned about the question of the Emperor and Empress coming to this country. His Majesty receives letter from people of all classes of life, known or unknown to him, saying much the matter is being discussed, not only in clubs but by working men, and that Labour Members of the House of Commons are expressing adverse opinions to the proposal... I feel sure that you appreciate how awkward it will be for our Royal Family who are closely connected with both the Emperor and Empress ... The King desires me to ask you whether after consulting the Prime Minister, Sir George Buchanan should not be communicated with a view to approaching the Russian Government to make some other place for the future residence of their Imperial Majesties.
>
> Stamfordham to Balfour, 6 April 1917

He must beg you to represent to the Prime Minister that from all he hears and reads in the press, the residence in this country of the ex-Emperor and Empress would be strongly resented by the public, and would undoubtedly compromise the position of the King and Queen from whom it would generally be assumed the invitation had emanated... Buchanan ought to be instructed to tell Miliukoff that the opposition to the Emperor and Empress coming here is so strong that we must be allowed to withdraw from the consent previously given to the Russian Government's proposal.

Stamfordham to Balfour 6 hours later

"This is getting silly Deepak. I thought George was dead keen on him coming to England. Now he's sending letters every few hours saying don't let the bastard in, like he was an illegal immigrant or something."

"It is very odd. Something clearly has got into him. He seems to be getting frantic about the whole thing. He's claiming it was because of all the letters he was getting, as if he took a blind bit of notice of anything the great unwashed thought. I don't believe a word of it, but whatever the reason it had results. "

And then, just as hope seemed in sight, a telegram arrived from England! It was the 10th April (N.S), and the memory of that day has remained vividly in my mind. There had been a certain amount of desultory shooting during the night, but my father had gone as usual to the Foreign Office, and when he had not come up for luncheon at one o'clock my mother, who never knew a moment's peace of mind when he was out of the house, grew anxious, and rang for William to ask if anything had happened.

"His Excellency came in a few moments ago," William replied. "He went straight into the Chancery, as he was told that there was an urgent telegram from England."

... There were, after all, telegrams from England every day, and there was no reason why this one should be of any special importance, and yet those moments of waiting stand out in my mind with a peculiar and unforgettable distinctness.

Then at last the big white doors were flung open and my father came into the room, and seeing his look, my mother gave a little exclamation of dismay. "Are you ill?" she exclaimed. "Has anything happened?"

He had sunk down in the chair in front of his desk, and put both hands to his forehead, in a gesture that was habitual to him when he was worried and anxious. "I have had news from England," he said, and his voice sounded flat and lifeless. "They refuse to let the Emperor come over!"

Meriel Buchanan, *The Dissolution of an Empire* p192

"Looks like George got his way."
"He did, and look what happened next."

I attended a service at the Russian Church in Welbeck Street in memory of dear Nicky, who I fear was shot last month by the Bolshevists. I was devoted to Nicky who was the kindest of men, a thorough gentleman: loved his country and people.

George V, *Diary*, 25 July 1918 (The King decreed a month of court mourning)

Was there ever a crueller murder and has this country ever before displayed such a callous indifference to a tragedy of this magnitude. What does it all mean? I am so thankful that the King and Queen attended the memorial service. I have not yet discovered that the PM .. [was] even represented, Where is our national sympathy, gratitude, common decency?

Stamfordham to Lord Esher

I hear from Russia that there is every probability that Alicky and the four daughters and the little boy were murdered at the same time as Nicky. It is too horrible and shows what fiends these Bolshevists are. For poor Alicky, perhaps it was best so. But those poor innocent children!

George V, *Diary*, August 1918

The murder shook my father's confidence in the innate decency of mankind ... My father had personally planned to rescue him with a British cruiser but in some way the plan was blocked. In any case it hurt my father that Britain had not raised a hand to save his Cousin Nicky. "Those politicians." he used to say, "If it had been one of their kind they would have acted soon enough."

Duke of Windsor (Edward VIII) *A Kings Story*

"Talk about crocodile tears Deepak! First he wants them to come, then he says they can't come, then when they get killed he's crying his eyes out, saying it's all the fault of the politicians and if it was up to him he'd have got them out with a gunship."

Deepak shook his head. "We have a classic case of denial here Spencer. As you say, first he wanted them to come. Then he changed his mind and seemed to be almost desperate that they didn't come. Then, when he found out that they had all been killed, he claimed he had wanted to rescue them all along but the politicians prevented him. What a shit. The idea that he was concerned about the working classes doesn't really make sense. I did a bit of research before you came and it turns out he was an old skinflint. He kept his workers on his estates on poverty wages. He was pretty dim, even by the standards of our monarchy, and preferred to stay at home pursuing his hobbies of stamp collecting and game shooting. Something else must have made him change his mind."

"All this Russian stuff is practically a hundred years old Deepak. What's it got to do with our boy Reuben Silver getting a bullet in the back of the head in Dogswell?"

"A very good question Spencer. I've been wondering that myself. And why encrypt it? This stuff has all got to be in the public domain."

We looked at the screen for a couple of minutes but we wasn't getting any wiser. Well I wasn't, anyway. Deepak decided to help me out.

"We should have a better look at this Nicholas the last."

How were we going to do that I wanted to know.

"The Internet Spencer. We all have access to the world wide web and I can log into university libraries with over a million books online. Omniscience is ours Spencer. We only have to know how to look."

Deepak bunged something into Google.

"Let's start with the fount of all wisdom, *Wikipedia*."

Up it come and we was looking at a bloke with a beard, wearing a uniform with what looked like a load of spaghetti around his neck. "Autocrat and Emperor of All the Russias" it said underneath. How many fucking Russias was there in them days—and where did they all go? Didn't look like *Wikipedia* was going to tell us. What it did tell us though was that the bloke was a walking fucking disaster:

Nicholas II ruled from 1 November 1894 until his enforced abdication on 2 March 1917. His reign saw Imperial Russia go from being one of the foremost great powers of the world to economic and military collapse.

Under his rule, Russia was humiliatingly defeated in the Russo-Japanese War, which saw the almost total annihilation of the Russian Baltic Fleet at the Battle of Tsushima. The Anglo-Russian Entente, designed to counter German attempts to gain influence in the Middle East, ended the Great Game between Russia and the United Kingdom. As head of state, Nicholas approved the Russian mobilization of August 1914, which marked the beginning of Russia's involvement in World War I, a war in which 3.3 million Russians were killed. The Imperial Army's severe losses and the High Command's incompetent handling of the war, along with other policies directed by Nicholas during his reign, are often cited as the leading causes of the fall of the Romanov dynasty.

Nicholas II abdicated following the February Revolution of 1917 during which he and his family were imprisoned first in the Alexander Palace at Tsarskoye Selo, then later in the Governor's Mansion in Tobolsk, and finally at the Ipatiev House in Yekaterinburg. In the spring of 1918, Nicholas was handed over to the local Ural soviet by commissar Vasili Yakovlev who was then presented with a written receipt as Nicholas was formally handed over like a parcel. Nicholas II; his wife, Alexandra Feodorovna; his son, Alexei Nikolaevich; his four daughters (Olga Nikolaevna, Tatiana Nikolaevna, Maria Nikolaevna and Anastasia Nikolaevna); the family's medical doctor, Evgeny Botkin; the Emperor's footman, Alexei Trupp; the Empress' maidservant, Anna Demidova; and the family's cook, Ivan Kharitonov were executed in the same room by the Bolsheviks on the night of 16/17 July 1918.

A bit further down the page there was a picture of Nicholas and—guess who?—George the Fifth. Talk about peas in a pod. Even their mothers couldn't probably tell them apart. It turned out they was cousins. Their mothers was sisters, daughters of the King of Denmark. Not only that but George was also a cousin of Nicholas's wife, the Alicky that he was moaning about. Queen Victoria was grandmother to both of them. Nothing like keeping it in the family.

I got to admit that this *Wikipedia* was a mine of information. Great big screenfuls of it. Most of it went over my head—lots of stuff about politics and wars. One bit did catch my eye though—Rasputin. I remember the song—"Ra, Ra Rasputin, lover of the Russian Queen" and all that—but I thought it was just a song. Turns out he was real. He was a monk who had some magic power of treating Nicholas's son who had haemophilia. Caught it from Queen Vic apparently. I was just about to say to Deepak that this was all very interesting but it wasn't getting us anywhere when something caught my eye in Wikipedia:

> At the time of his death, his net worth was $900 million, which is the inflation adjusted equivalent to $300 billion in 2012 dollars, thus making him one of the richest monarchs in human history

"What's all this about him being worth hundreds of billions then Deepak?"

He rolled his eyes.

"Well he didn't have it on him when he was shot. I think you should take that with a big pinch of salt Spencer. All his palaces and things were taken over by the Bolsheviks. They weren't too keen on paying compensation."

"But maybe he had money abroad—Swiss bank accounts, that sort of thing."

"There were always rumours. Several people in the thirties claimed to be one of his children who had somehow escaped the massacre and knew where the money was. They were all fakers. They've got the DNA evidence now. The whole family was killed in 1918. If there ever was any Tsarist gold it will be long gone now. Frankly you've got more chance of finding a pot of gold at the end of a rainbow."

10

I always like to keep the client in the picture. Makes them better payers. I went round to see Rachel Silver with the good news—we had got something. Didn't mention the bad news—we didn't have a clue what it was about.

"We're starting to get stuff from his computer but we need some help with passwords. Looks like he used a different one for every folder. We've got one folder cracked. He used your name as the password so we reckon he probably used something similar for the others—mother or father's name, pet's name, postcode, maybe a road name, that sort of thing. We think you may be able to help us out."

"His father's name was Hyman and his mother's was Miriam but you say you've managed to read something. What was it about?"

"Nothing, really. Well, nothing to do with what we're about. Just a load of stuff about King George the Fifth and the Russian Tsar, Nicholas the something or other. Seems Georgie-boy invited Nicky to come to England after the Revolution and then thought better of it. Poor old Nicky ended up with a bullet to the head. Can't say I was crying my eyes out when I read about it. I ain't much of a royalist. Anyway it was nearly a hundred years ago and a long, long way from Dogswell."

She looked to heaven and opened her arms wide, like she was a bit exasperated.

"Oh God, not that again! Reuben was obsessed with the fate of the Tsar and his family and was convinced that there were some murky dealings with George the Fifth who had reneged on an agreement to bring him to England. Reuben tried to explain to me why but I couldn't follow it. It was all to do with the government and Lloyd George and the Labour party and the revolutionaries and God knows who else. All absolutely ridiculous of course but that didn't stop Reuben from trying to prove it. He had a whole library on everything to do with it. Look, I'll show you."

We went into the next room, which was as she said, a library, bookshelves floor to ceiling. I took a look at some of the titles: *The Last Days of Imperial Russia*, *The Dissolution of an Empire*, *The Lost Fortune of the Tsars*, *The Murder of the Romanovs* and lots more where they came from.

"I see what you mean. He definitely had a thing for the Russian stuff. But if he had all these books why did he just put a few bits and pieces on his computer and encrypt them? They wasn't secret or anything was they?"

"Reuben was always making notes of things that interested him. It was his way of clarifying his thoughts. Why he encrypted these particular ones I have no idea. We didn't discuss the subject, mainly because I thought the whole thing so absurd. Unlike you Mr Weintraub, I *am* a monarchist and very much in favour of the Royal family. I thought his ideas were frankly unpatriotic, especially since this country saved his father's life. He was a Polish Jew who fled to Belgium and came here on almost the last boat to leave before the war. At one stage I thought Reuben was becoming, well, a little unhinged. He even suggested that one of King George's motives was to get his hands on the Tsar's stamp collection. Have you ever heard anything so ridiculous! I was beginning to get worried about him and this obsession. I suggested he might try to get some help."

"What sort of help?"

"Counselling, perhaps talking to a psychiatrist."

"I suppose he didn't?"

"No."

"So where did he get all these ideas from?"

"I don't really know. Reuben was always keen on history. It's what he read at Oxford and this particular era came to fascinate him. Maybe it was the Eastern European thing as his family came from there. I'm sure there were lots of things he didn't tell me because, as I said, I refused to talk about it, but I don't suppose we'll ever know what they were now."

"Probably not. Anyway, I don't think any of it matters. I don't think the Royal family or the Russian Tsars sent out a hit-man to do Reuben. It has to be someone else. Which brings me to another question. Did he have anything to do with the ENF?"

"The what?"

"The ENF. The English National Front. Bunch of roughnecks who go about waving flags and beating up immigrants and gays."

She didn't like that notion one bit. She leant back in the chair like a cat going on its hind legs.

"Absolutely not! Reuben would never have anything to do with people like that. Whatever gave you the idea?"

"That phone call you got was from a pay as you go mobile that was bought by a bloke named Steve Curting who is something of a big wheel is in the ENF. When we was trying to find Reuben I managed to track Curting down and asked him if he knew anything about Reuben. He said he'd never heard of him. I said that was a pity because Reuben had a wife and kiddies crying for him to come home. The look he gave me suggested that he knew there weren't no kiddies. He definitely knew something."

"Whatever you say Mr Weintraub, I can't imagine Reuben being mixed up with anything like that. His instincts were all the other way. He was rather left-wing in his youth, like most students. He grew out of it of course, especially after he joined the Bank, but he has always been liberal in his leanings. Besides, from what you say about these people, I imagine they are very anti-Semitic as well."

"You could say that. It does seem a bit odd. Maybe I should have another chat with Mr Curting. Look, there's one other thing I wanted to talk to you about, but it might be a bit delicate"

"What's that?"

"Well, I went to the place Reuben had been staying in Dogswell. It was flat in an estate. He got it off an Internet ad. It couldn't have been just a spur of the moment thing. He must have been planning it for a while. I don't want to be nosy, but any idea why?"

She sighed and I thought her eyes were watering up.

"I can't think of a reason. I know this might sound absurd but the more I find out the less I think I know—knew—Reuben. His mild obsession with kings and tsars was one thing, but he was obviously more troubled than I ever realised."

...

When I got back to the office I found Fanackapan in a strop. There was no petty cash and we'd run out of biscuits, tea and coffee. Talk about a crisis. I fished out a fiver and told her not to spend it all at once. She then plonked a load of papers on my desk.

"What's this?"

"It's all the bills you haven't paid for the last six months— rent, business rates, telephone, electricity for a start. You had better start paying or you'll be out on your ear."

I hadn't sorted out the bank so I couldn't write a cheque but I did have the Silver money.

"Will they take cash?"

"No, but if you give me the cash I'll put into our new ac- count and you can write cheques with them."

"What new account?"

"The one I set up with the building society across the road. I knew you wouldn't bother to get your account straight at the bank so that's why I set up the new one."

If there's one thing I hate it's fucking mind-readers but I had to give her a wedge and let her do the necessary. There was no tea in the office so I switched on my computer and started watching a few videos, mainly funnies. It was too early for any- thing raunchy. Then I got a ping as an email came in.

Dear Mr Weintraub,
Having thought about if further, I would be willing to talk to you. My contact details are below.
Yours
Marilyn Haigh

I'd almost forgotten about her. We'd found a message from her on Reuben Silver's iPad. When I first contacted her she said she didn't want to talk. Now she'd changed her mind. I didn't think there would be anything in it, but you never know.

11

Marilyn Haigh lived way out in the badlands of West London, not somewhere I go often. I had to take a train and a cab to get there. Her street was all mock-Tudorish semis, very quiet, very respectable. I pushed her doorbell and I heard it inside, playing some sort of tune. She opened the door and took me into her front room. She was about fifty, I'd guess, slim, not bad looking, dressed in a jumper and slacks. She had a neat haircut in a bob, nothing flash, and wasn't wearing no make up. I sat down and she asked me if I would like some tea.

When she went out I looked round the room. It was all very neat, light and airy. There was the usual furniture—a sofa, a couple of armchairs, a sideboard and a low table. You couldn't really say any of it was old or new. On the sideboard were a lot of framed photos, mainly of her and a bloke that I guessed was her husband.

She came back in with the tea and started talking.

"I was very sad to hear what happened to Mr Silver. Absolutely shocking. That's why I changed my mind about seeing you. He was such a nice man. Please give my condolences to Mrs Silver. I do understand what she must be going through."

"Of course. Thanks for seeing me. As I told you, I've been engaged by Mrs Silver to look into the background of her husband's death, Not to try and find the killer, obviously; that's the Police's job, but the Police aren't telling her much and she just wants to try and find out why anyone would want to kill her husband. So I'm talking to anyone who might be able to give us a clue."

"I understand of course, Mr Weintraub, but I'm not sure that I can be of much assistance. Mr Silver came to see me in connection with some research of a historical nature. That's all I can tell you about him."

"What sort of historical nature?"

"Well my husband, my late husband, was an acknowledged authority on the finances of the British Royal Family. He wrote a book, *the* book, on the subject. I'll get a copy for you."

She fished it out of a bookcase and gave it to me. It was called *Money and Monarchy* by Robert Haigh.

"This looks very impressive. What's it all about?"

"It's a definitive enquiry into the financial affairs of every British monarch from Queen Victoria onwards. It looks at their income, their expenditures, what tax, if any, that they paid, all those things. Needless to say, his book was most unwelcome in Royal circles. Their friends in the press made every effort to denigrate it."

"I bet they did. So why did Reuben Silver want to come and see you?"

"He had been doing some research on royal finances for a book he intended to write and had contacted me to see if there were any updates on Robert's book. I told him that there wasn't a great deal more. Robert had been working on the new edition but it was mostly adding details. The only thing new was that he had been following up some information that William Taft, who had been President and Chief Justice of the United States, had said that George the Fifth had received some of the proceeds of the sale of honours by Lloyd George and Maundy Gregory. "

"What do you mean, sale of honours?"

"It was a big scandal in the twenties. A lot of rich people wanted an honour, a knighthood or a peerage, and were prepared to pay for it. A man called Maundy Gregory, with the connivance of Lloyd George, sold the honours and the proceeds went to both the Liberal and Conservative parties. Gregory was eventually prosecuted."

That sounded a bit tasty. It's not every day you hear of kings trousering loot.

"So was George in on the deal?"

"Who knows? Robert was convinced that Taft had, made the allegation when he visited London in 1922, based presumably on what he had heard in British financial circles, but he hadn't been able to pin down who he had talked to. I doubt if we will ever know."

"Was Mr Silver interested in that?"

"I think so, though he said his main interest was in the period around the First World War. I gave him some more detailed background information that Robert had not included in the book. I was Robert's assistant so I am quite familiar with the material."

"Did you and Mr Silver talk about anything else?"

"Nothing more about Robert's work. We just chatted. As I said, Mr Silver was a very nice man, very sympathetic, and I was feeling very low after Robert's death."

"Yes, I'm sorry about that. Was it very sudden?"

She looked at me and I could see tears come into her eyes.

"Yes, very sudden."

"What was it, a heart attack?"

She looked away and said nothing for a few seconds.

"No, not a heart attack. He was found hanged."

That was a shocker. I didn't know what to say for a minute.

"That must really have been awful for you. Was it suicide?"

She shook her head and I could see the tears begin to roll down her cheeks.

"Mr Weintraub I really don't know. All the time I knew him Robert never said anything to me that he might contemplate suicide. Like everybody he had his ups and downs but he was never really depressed, certainly not suicidal. There was no note, nothing. He was found hanging in the nude in the little office he used in the centre of town. The police hinted that it might have been a sex game gone wrong, but Robert wasn't like that. He had no interest in exotic sex. Quite the contrary. The inquest verdict was misadventure, which means they just don't know. It's a complete mystery and it haunts my every waking minute."

...

I felt really sorry for Marilyn Haigh but my guess was the coppers was right. He was playing around, trying to give himself a big thrill and it went a bit far. She said he didn't like sex games but it's always the quiet ones. Whatever happened I didn't think it had anything to do with the Silver case.

I wanted to talk to Curting again. We needed to find him and the boy to help there was Gazzer. Finding Gazzer ain't always easy. I went round his place but Eth said she didn't know where he was. Eventually I tracked him down by accident when I saw him going into the Black Hart, a spit and sawdust boozer in a little alley off the High Street. When I went in he was sitting by himself in a corner nursing a pint. He was his usual cheery self.

"What do you fucking want?"

"I just want another word with your mate Curting, Gaz, and I thought you might help us get in touch."

"Fuck off."

He always did play hard to get.

"Don't take it like that Gaz. Look, it's important. I tell you what, I'll buy a couple more drinks and there's a pony in it for you as well if you can tell me where I could find him."

"No can do."

"Why not? He's one of your lot isn't he?"

"Nope."

"What do you mean no? I saw him at that meeting in the Pirates when you was there."

"He ain't one of my lot 'cos I ain't in the Front no more. I've been fucking expelled."

The mind boggled. What the fuck did you have to do to get expelled from the ENF?

"Expelled? How come?"

"Well, it was at the last meeting. The chairman said things was getting slack. We wasn't showing enough patriotism, doing enough marching and flying the flag and giving the towelheads a hard enough time and besides some of us was dressing sloppy. He was looking straight at me when he said it. Nobody says I ain't a patriot so I had to deck him, didn't I?"

"Put like that Gaz, who could argue? So they chucked you out?"

"Yeah, bastards!"

"Well there you are Gaz. Maybe you could start up your own outfit. Make it just what you want. Anyway, there must be somewhere where we can find Curting?"

He looked doubtful.

"The only place you might see him is at the sing song in the Pirates tomorrow night. He sometimes turns up."

...

I got there early. A lot better chance of getting some sense from Curting at the start than when he's totally pissed and carousing with a load of drunken ENFers. Just as I got there Gazzer turned up with Fifi in tow. That hound didn't look like he'd mellowed much since I last saw him.

"Whatya Gazzer. I thought you said you'd been chucked out. Have they let you in again?"

"Nah. I've just come along for the singing. I thought some of the lads might still be pleased to see me. And I'd like to hear what that bastard Curting has got to say for himself."

A couple of minutes later the boy himself, Curting, come round the corner. He looked puzzled for a few seconds before he recognised me. "Didn't I see you at our last meeting?" and then he spied Gazzer.

"Evening Gazzer. I heard you've been a naughty boy. Got yourself kicked out. Tut, tut."

Gazzer looked like he was going to blow up. Curting looked at the dog.

"Got a dog I see Gazzer. What's its name?"

"Fifi."

Curting come over all mimsy and limp-wristed.

"Oh Fifi is it? And it's a boy. Are you gay Fifi? Do you like to take it up the ..."

There was an explosion of growling and all of a sudden Curting was flat on his arse, yelling and screaming, with Fifi's size 20 gnashers round his ankle.

It looked like it was going to be fucking carnage but Gazzer eventually managed to pull Fifi off with the lead. He practically had to strangle him. He gave Curting a right earful.

"You should count yourself lucky Curting. He usually goes for the bollocks. And he don't like being called a poofter neither."

Curting got to his feet, trousers torn and blood around his ankle, still cursing.

"That fucking dog's mad! What's it got, rabies?"

I thought I'd better step in before things got completely out of hand.

"No, just bad breath. You'll live, probably. Since we're talking, I wanted to ask you about Reuben Silver. Last time you said you'd never heard of him, but we know that someone called his wife on a phone bought by you, wanting a couple of million quid as a ransom. And now he's been found with a bullet in his brain. In my book that could put you in the frame."

He was definitely rattled.

"What the fuck are you on about? I never heard of no ransom nor this bloke Silver."

Time to put a bit of pressure on.

"I don't believe you and I don't think Fifi does neither. As you seen, he's a sensitive soul and he don't like being lied to."

Curting looked around. I think he was working out his chances of getting inside the door of the pub before the dog. He must have come to the same conclusion as me—none.

"Look, OK, I phoned her but it was nothing to do with no ransom and I don't know nothing about murder. What do you think we are, criminals?"

I didn't bother answering that one.

"So why did you phone her then?"

He looked around again and made a face.

"We found out he was a big backer of *Spotlight*. We wanted to tell him to lay off if he knew what was good for him. He wasn't there when I phoned. His wife answered. I just asked where he was. She said he was out on business."

"So threatening someone is not criminal? That's a new one. And what's *Spotlight*?"

"*Spotlight* is one of these lefty magazines. Claims to 'expose' what it calls 'right-wing groups'. It's full of lies. Calls us Nazis and all sorts of other shit. We wasn't going to do nothing to Silver. It was just a little frightener."

"And you're not Nazis, of course?"

"No we are fucking not. We're English nationalists, like it says on the tin. People tell lies about us all the time. If we had the money we'd sue. But we haven't, so we have to find some other ways."

"So that's it. You just wanted to warn him off. And how did you know he backed this *Spotlight* rag?"

"Someone tipped off our head office. Anonymous. Come in a brown envelope."

Sometimes you get the impression that someone isn't lying about everything. I wasn't sure what he wasn't lying about but there didn't seem a lot of point trying to find out just then. Besides, he wasn't that bright; he probably didn't know that much.

"I'd go and see a doctor about that ankle if I was you. No knowing what Fifi's had in his mouth lately."

12

Since I know fuck all about politics, or about computers, I got Deepak over and we looked up *Spotlight* on the internet. It was a bit of a revelation. "*Spotlight* leads the fight against fascism and racism" it said on the banner and below it listed all the "fights" it had got itself into. Turns out that *Spotlight* was a bit of a bruiser. In good old Blighty we had the ENF and the BNP up to their usual tricks—rioting, torching mosques and the like. But that was nothing to what was happening abroad. According to them fascism was up to no good all over the place—France, Russia, Germany, Belgium and the rest; there was practically nowhere where the jackboot wasn't on the march. If *Spotlight* really was fighting that lot it would have needed a fucking army, but the website just mentioned a couple of people from some university I'd never heard of. Looked like maybe they was biting off more than they could chew.

"How do we get in touch with this lot Deepak? Maybe they could tell us if Silver really was backing them."

"I doubt it Spencer. They're probably very sensitive about that sort of thing for obvious reasons. But, if you want to try, there is a contact box. We could send them a message. You never know. They might reply. What do you want to say?"

I told him to play it straight. They must have heard of Silver's murder. Tell them that Silver's wife had asked us to help since she wasn't getting much information from the police. We had heard that he was a backer of *Spotlight*. Was that true?

About ten minutes later we got a reply: "Thank you for your message. We cannot enter into any discussions with you since we have no idea of your true identity."

I asked Deepak what we do now and he suggested sending them a link to my website to show them who I was. Deepak does the website. You have to have one these days. It's not at all bad. It's got a nice picture of me looking businesslike, tells the punters what we do and even has a few vox pops from satisfied customers. I do get a bit of business from it.

Another ten minutes and the reply came, this time from the website email: "I am afraid we cannot help. Some of our supporters wish to remain anonymous and we never confirm nor deny their support."

I took that as a definite maybe so I asked them if, just suppose he had been a supporter, could that possibly have been enough to have got him killed?

"There are always threats but mostly it's just bluff. As far as we know none of our supporters has ever been killed because of their support. The worst we have had is a few minor injuries on demonstrations, some of those inflicted by the police."

Glad to see the boys in blue are keeping up the good work. I wanted to ask a bit more about the ENF but this messaging was getting a bit tedious so I asked if we could phone them. They didn't do phones but said they could do Skype. I hadn't a clue about Skype until Deepak told me it was like a phone over the Internet. Did we do Skype?

"Sharon has it on her computer. She talks to her sister in Australia."

Fanackapan phones Australia! How much is that costing us? Deepak said it was OK, it was free, so we got her in and asked her for her Skype name. Turned out to be "BlondeBombshell7865". Give me strength!

A few clicks later and we all set up. The voice at the other end had a bit of a Northern twang. According to Deepak you can do video on Skype as well, but he had his turned off. Didn't want us to see his face. Understandable I suppose. I asked him what I should call him. He said "Al"

"What, just Al?"

"Yeah, Al. Al all the time."

"OK Al, let's kick off. I used to think the ENF was just a bunch of thugs and thickos but I'd heard that bloke Dimmuck talk and thought maybe there was bit more to them."

"In some ways you're right. All these groups have their hooligan element. Helps to keep up the profile but they'd get rid of them soon enough if they saw a sniff of power, just as Hitler had half the brownshirts shot when he became Chancellor. The thinking element of the ENF, and there is one, see themselves as part of a new movement on the right, not just in Britain but across Europe. They reject all that sixties stuff—not just hippy, lefty liberalism but the generation that came up with it. They say that they came up with a load of crazy, utopian ideas, partly as a knee-jerk reaction to fascism of the previous generation. They often call it 'cultural Marxism' and say that it promoted the breakdown of cultural norms right across the board and, worse, encouraged uncontrolled mass immigration and the rise of multiculturalism, which in turn led to a crisis of identity. The only way forward is to sweep away all those ideas and the corrupt generation that came up with them. They want to give the original people of the country back a strong sense of identity and reject most liberal reforms—gay rights, feminism, multiculturalism, all that."

"I see. Boys will be boys, girls will be girls, gays will be banged up and blacks will be chucked out. Sounds simple enough."

"It's not quite as simple as that. They have quite a sophisticated analysis, for a right-wing group anyway. They're not simply racists. Actually they would deny they are racists at all. They claim to respect all races, providing they live in their own countries. All Chinese should live in China, all Indians in India, all Africans in Africa and so on. They don't want people to come here and claim to be British while still behaving like they were back in their village. There's also another element to their thinking, a sort of pan-Europeanism, or more accurately pan-white Europeanism. "

"They've more or less got it now haven't they? It's the Common Market or the European Union or whatever it calls itself these days."

"Not at all. They think the European Union is infected with all the old liberal vices and is doomed, with the euro as a sort of slow-motion suicide pill."

"What, they expect Europe to go belly up and then they take over? Good luck with that one. Have you seen who they've got in the ENF?"

"Forget about the rank and file, it's the leadership and the backers that count. They do have a few true believers, Dimmuck is one, but there are also some very shady fellow travellers and they obviously have funds but it's been very difficult to for us to find out where they get their money. And then of course there's the security services."

"What do you mean, the security services?"

"All these groups have been pretty thoroughly infiltrated by MI5 and SO15, the police anti-terrorist squad. In some cases, and the ENF could be one, we think they are only kept going by the infiltrators."

"Revolution on the rates. That's a good one. Why would they want to do that?"

"The ostensible reason is that it is better for the groups to be visible and attracting recruits who can then be tracked, rather than going underground, out of sight. Then of course there's pulling the wool over the eyes of a gullible public. Look at all these nasty people we have to keep you safe from say the securocrats. Better pay up for us. But the real reason may be nostalgia for what they consider to have been a better, more heroic age when they did things that were actually worthwhile."

"What do you mean worthwhile? Stopping us getting blown up has got to be worthwhile, hasn't it?"

"For you maybe, but not for them. They don't consider a bunch of crazed religious fanatics as proper enemies. They much preferred the likes of the IRA, ordinary decent terrorists. At least you knew what they wanted. But their real desire is for something much grander—the Great Game."

"What's the Great Game? The Champions League in spying?"

"You might put it like that. The original Great Game was in central Asia between Russia and Britain in the eighteenth and nineteenth centuries. The Russians, expansionist as ever, were pushing down through Persia and the British feared they might invade India, the jewel in the British crown. So the British in turn looked to protect India's northern frontier by sending out spies and subverting rulers all over the Middle East and by invading Afghanistan several times, not altogether successfully."

"I heard we had form in Afghanistan. Don't learn much, do we Al?"

"It would seem not. But now they think that the Great Game is about to kick off again. The era of American hegemony is coming to an end. Soon we will be in a multi-polar world—the US, China, Europe, Russia and who knows what else. We will be in an age of statecraft, of shifting alliances, of deal and counter deal, of Kipling and le Carré, of double and triple agents, of perfidy as an art form. That's what really turns them on. They feel that they are uniquely qualified to play that game. Deep in the mindset of the security forces is the idea that they are somehow the guardians of the quintessential Britain, the keepers of the eternal flame. It's called the Deep State. Politicians and governments come and go, flitting almost mindlessly across the surface of the body politic, while they, the securocrats, do the heavy lifting, clear up the messes, eliminate the threats, explore the opportunities. But they can't do anything overtly at the moment. They need to find other means of exerting pressure. So they are reviving the idea of the front, an idea they picked up from the Communists in the Cold War of blessed memory."

This was beginning to do my head in. "What do you mean 'the front'?"

"Well, a front organisation is one that is ostensibly separate and independent but in reality they control or at the very least heavily influence. We can't be sure but there is some circumstantial evidence that there are connections between the ENF and elements in the security services. "

"What evidence?"

"Funding for a start. They're a lot better off than most right-wing groups but it's not clear where the money comes from. They claim it's all from the public donating but we very much doubt it. Then again, they always seem to get off lightly even when their members break the law and there have been a few favourable mentions of some of their policies in the press by known mouthpieces of the security services. It doesn't prove anything but that's the point of a front. Everything is deniable."

"OK Al, I'll take your word for it. Thanks for the info but I don't know where it gets us. I take it you don't think MI5 put a bullet in his head?"

"I very much doubt it. They prefer more subtle methods."

"Like what?"

"Well, he was a banker, wasn't he. If they wanted to get him they would probably cook up some financial scandal—fraud, money-laundering, that sort of thing. Another tactic is the sex scandal. They tend to use that for politicians they don't like. In any event, what would be their motive?"

"You've got us there Al. We can't see why anyone would want to kill him. The only thing odd about him seems to be that he was a bit hung up on something that happened a hundred years ago, when King George didn't want his cousin Nicky the Tsar to come here. I don't think either of them had anything to do with it. "

"If there's a royal connection then that puts things in a different light. Everything about royalty is secret forever unless they want it known. There is no right to know. The security services identify with the Crown, not the people, or parliament or democracy or anything like that. They have intervened time and again to protect the Crown from embarrassment or intrusion or simply to preserve their prerogatives. I would be a little circumspect if I were you."

After he hung up or clicked off or whatever the word is for it in Skypish, Dany, Deepak and me sat around trying to work out what exactly we had found out. Not a lot really. We didn't think something ancient was likely to bring the monarchy down. More's the pity Deepak said. If the ENF is a set up then those security boys have got more front than Brighton, but I've seen a lot of spy movies. That wasn't exactly news. They've been up to those sort of tricks for ever. As for the 'Great Game', don't make me laugh. We're talking Dogswell here. If the Russkies invaded Dogswell any British government with half a brain is going to say you're welcome to it Ivan. Take it away and don't fucking bring it back.

13

One thing I don't never do, hardly, is shag the client. More trouble that it's worth. For a start they always want a discount. Last one wanted it half-price, "after all we'd been to each other". All she'd been to me was a royal pain in the arse. Yap, yap, yap; she never fucking stopped. She was always on the phone or coming round to the office telling me what she was going to do with her old man when I found him or what she had just bought in the shops or where she was going out. There wasn't nothing that she wouldn't gab on about. Only did the business because I thought it might shut her up. Fat chance. I got even more earfuls of the same stuff plus a load of luvvie-duvvie crap on top. Turned my stomach. In the end getting rid of her at half-price was a bargain.

Afters, on the other hand, is different. Afters is a recognised perk of the profession. After the job is done and dusted and you have the spondulicks in your hot little hand, you're allowed to suggest a little glass of something to celebrate. If she says yes then it's game on and if I'm not snapping knicker elastic by the third glass of bubbly then I will be saying to myself, "Spencer, my son, you are definitely slipping."

We wasn't exactly at the afters stage yet with Rachel Silver. Truth to tell, we wasn't even at the before stage. She was lounging across a sofa in her drawing room, hair down, in her usual outfit of cream silk blouse, light-coloured skirt and the sort of fuck-me shoes that I almost couldn't take my eyes off. There was a little gold chain around her neck, giving off the sort of glow only money can buy. It can be tricky concentrating with a bit of a knob throb on, but I pride myself that I'm a professional. You've got to stick to the business. Some things definitely aren't on. I know the old story about a bit of posh fancying a bit of rough but there's posh and there's posh. And if I'm honest, there's rough and there's rough. It wasn't going to happen any time soon.

She was all affronted when I told her what Curting said.

"Are you saying that you are taking the word of that horrible man against mine?"

"No, no. Of course we know he's lying. Wouldn't know the truth if it bit him on the backside, if you'll pardon the expression. What about this *Spotlight* thing? Any mileage there?"

"Do you mean did he support it? Not to my knowledge. As I think I told you, he was mildly left-wing when he was a student; most students are, aren't they. By the time he joined the bank of course he had given up all that nonsense. On the other hand you say *Spotlight* is an anti-fascist magazine. That may well have appealed to him. He was very worried that anti-Semitism was on the rise all over Europe."

Maybe he did, maybe he didn't. We wasn't getting anywhere there. I thought I'd try a long shot.

"We talked to a bloke from *Spotlight* and he reckoned that the ENF might be mixed up with the security services, MI5 and all that. Was your husband or the bank involved with them at all?"

She looked shocked.

"No, of course not. Well, I suppose it depends what you mean by 'involved'. There are strict money-laundering regulations and the Bank has to report anything suspicious. I know that there were the occasional conversations with officials who I suppose could have been the security services. The Bank holds the personal accounts of some very high profile people and they are almost paranoid about their security. I have no idea who or what was involved. I did once ask Reuben and he made the usual joke about how he could tell me but then he would have to kill me."

"OK. Look Curting may have been lying about asking for money, the ransom and all that, but I don't think he was lying about *Spotlight*. He wouldn't have the wit to make it up. And he says they was tipped off. That sort of makes sense too, because how else would they find out? The informer must have had access either to your husband's accounts or to Spotlight's and I don't think getting into either would be that easy. The point is that, apart from all that weirdo Russian stuff on his computer, it's the only lead we've got. Is there anybody you think might know a bit more. Maybe someone at the Bank?"

"I doubt if they would tell you much. Like all banks they are very reticent about disclosing anything. On the other hand, you never know. I will talk to the chairman, Freddy Rosquevoir, who I know very well. If anyone can tell you anything he can, but I have no idea whether he would be willing to see you."

"OK, let's see if we can have a chat with this Freddy, what did you say his name was?"

"Rosquevoir, His real name is Ferdinand but all his friends, of whom he has many, call him Freddy."

"Foreign is he?"

"Well, yes, but that's rather more the rule than the exception in banking. The name sounds French but I believe his people came from somewhere in central Europe. On the other hand he was educated here, Harrow and Oxford, and then a spell in the Army, Blues and Royals naturally. Only the best for Freddy. He can pass for the perfect English gentleman, which is why he is where he is. Freddy is a born networker. He never forgets anyone he meets and they never forget him."

14

"Your choice of whisky Mr Weintraub? We have a few single malts here: Balvenie, Glenmorangie, Glenlivet, Laphroaig, although that one's a bit peaty for some tastes. Or maybe you would prefer a blend. Chivas Regal?"

I took the Chivas. Only one I'd ever heard of. We was sitting in Rosquevoir's office, all wood panels and high class pictures. He was one of these paint by numbers toffs. You had to admit he had it all. He was tall, six two at a guess, trim, hair darkish with a bit of grey and a face that even I would say was handsome. His suit must have cost more than my flat. Smooth talking didn't come into it. His way of talking could charm the knickers off a nun.

"Rachel Silver said you wanted to see me for an informal chat Mr Weintraub, or should I call you Spencer? You may call me Freddy. Everyone else does."

"Spencer's fine by me Freddy. I've been called worse."

"Haven't we all Spencer. Well, what is it that you would like to know? I must say we are all extremely distressed at what has happened to Reuben. And poor Rachel. She is simply distraught. We like to think of this bank as a family, but in Rachel's case that is particularly true. Her father was my predecessor as chairman."

He even did a very nice line in sympathy. Makes you sick.

"Well, there's a few things I'd like to straighten out if I could. As you know Mrs Silver has asked me get some background on what happened as the Police aren't telling her much. Not to find out who done it, you understand. That's for the Police, but just to see if I can find out where he went and why he ended up in Dogswell. I know that area well. It's my manor as you might say. If we could start at the beginning, how was he doing at work? Was he in any sort of trouble?"

He shook his head. "On the contrary, Reuben was one of our stars. He had a first class degree and the highest possible banking qualifications. Not only that but he had a way of winning a client's confidence and coming up with deals that they believed were the best possible for them. People like that are very hard to find Spencer, even harder to replace, I don't mind telling you."

"Fine. We are also trying to find out whether he gave money to a magazine called *Spotlight* that writes about right-wing and fascist politics. Would you have any idea?"

"Ah, there I can help you. Rachel mentioned this to me and I took a look at Reuben's expense account. We allow directors to make donations to their favourite causes from their accounts, within reason of course. It turned out that Reuben did indeed make a couple of donations to *Spotlight* last year."

"Could you tell me how much?"

"I'd rather not, if you don't mind, but it was a significant amount."

"What, like a hundred grand?"

"Oh no, nothing like that."

"Well a few grand then?"

"I think you get my drift Spencer."

I did get his "drift". So Curting wasn't lying about *Spotlight*. Maybe he wasn't lying about other things too.

"Isn't it a bit unusual for one of your lot to be giving money to a lefty rag? Was Reuben a bit of a red under the bonnet, so to speak?"

He laughed. "Well I suppose it is a bit unusual. Reuben presumably had his reasons. I have never heard him express any strong party political views although he did say to me that he had voted Conservative at the last General Election. But just voting for them does not mean endorsing their simple-minded nostrums. On the contrary. Reuben in particular had a very sophisticated approach to politics. It may surprise you Spencer that we in the City are Marxists, though I grant you that many of our number do not realise that they are disciples of the one true prophet. Under capitalism there is an eternal, ineradicable struggle between capital and labour, something that Marx saw

more clearly than anyone else before or since. There is no denying the brilliance of his analysis. The only question is what conclusions are to be drawn from that analysis—in short what side
are you on. We have no doubt which side we are on—the winning side."

I'm not big on political theory but Freddy had to be taking
the piss.

"Come off it Freddy. I've got a mate who's a big Marxist and
he says Marx predicted the collapse of capitalism and when that
day comes you and your lot will be first up against the wall, no
disrespect of course."

That made him laugh even more.

"Ah yes Spencer, vulgar Marxism, always banging its head
against the facts. Marx and Engels when they wrote the *Com-
munist Manifesto,* did imagine they were signing the death warrant of capitalism. In reality they wrote a love letter to its dyna-
mism, its sublime powers of creation and destruction. And
would you like a final irony? Both ended their lives as English
gentlemen. Engels even asked for his ashes to be scattered in the
sea off his favourite seaside resort, Eastbourne. Have you ever
been to Eastbourne Spencer, that most petit-bourgeois of bor-
oughs? Go there and you will find no statue, no plaque, no *Frie-
drichengelstrasse,* no reminder of any sort of the only world-
historical figure who ever expressed any affection for the place.
How quintessentially English."

"So what are you saying Freddy? Waving the Red Flag helps
you line your pockets? I don't believe it."

"Not quite Spencer. As George Orwell put it in *1984*: 'He
who controls the past controls the future. He who controls the
present controls the past.' Finance controls the present Spencer
with our single, simple message—freedom. Admittedly it is the
freedom to do what you can afford, but what other real freedom
is there? It is the triumph of the market. And who can deny our
success? There is now no intellectually coherent opposition to
our form of capitalism—monopoly financial capitalism. No
element of society now rejects its writ. There is no one left that
can even give us a game—no Lenin, no Trotsky, no Gramsci, no

Stalin, not even, God help us, a Sartre. As Richard Nixon put it in his one great contribution to the theory of economics: 'When you've got them by the balls, the hearts and minds will follow.'"

"That last bit I can understand Freddy. It's much the same in my line of work, but you don't take all that intellectual bollocks seriously do you?"

"On the contrary Spencer, ideology makes the financial as well as the political weather. We rewrite the past in our own image and likeness, so that the future is ours too. Who now celebrates the past triumphs of labour? Who can now sing the *Internationale* without irony? 'Arise, ye starvelings from your slumbers.' One can only laugh. You might remember that in *1984* Orwell said that if you want a picture of the future, imagine a boot stamping on a human face—forever. So crude. We take a more enlightened view. Our vision is of a face pressed up against a window, looking in—forever."

That sounded like bollocks to me as well, so I ignored it.

"I don't know whether Mrs Silver told you about this but she says she was contacted by someone just after her husband went missing asking her to pay a ransom. We found out that this person was someone called Steve Curting who is a member of the English National Front. We talked to Curting and he admitted making the phone call but said he didn't know nothing about a ransom. He says they were tipped off about the *Spotlight* donation and just wanted to put the frightners on Reuben Silver."

"Yes, Rachel did tell me about the ransom demand. I have heard of the ENF of course, a very nasty bunch, but I must say I find this ransom thing absolutely bizarre. As far as I know there's absolutely no evidence that he was kidnapped or anything like that."

"What about the tip off? Could it have come from here.?"

When you ask a simple question you have to look them straight in the face, looking for the tell. There was no tell with Freddy. He still had that caviar wouldn't melt in his mouth expression.

"Absolutely not. All our employees are absolutely trustworthy. Most have been here years, even decades. Discretion is our watchword. This bank did not prosper by talking out of turn. Besides, directors' accounts are only scrutinised by other directors and our chief accountant—and I can absolutely vouch for them."

It was "absolutely" this and "absolutely" that. Looked like I was going to get absolutely nowhere on that one so I thought I'd try another tack.

"Look, Mrs Silver is my client and all that, so I don't want to pry, but I do a lot of this sort of work. Not usually around places like this, but I reckon human nature don't change that much. If a bloke does a runner it's usually for one of two reasons—money or a woman. You tell me it's not money. As it happens, I talked to a publican who said he saw Reuben in his pub in Dogswell a couple of nights before he was killed with a woman who he described as a real looker. That suggests to me that he was having an affair."

He gave me the sort of look he probably gives clients when he wants to put half a million on his fee.

"We're men of the world in banking Spencer. Money is an aphrodisiac as has often been remarked. Every million you make takes a year off your age, so they say. We're no stranger to affairs, divorces, separations, whatever. They're an occupational hazard; they go with the territory. However in Reuben's case I would be astonished if he was having an affair. You see we have ways of detecting these things, for our own security naturally. It's not that we're prudish, but it wouldn't do if, say, one of our senior staff was having an affair with the wife of one of our clients—wouldn't do at all. There are always tell-tale signs—more long lunches, a sudden interest in theatre, opera, art galleries, the extra day on overseas trips, another mobile phone. These things are very difficult to conceal completely, especially from their PAs. The PAs, and I don't think you will be surprised by this Spencer, are instructed to report anything of that sort in absolute confidentiality to our Director of Security."

"Is that Jack Dapper?"

He gave me that look again.

"No, Inspector Dapper takes care of other aspects of our security. Our deputy chairman Bernard Cadogan handles all financial security matters, liases with the financial authorities and so on. He has a security background. As I was saying, we can nearly always spot the signs and there were absolutely no signs that Reuben was having an affair, none whatsoever."

Well if he was lilywhite, what about his other half?

"If that's the case do you think he might have thought that Mrs Silver was having an affair and that set him off?"

He shook his head.

"I can't imagine so. Rachel is a very beautiful woman, as no doubt you have noticed, and she has always had plenty of admirers, but I've never had any reason to doubt that they were happily married. To be honest some of us, myself included, were a little surprised that she did decide to marry Reuben, but there you are. There's no telling the heart's reasons, is there Spencer?"

If he meant that there's never any shortage of people doing the stupidest things then I suppose he was right but I didn't buy all of it. These people didn't get to be that rich by being stupid. According to Rosquevoir everything was hunky-dory but Reuben Silver didn't do a runner just because he fancied a few weeks in sunny Dogswell.

"Well what about all the Russian stuff that he kept boning up on. I got the impression from Mrs Silver that she thought he might be going a bit mental over it—seeing plots, conspiracies, stuff like that. Could that have set him off?"

Another of those looks.

"I hardly think so. I think you may be misinterpreting what Rachel was telling you. Reuben was something of a historian. He had a first class history degree and since his family came from Eastern Europe he took a keen interest in the history of that region. I find that entirely laudable. Banking—let's not beat about the bush, making money—can become an all-consuming obsession. 'For the love of money is the root of all evil.' as it says in the Bible. Far too many in our industry are just out to make a quick buck, so it's most refreshing to come across a well rounded individual, someone with a hinterland."

"OK Freddy, I take your point that it's nice to have someone in your firm who isn't just a greedy bastard, but what was all the Russian stuff about?"

"Reuben told me some time ago that he was thinking of writing a book about what happened to the fortunes of all those royal dynasties that disappeared at the end of the First World War. Our Bank, as I'm sure you know, held the accounts of many of the crowned heads and noble families of Europe and Reuben asked if he could look through our archives to see what was there. I thought it was an absolutely fascinating idea and gave him every encouragement. After all, what a cast of characters. Boris of Bulgaria, Ludwig of Bavaria, Franz-Josef of Austria, all those kings and princelings of the German Empire and of course the biggest fish of all, Nicholas the Second, Tsar of all the Russias."

There it goes again, 'Tsar of all the Russias'. I still haven't found out how many Russias there was in them days and what the fuck happened to all the others.

"So Reuben was writing a book. Did you talk to him about it?"

"Several times. I was all the more interested because we share a background. Our fathers both came from central Europe, what used to be called *Mitteleuropa*. People rarely talk about *Mitteleuropa* now, that part of Europe from the Baltic to the Black Sea, but once it was the intellectual powerhouse of Europe, with Vienna as its cultural capital. For Reuben the idea of *Mitteleuropa* had an enduring fascination. As he saw it, its language was German but its soul was Jewish. Just as Egypt was the gift of the Nile, so *Mitteleuropa* was the gift of the Jews. They were the stream running through it that fertilised its banks, that gave it its ideas, its literature, its music, its art. For Reuben Jewishness was not simply a matter of blood but had an almost metaphysical quality. As he put it, it was 'a community of fate.' A community that could claim Freud, Einstein, Wittgenstein, Mahler, Schoenberg, Kafka, Mendelssohn among many others. I think he saw himself in another life as a leading intellectual in *belle époque* Vienna. Instead he became a banker in England in what, if I can coin a phrase, has been something of a *mal époque* for bankers. A worse fate of course was in store for his co-religionists. As Reuben saw it, *Mitteleuropa* died with its Jews. And with their loss the German language, in which most of the central ideas of the twentieth century had been first expressed, was reduced to a provincial *patois*. *Mitteleuropa*, he once said to me, was now nothing but a small-minded intellectual backwater, its *lingua franca* English, its defining cultural expression the Eurovision song contest."

He was beginning to lose me there. I couldn't keep up.

"So let me get this right Freddy. What you're saying is that Reuben Silver was a bit of an oddball among all you get-rich-quick boys?"

"I suppose you could put it like that Spencer, although I like to think that I too have a hinterland. My particular passion is music. I collect early music autographed scores, mainly English. As a matter of fact I have just acquired a very fine set of scores for keyboard and *viola da gamba* by Purcell, in his own hand naturally. Some of them have never been played before, certainly not in modern times. I'm a patron of the London Early Music Ensemble and they have honoured me by asking me to be the guest conductor for the first performance of one of them, an air in D-minor. I can't tell you how much I'm looking forward to it."

I was beginning to think all this was bollocks too, but he seemed to be getting a bit misty-eyed, so maybe it wasn't.

"So Reuben was mugging up all this stuff on Russia to write a book, nothing more to it?"

"Yes, exactly that. Reuben did once tell me that he had looked in our archives and discovered that some members of the Russian nobility had held accounts here before the First World War. We had a bit of a chuckle over the notion that there might be a pot of tsarist gold lurking somewhere in our vaults. A most amusing idea, but unfortunately Spencer, I have to tell you that there is not."

As I was getting up to go I noticed he had a lot of pictures in frames on a sideboard. Most of them were of him with nobs, snobs and celebs, but a few were of him in his army days.

"I heard you was in the Army Freddy. What was it like?"

"Terrific Spencer. I was in the Blues and Royals, Household Cavalry. Enjoyed every minute of it. Finest body of men in the world. Do anything for you. Absolutely devoted to Queen and Country."

"What was you then, a general?"

He burst out laughing.

"Not quite. I was on a Short Service Commission. Just made Captain, which actually was quite good going, if I say so my-self."

The pictures was mainly of him and his mates in uniform looking very smart. There was one of him lounging on a camp bed with several squaddies looking on. They was all in fatigues in what looked like a jungle. I pointed to it.

"Where was that Freddy?"

"Can't say I'm afraid Spencer. All a bit hush-hush still. Rather silly I agree, but there you are. I don't make the rules."

"So you got up to a few things you don't want nobody to know about."

"Put it this way Spencer. Sometimes you have to get your hands dirty for the greater good. In the Army you go where you are sent and do what you are told."

Fair enough I thought. Somebody's got to keep some things secret.

"Do you still see your old army mates then?"

"Of course Spencer. We meet very regularly. Being in the Army is a bond for life. A bond for life."

15

"You've got some more for us then Deepak?"

He was bent over the screen banging on the keyboard.

"Yes, but it's getting harder Spencer. He seems to be using random passwords. We're having to try a dictionary attack. It's taking a lot longer."

I had visions of him chucking books at the screen.

"What's a dictionary attack?"

"We try all the words from the dictionary. Start with the short ones and work up."

"And if that don't work?"

"Then it's brute force."

"You kick it to death?"

"No, we try combinations of characters—letters, numbers, symbols. That does take time. Sami here is our encryption expert."

Sami was God's gift to women. About five-four, frog eye glasses, terminal acne, hair like greasy spaghetti down to his shoulders and wearing a dirty T-shirt that had writing on it across the front: '1f u c4n r34d th1s u r34lly n33d t0 g37 l41d'. Your guess is as good as mine.

"OK Sami, what have you got this time?"

"It...it...it's a b...b...bit different from the first one."

He had a bit of a problem getting the words out. He kept looking at the floor as he was trying and then looked up at you when he managed it, like a little spaniel.

"Oh yeah. What's it called?"

"T...t...two"

"What two as in number two."

"Y...yes, just the figure 2."

"That's helpful. So what does it say?"

"T...t...ake a look."

I hear the sound of dogs coming from the east and all is lost. Yet I have slipped their nets to reach the second Troy and as it is written upon this rock I will build my golden empire."

Dany and I just looked at it. What the fuck... Rachel Silver thought her old man was going round the bend and that just about settled it. Either that or he was on something a lot stronger than I've ever had. Then Sami said something.

"C...could be a cryptic puzzle."

"Well I'm fucking puzzled Sami, that's for sure. What are you talking about?"

"Have you ever looked at crossword puzzles in the newspapers? When you first see the clues and then the answers they don't seem to make sense. You don't read a clue as a single thing. You have to break it down into bits and then put the bits together to get the answer."

He didn't stammer that time. Seems like when he had something to say it comes out OK.

"So our top bankers have nothing better to do than playing crossword puzzles. No wonder they fucked the country up big time."

Deepak joined in. "I wouldn't knock crosswords if I were you Spencer. Alan Turing, who cracked the German Enigma code, used crosswords to select the best decoders. Sami is very good at puzzles."

I was a long way from being convinced but what the fuck, we didn't have nothing else to go on.

"OK Sami, show us how good you are. Break that down and see what you come up with."

His eyes blinked under those big glasses.

"W...Well I suppose you could start with the 'sound of dogs coming from the east'. That might be a dog from there with a distinctive sound, say a wolfhound or a husky. The 'second Troy' shouldn't be too difficult. Let's have a look in Google."

The Google page come up with a whole lot of stuff about a poem *No Second Troy* by some tosser called William Butler

Yeats. As far as I could make out it was all about him not getting a girl called Maude. She wouldn't come into his garden. I'm not fucking surprised. You definitely wouldn't get a legover down Dogswell if you spouted that sort of shit.

"So that's what you've come up with Sami. A lovesick husky howling at the moon."

Sami started to open his mouth when Dany chipped in.

"I seem to remember from my Sunday School that 'upon this rock I will build' or something like it is in the Bible somewhere."

"That's not a lot of help Dany. The Bible's a big book. How are we going to find it?"

Sami was on it in a flash. "Most versions of the Bible are online. Which one do you think we should be looking at."

I'm not sure Dany believes in God but he likes that old time Caribbean religion.

"There's only one, the King James version."

In a couple of clicks Sami had the search going and up it come:

> Matthew 16:18: And I say also unto thee, That thou art Peter, and upon this rock I will build my church; and the gates of hell shall not prevail against it.

Dany gave a big smile. "Told you. Sunday School comes in useful sometimes."

I asked Sami if we was looking for a church.

Sami seemed to think a bit different. "Maybe, but I think it's more likely that we're looking for someone called Peter. That passage from Mathew is a pun on the Latin word *petrus* which means 'rock'."

That clicked with me too. "I think that's right. My Mum's a Catholic. She used to make me go to catechism classes. I remember the priest telling me that St Peter was the first pope and his name meant rock in Latin. So I said he should really be called Pope Rocky and he give me a clip round the ear for being cheeky to God."

Sami was now getting into things. "This second Troy thing must mean something. Let's give it another go." He bashed some more into his computer. "Ah, this looks better. There's a 12th century poem by someone called Geoffrey of Monmouth which mentions it:"

> Brutus! there lies beyond the Gallic bounds
> An island which the western sea surrounds,
> By giants once possessed, now few remain
> To bar thy entrance, or obstruct thy reign.
> To reach that happy shore thy sails employ
> There fate decrees to raise a second Troy
> And found an empire in thy royal lines
> Which time shall ne'er destroy, nor bounds confine.

He was on a bit of a roll now. "An island 'beyond the Gallic bounds'. That must be Britain. This is a Peter who 'has slipped their nets' and comes to Britain after 'all is lost' That could be a war or revolution, something like that. The Georgev file mentioned the Russian revolution and we have 'coming from the east' here so that would fit. It looks like our Peter might be a Russian who fled the revolution. So now it's the 'the sound of dogs', not 'dogs coming from the east' we need to consider. That could be a bark or a howl. Let's see what the Russian for a dog bark is." He was on the computer again. "'lay'. OK, 'I hear the sound of dogs', that could be something to do with his surname. It's presumably a Russian name so let's try Peter Layov." The screen filled up but he didn't think much of it. "Maybe Peter Layovsky. " Same result again and the same with a few others he tried. "No good there, so maybe we should use the English. Let's try Barkov or Barkovsky." Again he got no joy.

Dany always tries to be helpful. "Why not just try 'Bark'.

Sami was a bit scornful. "Bark doesn't sound very Russian does it?" but just to humour Dany he tried it and bingo. There it was in *Wikipedia*:

Pyotr Lvovich Bark later Sir Peter Bark, (18 April 1869—16 January 1937) was a Russian statesman

There was even a picture of him, a tubby bloke with great big curly moustaches. I had to admit this Bark fitted the picture. We found a bit more stuff about him on the Internet. His name was German, not Russian. He was Nicky the Tsar's last Finance Minister and was with him until Nicky was kicked out. He was then imprisoned by the revolutionaries but was let out and came to England in 1920 and didn't he do well here. He picked up a knighthood from King George and ran a number of banks, courtesy of the Bank of England. As Sami said, running banks fitted with 'my golden empire'.

Deepak thought all this was a bit suspicious. He got back on his computer.

"He wasn't exactly your average refugee Spencer. According to Debretts, which says it's 'the trusted source on British social skills, etiquette and style', that knighthood, something called a Knight Grand Cross of the Royal Victorian Order would you believe, is the personal gift of the King and is given for services to him. He must have done something special for George to deserve it. Almost all the other ones on the list are royals of some sort. I think we should try to find out more about him."

I wasn't that keen. "That's all very interesting Deepak, but what's it got to do with Silver getting murdered. We'd be wasting our time."

"If you say so Spencer but Silver obviously thought something about this guy Bark was important because he encrypted it and then wrapped it in a riddle."

Dany agreed and, when I thought about it, Rachel Silver said she wanted any information about what was going on and she was paying, so why not? That's the sort of argument that makes sense to me.

"OK. Let's see what we can find out."

Sami then spoke up. "I think there might be something else because of that phrase 'as it is written'. Maybe something he wrote."

Deepak hit the keyboard again and for the next quarter of an hour or so we waited as he looked at what he was getting.

"There's very little more of interest. The only thing I can find is that there are some of his papers at Southwark University. That could be they are what you were talking about Sami."

"Can we have a look at them?"

Deepak did some more on the computer.

"They're not online. You have to go there to see them. They are in something called the Bazalgette Memorial Library"

"Southwark University, that's at the Elephant isn't it? That's not far. Why don't we pop along and take a look."

Deepak scrolled down the screen.

"It's not quite as simple as that. They are in their special collections. You have to make an appointment to see them and you are supposed to be a *bona fide* researcher."

Nothing like the present, I thought.

"Right, let's make an appointment. Now who looks like a student round here?" We all turned to look at Sami. "OK Sami, off you go, but for fuck's sake get yourself a clean T-shirt with nothing rude on it."

...

I thought I'd pay another visit to The Pirates. Something about that place bugged me. A great big pub surrounded by houses with not another for at least half a mile, but when I was in only the ENF crowd was there. I didn't see no one else. Admittedly that bunch of scumbags would put anyone off, but the place was big enough to get away from them. Most pubs have their regulars and regulars never seem to mind what else is going on as long as they can sit there with their pints.

It was late afternoon when I got there. No one at all in. I ordered a pint of the only real ale they had, Badger's Nadgers. To be fair it wasn't bad. Some of the pubs round here keep their ale in the barrel for months. Tastes worse than vinegar. A decent price too, two fifty. There are pubs up in town that charge close to a fiver. That's outrageous. Time was when you could get hung for less.

The barman was your typical pub landlord—probably about fifty but looked about sixty five, bald, big paunch and walked with a swing-arse shuffle. The one thing landlords have to be is talkative and as I was the only one in he had to talk to me. He said his name was Bob.

"Bit quiet at the moment Bob."

He shook his head.

"It's always fucking quiet. You count as a rush."

"That's a shame. Why's that?"

"Pub's got a reputation, hasn't it."

"What, you mean the ENF crowd?"

"Yeah, all that singing and swearing and fighting too sometimes. Puts people off. No one wants to use the place."

"Well at least you've got their custom."

He snorted at that. "Custom? You've got to be joking. Wouldn't keep a fly in shit. Most of them have got even less money that they have manners. Half of them ask for credit. Custom like that I can get any day. They come in on Fridays shouting their heads off and the rest of the week it's like a fucking graveyard. "

"Well why don't you get rid of them Bob? Bar them, tart the place up a bit and you'll soon get a better class of punter. Look at this place. It would scrub up lovely."

That was true. I had time to have a good look this time. Place must have cost a fortune when it was first built. You couldn't get nothing like it these days. Wood panelling everywhere, carved bar, fancy windows, but all tatty now.

He sighed, shook his head and put on a sad face.

"Yeah, it was built for the heroes, like the houses."

That was news to me. Bit of a shortage of heroes in Dogswell these days.

"What heroes—and what houses come to that?"

"The soldiers that come back from the First World War. 'Homes for heroes', that's what they called the houses round here, and the pub was built for them too, so they could drink in style."

"All the better to do it up then Bob. Let the people raise a glass in their memory."

He looked even sadder.

"I wanted to but I wasn't allowed."

"What do you mean, you wasn't allowed?"

"The pub company. They wouldn't have it. Told me to keep things going they way they are. I pointed out to them the pub was losing money but they didn't seem to care. Normally if a pub is losing then they shut it down quick and turn it into flats. They make a lot more money that way. It's getting to the point where the working man won't have nowhere to go for a pint round here soon. I asked them if they was going to shut The Pirates but they said no. It's one of their 'flagship' pubs they told me. That's crap. Fuck knows what they think they're doing."

"So why don't they do the place up if it's supposed to be a flagship?"

"You may well ask. I had the estate manager—he looks after all the company's buildings—here a while back. His name's Stenson, Henry Stenson. He said the electrics needed doing. Maybe they did, maybe they didn't, but I told him to take a look round. What this place really needs is a lick of paint, new carpets and furniture, all that. He just shrugged and said they didn't have the budget for it. They was in and out in a couple of days doing the electrics and when they was finished it didn't seem to make no difference. Some lights still didn't work. And then Stenson bought in a policeman."

"What sort of policeman?"

"I dunno. What sort are there? He said his name was Inspector Babcock. He was a detective, plain clothes. Said he was there to check on the license. Poked his nose in everywhere. Asked me about what happened in the pub, who comes in, things like that."

"Sound a bit OTT. Have you ever had a copper ask about the license before?"

"No, never. They don't want to know unless there's a lot of trouble. It's the Council that does the licensing."

"There you are Bob. One of life's little mysteries."

He agreed and pulled me another pint, on the house.

...

I went back home to Weintraub Towers. Actually it's not a tower but the top floor of a maisonette block. Used to be Council. I bought it off a bloke who got it off the Council and then set up a little drug dealing business in it. He got caught and had to sell up and yours truly bought it for a very nice little price. Mind you, the place was an absolute tip. Cost me a fortune to get it into shape.

I fancied something to eat and looked inside the fridge. Just a couple of cheapo pizzas from the local supermarket, a quid each. God knows what was in them but I wasn't exactly flush when I bought them. I had a bit more now with the first of the Silver money, so I thought about a Chinky takeaway, but waste not want not, so I fished one out, put it in the oven, opened a can of beer and turned the TV on.

It was one of them bonnet and bodice serials. I'm not a big fan but as far as I can see there are two types: one where the bodices come off and one where they stay on. This was a stay on. All they seemed to do was ride round in carriages, complain about the servants and fall in love. Just like Dogswell. Dany is big on love. He has to be. His wife waited for him all the time he was inside and didn't shack up with no one else. He says I should try it. I told him that my definition of being in love was when you didn't want to kick her out of bed after you'd done shagging. He said that was idiotic. Maybe he's right. So I cheered myself up by thinking that once the Silver business was done I would be well flush and ready to go on the town. Love would be mine.

The pizza came out of the oven burned. It was just about eatable. I started thinking about the Pirates and the more I thought the more I reckoned something funny was going on. I gave Jimmy Dalrymple a ring.

"Jimmy, Spencer."

"Hiya Spence, what's up?"

"Dunno Jimmy, it may be nothing, but do you have a DI called Babcock at Dogswell?"

"No, definitely not. Never heard of him."

"Have you ever had to talk to a publican about his license?"

"Nah, why would we do that? We've got enough on our hands without pissing about with pub licenses. The only time we would go to a pub on police business would be if there was trouble."

"Thought so. So where might this Babcock come from?"

"Fuck knows Spence. They've got all sorts of special units now for everything you could think of and some you couldn't. They've even got one for art thefts, stolen pictures and that sort of thing."

"I bet that lot don't come to Dogswell too often, Jimmy. Anyway, thanks for the info. See you around."

So what was this Inspector Babcock after? Why had he bothered to come all the way to Dogswell to sniff around an old, dead-beat pub? Probably none of my business, but I couldn't help asking. I had another beer to help me think about it.

...

Sami got back the next afternoon from looking at Bark's papers so we went over to see what he'd got.

"Anything interesting Sami?"

"I...I...I'm not sure. The papers were his memoirs of his time in the Russian civil service, right up to the revolution. They were typescript, so I assume they hadn't been published. I'm not surprised because they were mostly pretty dull. Bark was obviously quite an important person. He was over here a few times during the war negotiating loans for Russia with banks like Barings. When he came he used to have a guard of honour meet him at Waterloo. He also delivered personal messages from the Tsar to King George."

"That *is* interesting. Did he say what was in them?"

"No."

Deepak joined in. "He probably didn't know. I expect they were sealed. Monarchs don't generally want their subjects to know what they say to each other. If they did they'd realise how stupid and ordinary their rulers were."

Deepak does go on. Anyway, I wanted to know what else Sami found out.

"A lot of it was about internal Russian politics. They were always trying to reform agriculture. During the war they tried to clamp down on vodka producers because many Russian soldiers were getting too drunk to fight. It didn't work. There was one passage that I thought was interesting but I'm not absolutely sure because it was in French."

"Why French?"

"I don't know. There were 28 chapters. The first 20 were in English and the last eight, which were about what went on during the war, were in French. There didn't seem to be any reason for the switch. My French is pretty bad. I only scraped a GCSE pass at school, but there was something about secrets in one of the chapters so I took a photocopy."

He put the photocopies on the table and we all took a look but none of us was any better at French than Sami, in my case a lot worse. "Wee wee monsewer" is about all I can manage.

Sami pointed to the first line of the passage he thought was interesting.

Le lundi 20 février je reçue un mot de l'empereur me demandé de lui envoyer le mercredi matin, 22 février, 200,000 roubles des fonds secrets qui étaient à la disposition du souverain.

"Those words *fonds secrets* mean 'secret funds'. I think Bark is saying that he arranged for secret funds of 200,000 rubles to be paid to the Emperor, Nicholas."

That did sound worth another look so I said we needed to get a translation. Deepak said we could try Google Translate. What the fuck was that?

"It's a quick and dirty online translation service Spencer, all done by computer. You can put a text in almost any language into it and it will translate it into English. It won't exactly be polished but it should give us the gist. First we have to scan and OCR the photocopies."

Google get everywhere, don't they. I didn't bother to ask what OCR was. If you keep asking questions people might get the idea that you're stupid. Turns out that it converts the page into a word processor file. Deepak made a few corrections and then bunged it into a box on the Google Translate web site. Up it come in English, more or less:

> Monday, February 20, I received a note from the Emperor asked me to send him on Wednesday morning, February 22, 200,000 rubles secret funds that were available to the sovereign. Our budget had been made containing a secret funds. When I entered the Ministry of Finance, the secret funds had 6 million rubles that were gradually increased to 10 million. During three years during which I was ministry, this was the first time that the Emperor asked me to send him a secret funds.
>
> Knowing that the Emperor had to leave Wednesday night, I raised him myself money at 11am. The Emperor was surprised to see me and told me that I would not have bothered me to bring him the sum requested. Although he was conscious, he was not showing nervousness. He conscientiously signed the receipt that I had prepared and kept me with him for fifteen minutes. When I bade farewell my heart sank, but I was far from thinking I saw the Emperor for the last time.
>
> The day after the departure of the Emperor, Thursday 23 February, there were disturbances in Petrograd.

Deepak was right. The translation was a bit rough but we did get the gist. Nicky the Tsar had a secret slush fund that he could dip into at any time. He just had to ask Bark.

"This 200,000 rubles. What's that worth in real money Deepak?"

Deepak got onto his computer. It didn't take him long. It's amazing what you can find out on the Internet these days.

"It was worth about £20,000 in 1917, which would be just under £1 million today."

"So this secret fund that had 10 million rubles in it. What would that be worth today?"

"Pushing £50 million."

"That is quite a tidy sum Deepak. What happened to it?"

We both looked at Sami. He just shrugged.

"I.. I...I know my French is bad but I don't think Bark wrote any more about secret funds."

Deepak pointed out that Nicky abdicated less than a week later. "It's very odd. According to Bark, this was the first time that Nicholas had asked for money from the secret fund. What would he need that much cash for? Monarchs don't need to carry money. Who is going to ask them to pay? Did he have an idea that something was going to happen and he might need it to get out of a tricky situation?"

That made sense to me. "Good point Deepak, and £50 million would come in very handy if he had to do a runner and get out of Russia, which he very nearly did, only for cousin George to scupper it."

That set Sami thinking. "The more I think about it, the more odd that story about the secret fund is. If you read his memoirs, Bark comes across as the archetypal civil servant. He's not in it for the money. He was working in a private bank and took a big pay cut to go into the Ministry of Finance. Even the Tsar asked him why and Bark said he preferred to be in public service. He was very discreet and appeared to be devoted to Tsar and empire. Then he seems to act out of character by being indiscreet and revealing that the Tsar took money from the secret fund."

Deepak nodded. "I agree Sami. It is very odd and it's not the only thing unusual about our Mister Bark. I've been doing a bit of digging. He may have looked on the surface like a boring civil servant but he was clearly something of an operator. He got his wife and family out of Russia in 1919 on a British cruiser. That must have taken some clout because that ship was packed with the top Russian nobility, including the Empress Marie, mother of Nicholas and sister of Queen Alexandra, George's mother. After the Versailles Conference, he and his family come to England and he is almost immediately taken up by King George. He was a regular visitor to Buckingham palace and was the goto guy who sorted out the affairs of any of George's Russian relations who had ended up in England. He was mentioned several times in George's diary, such as when he received his gongs. The British banking establishment was equally welcoming. Barings loaned him over £16,000, worth about £800,000 today and Montagu Norman, the governor of the Bank of England, seemed to take a particular shine to him. I've got a list of the directorships which the bank gave him—the Anglo-Czechoslovakian Bank, the Banque de Pays de L'Europe Centrale, the Croatian Discount Bank and the British and Hungarian Bank. Then in 1926 the Bank of England incorporated all that lot into the Anglo-International Bank and Bark was made managing director. Some might think he was a lucky boy. It's not every refugee that gets a knighthood and his very own bank."

Difficult to argue with that. "So are you saying Deepak that Bark had some sort of hold over the Bank of England and George?"

"That's one possible explanation. Or then again, maybe he had the keys to the safe. There were always rumours about tsarist gold in vaults somewhere in London or Paris or New York. And what happened to that Secret Fund? The other question of course is why did Silver encrypt the reference to Bark and then wrap it in a puzzle? Was it just some little game he was playing with himself or was he trying to hide it from someone? And if so, who? "

"All very interesting Deepak, but we still have the same question: has it got anything to do with why Silver got killed?

16

If there's one bastard in this world you're better off not getting the wrong side of it's Thacker, Superintendent Norman Thacker, the Lord of Dogswell Nick. He's old school. Very old school. Fucking prehistoric. He's the last of a dying breed. Once he's gone they'll put in a bunch of pen pushers, box tickers and computer bashers. Thacker don't like computers. Says he hasn't never seen one feel a collar yet. And don't get him on Scotland Yard neither. He thinks they're a bunch of officious, time serving, cover their arse merchants, who couldn't catch a criminal to save their lives. Him and Jack Dapper both.

There I was looking straight at his ugly mug and, more to the point, there he was looking straight at mine. He was having me in to his nick for one of his "chats". Chats to Thacker was like thumbscrews and the rack was in the olden days, before all the PACE bollocks. He would chat away until you coughed for whatever it was he wanted you to cough for and then, if he felt in a good mood, he would charge you. Otherwise he would let you go and let everyone you had grassed up know, so they could sort you out.

"Now Mr Winebar, this is just a chat, just between you and me. You're not under arrest and you're free to go at any time, which means when I say you can go."

"What exactly did you want to chat about Mr Thacker?"

"Superintendent Thacker to you Mr Winebar, Superintendent. Let's have a bit of respect. You're in enough trouble already."

"I beg your pardon Superintendent. No disrespect intended. What's this trouble I'm supposed to be in?"

"Don't come the innocent with me *Mister* Winebar. You know exactly what I'm talking about. A certain Mr Reuben Silver, a member of the Hebrew fraternity so I'm told, come to a very sticky end in this manor, with a bullet in the back of his head. That's not the sort of thing we like to see round here. Gives the neighbourhood a bad name. So I'm going to find out who done it."

"And?"

"And a little dicky bird tells me you've been nosing round lately, asking about him. Now I know I'm paid to be suspicious but that is suspicious in anyone's book."

Normally I plead client confidentiality to that sort of question but this wasn't really the time.

"That's right. His wife is one of my clients. He'd disappeared and she asked me to find out where he was."

He gave a big snort. "Oh it's Little Bo Peep is it? Little Mrs Silver has lost her husband and doesn't know where to find him. So what does she do? She hires the cream of Dogswell to sniff him out. Listen sunshine, I have met the fragrant Mrs Silver. She could afford the best and you are definitely not the best. So there's more to it than that and we are going to sit here until you tell me exactly what that is."

"There's nothing more to it. She turned up in my office, said her husband was missing and wanted me to find him. That's what I do. I find people."

"I know what you do. You find lots of things, like bouncers for the clubs round here. And I know where you find them. That's not all you do is it? We know all about your little games—a little muscle here, a bit of a threat there. All in a good cause you would say, but I would say there's the law Mr Winebar and one of these days the law is going to come down on you so hard your goolies will squirt out your arsehole."

Truth to tell, hand on heart, we've all done a few things we'd rather the law didn't know about, but I didn't think he was going to nick me for them just then. I hadn't really twigged what he was on about.

"Always act in my client's best interest Superintendent. Satisfaction guaranteed or your money back."

"You should be in politics Mr Winebar. You could tell porkies for England. Now let me put to you a little theory I have. You do your job and find him and then think to yourself that here's a rich man on the run and maybe he don't want to be found and he's willing to pay a few bob to make sure he isn't."

"Come off it Superintendent. That wouldn't be ethical. What makes you think I'd do a thing like that?"

He raised his eyes to Heaven.

"Ethical! Now I've heard it all. Do not make me laugh Mr Winebar. My doctor says it's very bad for my constitution. Why would I think you would do a thing like that? Because that's the sort of thing you do. I've got a couple of statements here that say so and I could get plenty more. There's the case of Miss Mylene Sturridge who asked you to trace her paramour, one Marlon Bridgewater, a person well known to us here, who she says done her very wrong. Only having taken her shilling you took another score off Bridgewater and allowed him to scarper, without telling Miss Sturridge."

"The reason I done that Superintendant is that I found out that her two brothers were going to kill him for what he done to her. If I'd told her where he was you'd have had a murder on your hands. You wouldn't want that."

He gave a right snort.

"Quite the humanitarian aren't you Mr Winebar. You take a slice off both sides and you want a medal for it. And now you land yourself a little job where both parties are rich as Croesus. You must have thought it was Christmas come early. You sting her, for twice your usual rate I wouldn't doubt, and when you find him you tell him that your discretion can be had for a price. What could be nicer? Only maybe he don't play ball, or he don't come up with what you think is enough, so you try to twist his arm a bit

Whatever else you say about Thacker, he is no mug. He knows the way they think round here, me included. This was getting serious. It's one thing to be accused of bending a few rules but the way Thacker was talking he was fitting me up for murder.

"Are you trying to say I killed him Superintendent? That's ridiculous. You couldn't pay me enough money to do that sort of thing. "

He pulled one of his very unfunny grins.

"Oh I don't think you done it yourself Mr Winebar. You're far too fly for that. But you know one or two what would. Bung them a grand and they'd fry their grandmothers. Maybe you told them just to rough him up a bit, but things got out of hand—trigger finger slipped, that sort of thing."

"No, no, you've got it all wrong. It wasn't like that. We was looking for him but we hadn't found him. You can ask my associate Dany Bullimore, or you could ask Jim Madgewick at the King William pub. You know Jim. He'll tell you that I showed him a picture of Reuben Silver and asked if he'd seen him. It was only after that that I found out he'd been shot."

He give me one of his special smiles, the one that could kill a crocodile at twenty paces.

"Oh yes, I know Jim. Jim and I go way back. In fact I probably know more about Jim than he knows himself. I'll have a word with Jim and I think he'll agree with me. 'Jim,' I'll say to him, 'would you agree with me that when Mr Winebar comes into your pub, orders a few drinks and then, just by the way, pulls out a picture and asks if you've seen the gentleman in question, who was already dead at the time, that it looks like he was trying to cook up an alibi?' 'I would Gov.' he'll say. Jim still calls me Gov after all this time—bit of respect, without needing reminding, unlike some."

Things wasn't getting any better. Much more of this and even I would be wondering whether I'd done it.

"What can I say Superintendent. It was just a job. I was trying to find him. I had no idea he was dead."

"Really? So maybe you could tell me what you was doing the night he was shot."

"I can't really remember. I'd have to have a look at my diary."

That set him off. I thought he was actually going to laugh.

"Your diary eh? Not a word of a lie there of course. Better than the Bible I expect. Was you feeding the five thousand that night or just curing a few unfortunates of leprosy?"

As it happened I knew exactly where I was that night. I was paying serious attention to a lady who just happened to be the missus of one of his sergeants. Her old man had told her he was on night duty but I knew he was up to his usual tricks. He was giving it to the old lady of one of the lags he sent down. He was always at it. His technique was simple enough. If he fancied it he would and go round and either she still wanted her old man, in which case he would say that he would put in a good word and maybe get him a cushy number on the block. Otherwise, if she had had enough of hubby, he would tell her that he would make sure he didn't give her a hard time when he come out. He usually had three or four at a time on the go. I knew Thacker wouldn't exactly be best pleased to find out what either of us was up to, so I thought I'd have to try a diversion.

"Look Superintendent, you've got it all wrong. I had absolutely no reason to hurt Reuben Silver but I can tell you who might have, the ENF."

"Those toerags who keep on marching round with their flags causing trouble? What have they got to do with it?"

"They found out he'd bunged a few grand to this magazine *Spotlight*, which runs stories about what a bunch of racists and fascists they are. They wanted to put the frighteners on him."

"And how do you know this?"

"I can't reveal my sources Superintendent, you know that, but I can tell you it's absolutely kosher. Maybe you could ask Mrs Silver. She might know."

"Come off it Winebar. Client confidentiality my arse. You ain't a lawyer or a priest. And even if you was we have our little ways of getting you to talk."

"Is that so Superintendent? Someone did tell me thumbscrews was back in fashion."

"We can but dream Mr Winebar but we don't usually need to go to those lengths. If you was lawyer I would just put a quiet word in to the Law Society about how you was a bit too close to one or two of your dodgier clients. Money, drugs, women, you know the drill. And if you was a priest we only need mention two words—little boys. Don't matter what you say. Everyone thinks you're all at it. After that you'll sing louder than Tommy Tucker. As for you, where do I start? Let's try accessory to murder and then there's all those other dodges and wheezes you get up to round here. If we put our minds to it you'd be lucky to get out before Hell freezes over."

He wasn't going to give up. I didn't have no choice about telling him.

"OK Superintendent, you win. This is how it happened. When Mrs Silver first came to see me she said that she's had a phone call saying her husband had been kidnapped and she was to wait for instructions about how to pay the ransom. She never got no instructions. The phone was a pay-as-you-go but we traced it and found out that it was bought by a bloke called Steve Curting who was an ENF heavy. When I asked him about it he said he didn't know nothing about a ransom but did admit phoning Silver's home number to put the frighteners on him because he had given a few grand to *Spotlight*. I asked him how he knew Silver had given the money and he said they'd had a tip-off, something about a brown envelope. That's all I know."

He leaned over and looked me in the eye for about 20 seconds.

"So, let's get this straight. Mrs Silver told you she'd had a phone call asking for a ransom and you found out the phone belonged to this Curting. What if I tell you that we have interviewed Mrs Silver and she's denied getting any news or having any contact from anyone about her husband all the time he was missing. We've also looked at her phone records. First thing we do with these cases. There wasn't no calls from a pay-as-you- go phone. All the numbers check out—family, friends, business and the rest. What have you got to say to that?"

I had to admit that was a bit of a choker. First time I tell the truth and he calls me a liar.

"No, no, you're wrong there Superintendent. We got hold of the phone records. That number was definitely there and we traced it to Curting. Why would I make it up?"

"Why your sort do anything is always a mystery to me Mr Winebar. You say you got the number off her phone records.

That means you've just admitted to a criminal offence. Only you couldn't have committed it because the number wasn't there. I think I might give this one to our friends at the CPS, the Criminal Protection Service as we call them here. That should give them something to think about instead of their usual—finding ways to let all the murderers, rapists and muggers we catch back on the streets."

"Well what about *Spotlight* then? They should have a record of what Silver gave."

"Ah yes. Mrs Silver mentioned that you had told her about this *Spotlight* thing but she didn't know nothing about it. We've talked to that *Spotlight* outfit. Tricky to track down and very cagey with it when we did. They didn't have no record of anyone called Silver giving them money."

"Maybe he did it anonymous."

"And maybe he didn't. Don't help you·very much though, does it?"

"What about the bank then? Its chief, Freddy Roswhathisname, told me that Silver had given the money."

"Oh it's 'Freddy' is it. We are moving up in the world. The bank says that charitable donations are matters for individuals and we didn't find nothing in Silver's bank records."

"What about Curting. Have you asked him?"

"From what I remember he's some sort of lowlife that hangs around these parts. We'll find him but I can tell you now that sort would deny their mother if they thought it would get them off a parking fine. You won't get nothing there. So what have we got now? A kidnapping that nobody heard of, a phone call that never happened and a donation that nobody knows nothing about. Don't look too convincing does it?"

No it didn't and he was just getting started.

"Let me tell you what I think might have happened. Hubby Silver done a runner, we all agree on that. Why, we don't know yet. Let's assume that the fragrant Mrs. Silver is pure as the driven snow, as she may well be. She just wants him back so she decides to get someone to look for him. I asked her why she didn't hire one of the big private agencies and she said that she had an idea that he might be hiding out in Dogswell and she thought a local man would be better. So I asked her why she picked Mr Winebar, a person well known to many of us round here, and she said—and I am not making this up—'because I thought he was Jewish'. "

I didn't bother to butt in. I didn't think he'd buy the Jack Charlton line.

"Didn't she want to have a good look at your John Thomas to make sure you was properly scalped? No? Thought not. She's far too ladylike. I go back to what I just said to you. Our Mr Winebar, Jewish or not, takes the money and goes looking and, amazing to all of us, he actually finds the bugger. So now he thinks to himself: my bread could be buttered on both sides here. Let's see what it's worth to rich hubby not to tell rich wife where he is. Only he don't do it himself just in case it gets back to the wife and he don't get paid by her. So he gets another scumbag to do it and things go wrong and we all know what happened then."

Beam me up Scotty. Things was getting sticky. All I could do was try and bluster.

"That's all cock if you don't mind me saying so Superintendent. You haven't got a shred of evidence for any of it."

"Evidence? Don't make me laugh. Half the villains in Wormwood Scrubs are banged up on less evidence than I've got on you already—and I'll get plenty more, believe me. Do yourself a favour and tell me exactly what happened."

"Nothing happened, or rather it happened as I said. We was looking for him, we nearly found him but he got killed before we did. I've no idea who done it."

Thacker sat looking at me, playing with his fingers on the table. He stared at me for about half a minute. "Right, you can go for the moment, but watch your step because we'll be watching you."

We went out into the incident room. There was the usual bunch of detectives peering into computer screens, pretending to look busy, and a few uniforms lounging about. Thacker rapped on a desk.

"Listen everybody. As some of you probably know, this is Mr Winebar. He's been helping us with our enquiries so I want you all to be helpful to him. If you see him parking his car, help him to make sure he isn't accidentally parking on a yellow line. Or if you see him on the street you can help him make sure he hasn't accidentally come out with a dangerous weapon in his pocket. We all help each other round here. I'm sure he don't like criminals and murderers any more than we do, do you Mr Winebar?"

Nothing for it but to go with the flow.

"Castration's too good for them Superintendent."

Thacker turned his head sharpish. I think he was a bit surprised.

"Now that's what I call the right attitude, Mr Winebar. I will take your very helpful suggestion along to the next meeting of the Superintendents Association. I expect they will want to put it to the Home Secretary. He's always looking for a bit of red meat to toss to the papers."

Everyone pretended to laugh. More than their jobs worth not to. Thacker then put a stop to it.

"Things are looking a bit slack round here. I want this miserable bastard caught and I want him caught quick. You all had better look lively or I'll get a new bunch in what can do the job properly. You, what are you doing?" He pointed to a uniform who looked about seventeen. I thought he was going to cry.

"I'm looking through directives from Scotland Yard on the organisation of a murder enquiry sir."

Thacker put on his thunder face.

"Wash your mouth out constable! We don't allow language like that around here." He looked right down his nose at the poor bastard's face. "What's your name constable?"

"ZP3215 Carstairs sir."

Knicker wetting time for Carstairs. Thacker licked his lips.

"Ah yes, Carstairs. You're one of them new brooms Carstairs, aren't you? They tell me your sort is going to take over from all us old has-beens. So you went to college and got a bit of education, unlike the rest of these pig-ignorant drongos. What was you learned there?"

"I, I read sociology sir."

Thacker did his cheesy grin again.

"A copper what can read. That's got to be a first for Dogswell. What did you say you was reading?"

"Sociology sir."

"So-shee-ology, So-shee-ology." He rolled it round his mouth like it was a big gobstopper. "I thought that was a Japanese restaurant?"

Carstairs gave a little whinny, like a donkey taken up the arse with a cucumber. Everyone else tried to keep in the giggles.

"You must be thinking of sushi sir. Sociology is the study of social interactions. It's the study of human beings really."

Thacker shook his head in a bit sad, bit seen it all before, sort of way.

"Well I never. Human beans eh, human beans. Ain't seen one of them round here for years. Anyone else clapped eyes on a human bean round here lately?"

We all knew enough to keep shtum.

"Maybe the sergeant can help us out." He turned to the custody sergeant. "Have you by any chance, sergeant, got any human beans banged up in your cells?"

The sergeant flipped through his book, pretending to look.

"Don't think so Gov. All we got are a couple of drunks, a couple of druggies, one soliciting, two stabbings and a taking and driving away. Quiet really."

Thacker turned back towards Carstairs.

"There you are Constable Carstairs. We've got druggies in Dogswell; we've got drunks in Dogswell; we've got whores in Dogswell; we've got psychos and God knows what else in Dogswell but we ain't got no human beans in Dogswell. They don't come this far south."

17

Dogswell nick is very new and very big. It sits right in the middle of the High Street and looks a bit like Colditz, only without that friendly, welcoming air. They knocked down an old department store to build it. You used to be able to get everything there from a pair of socks to a three piece suite. Now you just get a ten-stretch, if you're lucky. I walked out of there after the going over from Thacker. It was a nice afternoon, bright sunshine, but I didn't exactly feel cheerful. I needed a drink so I called Dany and we met up in the KB.

"This is a fucking nightmare Dany. Thacker is within a gnat's bollock of doing me for Silver's murder. I've got to get out of this."

Dany didn't seem too worried.

"He can't do that. I know Thacker. He's just bluffing. Ten to one he knows you didn't do it."

"Ten to one you're right Dany but that don't make no difference to Thacker. Guilty till proven guilty is the way he thinks. He's got to get somebody for it and if he can't find no one else it's going to be me. I'm going to have to get out, skip the country."

"That's a bit drastic Spencer. Where are you going to go?"

"Fuck knows, but it ain't as if I'm not spoiled for choice. It's ridiculous how many countries there is in the world today. I was watching the Eurovision Song Contest the other night. They got countries coming out their ears. Never used to be like that. I used to have to watch it years ago with my old Mum. She loved that tosser with the rug. 'That's Terry, ' she would say, 'I love him.' In them days there was a lot fewer countries and Ireland always used to win. Some fat mick from Ballybogshit or wherever would come out and sing about his mammy and they would bung him the gong and tell the rest to fuck off till next year. Now it's all different. No sign of a fat mick anywhere. The winners was a bloke and a couple of tarts who waggled around like they had food mixers up their arses and come from somewhere called Lissooania."

"Where's that? Never heard of it."

"Fuck knows. It sounds like a disease, the sort that Tony Hancock used to go on about:"

> *- I haven't been feeling too good lately Doc. Any idea what's wrong?*
> *- You've got a touch of Lissooania, old boy. Lot of it about.*
> *- That sounds bad Doc. How long have I got?*
> *- Oh, nothing to worry about old boy. Might make you want to shake your arse a bit, but you should be right as rain in a few days.*

I mean, say what you like about the Krauts—two world wars and one world cup and all that; they definitely do not like it up 'em—but at least Germany is a proper country. You know where it is. Cross the Channel and keep going straight. Can't miss it. That's what they told Montgomery anyway. But Lissooania? Who come up with that one?

"So any idea of where you might go?"

"Not really. Maybe Kazakhstan."

"You really are desperate Spence. I saw a film about there once. They're all mad."

"Yeah, but it's a long way away and very big. Thacker would never find me there."

"Neither would anyone else. I've got a better idea—Northern Cyprus."

"Northern Cyprus. That's in the Med isn't it? Tell me more."

"It's a breakaway from the other bit of Cyprus. Only recognised by Turkey. Better still, there's no extradition. There's a good few villains from around here hiding out there."

"That is a peach of an idea Dany my son. I definitely want some of that. I can see myself now, on the lounger, by the pool, glass of vino in one hand and two fingers up to Thacker with the other. When's the next plane?"

Thinking about it, of course, it wouldn't be quite so easy. I hope they understand English if you shout loud enough because I don't speak a word of Cyprusish or whatever they talk there. And then you need to take a few bob with you to get you started in a foreign land. I wasn't exactly flush although I was owed by Rachel Silver plus a couple of other clients who hadn't paid up for at least six months and with who strong words, if not worse, would have to be had. So I would have to postpone my little vacation on the Med for a while. Still, no harm in dreaming. Dany and I got to talking about how I'd need a whole new wardrobe to wear out there. He always goes for something loud—Hawaiian shirts, great big patterned shorts. All his lot are like that. I like something a bit more understated, a bit classier. We was just talking about what type of swimming trunks I should have when Deepak's app went off. He had put this app on my phone because he's a bit paranoid about actually making phone calls. When it goes off it means he's got something for me.

We didn't get there for a while. To be honest, choosing between sinking a few in the KB and contemplating a life of sun and all the rest or watching a load of bollocks on a computer screen wasn't exactly hard. So we was just that little bit squiffy when we turned up, which didn't exactly please Deepak. He was a bit short with me.

"Spencer, are you sure you want to look at this now?"

"Yeah, yeah. Sorry about the wait Deepak. We got a bit carried away planning my holidays. I'm definitely up for it now. Let's have a look. What did you say it was about?"

"It seems you have another riddle Spencer."

> With swords they entered the door to the sublime. That was their crime and their punishment obscured by his eminence will be for the second to be given to the third and they shall see glory in saintly wisdom.

"Looks like another one for Sami Deepak. Is he here?"

"He's just come in." He called across the room and Sami poked his head out from behind a big screen. He sidled over to our screen took a long look.

"L...l..let's start with 'd...d...door to the s...s...sublime' and see where we get." He put it into the search engine and the first thing that came up was a *Wikipedia* entry

> The Sublime Porte, also known as the Ottoman Porte or High Porte is a metonym for the central government of the Ottoman Empire. Porte is French for "gate". When Sultan Suleiman the Magnificent sealed an alliance with King Francis I of France in 1536, the French diplomats walked through the monumental gate or Bab-i Ali in order to reach the Vizierate of Constantinople, seat of the Sultan's government.

That had to be way off beam.

"Looks like the start of *Ali Baba and the Forty Thieves* Sami. Shall we try something else?"

Deepak thought different.

"I wouldn't dismiss it so easily Spencer. It might be a reference to the Ottoman Empire, or maybe to the city of Constantinople. 'With swords they entered' sounds like a battle or a war of some sort. Let's take a look at Constantinople."

Up it come *in Wikipedia*. There was a load of stuff about the Roman Empire and then it turned out that in 1453 the Turks invaded and killed a load of Christians. That seemed to fit the bit about swords and it definitely looked like a crime but what was this punishment about second being given to the third?"

Dany thought he'd join in. "Crime and Punishment sounds like a good title for a book."

I thought Dany was all to fuck as usual. "Yeah, Agatha Christie: 'Hercule Poirot twiddled his moustaches as he contemplated a suitable punishment for this dastardly crime. Ze Turks must pay for taking Constantinople.'"

Sami though thought otherwise. "I th...th...think you may be right Dany. There is a well known novel called *Crime and Pun-*

ishment, though it's by Fyodor Dostoyevsky, not Agatha Christie."

So who was this Dostiewhatsit tosser I wanted to know and what had his book got to do with Constantinople? Sami said he was a Russian. He had read the book and it was about some student knocking off a pawnbroker. So where did that get us?

"Maybe Dostoyevsky had something to say about Constantinople." suggested Deepak.

It turned out he did. A quick Internet search turned up something from his diary:

> Yes, Constantinople should belong to us, not only because this city is a famous harbour, a narrow, a "world centre", "the omphalos of the earth"; not only because today is necessarily recognised by all that Russia, that giant, comes, at last, out of his isolation, where he had been growing and came to touch the ceiling, and now goes ahead to the open air, breathing the free air of the seas and of the oceans. What I want rather is to offer a view, exceptionally important by itself, according to which, Constantinople can not but belong to Russia!

Talk about a pile of airy-fairy shit. I had to read it about three times before I could work out what he was on about. The Russians was in it now but why did they want to get their hands on Constantinople? After a bit more digging we found out that Constantinople was the centre of their sort of Christianity, called "Orthodox". I suppose that makes the rest of them unorthodox. Fine by me but has anyone told the Pope? They wanted to get it back for the Christians from the Turks who was Muslim. Sami said that was where that phrase 'saintly wisdom' came in. Saint Sophia, which he said meant holy wisdom, was the cathedral in Constantinople but the Turks turned it into a mosque. The Russians wanted to turn it back. But there was a lot more to it than that, as Deepak and Sami quickly found out. The Russians wanted Constantinople because they could then get their ships into the eastern Mediterranean and that would threaten the Suez

Canal and cause big headaches for the British, so we didn't like that at all. There was even a song about it:

> *We don't want to fight but by Jingo if we do,*
> *We've got the ships, we've got the men, we've got the money too,*
> *We've fought the Bear before, and while we're Britons true,*
> *The Russians shall not have Constantinople.*

"They were singing that in 1878 Spencer. That's where the word 'jingoism' comes from."

"What's jingoism, ringing bells or something?"

"No, it means ultra-nationalism, my country right or wrong. Think England football supporters on a bad day, or Dogswell supporters on any day. British policy was to stop the Russians getting their hands on Constantinople at all costs."

Sami brought us back to the puzzle. "We still haven't worked out what 'second to be given to the third' is. Let's see what searching for 'Constantinople' and 'second' gives us."

We had to scrabble around a bit. There was a few false leads but eventually Sami found something that he thought was interesting.

"C...C...Constantinople was called the s...s...second Rome. We should look for somewhere called the third."

We looked and sure enough there it was in *Wikipedia*:

> Within decades after the capture of Constantinople by Mehmed II of the Ottoman Empire on 29 May 1453, some Eastern Orthodox people were nominating Moscow as the "Third Rome"

That would seem to mean that Constantinople was being given to Moscow, but who was giving it and why? It didn't take a lot to find out. It was us:

Aide-mémoire from Russian Foreign Minister to British and French ambassadors at Petrograd, 19 February / 4 March 1915

The course of recent events leads His Majesty Emperor Nicholas to think that the question of Constantinople and of the Straits must be definitely solved, according to the time-honoured aspirations of Russia.

Every solution will be inadequate and precarious if the city of Constantinople, the western bank of the Bosphorus, of the Sea of Marmara and of the Dardanelles, as well as southern Thrace to the Enez-Midye line, should henceforth not be incorporated into the Russian Empire.

Similarly, and by strategic necessity, that part of the Asiatic shore that lies between the Bosphorus, the Sakarya River and a point to be determined on the Gulf of Izmit, and the islands of the Sea of Marmara, the Imbros Islands and the Tenedos Islands must be incorporated into the (Russian) Empire

The special interests of France and Great Britain in the above region will be scrupulously respected.

The Imperial Government entertains the hope that the above consideration will be sympathetically received by the two Allied Governments. The said Allied Governments are assured similar understandings on the part of the Imperial Government for the realization of plans which they may frame with reference to other regions of the Ottoman Empire or elsewhere."

British aide-mémoire to the Russian Government, 27 February / 12 March 1915

Subject to the war being carried on and brought to a successful conclusion, and to desiderata of Great Britain and France in the Ottoman Empire and elsewhere being realised, as indicated in the Russian communication herein referred to, His Majesty's Government will agree to the Russian Government's aide-mémoire relative to

Constantinople and the Straits, the text of which was communicated to His Britannic Majesty's Ambassador by his Excellency M. Sazonof on February 19 / March 4 instant."

What was that all about? One minute we was going to punch the Russkies on the nose, by jingo, if they so much as looked at Constantinople. The next we was handing it to them on a plate. Wasn't there a stink about it? Deepak pointed to another bit of text further down the screen.

"It seems like they expected one. They sent a follow up note. Look what it says."

That document involves a complete reversal of the traditional policy of His Majesty's Government, and is in direct opposition to the opinions and sentiments at one time universally held in England and which have still by no means died out.

"Fuck me Deepak, That's one big reverse ferret as they used to say in Fleet Street. Something must have really got into them."

Sami nodded. "There's another qu.. qu..question. I'm puzzled by that phrase 'obscured by his eminence'. 'His Eminence' is usually a Roman Catholic cardinal but I doubt if any cardinal was involved." He thought for a minute and the rest of us thought with him, but we wasn't coming up with much, so he went on. "The only other usage of 'eminence' I can think of is in French, *éminence grise*, grey eminence in English, which means someone operating behind the scenes."

It was Deepak who got it first.

"That's it, Grey. It's Sir Edward Grey again, the British Foreign Secretary. He was certainly eminent and he was known to keep his cards very close to his chest. 'Obscured by his eminence' probably means that he kept the agreement secret. Let's see."

He was off in his travels round cyberspace again. After a few minutes he reckoned he had found it.

"Yes, there it is, and the person saying so is none other than Winston Churchill. It's in his book, *The World Crisis*:

> The supreme need of encouraging Russia in the midst of her disasters and defeats had led Sir Edward Grey, as early as November 14, 1914, to instruct Sir George Buchanan to inform M Sazanoff that the British Government recognised that 'the question of the Straits and of Constantinople should be settled in conformity with Russian desires.' At the time this had remained a complete secret."

The things they did in them days. I don't think they could have got away with it now.

"If I'm reading this right Deepak, somebody is definitely having a laugh. Not only was we doing the exact opposite of what we always said we was going to do but, according to Winston Churchill, nobody knew about it. How come?"

"You may well ask Spencer. It looks like the main reason as Churchill said was that the war was going badly for the Russians and this was an incentive for them to keep going, but it was a very dangerous game, as Sir Edward Grey obviously realised. Keeping the Russians out of Constantinople had been British policy for nearly a century, which is why he had to keep it secret even from those like Churchill who were in the Cabinet. This was the arrogant high point of imperialism—two countries discussing dismembering a third without so much as a by your leave. Well the Ottoman and Russian Empires soon bit the dust and the British didn't last much longer either. Serves them all right."

"Yes, but what I want to know Deepak is where is this getting us? We've had King George who obviously welshed on his cousin Nicky and then pretended that he didn't. We've had this bloke Bark who seemed to be in with everybody, Georgie, Nicky and the Bank of England, though nobody seems to know how or why. And now we've got this stuff about Constantinople. What's any of it got to do with anything?"

"Our Mr Silver was obviously deep into some conspiracy theories but quite what is not at all clear. There's an obvious link between George and Bark but where Constantinople comes into it I have no idea. Maybe it will become a bit clearer when we decrypt the rest of his files."

"Or maybe it won't. Something very odd was going on in that bloke's head."

18

Me and Dany had just got back to the KB and was about to have a well earned drink after learning more than we ever fucking wanted to know about Constantinople when we got another ping from the app. We both reckoned we'd had enough of computers for one day and decided we'd go over there next morning..

When we got there Deepak was sitting there as usual, with Sami and another of his mates in a corner, and half a dozen screens all flickering away. How they make any sense of that stuff beats me. Another fucking universe. It can't do your eyes no good, nor your sex life neither.

"You ought to get out more Deepak. You're working too hard. Get yourself a girlfriend."

"That's what my mother says Spencer. She's always trying to get me hitched. 'You must think about getting married Deepak. People are beginning to talk. Just give me the word and I will fix you up with a nice girl.'"

"There you are. Mothers aren't always wrong."

"I've got better things to do with my time Spencer. Unlike some people I'm not entirely obsessed with sex."

"You mean you're gay?"

"No! In my experience most gay men *are* entirely obsessed with sex."

"You've got a point there old son. Anyway I didn't come here to discuss your love life. What have you got for us?"

"I think this one might be a real puzzle Spencer." He pointed to the screen. On it was a drawing of an old bloke with a long beard and a pointy hat.

"That's it, just a picture?"

I turned to our puzzle expert. "You got any ideas Sami?"

He had on another of his T-shirts with a slogan. Maybe this was the clean one. It said " Software is like sex: It's better when it's free." I suppose a boy shouldn't give up hope.

"W...w...well, it's a wizard. Presumably that's a clue. There may be a message hidden inside it."

"What do you mean, hidden inside it? Where? In his beard?"

"N...n...no. In the file itself. We need to open it with a text editor."

He opened some program and all of a sudden instead of a bloke with a beard there was a shitload of symbols and characters spread all across the screen.

"What the fuck is all that Sami?"

"Most of it is encoding for the picture, but look at the bottom. There are some characters there that aren't."

I looked but I couldn't see no difference. Sami had to point it out to me. It was a string of figures that looked something like 102:20, 148:18, 183:32 and a few more.

"It's just numbers Sami. What does it mean?"

"It l...l...looks like a one-time pad."

"A what?"

"A one time pad. S...s...secret agents use it. You have a text, maybe a book or a newspaper article, and the numbers indicate a letter or a word on a page. Put them together and you have the message. Unless you have the text it's unbreakable."

"OK, so what's this text?"

"I d...d..don't know. There's doesn't seem to be anything here to identify it."

"So you're saying we're fucked on this one."

"Y...y...yes, unless there's another clue in the picture."

Deepak then came up with an idea. "Maybe it's a book about wizards like the ones in the Harry Potter books, or Gandalf in *Lord of the Rings* or Merlin in tales of King Arthur and the Knights of the Round Table."

"Worth a try Deepak. Anybody got these books?"

It turned out that they did. Dany's kids love Harry Potter so they had all of them and Sami had a copy of *Lord of the Rings*— why wasn't I surprised? They went to get them and Sami said he'd pop into the library to see if he could pick up any books about King Arthur.

...

About an hour later everyone was back with the books. So what do we do now I asked Sami.

"I th... th...think the first number of each element is the page and the second is the line."

We tried it with *Lord of the Rings*. Up popped:

> "My dear and most beloved hobbit!" said Frodo, deeply moved.

That didn't look too promising and the Harry Potter and King Arthur books were just as useless. It looked like we was going to draw a blank when Sami looked at the picture again and said, "The face is cut away. It's a sort of mask. Maybe that's the clue."

He tried 'Gandalf's mask' in Google but didn't come up with anything and then 'Merlin's mask'. This time he hit something. *The Mask of Merlin: A Critical Biography of David Lloyd George,* a book by someone called Donald McCormick.

I was racking my brains trying to remember where I'd heard that name Lloyd George before when Deepak put me straight.

"He was the British Prime Minister in the First World War Spencer. This looks a bit more promising. He's was mentioned in the first file of Silver's that Sami decrypted."

"Oh, I remember now. He was a bit of a ladies' man wasn't he? Knew everyone's mother so they say. Anyway, as you say, this one looks worth a try. Can we get hold of a copy?"

We could. There was a digital version on some website. We downloaded it and tried the first reference.

> While at the Ministry of Munitions, Lloyd George was once again the friend of big business and the industrial-financial oligarchies with whom he curried favour when at the Board of Trade. He was caught up too deeply in

the mesh of international armaments intrigues to be a free agent. For the man to whom he turned for help and advice was Sir Basil Zaharoff, chief agent of the Vickers Company, with a roving commission to go where he liked and sell arms to whomever he could at a commission. When war came in 1914 Zaharoff was at the zenith of his power and, with the aid of Lloyd George, soon filled the role of unofficial chief inter-Allied munitions agent.

Then it went on to say that Lloyd George made his name by using this Zaharoff to help him sort out the shell shortage for the army which was in danger of losing us the war. But Zaharoff was a wily old bird. He was keeping tabs on Lloyd George.

Zaharoff ... took steps to find out all about Lloyd George, his weaknesses and secrets, and the man he employed to do this was none other than Arthur Maundy Gregory, the honours tout. Gregory had long been closely associated with Sir Basil Thomson, Head of the Metropolitan Police Criminal Investigation Branch, the enforcer for the Secret Intelligence Service (SIS), on counter espionage work and, according to Thomson, Gregory informed him that he had discovered that sometime during the early nineties Lloyd George had had a brief liaison with Zaharoff s English wife.

"This is a bit tasty Deepak. Wasn't Boris Whathisname Frankenstein in the pictures? If Lloyd George was getting up to his usual legover antics with his wife he could have sunk his fangs into him and turned him into a zombie. Might have done wonders for the war effort."

"I shouldn't dignify that with a response Spencer. Boris Karloff was the actor, not Zaharoff. And while we're at it, Frankenstein was not the monster. He was its creator. Oh, and zombies don't exist. Apart from that, you're spot on."

Deepak always does take things a bit literal. Best to leave it, so we checked the next reference.

> Once he was embroiled with Zaharoff, Lloyd George was automatically in trouble with the French, with whom the arms magnate was now on the worst possible terms largely through his own doubledealing. One of the British Premier's first aims was to sabotage the Sykes-Picot plan, to which Zaharoff strongly objected, by provoking a rupture with France.

I thought getting up the noses of the Frogs was pretty much par for the course for our prime ministers, but what was this Sykes-Picot bollocks? We looked it up and it turned out that us and the French had agreed to carve up the Middle East between us, with a little bit to the Russians, once we'd won the war and taken it off the Turks. We was pretty free with other peoples' countries in them days. But why did he want to sabotage it? We got the answer in the next reference.

> Sir Basil Thompson in the course of his probes into Bolshevik activities had discovered documents which incriminated servants of the Crown as secret agents of Sir Basil Zaharoff *with the knowledge of Lloyd George*. Thomson had certain suspects followed, and then learned that Zaharoff, the man who had lavished presents on the Czar and his family, had established links with the Bolsheviks, It was purely a temporary arrangement by which Zaharoff sought to divert munitions supplies intended for the White Russians so that they could be delivered to Greece and certain Balkan countries for ultimate use against the Turks. Zaharoff had by devious means done his utmost both in London and Paris to call off the campaign against the Bolsheviks. Not, of course, that he was pro-Communist, but simply that he wanted the arms to carve an empire for Greece in the Balkans. Zaharoff knew that if the White Russians won, they

might agitate for Constantinople, as promised to them in the Sykes-Picot Agreement. He wanted Constantinople for Greece and he had received an assurance from the Bolsheviks that they would make no claim for this city.

There was a lot of dirty dealing in them days. So what happened? We spent the next hour or so finding out. What a mess. The Greeks wanted Constantinople because since Roman times it had been the most important Greek city. They also wanted a lot of the coastal regions of Turkey, which they called Asia Minor. Greeks had been living there for over two thousand years. At the end of the war the Russian and Ottoman empires had gone, so in 1919 the Greeks decided to try their luck and invaded. Lloyd George was backing them all the way, but the rest of the British Government was dead against. At first the Greeks did well but by 1922 the Turks had got their act together and smashed them completely. It was the biggest disaster in Greek history. A million Greeks were kicked out of Asia Minor and had to go and live in Greece.

It looked like Constantinople was a bit of a curse. Everyone who wanted it come a cropper. I suppose that's history for you. One fucking thing after another. Then Dany, who as usual hadn't said much, started up.

"This history stuff is all very interesting but I think we may be missing something. As they tell you on my Psychology and Law course, the thing to look for is why people do things, not just what they've done."

Both Deepak and me just looked at him. This was news to us.

"How long have you been doing this course Dany?"

"In the second year now. It's the Open University degree in Psychology and Law. I started it when I was in prison."

First time I've had the Open University in my corner but I'm always willing to listen.

"OK Sigmund. Let's have your take on things."

"We haven't asked why he encrypted the files at the Bank."

"Because he didn't want someone at the Bank to see them."

"But why the puzzles rather than just plain text? Did he think someone was reading his files even though they were encrypted?"

"That's a point Dany. What do you think Sami?"

"It w...w...would be possible using the same techniques as us, or if they had the passwords."

"So why write them at the Bank in the first place?" said Dany. "Why not do it at home if you wanted to prevent anyone at the Bank seeing them?"

"He didn't have a computer at home."

"Oh come off it Spence. He was a banker. How much does a computer cost? No, I reckon that the reason was because he didn't want his wife to see them, but if he encrypted them she would get suspicious that he was hiding something."

"He didn't want her to see it because she thought it was making him go loopy."

"I don't buy that. He could have easily explained it away. Didn't your mate Freddy Rosquevoir say that he thought an outside interest was a good thing for a banker? There had to be something in there that he didn't want her to see. And another thing, why did she keep you on after her husband was killed? You're not a private investigator, as you say yourself."

"She wanted to know what was happening. The police wasn't telling her nothing."

"I don't buy that either. The police can't get away with that attitude nowadays, even Thacker can't. There'll be a family liaison office and they have to keep the victim's family informed, at least up to a point. The only reason they might keep things back is if she was under suspicion. Do you think she was?"

"Don't think so. Thacker is suspicious of everyone but I don't think he had her in the frame."

"Then she must have been hoping that you would find something."

"What?"

"Good question Spence, to which we don't have a good answer."

19

We was back to Square One, or rather One Baring Square. She was in her "office" sitting behind a massive desk that you could have landed a plane on.

"What do you mean you want to finish? Isn't my money good enough for you?"

It ain't every day I turn money down. To be honest it hadn't never happened before and mine, I don't mind admitting, can be a very dodgy business. But things was getting a bit out of hand.

"It's not the money any more. The Police are now looking like they might want to fit me up for something, maybe even the murder. I really don't need that. And besides, from what they tell me, you haven't been straight with me neither."

She looked almost shocked.

"What! That's absolutely absurd! I really don't know what has got into the Police these days. It's that dreadful man—what's his name?—Thackeray..."

"Thacker."

"Thacker, that's right. He has been to see me twice, asking all sorts of intrusive questions, as I think I mentioned to you. The last time he even insinuated that I might know something about Reuben's murder that I wasn't telling him. I was absolutely furious. The moment he had gone I called my solicitor and we consulted a top QC. A very stiff letter was sent to the Commissioner of the Metropolitan Police about the behaviour of Superintendent Thacker. I expect him to be told in no uncertain terms to mend his ways in future."

I had a good laugh about that. I know which side my money was on.

"Good luck with that one. In my experience, one word from Scotland Yard and Thacker does what he likes. Or rather, in my case, what he don't like and he definitely don't like me. He also told me, and this is the real choker, that you said you hadn't had no word about Reuben all the time he was missing and that there wasn't no record of any pay-as-you go phone calling you. I know that last bit isn't true because we found out the phone call was from Curting. So what gives?"

She come over all apologetic. She knew she'd been caught out.

"I'm really sorry about that. I realise now it has put you in a very difficult position. Freddy called me and asked me to say absolutely nothing to the police. You must see it from his point of view. The Bank has many very important and influential customers. Discretion is all important. to it He wants to avoid any hint of scandal. He said he had been talking to someone very senior in the Police and they had told him that they believed it was just a random murder, probably a robbery gone wrong. Poor Reuben just happened to be in the wrong place at the wrong time. He said that the Police had assured him that they were confident of making an arrest very soon. In the circumstances he thought it was best for all of us to say nothing, let the police catch the culprit and let justice take its course."

"And what about the phone call? How did you make that go away?"

She come on full-frontal offended.

"I didn't make anything go away. How could I? I've no idea how these things work. Maybe Thacker wasn't telling the truth. Maybe he was just trying to scare you."

That thought had occurred to me but there was something about the way Thacker had put it that made me think he wasn't just trying to put the wind up me. Still, it was a possibility.

"What about your pal Freddy? He knew about the phone call but he told you to say nothing. He must have known the Police would look at your phone records. First thing they do, as Thacker told me. Maybe he has ways of making it go away."

"Nonsense, Freddy wouldn't do anything like that. I don't imagine he knows any more about telephone systems than I do and anyway he wouldn't do anything illegal."

"I thought you said he was a banker?"

"Please, spare me the tired clichés about bankers."

"Oh, tired is it? What I'm getting tired of is being messed about. First by you for telling me one thing and the coppers another and then by Thacker threatening to do me for the murder if he can't get no one else. If I was suspicious I'd be beginning to think that you and Freddy was setting me up."

I think that shook her a little bit. She looked at me for a few seconds and then come over sympathetic.

"No, no, absolutely not. You mustn't believe that. I'm truly sorry if anything I, or Freddy for that matter, have done has made things difficult for you, but you're innocent. You haven't done anything so you've nothing to fear."

Sometimes you just want to give up. Where to start?

"I really don't think you know how the law works. Have you got any idea how many people are locked up for things they haven't done? Don't get me wrong. Nearly all of them have done something. Usually they should have been banged up for longer than they actually got, but either they're too fly or, more often than not, the coppers are too stupid or lazy to get the evidence for what they actually did so they have to fit them up for something else. It's a fair cop as they used to say in detective books."

Time for her to be shocked again.

"No, no. I won't believe a word of it. We are always told that British justice is the finest in the world and I firmly believe that it is."

"Believe what you want but I can tell you that if Thacker wants to fit me up he'll find a way to do it. And the more I keep working on this case the more he'll want to do it. He's like that. He's a mean bastard, if you'll pardon my language. I really don't want to give him the excuse. I'm looking for an out from here. I've got my eye on a nice little spot in the Med. Sunshine, bottle of vino, lie back by the pool and forget all about Thacker and everything else."

Her expression completely changed. She gave me an imploring look, then her face crumpled. I thought she might be going to cry.

"Please, please, there's nobody else I can turn to. Do you have any idea what I'm going through? My husband has been murdered. Nobody can possibly understand the hurt. I try to keep myself together but sometimes the grief just overwhelms me. I just collapse. I lie on a bed and cry for hours. Nothing makes sense any more. I want someone to tell me why. What could he possibly have done that someone would want to kill him? Who could hate him that much? Freddy wants me to say nothing. The Police are not telling me anything and so I'm desperate. Anything, any little thing, however trivial, would be a comfort. Something that helps me believe that, however slowly, we were getting to the truth. Can't you see that? I don't care what it costs. Won't you please help me?"

Two things I've always been a sucker for—cash money and a damsel in distress. Got me into more trouble than I even dare think about. And here they were wrapped up in one. What could I say?

"Look, I'd really like to help but, as I said, I don't think there's any more I can do."

She wasn't giving up.

"Please, can we just go over where you have got to so far. Maybe that will give us some ideas."

I didn't see us coming up with much in the way of ideas but I wanted to wrap things up and get paid so I'd brought over my report and all the other bits and pieces we had like print-outs of the stuff we'd got off the hard drive. I put them on the desk.

"I'm not sure we're much further on than last time. If anything we seem to be going backwards. Your friend Freddy told me that Reuben made a couple of donations to *Spotlight* but the coppers say they can't find any record. That doesn't necessarily mean much. We know that Curting made a phone call to you, although the coppers say there's no record of it now. That we can check out from our own sources. Curting says he didn't say nothing about a ransom, he just wanted to put the frighteners on about *Spotlight*. You said he did. I believe you naturally. Curting said he doesn't know who tipped them off about *Spotlight*. Friend Freddy said it definitely wasn't anyone in the Bank. The guy from *Spotlight* said it might have come from the security services because he thought there might be a link between them and the ENF. Then there's all the Russian stuff on his computer. It looks like a load of old cobblers to me but our mate Deepak, who's not just the dog's whatsits in computers but he's a bit of a Russian Revolution buff, is getting right into it. He thinks Reuben thought he was on to a big conspiracy."

"What do you mean, conspiracy?"

"We're not really sure yet." I tried to tell her about King George and Bark and Lloyd George and Constantinople and Zaharoff and the rest. Not sure I got it all right. She didn't seem that impressed.

"You are beginning to sound like Reuben. It all sounds highly unlikely to me. Besides it was nearly a hundred years ago. What on earth has it to do with Reuben's murder?"

"You've got me there. I can't see any connection. The only mystery is why it's all encrypted and then put into puzzles. This stuff is not exactly top secret. It all seems to come from books and the Internet. It don't make sense. The only thing I can think of is he might be trying to hide it from someone at the Bank. Any idea who or why?"

"No."

"Could he have been poking around in old Bank business and didn't want nobody else to see? I seem to remember friend Freddy telling me that Reuben had told him about some Russian nobs who had accounts at the Bank before the First World War. Could that have anything to do with it?"

"I very much doubt it. Besides any money in those accounts would be long gone by now."

"Yep, that's more or less what Freddy said. But if there was something there besides money is there anyone that could tell us?"

"Well, they do have an archivist."

"A what?"

"An archivist, someone who looks after old files and records. A sort of guardian of the Bank's history, if you like. A few years ago they commissioned a history of the Bank by a very distinguished writer. I think we have a copy somewhere."

"Must be riveting. Could we talk to this archivist?"

"Again, I doubt it. As I keep telling you, the Bank is very discreet. It very rarely discusses anything about its accounts, even very old ones."

Looked like we had a bit of a dead end there and we wasn't likely to get much further with the *Spotlight* thing either unless maybe we could rustle up a contact at MI5. Still, I thought I might as well earn a few bob more by looking busy while I sorted out my escape to the sun.

20

"You always were a sucker for a pretty face Spencer."

For a jailbird Dany has a fucking big streak of morality. We was sitting in the office wondering how we might stretch our little earner.

"What are you talking about?"

"You still seem to take her at her word, that she's just the grieving widow and nobody is telling her what's going on so she needs you as a knight errant to keep her in the picture. But I think there's more to it."

"Such as? I think all this university stuff may be going to your head Dany. We should call you Prof. "

"Well for a start, you remember when I was looking at the cctv from Ali's and I saw that she drove off in a top of the range Merc. It came near enough to the shop that I could make out the number. I had it checked and it was registered to her husband at their address."

"So she come here in her own car. So what?"

"You told me that she'd said she'd come in a cab. Why would she say that if she hadn't?"

"She said she looked me up in Yellow Pages, I thought she said she got a cab to take her here. Maybe she just asked the cabbie the way and drove herself."

"Come off it Spence. Those cars have satnav and all the gizmos. She would just have to put your address in and the thing would practically drive itself here. And then there's the business of Curting's phone call. She first tells you that he wanted a ransom. Curting says he only wanted to put the frightners on. Who do we believe? Then she drops you in it with Thacker by saying she hadn't had any contact from anyone after her husband disappeared. We know there was a phone call but Thacker said there wasn't. He could be lying but I don't see it. Why would he? You haven't been interviewed properly yet but if you were it would all be on the tape and if it came to court he'd have to produce the phone records. He couldn't chance it. That record must have been deleted and I bet she knew it."

"You could be right Dany, but who could have done it and why?"

"That is the big question Spence. I've no idea. We could ask Billy the Bone. He might know."

....

Billy is not the easiest bastard to contact. He works for a big phone company—no names, no you know what—so obviously you can't phone him. You phone his wife saying you've got an urgent job needs doing. She gets on to him and if you're lucky she calls back telling you where and when to meet up. A couple of hours later we get the call saying to meet in a pub in Croydon, not somewhere I go often, for reasons that would be obvious to anyone who's ever been there.

By the time we got to the plastic and glass shithole that is the unlovely city of Croydon it was well after five, so all the office workers was getting the hell out of town and the pub was almost deserted. Billy was sitting in a corner, nursing a pint and looking his usual miserable self. He's bald, paunchy and has one of them mouths that turns down at both ends. Everything is always too much for Billy. He don't like nobody much and nobody much likes him. On the other hand he really likes a bung and to be fair he must be good at what he does because he nearly always comes up with the goods when I ask. As usual he wasn't that pleased to see us.

"You bastards could have put me right in it. We've had investigators sniffing around wanting to know who was checking on that number you asked me about. Someone is in big trouble."

"Sorry to hear that Billy. What have they been doing to you?"

"Not me. Nobody's said nothing to me yet. They'd have to get up very early to catch me, but I have to be very careful. All our system access is logged. I didn't use my own password. I used my supervisor's. Stupid bugger leaves it on a notepad in his desk drawer because he can't remember it. He's been given a right roasting. Could be for the chop."

"We'll send him flowers. Look Billy, we wanted to have a chat with you because a call made from that phone to one of our clients has been deleted from her records. How could that be done? Could you do it?"

Ho looked at me like I had gone mad all of a sudden.

"No way. Technically it's possible but I wouldn't touch it. If we could delete them we could have free calls for ourselves and all our mates, couldn't we. Don't imagine the powers that be hadn't thought of that one. If that call was deleted it was done by someone a long way up from me. And don't ask me to check, neither. I can see what you're thinking. There's no way I'm going to get involved. More than my job's worth."

"Fair enough Billy, I take your point, but there must be talk at your place about why these investigators are sniffing around. What do you think they're after?"

"Who fucking knows? There's a lot of talk around, most of it bollocks. I heard somebody reckon that one of our blokes had tapped into some financial outfits and was tipping off some of the wide boys in the City if there was going to a big deal so they could get in quick. The only thing I know for certain is that number you asked me about has been blanked."

"Blanked?"

"Yeah, blanked. If you try and look it up on the system it's not there."

"And you've tried?"

"No I fucking haven't. I told you everything's logged. I just heard it from a reliable source. Not saying who."

"Does that sort of thing happen often?"

"More often than you might think."

"Who can do it?"

"Old Bill, spooks, Home Office, take your pick. All sorts of nosy bastards can do what they like. Fucking disgrace. Call this a free country?"

21

"You won't believe this Spence, but I got an email this morning from Jack Dapper."

"What did he want?"

"That's the funny thing Spence. He didn't really want anything. He just said he'd enjoyed our last 'little chat' and asked if I wanted to pop round sometime and talk over old times again. I think he must be lonely."

"The tears are rolling down my leg Dany. Are you going to take him up on his kind offer?"

"You must be joking. I don't go for all that 'good old times' stuff. Mostly I remember being called all sorts of names by my so-called colleagues and when I threatened to smack someone they'd say something like 'Can't you coons take a joke Dany?'"

Well, that's what you used to get for being black in them days. Can't say them things now of course, not if you don't want to have the Racial Equality lot stuffing a writ up your arse. Anyway, I had to agree with Dany. Who'd want to sit there watching Jack Dapper knock back the scotch and listen to him saying how much better things was when he and his like was in charge? Then another thought occurred to me.

"Dany, you remember that I mentioned to you about what Rachel Silver had told me —- that the Bank had someone called an archivist who looked after all their old records?"

"Vaguely"

"Well, she said we wouldn't be able to talk to him, or maybe it's a her, because the Bank wouldn't allow it. If you and I go along and chew the fat with Jack, maybe he could help us to have a chat with this archivist."

"Why on earth would we want to talk about old bank records? Paint drying would be more interesting."

"I know, I know. It's probably nothing but Reuben Silver apparently found out that there was Russian nobs who had accounts there before the First World War. That might have something to do with all this Russian stuff on his computer. Anyway, that's not the point. In our business Dany, information is money. Anything we find out, even if we think it's sweet FA, means I can stick a few bob more on the Silver invoice. I think we ought to bring Deepak along as well. He seems to know about this sort of stuff. You and me haven't got a clue."

Dany's no mug. He saw the point. He picked up the phone and put it on speaker. It rang and then there was a grunt at the other end.

"Jack?"

"Who's that?"

"It's Dany Bullimore Jack. I got your email. I thought I might take you up on your offer."

He sounded surprised.

"Yeah, yeah, Dany, that's fine. When do you want to come?"

"Tomorrow afternoon would be good for me Jack. Can I bring Spencer and Deepak?"

"Do you have to?"

"We are a bit of a team at the moment Jack. Anyway Spencer goes way back too. He's got plenty of good stories You'll enjoy them."

There was another grunt.

"OK, OK. See you then."

There was security stickers ready waiting for us at the Bank reception and a little fat bloke in uniform took us up to Jack's office. He was already half cut, sitting there with a big glass of Scotland's finest in front of him and a couple of empty glasses into which he poured big shots of the same as we come in. Then he fished out a carton of orange juice for Deepak. Very thoughtful.

"Nice to see you again Dany ... and you too Spencer ... and you, er ..."

"Deepak."

"Deepak."

He handed us our drinks and didn't wait for us to ask him how he was. He started telling us before we had sat down.

"I'm finished with this job! I've had it up to here. Those poncey bastards look down their noses at me like I was some sort of toad just crawled in from the slime. They've got no fucking idea what goes on round here. They're being ripped off right left and centre and it serves them fucking right. I used to crack down on all that sort of stuff but now I don't give a flying fuck no more."

We just nodded, all sympathies. There was no stopping him.

"You take that Froggy chef we got here. All those bankers want their fancy kwee-zeen as they call it, with all the best wines in their deluxe dining rooms. Do they know that he orders twice as much as he needs and that he and his wife have got a little restaurant in Soho where all the extras go? Do they fuck. And he ain't the only one. They're all at it round here and I don't give a shit no more."

He looked at us as if he expected some sort of response. I had to say something.

"Someone taking something off a banker. That's a turn up for the book eh Jack? Whatever is the world coming to?"

He was too pissed to realise that I was taking the piss. He just kept droning on. I thought I might as well try and get something useful out of him.

"Jack, you know we're doing a bit of work for Rachel Silver. She just wants top know why her husband got killed. The police aren't telling her nothing. You know Thacker. He probably thinks she's mixed up in it. He definitely thinks I am and I swear to you I'm as innocent as a convent full of nuns. You remember that computer drive you so kindly let us have, Well there was a lot of stuff about Russia and the First World War on it. Nothing secret or confidential but we can't make head nor tail of it. We did hear that Reuben Silver found out that some Russian bigwigs had accounts at the bank back then. Rachel Silver told us the Bank had someone called an archivist who would know all about that sort of thing and we thought we could have a chat with him and maybe he could help us out on a few things."

He pulled a face. "Archivist? What the fuck's that? I ain't heard of nothing called an archivist round here."

"Rachel Silver says the Bank definitely has one."

He picked up a book from his desk. "OK, OK. Let's see what our phone book says. How do you spell it?"

Dany piped up. "A-R-C-H-I-V-I-S-T." Fucking walking dictionary he is.

Jack ran his finger down the page. "Fuck me. Here it is: Archivist. So that's what that little toerag does." He picked up the phone, "Terry, get in here."

A couple of seconds later the door opened and a boy, couldn't have been more than seventeen, come in. He was dressed smart—sharp suit, narrow tie, hair slicked down.

"Yes Mr Dapper?"

"Terry, I want you to find that smelly little turdface Milton Freeman, calls himself an 'archivist' apparently, and tell him to get his arse in here pronto."

"Yes Mr Dapper."

And with that he was gone, like in a puff of smoke. Dapper looked at the door he'd just gone out of and nodded.

"Smart boy that. About the only one I can rely on in this place. He's the post boy. Goes into all the offices with the post so I get him to keep his ears and eyes open for anything tasty. You wouldn't hardly believe the things he comes back with. Thanks to him I know everything what goes on in this place. Who's doing what to who, with who. They're all at it. I tell you, Wormwood Scrubs is a choir of angels compared to this lot. I drop a little hint now and then that I know what's going on so they can't even think of sacking me. When I go, and it'll be soon, I'm going to cop a packet for keeping my mouth shut. And I'll make sure Terry gets something for his trouble. You've got to look after your own. That boy would make a good copper. I've told him I'll put in a good word if he ever wants to go for it.

"It was Terry what told me that this toerag Freeman was watching porn on his computer when he was supposed to be working. Nothing too nasty—tits, fannies, willies and a bit of girl on girl. Just wanking fodder really, but we can't have that sort of thing going on in this Bank can we? What would the directors say if they could get their hands out of the till and their cocks out of their mistresses long enough to take any notice? I give him the mother and father of a bollocking. You should have seen him rolling around on the floor, begging for mercy, wet coming from every fucking orifice. It was all I could do to keep a straight face. Didn't sack him though because he told me about a couple of other scallywags what was nicking stationery and stuff and selling it on their stall down Petticoat Lane. I like to make an easy kill every now and then. Keeps the bosses happy. So I had them out the door double quick and told him to watch his step. The little bastard will do anything I say now. You ask him what you want and I'll make sure he tells you."

That was a turn up. Some people say I was born lucky but I always say you make your own luck. Whatever. Grab it while it's there say I. Just then Terry opened the door and in come something that looked like a spare prick in a fifties sitcom—dark grey suit that had seen better days, round specs and a pudding basin haircut. A budding banker he wasn't. He looked like a mouse that thought a cat was waiting round the corner. Jack was all welcomes.

"Ah, Mr Freeman, good of you to come. Can I introduce you to some friends of mine, Mr Dany Bullimore, Mr Spencer, er, Weintraub and Mr Deepak. They're gentlemen scholars as you can see and they'd like to talk to you."

His nose twitched. "What about?"

"That's for them to ask, but we know each other, don't we, and I'm sure you'll be very helpful to them, won't you?"

"I'll try."

"I know you will. You'll try very hard. Now I understand that you're an archivist. Could you just tell me and these gentlemen what an archivist does to earn all the money we must be paying you."

He blinked about ten times.

"The Bank is one of the oldest in the country. It was founded in the seventeenth century and the records go back till then. It's one of the most important collections of financial documents in the world. I look after all the records, catalogue them, keep them in order so to speak, and assist historians and other academics in their researches. My master's dissertation was on nineteenth century financial systems so I find it very interesting work."

Whatever turns you on. I thought we had better get down to our own bit of research.

"Must be fascinating. We're interested in some Russian stuff. I heard that some Russian big nobs—dukes, earls or whatever they had there—had accounts with the Bank before the First World War."

He looked at us a bit suspicious.

"That is possible. The Bank, as I expect you know, has always catered for the wealthy and well-connected, not just from Britain but from all over the world. Before 1914 many of the crowned heads of Europe and the nobility had accounts here. Who exactly did you have in mind?"

I thought we might as well cut to the chase.

"We're doing a bit of research on behalf of Mrs Rachel Silver. You know of course what happened to her husband?"

"Yes, very sad."

"He was was doing some research for a book he was writing and he found out about these old accounts at the Bank. Now I don't suppose he went rummaging about in your old files by himself. He probably wouldn't have known where to start. He must have had a bit of help and who better to help him but your good self?"

He started blinking again and looking around at each of us.

"Well now you mention it, he did ask me and we did indeed find some records, a couple of archdukes if I remember. Nothing terribly interesting."

You get the impression sometimes that someone is holding something back. Pissed as he was, Jack obviously thought the same thing. Once a copper.

"Now then Mr Freeman, I did ask you nicely to cooperate with these gentlemen. I think I detect from your tone of voice that you're not telling us what you know. Now I'm going to ask you again, just this once. You wouldn't want me to take it further would you?"

"Well, I, I would like to be, er, helpful, of course. I'm not quite sure what you are looking for. Could you be a little more specific?"

I thought we might as well be obliging.

"Mr Silver was particularly interested in what happened in 1917 when the Russian Tsar Nicky gets kicked off his throne and asks his cousin George, our King George the Fifth, to let him come here. George first of all says yes and then changes his mind and nobody's sure why. So does the Bank have any records about the Tsar around that time?"

"I don't know. I suppose I could take look in the archives for you but it would take some time and there might be nothing there. It was a long time ago and some records might have disappeared even if they once existed."

He was a terrible liar. Even as he said it you could see his eyes staring and his nose twitching like a rabbit about to get it in the neck from a hungry fox. I pushed him on.

"I don't think you're telling us the truth Milton. I think you and Mr Silver found something in your archives that you're not telling us about."

"I, I, well even if there was something I couldn't say what it was. All our records are very confidential. It would be more than my job's worth to tell you."

Jack chipped in.

"It's more than your job's worth not to tell us. So be a good boy Milton and cough up. If you do we won't say a dicky bird to no one. That's a promise."

He was shaking now.

"Well, Mr Silver told me that he had studied history at university and had become interested in the Bank's dealings with pre-revolutionary Russia. As you mentioned, he thought he might write a book on the subject and asked me if I would look in our records and let him see anything I thought would be of interest. I discovered that several members of the Imperial family did have private accounts here in the nineteenth and early twentieth centuries."

Deepak decided he would ask a question.

"Were they all closed at the outbreak of the war?"

Milton looked a bit surprised.

"Yes they were, or at least most of them were. How did you know?

"The Tsar gave orders for all foreign accounts held by members of the Russian nobility to be closed and the money sent back to Russia to help the war effort. You said most of them. Which ones were still open?"

"There were a few minor members of the nobility who kept their accounts on. I think some of them may have had property in England or France."

"Any others?"

"Just one."

"And who was that?"

"I don't know."

"You don't know. Why not?"

"I'm not even sure it referred to a person. It was just called 'Amto'."

"Amto. What does that mean?"

"I have no idea."

"So how do you know it had anything to do with Russia?"

"It was clear from some of the correspondence that there was a connection with the Imperial family but I don't know exactly what."

"Was there any money in it?"

"To start with, yes. I didn't do an exact reckoning but there were certainly tens of thousands of pounds in 1914, perhaps a hundred thousand or even more, but almost all of it was withdrawn at the start of the war"

"Was it active during the war?"

"There didn't seem to have been much, if any, activity until early 1917 when quite a lot of money was paid in."

"Quite a lot. How much?"

"I'm not sure. From memory, several million roubles, which was converted into sterling."

"What happened to it?"

"The account was closed sometime in 1917. There doesn't seem to be a record of where the money went."

"Why not?"

"I don't know. These were old records. Maybe documents were lost or misplaced."

"So where did this money come from in 1917?"

"From Russia, the Foreign Finance Ministry in Petrograd."

"So it was official Russian state money. Who were the signatories on the account?"

"I don't know."

"You don't know or you're not telling us?"

Milton started wriggling again.

"To be honest I didn't look at the records in any detail. I gave them to Mr Silver. He preferred to do his own research. He might have known who the signatories were."

Deepak paused for a few seconds. "Does the name Peter Bark mean anything to you?"

"Yes. Mr Silver mentioned him to me. He was Tsar Nicholas's last Finance Minister. His name may have cropped up in some of the documents in the Amto file "

"May have cropped up. How so?"

"I don't really remember but it would hardly be surprising. As Finance Minister he would be ultimately responsible for payments from his ministry. I understood from Mr Silver that he spent a lot of time negotiating war loans for Russia with Barings and came over to this country several times during the war."

I decided to chip in again.

"This Amto. Maybe it's the name of a Russian or maybe something in Russian."

Milton shook his head

"I doubt it. I asked more or less the same question to Mr Silver, who as you know was well informed in these matters, and he said he couldn't think what it might refer to."

"Well, could we take a look at these records? Maybe that would give us a clue."

He shook his head again.

"I'm afraid not. They've been removed."

"Removed? By who?"

"Mr Cadogan. He's responsible for financial security matters at the Bank. Following Mr Silver's, er, death, he asked all staff who had any recent dealings with Mr Silver to inform him so that he could inform the police. I told him about our researches and he thought they were very unlikely to be relevant but it was best to collect them just in case the police wanted to see them."

At the mention of Cadogan Jack gave a big snort.

"Cadogan! What does he fucking know about security?"

Seems he knew enough to get his hands on those records, whatever they was. Something was going on here, though fuck knows what, but I didn't think Mr Cadogan would be kind enough to tell us. There wasn't much else we was going to get out of Milton so I told Jack and he told Milton to fuck off in his usual friendly fashion and we decided to go too.

Jack was all affable as he took us to the lifts.

"You must pop in again lads and definitely make sure you come to my leaving do when I sort it out. I'm going to make sure these bastards pay for the biggest and best leaving do in history. It'll clean them right out."

Just as we got out of the building my phone rang. It was Jimmy Dalrymple.

"Brace yourself Spencer. I have big news. Thacker has got someone for the Silver hit."

Big news indeed. "Yeah. Anyone we know?"

"Steve Curting."

22

"Robbery? You must be fucking joking."

We was sitting in my office, me, Dany and Jimmy Dalrymple, after we got back from seeing Jack Dapper. Jimmy was giving us the SP on Silver.

"That's what they're saying Spence, honest. I was down with Thacker's crew in the Butcher's Arms and they was all celebrating. They reckon they've nailed him. The story is that Silver was in that little Indian mini-market in Clissold Street buying a few things and when he took his wallet out the shopkeeper saw he had a wad of cash in it, hundreds at least, maybe a grand or more. Curting was right behind him at the checkout and he must have seen it as well. They've got both of them on cctv in the shop and the shopkeeper ID'd Curting as well. They've also got him on the Nightingale Street cctv, round the corner from the park about the time they reckon Silver was shot. They're saying that Curting followed Silver and tried to rob him. He forced him into the park so no one could see what was happening and then shot him. Might have been a bit of an accident. I mean, who'd shoot someone for a measly grand? Some of them reckon he might get off with manslaughter if he plays his cards right, but they definitely reckon he done it. "

Dany wasn't exactly convinced.

"That don't sound like an open and shut case to me Jimmy. Have they got the gun?"

"No."

"Anyone hear or see anything?"

"Doesn't look like it."

"Any cctv in the park?"

"No. Only about a hundred yards up the street and it wasn't working."

"How unfortunate. Any cctv after he was supposed to have done it?"

"Don't think so."

Any forensics?"

"Not of Curting, no. They told me they didn't even find the cartridge case. They've had a lot of Plod on it doing the usual—house to house, going through bins and drains and the rest. Don't think they've come up with much. "

Watertight it wasn't. Dany was right.

"So if I've got this right, Silver just happened to be in a shop and took out his wallet which just happened to have a load of cash in it and Curting just happened to be in the same shop and just happened to have a gun on him and just happened to fancy helping himself to the cash and followed Silver and shot him all unplanned and maybe accidental but somehow left the scene clean as a whistle and nobody seen him. Sound likely to you?"

Jimmy just shrugged.

"You could put it like that Spence but I'm just telling you what they was saying. Curting's got plenty of form—GBH, robbery. They all reckon with what they've got Thacker will get him to cough."

"Anyone mention *Spotlight*?"

"What's that?"

"It's a magazine. Specialises in exposing what it thinks are right-wing and fascist organisations like the ENF. Silver gave them a few grand. Curting was a member of the ENF and someone tipped them off about Silver. That could give him a motive. I told Thacker about it but he said there wasn't no evidence for any money from Silver. Now he does Curting. There's got to be a connection somewhere."

"Nobody mentioned no *Spotlight* to me Spence. As I said, they all think they've got Curting well stitched up. Don't need nothing more."

"Well it don't smell right to me but ours not to reason why. If Thacker has got this thing wrapped up then the best thing I can do now is go and see the very rich Mrs Silver with the biggest bill I think I can get away with."

....

I went to see her the next morning. She was a bit more cheerful than last time, invited me into her big front room and the housekeeper bought us coffee. I went through all the stuff we'd done for her. She didn't seem that interested, but she didn't make no objection to the bill neither.

"You will take a cheque this time?"

As a matter of fact, I would. My financial affairs was in a lot better shape. I was doing everything through our new account and the old bank could wait for their money. A cheque was no problem. Mostly she just wanted to talk about the arrest.

"I must say it came as something of a relief. When it's all over maybe I can get something like closure although the pain will never completely go away. I'm sure the trial will be an awful ordeal. Freddy came to see me last night and he was a great comfort. It looks like he and the police were right after all. It was just a robbery. Poor Reuben was simply in the wrong place at the wrong time. I can't help thinking about it, how he must have felt. The horror. I keep trying to put it out of my mind but it keeps sweeping back, like a wave, going through me and reducing me to helplessness. I just have to sit down and cry."

I must have looked a bit concerned because she looked at me and laughed.

"Don't worry, I'm not about to burst into tears. I've done my crying for today. Actually, I often find that a good weep can improve the mood. As you can see I'm quite cheerful now. I do want to thank you for all you've done. It was a great help and comfort at a time when I needed it. I know you must think Reuben was a bit odd, what with all his theories about ancient conspiracies, but you have to remember where he came from. For his parents and grandparents there really were people out to get them. The pogrom was an ever-present threat. Some of that ancestral fear and distrust never really left him, even though he was born and brought up in a country where there was nothing to fear. But you must believe me when I say that Reuben was a good man, the best I have ever known. I can't begin to say how much I miss him."

"I understand. I hope you get over it eventually. By the way, you were right about the Bank having an archivist. We managed to talk to him. He told us that Reuben had been doing a bit of digging in the Bank's old accounts. He found one called Amto. Mean anything to you?"

"Amto? I don't think so. Who or what was it?"

"We don't know but it definitely had something to do with the Russian royal family. There was quite a bit of money went in in 1917 then it all went out again, but we don't know where. We think this Peter Bark, who I told you about before, had something to do with it. Reuben maybe knew but we couldn't see any of the records because someone called Cadogan had taken them all."

"You mean Bernard Cadogan, the Deputy Chairman."

"That's the bloke. Said he was minding them in case the Police needed to see them."

I thought I saw a bit of a frown cross her face but then she just shook her head and gave me a smile.

"All very mysterious but all in the past. Anyway Spencer I just want to thank you for all you have done. You have been a big help at a most awful time."

Calling me Spencer now, but I didn't fool myself to thinking that I was getting somewhere. Still, since this was probably the last time I was going to see her, I thought it would be nice to have a little memento of the occasion.

"Glad to be of service. Now it's all over, I like to have a record of our cases, so would you mind if I took a selfie with you, for our records?"

"Pardon?"

"A selfie, you and me, with my phone. I like to have a picture of all our clients."

"Oh I see. Yes, of course."

I went over and put one arm round her while the other held up the phone. She didn't exactly snuggle up but she didn't go all stiff neither. Our heads were close, not touching but close. I thought to myself, "You never know Spencer. Maybe in another life." and took the picture. It come out very nice.

I left her place wishing all my cases could be like that. It may have had its ups and downs but a nice wad at the end makes up for a lot. I even had enough left over to check out Northern Cyprus, just in case it might come in handy another time. Dany and I decided it was time to celebrate and we went to the KB. They keep a bit of champagne in the fridge so we had a bottle. The label said "Krug". The new barman has a college degree— don't ask what he's doing behind a bar—and he said it didn't rhyme with bug but was pronounced "Kroog". I can't be doing with that. I'm paying for it and it's Krug like bug as far as I'm concerned. While we was sitting there drinking, Jim come over and asked us what the celebrations was for. I told him.

"I did hear about it Spencer. Thacker came to see me and he was asking about you."

"I know Jim. He told me while he was tying my goolies in knots."

He knew what I was talking about.

"Yeah. I don't think landed you in anything but you know what Thacker's like. That bastard knows too much. He and I never got on when we was coppers and it ain't got any better since. I wasn't going to tell him nothing, come what may."

Thacker rubbed them all up the same way. No copper liked him because he wouldn't even take a little drink. The last thing you want in this world is a copper that's too honest. It's not natural.

"Nuff said Jim. No harm done. We done very nicely out of it in the end. Sit down and have a drink with us."

We was chatting away. I told him a bit more about the case. Not too much; you've got to keep a bit of client confidentiality. We got onto the subject of the lovely Mrs Silver.

"As a matter of fact Jim, I have a picture of her and me taken this very day. Would you like a shuftie?"

I pulled out my phone and showed him. He cast an eye over it and then stared, hard.

"Fuck me, it's her!"

Dany and I both nearly choked on our bubbly.

"Who?"

"The one who was with that bloke Silver the night they came in here. The one I told you about."

"Are you sure?"

"Of course I'm sure. She's too good looking to forget."

23

Dany and me spent the rest of the evening talking about it but we didn't reach no definite conclusions. A couple of things was clear. She didn't turn up at my office by accident. She must have known that he was around here somewhere, but she must have lost contact somehow, otherwise why would she shell out to get us to find him? And the kidnapping story was crap. Curting was telling the truth about that, whether he killed Silver or not—and we both rather thought he didn't. If Jimmy D was to be believed, the case was shaky although he might have had something to do with it. Maybe I wasn't the only one looking for Silver. It could be the ENF was after him as well and Curting tipped them off when he saw him. But Curting was no professional gunman. He was your typical Dogswell low-rent, mini-brained scumbag. A fist in the face, yes. A bullet to the back of the head? Don't think so. Even if he ever done it, it would be a complete mess. Whoever killed Silver didn't leave nothing behind. They knew what they was doing. None of it stood up, but then what did we care? It wasn't none of our business no more.

Dany didn't quite see it like that. He still wanted to know why Silver did what he done.

"It's almost like he knew he was being watched and was taunting whoever was watching him with these puzzles. But if that was the case, why encrypt them? Nobody could read them without the password. And what was he trying to say with them? He seems to be playing a very elaborate game. Maybe he was under a lot of pressure. I think he might have been heading for a breakdown."

"You could be right Dany. Something very weird was going on in his head. Maybe those puzzles were a cry for help. Then someone decided to help him by shooting him."

"Don't be flippant Spencer, for God's sake. This is a man's life we're talking about. He may have been heading for a crack-up but the puzzles were the product of a rational mind. He must have been trying to say something with them and the question is whether that got him killed?"

"Good question Dany, but as I say, it's one we don't have to worry about no more."

...

Next morning I come into the office feeling a lot more chipper than usual. I did something I don't never normally do—looked at my bank statement on the computer. It didn't look too bad at all. No sign of red and enough in the black to keep me going for a while. I was even going to tell Fanackapan that she could take the rest of the day off when she come in saying there was a couple of gentlemen to see me. That was a surprise. You don't get too many "gentlemen" in Dogswell. "Show 'em in." I said, thinking to myself that business was definitely perking up.

They looked the gentlemen part all right—suits and ties, even had shiny shoes. Nobody has shiny shoes round here. Mostly they wear trainers, usually white ones, and when they get dirty they just throw them away and nick another pair. I spotted one for the boss straight away. He had a sharper suit, poncier tie and probably shinier shoes if I'd bothered to check. He spoke before I had a chance to open my mouth.

"Mr Reginald Nutbeam, otherwise known as Mr Spencer Weintraub?"

I was taken aback as they say, and afront come to that. What was this all about?

"Who wants to know?"

"Mr Nutbeam, or would you prefer Weintraub?"

"Spencer Weintraub is my professional name. Best to use that."

He plonked a business card down on my desk." Very well Mr Weintraub, my name is Addison and this is my colleague Mr Bennett." Bennett put another card on the table. "We're from the, ah, Treasury."

"What's that?"

Addison looked surprised.

"It's a Department of State Mr Weintraub, part of the Government. It manages the country's finances and, with the Bank of England, oversees the banking system. We are from the Treasury Solicitor's Department. It deals with the legal side of things."

Fuck me I thought. The banks get away with billions and the little man gets it in the neck.

"If this is about my tax, my accountant is on it right now. It's not that easy being a small business you know. Give us a break."

He didn't exactly laugh or even grin, but he seemed to find that a bit funny.

"No, no, Mr Weintraub. This has nothing to do with your personal finances. We understand that you have had dealings recently with the bank of Goldbury & Newman."

How did he know? I had to be a bit careful.

"Not exactly. I had a client who had connections there but that's confidential. I can't discuss it with you."

He didn't look too impressed.

"I'm afraid you may have to Mr Weintraub. You see, as you may know, the Bank has a number of, shall we say, high profile account holders, people who are very important to the country. Disclosure of their personal details, including their financial affairs, might affect national security and as a result the directors of the Bank are required to sign the Official Secrets Act. Signing, of course, merely emphasises their obligations. Anybody, including members of the public, who possesses or hands on an official secret without authorisation can be prosecuted, whether they have signed or not, and the penalties can be severe. "

This was well out of order. Me, national security? They had to be joking.

"What's that got to do with me? I wouldn't know an official secret if it took me up the backside, if you'll pardon the expression."

He gave me what I suppose was his official stare,

"I don't want to split hairs Mr Weintraub but what you know and what you realise you know may be two different things. However, as far as the Act is concerned, possession is all that counts. If you are in possession of an official secret without authorisation then you are guilty under the Act and any attempt to act on or disseminate that information would compound the seriousness of the offence."

This was getting my goat. It had to be a wind-up. What the fuck was I supposed to have done?

"Guilty of what? I don't know nothing and I ain't done nothing and I'm not telling you nothing confidential about my clients. If I started doing that I wouldn't have a business."

That didn't seem to put him off.

"Mr Weintraub, I understand that you were acting in, ah, a professional capacity for Mrs Rachel Silver who believed that her husband, the late Mr Reuben Silver, was missing. Is that correct?"

I didn't say nothing, just shrugged.

"I take it from your response that you are not denying it. Mr Silver, as I'm sure you know, was a director of Goldbury & Newman and therefore in a position of considerable trust and his possible disappearance was a matter of concern not just for his family and for the Bank but for those concerned with national security. Now I understand that you and two associates paid two visits to the offices of Goldbury & Newman. Is that correct?"

"If you know, why ask me?"

Then the other one leaned forward. He had a harder face and his expression hadn't changed the whole time he was sitting there.

"Can I emphasise Mr Weintraub what my colleague has been saying. We are being very serious. If you were to be charged with an act detrimental to national security then you could be tried under absolute secrecy. No mention or account of the trial would be allowed. You would not be allowed to hear the evidence against you and you could only be represented by a vetted advocate whom you would not be allowed to chose.

The jury would also be vetted and be unlikely to be sympathetic and if you were found guilty there would be no mention of that fact nor of your the sentence nor where it might be served. In short, as far was the world was concerned, you would have disappeared without trace."

I bet he really knows how to show a girl a good time. Something told me I might have to loosen up a bit. The first one, Addison, started up again.

"I'm sure it won't come to anything like that Mr Weintraub, as long as you cooperate with us to clear up a few things. I understand that your two associates were, ah," he looked down a notebook he was holding, "Mr Danilbert Bullimore and Mr Deepak Nandy. What was the purpose of your visits?"

"Nothing much really. We just went along to see one of Dany's, Mr Bullimore's, old mates. He and Dany go way back"

"That would be Inspector James Dapper, head of the Bank's security."

"Yeah, that's right."

"Mr Bullimore is an ex-policeman, which may explain his connection to Inspector Dapper, but I understand he has a criminal record. He was jailed for four years for corruption."

Somebody had been doing their homework. I was beginning to not like where this was going.

"Yeah that's true. He took a very silly drink and got sent down for it. But he done his time and paid his dues. Everyone deserves a second chance."

"And Mr Nandy is a computer expert and a member of the self-styled 'Revolutionary Cyberworkers Collective', which in common parlance might be described as a bunch of hackers."

"I don't know nothing about hackers. Fact is, I don't know nothing about computers full stop. Deepak is mustard when it comes to computers. He does my website and sorts me out when they go wrong, which they quite often do, but I'm sure he don't do nothing illegal."

He give me one of those 'what do you take me for' stares.

"On your own admission Mr Weintraub you know nothing about computers so you are hardly in a position to know whether he does anything illegal or not. Could I put it to you that a convicted felon, an accomplished computer hacker and yourself, a self-styled 'location agent', are curious company for a distinguished ex-policeman in a very senior position, responsible for security in a bank."

"Yeah, you could put it like that. You can twist anything if you try hard enough, but we just went along for a chat. Why don't you ask Jack Dapper? He'll tell you the same."

That was winging it a bit. No knowing what Jack would say, especially if he'd had a few.

"We have talked to Inspector Dapper. He confirmed that he knew about Mr Bullimore's conviction but like you he believes in giving people a second chance and invited him in for a discussion about his future. Very charitable of him. He also said that he knew nothing about you and Mr Nandy and that Mr Bullimore had asked if you could come with him. Why would Mr Bullimore have wanted you both to accompany him?"

Good old Jack. I thought he might have bad-mouthed me but I was betting that he hadn't told them nothing about what we was after. Wouldn't have done him no good and anyway he wouldn't have liked their attitude any more than I did. He'd come up against every London villain for the last thirty years so he could take on these two with his eyes shut and both hands tied behind his back.

"Like I said, me, Dany and Deepak are mates and we was going to see an old mate of Dany's. Just a social call really, Besides, truth to tell, we all fancied seeing the inside of a posh bank. We wouldn't normally get the chance."

He looked at me like he didn't believe a word I was saying.

"Just a 'social call' and despite the fact that you had been contracted by Mrs Silver to find her husband you didn't ask about him?"

"Well, OK, yes, we did talk about him. Would have been funny if we didn't. But Jack didn't know no more than anyone else why he got killed. Why would he?"

The other one, Bennett, had been taking notes all along. He looked up and started asking the questions.

"Did you discuss any of the clients of the Bank, past or present?"

Clients? How would I know who the fuck they might be, though I bet not many of them come from Dogswell?

"No. Wouldn't know who they were."

"What about with Mrs Silver? Did any client's names or the names of prominent people come up in your discussions with her?"

"No, don't think so."

Bennett leaned across towards me and gave me a long hard stare.

"Can I emphasis once again Mr Weintraub the seriousness of the situation. From what we know about you you could not be described as a reliable or trustworthy individual."

I wasn't having that.

"Not reliable or trustworthy. Who says so?"

He shook his head.

"Mr Weintraub, I'm sure even you do not imagine that your activities have gone unnoticed by the authorities. Please do not insult our intelligence, or yours. I will ask you once again and this time please tell the plain, unvarnished truth. Did you discuss any of the Bank's clients with Mrs Silver or in any way come into possession of any information about those clients?"

"No, I already told you."

"None at all?"

"No, unless you're talking about that old Russian stuff."

"Old Russian stuff?"

"Yeah, Reuben Silver had a bee in his bonnet about how King George the Fifth done the dirty on his cousin Nicky, the Tsar of Russia. Nicky was supposed to come over here after the Revolution. George first of all said yes and then changed his mind and in the end Nicky got shot by the commies. Mrs Silver told me her husband was a bit loopy about it. She didn't think much of it at all and showed me shelf loads of books he had on the subject. Anyway, it was a hundred years ago. What's it got to do with anything now?"

They looked at each other and then Bennett said, "You may well be right Mr Weintraub, that those events are all in the dim and distant past, but you would be well advised not to discuss any of the Bank's business, past or present, with anyone not authorised to discuss it. I can tell you that their number is very limited and does not include, without dispensation from the appropriate authorities, the local police. Thank you for your cooperation. We'll see ourselves out."

After they was gone I sat for five minutes trying to work out what the fuck they was on about. They was definitely after something. You don't come down to deepest Dogswell on the off chance that yours truly might have an official secret or two lying around. If I had an official secret it was so secret even I didn't know what it was. Then I thought I'd better have a word with Deepak. He might be on their list for a visit.

24

"Spooks? What do you mean spooks?"

For once Deepak had stopped playing with his computers and was listening to what I was saying.

"The address and telephone number on the cards they gave you seem to be legit. I've just checked. But the Treasury Solicitor's Department doesn't do official secret stuff. I've just looked it up. It does mostly commercial and political stuff like negotiating European laws and gets involved in money laundering cases. Those two weren't from there or if they were they must have been under cover. They must be spooks, spies of some sort."

"Where from?"

"Who knows? MI5, Special Branch—or SO15, the Counter Terrorism Command as it calls itself nowadays—or maybe some other government department. Take your pick. There are so many laws now that let officialdom spy on the public. They must have been fairly high up the food chain though to use the Treasury as cover."

"Yeah, but why me? Mickey Mouse knows more secrets than I do."

"That's almost certainly true Spencer. Disney have been accused of tracking every visitor to Disneyland and passing on data to God knows who."

"You know what I mean Deepak. There's fuck all I can tell them even if I wanted to. On the other hand you've got all this computer stuff. They already know about you. What if they turn up here? You see TV pictures of the cops carrying away people's computers. What are they going to find if they take yours?"

Deepak just laughed.

"I wouldn't worry about that Spencer. Our business is computer security. We're poachers turned gamekeepers. You don't imagine that we can keep going on the pittance you pay us for your website. We advise firms on how to keep their IT systems secure, so we know a thing or two about making sure our own are bullet proof. We don't keep anything remotely sensitive here. We don't use the Internet directly. We run a virtual private network through proxy servers to servers located in countries where a British writ is about as much use as a chocolate teapot. We use special browsers with all tracking turned off. Everything is encrypted and if we do need to run anything here then our machines are virtualized."

"What's that mean?"

"Each computer can run several virtual computers inside it. We can just fire up an instance, run what we want to and then shut that instance down and wipe it. It's as if it never existed. If they take our computers all they'll find are some harmless bits of HTML like your website. Everything is backed up on our private cloud and we'll be back online in an hour."

I didn't understand much of that though I took it that Deepak thought he and his computers was bomb-proof. I hoped he was right. Then I told him about Rachel Silver and how Jim had recognised her from the selfie. What did he think?

"Very interesting Spencer. Things gets murkier and murkier and not a lot of it makes sense."

You could say that again. Mind you, in my experience there's a lot less sense in this world than there ought to be. In these parts it's usually better to find out what's going on below the neck, well below, rather than above it if you want to know what's really happening. Follow the shag, as my mate Tony used to say.

"So that's it Deepak? One of life's little mysteries. We just leave it at that."

"You said yourself it's no longer any of your business. Just take the money and run."

"I did think it wasn't my business no longer but it looks like somebody still does. When these spooks as you called them turn up in my office and start asking funny questions I want to know why. Call me suspicious but I was definitely sure they was lining me up for something, only I don't have a clue what it was, except that it looked like it had something to do with Silver and the Bank."

"Maybe so Spencer, but we haven't got much to go on. If there are any clues as to what really happened I'm coming round to the idea that they may be in all the stuff on his computer. As it happens, there was one last file on Silver's disk, so I thought we would decrypt it, for old times sake if nothing else? Take a look."

> The French dance to all quarters and proclaim their intent. The magus from beyond our marches pays court to the eternal wanderer and with a quick tug on the heartstrings they go on to victory.

Another fucking puzzle. That called for Sami again. He come out from his usual hiding place, behind a big screen and flashed us yet another T-shirt. This one said "Roses are #FF0000, Violets are #0000FF." You work it out.

"So what do you make of this Sami?"

He blinked several times. Maybe blinking makes his brain work better. You can never tell with blokes like Sami. His brain's on a different planet.

"I th...th...ink we should start with 'F...F...French dance'. What French dances are there?"

I thought I could help. "The Can-Can. All legs in the air and knickers showing."

Sami looked a bit doubtful. Dany put his two pence in. "How about 'ballet'? That's a French word isn't it?"

Sami nodded and fiddled with the computer. "That's a possibility. Also 'bal' is French for a dance, like ball in English. The dance is to 'all quarters'. That probably means four, or maybe it's four in French, 'quatre'."

"So what have we got? Four balls? Four ballets?"

"Maybe, or perhaps it's the other way round, 'bal quatre' or something like that."

It was Deepak who came up with it. "How about Bal four— Balfour? He's been mentioned before. He was the British Foreign Secretary when the Tsar was supposed to come to England."

Sami went to the next bit. "W...w...we have 'proclaims their intent'. Did Balfour proclaim something, maybe about the Tsar?"

Again Deepak was on it. "The Balfour Declaration, of course. Let's bring it up. Here it is, made on the second of November 1917:

> *His Majesty's Government view with favour the establishment in Palestine of a national home for the Jewish people, and will use their best endeavours to facilitate the achievement of this object, it being clearly understood that nothing shall be done which may prejudice the civil and religious rights of existing non-Jewish communities in Palestine, or the rights and political status enjoyed by Jews in any other country"*

We all stared at it for a while. I had to ask the first question.

"Let me get this straight Deepak. We said we would give Palestine to the Jews. Was it part of the Empire?"

"Not of the British Empire Spencer. It was part of the Turkish Ottoman Empire at the time. The Ottomans were allied to the Germans so Britain was at war with them. Not only that, but the Brits had previously promised Palestine to the Arabs in return for the Arabs joining the fight against the Ottomans. Lawrence of Arabia and all that. On top of that Palestine was included in the Sykes-Picot agreement and the French were claiming part of it.

"So we was giving it away to two lots, without asking the Frogs, even though we didn't have it in the first place?"

"That's about it Spencer and you're not exactly the first to make that point. I think if we do a quick search of the Internet we'll find many of the same opinion." he tapped the keys. "Here's one:"

Thus, by a stroke of the imperial pen, the Promised
Land became twice-promised. Even by the standards of
Perfidious Albion, this was an extraordinary tale of dou-
ble-dealing and betrayal ... Rarely in the annals of the
British Empire has such a short document produced
such far-reaching consequences.

"He's not exaggerating. The consequences for the Middle
East have been convulsive and will be with us for decades,
maybe even centuries, to come. Not that it benefited the British." He tweaked the search terms. "Take a look at what other
commentators said."

He was right. Most of them agreed that we ballsed up big
time. As one writer put it, "Measured by British interests alone it
is one of the greatest mistakes in our imperial history." We
seemed to have pissed off everybody in that part of the world.

Sami pointed out that the Balfour Declaration was just the
first bit of the puzzle. We still had the rest of it. "The magus
from beyond our marches pays court to the eternal wanderer."
What did that mean?

"M...m...magus is another name for sorcerer or a magician.
'Beyond our marches' might mean that he is out of reach somehow, maybe a hermit, or maybe there's another meaning for
'march'."

That was worth a try. We looked it up and Deepak spotted it
first. "'Marches: the border districts between England and
Wales.' If he is beyond our marches he's in Wales, so we're
must be talking about a Welsh magician. Let's have a look."

All we got were a few conjurors, Welsh of course. Try something else, suggested Sami, maybe 'wizard'. In went 'Welsh
wizard' to the search engine and the first thing that pops out
was 'Lloyd George'. He does keep cropping up. So what about
the 'eternal wanderer?

Dany joined in. "I think that means Jews."

I asked him how he worked that out.

"My Sunday School again Spence. Our pastor told us about the Wandering Jew who was cursed for denying Christ and had to wander the earth until the Second Coming."

"That makes sense Dany." said Deepak, "Lloyd George was Prime Minister at the time. He was 'paying court' to the Jews with the Balfour Declaration but he was after something. There had to be a motive. The British weren't doing it out of the goodness of their hearts, because they felt sorry for a persecuted people. I think we should be able to find something which demonstrates that." He started searching. "Ah yes, here's something from Lloyd George's *Memoirs of the Peace Conference*:"

> It was believed, also, that such a declaration would have a potent influence upon world Jewry outside Russia, and secure for the Entente the aid of Jewish financial interests. In America, their aid in this respect would have a special value when the Allies had almost exhausted the gold and marketable securities available for American purchases. Such were the chief considerations which, in 1917, impelled the British Government towards making a contract with Jewry.

"There it is in black and white." Deepak continued, "Lloyd George bought the hoary old myth that 'World Jewry' was an organised conspiracy and Jews had all the money. He thought that getting them onside would help him win the war." He turned to Sami, "So what about the last bit of the puzzle Sami, 'with a quick tug on the heartstrings they go on to victory'? Are we talking some sexual intrigue here?"

Sami blinked several times. Something was definitely going on.

"I th...th...think it may be a bad pun. What's another word for ' quick tug'?"

I like a bit of word play so I thought I'd try. "Jerk?"

"No."

"Yank? Yeah, that must be it, 'Yank' as in American. With the Americans we go on to victory in the war. Simple."

Sami didn't look totally convinced. "There's still that word 'heartstrings'. It must mean something."

"We was sweethearts with the Yanks then. That's probably it."

Deepak wasn't convinced neither. "I think Silver is trying to tell us something. It's often the last bit of the puzzle that's the hardest. We need to do some more research."

Deepak and Sami started bashing the keys and nattering to each other. Dany and me decided we couldn't help much, so we buggered off to the KB for a bit of refreshment. A couple of hours later I got a ping on the app.

"So you've solved it then?" I said to them both as we came in. Deepak nodded.

"We think we know what the reference to heartstrings is but things are a bit more complicated than we thought at first. We need to go back to 1903. Lloyd George's connection with Zionism started then when he acted as counsel to Theodor Herzl, the founder of Zionism, over the British government's proposal to offer a home for the Jews in Uganda. The idea was abandoned but Lloyd George remained very sympathetic to Zionist aims. Arthur Balfour, then Prime Minister and MP for a Manchester constituency, first met Chaim Weizmann, who was then a professor of chemistry at the University of Manchester, in 1904. Balfour was also in favour of the Uganda proposal. Neither Lloyd George nor Balfour were particularly sympathetic to Jews. In fact they held the usual anti-semitic opinions of the time. They saw Zionism as a way of solving what they thought was the Jewish problem by allowing Jews to settle in their own country, far away from Britain."

So the Zionist idea went back a long time but why, I asked him, did it come up again in the middle of the war?

"In the war you had an extraordinary set of coincidences. Chaim Weizmann developed the ABE fermentation process that produces acetone, which was crucial to the production of explosives that allowed Lloyd George and Zaharoff to eliminate the ammunition shortage that had almost led to British defeat in 1916. Lloyd George became Prime Minister as a result, Balfour became Foreign Secretary and Weizmann became president of the British Zionist Organisation and had the ear of both. Balfour and Lloyd George, like most of the British establishment, were convinced of the power and influence of 'World Jewry' and became convinced too that they could swing Jewish support behind the Allies in both Russia and the USA if Britain espoused the Zionist cause."

"Yeah, we already know that Deepak. What about the heartstrings?"

"In the United States, the Zionist Supreme Court Justice Louis Brandeis was extremely influential with President Woodrow Wilson. This is where we think the reference to 'heartstrings' comes in. According to more than one source Wilson had been blackmailed for $40,000 for some hot love letters he had written to his neighbour's wife when he was President of Princeton. He did not have the money and the lawyer, one Samuel Untermeyer, acting as go-between said he would provide it if Wilson would appoint to the next vacancy on the Supreme Court someone put forward by Untermeyer. The money was paid, the letters returned, and Brandeis was nominated.

"Wilson had originally been elected on a promise to keep the US out of the war and there was considerable anti-war sentiment in Congress. Brandeis and the Zionists were prepared to urge the US to enter the war on the Allied side but they needed some incentive if they were to persuade Wilson. They got it with the Balfour Declaration. That was only revealed ten years later by Samuel Landman, who was secretary to Weizmann and later secretary of the World Zionist Organization. Take a look at what he wrote:"

> The only way (which proved so to be) to induce the American President to come into the war was to secure the cooperation of Zionist Jews by promising them Palestine, and thus enlist and mobilize the hitherto unsuspectedly powerful forces of Zionist Jews in America and elsewhere in favour of the Allies on a *quid pro quo* contract basis. Then one morning Baron Furness, one of

England's unostentatious representatives, brought to 44 East 23rd Street, at that time headquarters of the Zionist Organization, the final draft ready for issue. The language of the declaration accepted by the English Zionists based as it was on the theory of discontent was unacceptable to me. I informed Justice Brandeis of my views, called in Dr. Schmarya Levin and proceeded to change the text. ... Thus, as will be seen, the Zionists having carried out their part, and greatly helped to bring America in, the Balfour Declaration of 1917 was but the public confirmation of the necessarily secret "gentlemens'" agreement of 1916, made with the previous knowledge, acquiescence, and or approval of the Arabs, and of the British, and of the French and other Allied governments, and not merely a voluntary, altruistic and romantic gesture on the part of Great Britain as certain people either through pardonable ignorance assume or unpardonable ill-will would represent or rather misrepresent.

Here we was going again. What's it all got to do with anything? These things happened nearly a hundred years ago, like all the other stuff on his computer. Where's it getting us? Deepak as usual thought he had an answer.

"That's a good question Spencer, to which I can't give a definitive answer, but I've been doing a lot of digging and at least I think we can see some sort of thread running through what Silver wrote."

"We can?"

"Yes. Whose name keeps cropping up time and again?"

"You tell me. There's so many fuckers mentioned I lose track. My brain hurts."

"Lloyd George."

"OK, he does get a few mentions but he was Prime Minister at the time, so he was bound to be where the action was. So what?"

"Oh, he's much more than just another actor. Silver clearly thinks he's the spider at the centre of the web. Lloyd George was known as a statesman and a schemer and it's the schemer we have here."

Deepak leaned back in his chair and looked at me in a bit superior way. I think maybe he was coming the Sherlock Holmes—elementary my dear Spencer.

"Let's go back to the George V. file You remember we all agreed that George's explanation for why he changed his mind about allowing Nicholas in, that he was worried that it might antagonise the workers, was a load of crap. He was a deeply unimaginative man and the idea that he was in daily communion with the working classes is laughable. As you said, someone had obviously got to him. Well, who might that be."

"I dunno. Who did he talk to? The Queen? All those flunkeys? Could be anyone."

"Not quite. It had to be someone who he saw in private because even now nobody really knows why he did it and if anyone else knew it would have come out by now. And it would have to be someone whose advice he couldn't ignore."

"OK, so who are we talking about?"

"There's really only one person it could be, the Prime Minister, Lloyd George. All prime ministers have a meeting in private every week with the monarch. There are no notes taken and nobody is ever allowed to know what they talk about."

"That don't make sense. The government, Lloyd George's government, agreed to let him come. It was Georgie boy that changed his mind.

"Yes, but it was a coalition government. Lloyd George was a Liberal but there were a number of Tories in the Cabinet and he relied on the support of Lord Northcliffe and the Tory press. They were all in favour of the Tsar coming to England. He couldn't afford to oppose it openly. He would have to get someone else to do it and the only person with enough influence would be the King."

"Even if I buy that Deepak, why would he do it? What difference would Nicky coming to England make to Lloyd George?"

"That's what we are beginning to see. Everyone agrees that if the Tsar came there might have been a bit of opposition in Britain but it would have died down. The idea that if he came George would soon be swinging from a lamppost outside Buckingham Palace is laughable, unfortunately. However I think the real problem was the effect on Russia. There have been lots of cases in European history where exiled kings have returned. We had one here with Charles the Second. Cromwell cut off his father's head but after Cromwell died they invited Charles back and we haven't been able to get rid of his benighted progeny since. Nicholas in exile would have been a rallying cry for Russian monarchists. If the Provisional Government collapsed, as often looked likely, then one possible alternative would be a return of the monarchy. As it happened it did collapse and the Bolsheviks seized power. If you know anything about Russian history you'll know that there was a civil war. The opposition, the Whites, contained a lot of monarchists. A living Tsar would have been something that would have united them. The Whites very nearly won. Either way, if the Whites or the monarchy returned then the claim to Constantinople might be revived."

"And your point is Deepak?"

"That was something that Lloyd George was determined to prevent, for a number of reasons. First, if *The Mask of Merlin* is to be believed, he was in hock to the arms dealer Basil Zaharoff, one of the richest men in the world, and Zaharoff wanted Constantinople for Greece, not Russia. Then there is the fact that by 1917 the war was turning bad. The big offensives on the Western Front were getting nowhere. There were mutinies in the French and British armies and the Russian army was near collapse. He was desperate to keep the Russians in the war and if possible bring the Americans in as well, otherwise there was a real possibility that the Germans would win. What was he to do?"

"Don't ask me. I've no fucking idea. That's what prime ministers get paid for I suppose."

"He has to look for new allies because the existing ones, the French and Russians, are near the end of their tether, and he thinks he may have found a couple: socialists and Jews. In some cases they're the same thing — Jewish socialists. But Tsarist Russia was notorious for its anti-semitism and its belief in autocracy. The Tsar coming to England would send all the wrong signals."

I could just about follow his argument although it had an awful lot of what-ifs.

"Are you sure Lloyd George was at the bottom of it? Georgie was dead keen that cousin Nicky should come. How could Lloyd George get him to change his mind?"

"Here's some evidence. Do you remember in Silver's George V file there was an excerpt from the book *Dissolution of an Empire* by Meriel Buchanan, who was the daughter of Sir George Buchanan, the British Ambassador to Russia at the time? I got hold of a copy and there's another passage which might give us the answer." He picked up a book on his desk and opened it. "I didn't think much of it when I first read it because I thought she was just standing up for her father, but now I think she was on to something. Here it is. Take a look:"

> That day I remember Mr. Lloyd George's name was not mentioned, and it was only much later that my father told me that the whole plan of the Emperor's journey to England had been wrecked because Mr. Lloyd George had warned the King that the feeling in the country was violently against the Russian Imperial family, that the Labour members had sworn to create trouble if they were received, and that it would be very unwise to risk offending them at that critical juncture of the war.

"There's also another passage which is, to say the least, intriguing."

> Those who knew him and were with him through those dark and anxious days know the integrity with which he faced the situation, and know, too, how easy it would have been for him to justify himself, and how it was only

loyalty to what he considered was his duty, which kept him silent. Later on, when he had retired from the Diplomatic Service, he had, I know, the intention of including in his book the truth about the attempt that was made to get the Imperial family out of Russia, but he was told at the Foreign Office, where he had gone to examine some of the documents, that if be did so, he would not only be charged with an Infringement of the Official Secrets Act, but would have his pension stopped, and as he was a poor man, and had also suffered the loss of the greater part of his personal estate and possessions owing to the Revolution, he decided to hold his hand. The account he gives of the promise of the British Government to receive the Emperor in England, and the way in which, afraid of a few extremist Members of the House, they were persuaded to take no further action, is therefore a deliberate attempt to suppress the true facts, and thus save those who were responsible from criticism and contempt.

"OK Deepak, but she was just a girl. What would she really know? Her father was right pissed off. He would want to blame somebody and Lloyd George would be the obvious choice."

"That's a fair point Spencer. The same thing occurred to us, so we did a bit more digging. There's an intriguing little nugget in the biography of George V by Kenneth Rose, which is generally reckoned to be the definitive work on the subject. Lloyd George ran rings round the King. He thought he was stupid. He was always rejecting George's requests, for example to favour generals who insisted on sending thousands to the slaughter. Rose says that throughout the war there was only one important matter in which the King persuaded Lloyd George to change his mind and that was, and I quote, 'the most perplexing act of his reign: the abandonment of a loyal ally and much-loved cousin to degradation and death.'

"Now why just that one instance? Lloyd George was probably the wiliest, most manipulative politician of his era. Machiavelli could have learned a thing or two from him. Whether or not Nicholas came to Britain was a big deal. Is it really credible that Lloyd George would have let the King have his way on something so potentially important? My guess is that it was the other way round. Lloyd George inveigled George to change his mind. Look at what happened. Initially George was all for Nicholas coming to England, then he became vehemently against. He was panicking, sending messages to the Government every few hours. Then look at everyone who enquired about it. Buchanan the ambassador was threatened with the Official Secrets Act and loss of his pension. According to Rose, when Lloyd George wanted to write his war memoirs he was told by the Cabinet Secretary at the time to suppress all mention of the events and when he asked to see the telegrams about them he was told they were not available. The Royal Archives contain almost no documents dealing with what happened to the Tsar between March 1917 and May 1918. All telegrams sent from the Palace dealing with Nicholas appear to have been removed. All that smacks of a cover-up."

"So what are you saying Deepak? You think Lloyd George blackmailed George?"

"Blackmail or arm twisting? At the very least it must have been something that George found very persuasive. And here's another twist. I should have mentioned this before. When we first got the disk for Silver's computer we ran a few checks on it for viruses and malware and didn't find anything. Yesterday we ran some more beefed up checks and did find something. It was disguised as an operating system file which is why we didn't spot it before."

"Fuck me. What did it do?"

"We're fairly certain it's a keystroke logger."

"A what?"

"A keystroke logger. It records everything you input on your keyboard like, for example, when you type in a password."

Dany was quick onto it.

"Let me get this straight. Everything he typed in was being recorded. That means someone was spying on him and had all his passwords. He needn't have bothered encrypting anything because they could get in any time they wanted."

"That's about it."

"Who could have done it?" I wanted to know. "Hackers? The Russians, Chinese, maybe the North Koreans? They're supposed to be all over the Internet right now."

Deepak shook his head. "I can't see it being anything external. These banks have super high cyber security. They have to. Imagine the fuss if one of their celebrity customers, or even worse, royalty, had their account hacked and money taken. The bank would never recover. No, I'm fairly certain this was an inside job. Someone with administrative privileges on their network put the logger onto Silver's computer and then suppressed any anti-malware routines to make sure it wasn't picked up. It was someone at the Bank who was spying on him."

Just then my phone rang. Jimmy Dalrymple. Always the bad penny.

"Hi Jimmy. I'm right in the middle of something now. Can this wait?"

"Just a quickie Spence. I thought you'd like to know Curting's just been released."

"What! Why?"

"The little toerag managed to get himself a very expensive brief. Fuck knows who's paying for it. Anyway the word come down from on high—the CPS and some bigwig at the Yard—that he had to be let go. Not enough evidence they say. There's something funny going on. Thacker is doing his pieces."

I gave the good news to the other two. Dany was the first to cotton on to what it might mean.

"If Curting's out of the frame then Thacker is going to be looking for someone else to put back in it. Could be you again Spence."

25

There's no two ways about it. Thacker is a bad bastard. And he don't get no nicer when he thinks he's been shafted. He makes sure anyone and everyone gets a piece of his mind. It was just my bad luck to be one of them anyones. Dany was right. Next morning one of his constables, Carstairs the college boy, come round asking me to come and see Thacker for another of his 'chats'. He asked very nicely. I didn't like to say no in case he started crying.

"Now then *Mister* Winebar, I want you to tell me again about your dealings with that low-life scumbag, liar and, despite what the Criminal Protection Service and, God help me, Scotland Yard, say, murderer, Curting."

"I've already told you Superintendent, I didn't have no 'dealings' with him. I found out that he made a phone call to Rachel Silver before her husband was killed, that's all."

"So you say, but when we checked there was no trace of that call and Mrs Silver said she didn't remember a call neither. So what am I to make of it? I have to ask myself whether the phone company is fiddling with its records and the grieving widow is lying through her teeth or whether our Mr Winebar is telling his usual porkies. What side of the question do you think I'm likely to come down on?"

He's a big man with a big face and a big nose and he wears a suit a bit too tight for him and he was sweating. He looked at me with his usual expression that said he didn't believe a word I was saying.

"I'm telling the truth Superintendent. I don't know what else to say."

"You said that you never had dealings with him but I happen to know you met him at least once is the company of one Winston Montgomery Biggs."

This was getting silly. I was being set up for something I hadn't done with somebody I'd never heard of.

"I don't know what you're talking about. I don't know no Winston Montgomery Biggs."

Thacker give me one of his no-smile smiles.

"Oh I think you do. I heard you met him a few times. He's well known in this manor and I think there was a dog involved as well."

That's when a light bulb went on in my head?

"Are you talking about Gazzer Biggs, ENF member, likes to think he's a hard man, lots of tattoos?"

"That would fit his description, yes."

Winston Montgomery?? You could have knocked me down with a gnat fart. What was his Mum and Dad thinking?

"Well yeah. I did see both of them outside one of the ENF meetings. I wanted to find out a bit more about this phone call you say never happened."

"And did you?"

"Yeah, with a bit of help from the dog."

"The dog?"

"Yeah, Fifi."

"Fifi?"

What could I say? I wouldn't know where to begin.

"Ask Gazzer. You wouldn't believe it from me."

"So what did you find out about this phone call?"

"That's when he admitted that he'd tried to put the frightners on Silver about his donation to that magazine, *Spotlight*. They got a tip off in the post. I already told you all this. Look, I made a few enquires of my own. That phone record has been wiped. I'm told it happens more often than you might think."

"Is that so? I didn't realise you was an expert on phone systems. Anyway, Reuben Silver seems to have done a runner before you say Curting tried to phone him. Something else seemed to have frightened him. Have your 'enquiries' turned up anything?"

I had to think hard what I was going to tell him. Couldn't say too much else I'd be in more trouble than I was already.

"Maybe. I think he was being spied on by his bank."

"Spied on by his bank? What makes you think that?"

"Well, it's an internetty hacker sort of thing. I'm told by some computer boffins that the word is that his own bank had hacked into his computer."

Thacker rolled his eyes

"Now you're an expert on computers. Is there no end to your talents? Why do you think his own bank would do a thing like that? Did he have his hand in the till?"

"Shouldn't have thought so. Anyway stealing's legal for bankers, ain't it. It's what they do. No need for him to do anything illegal."

"If I want advice on what's legal or not I'll ask a lawyer, not a low-life like you. Now I'll ask you again, why do you think his bank would spy on him?"

I thought I might as well bite the bullet. After all, he wasn't going to believe nothing I said anyway.

"I don't really know Superintendent but I think it may have something to do with King George the Fifth and the Tsar of Russia."

Thacker must have heard most things in his time but the way he looked at me I'll be willing to bet he never heard that one before.

"King George the Fifth and the Tsar of Russia. Of course. Why didn't I think of them before? I tell you what we'll do. We'll put out an all-points bulletin, pull them both in and put them on an ID parade so you can pick out the guilty one. Oh I forgot. They're dead. Never mind, we'll have both of them dug up and you can tell us which one done it from beyond the grave."

Things hadn't started too well so I thought I'd better explain a bit more, though I have to admit history wasn't my best subject at school.

"No, it was all to do with the fact that George the Fifth did the dirty on his cousin Nicky the Tsar. He first of all said Nicky could come here after the Commies got in in Russia and then changed his mind so Nicky and his family all got shot."

That set him off good and proper. He looked at me like I'd gone fucking mad. Thinking about it I could see his point. I thought I'd better get in again before he could give me both barrels.

"Look Superintendent let me explain a bit more. It's not about them as such. All that stuff was a hundred years ago. It's that Reuben Silver had an obsession about them. He had hundreds of books all about what happened. His wife thought it was affecting his mind, maybe he was even going mad. Maybe the Bank twigged too, so they thought they'd better keep an eye on him and bugged his computer. I mean, it wouldn't do to have anything about all their posh customers getting out, would it?"

That didn't seem to make too much difference, Thacker was still looking at me like I was off my rocker.

"So have you any evidence that they was bugging him?"

I couldn't admit that we had the hard disk so I just had to blag it again.

"Not as such Superintendent, only what I picked up on the Internet grapevine but I'm told it's kosher."

Even I have to admit that didn't sound convincing. Thacker wasn't having none of it.

"So you haven't got no evidence but I'll tell you what we've got. We know Curting had something to do with it. We've got good cctv and ID from the shopkeeper. At first we thought it might be just a street robbery. Curting saw Silver had a wad of cash on him and thought he'd help himself, only it went wrong and Silver got shot. Now we know that you and Curting was, shall we say, acquainted and that you was employed by Mrs Silver to find her old man, who had upped sticks and left the marital home because he wanted a divorce."

That was a bombshell. Where did that come from?

"I don't say nothing about no divorce. Who told you that?"

"Oh dear, didn't the fragrant Mrs Silver take you into her confidence? He wanted a divorce and they was arguing over how to split the money because, as I understand it, most of it come from her family."

That was hard to believe. I've been at this game a good while and when a woman comes to me looking for her old man the first thing I ask them is how have they been getting on lately. I like to think I can spot a lie a hundred miles off and if Rachel Silver was lying about that she was fucking good at it. Mind you, she had lied about other things, so just maybe Thacker was right.

"I can't really believe she told you that Superintendent. You must have got it from someone else and they could be pulling the wool."

"You have your sources Mr Winebar, I have mine. Let's just say there are some people not unconnected with the legal profession who know what side their bread is buttered. Anyway, whether you knew about the divorce or not, you was on to a nice little earner, so you thought you'd speed up things and ask a few of the usual Dogswell scumbags to keep their eyes open for Silver. Curting got lucky only he decided to push his luck and things went too far. When you found out you thought you had better shop Curting by dropping him in it with me and making up cock and bull stories about magazines and donations. How does that sound to you?"

Didn't sound too good at all. I knew it was bollocks and I was pretty sure Thacker was just fishing. He didn't really have much solid evidence but the way he worked he wouldn't have too much trouble in twisting it into a story a jury would believe.

"That's crap Superintendent, if you don't mind me saying so. If your evidence is so good how come you had to let Curting go?"

I knew I'd hit a sore spot. You could see his face come over all glowery.

"Ours is not to question the great and the good of the Criminal Protection Service and Scotland Yard Mr Winebar. Ours is merely to obey. But if I have anything to do with it his liberty will be only temporary." He banged his fist on the table, "Only temporary."

I wouldn't be sure about that. I thought I'd push him a bit further.

"Look Superintendent, something funny is definitely going on. I heard that Curting got himself a very fancy brief, not something his sort could usually afford, and then the word come from on high to let him go. I think you agree with me that something smells."

He didn't try to deny it. "You've been talking to one of our gobby coppers."

"No names, no pack drill Superintendent. But let me tell you what happened to me yesterday. I got a visit from a couple of blokes that said they was from the Treasury." I fished out the card Addison had give me and showed it to him.

"The Treasury eh? You been fiddling your taxes again. Tut, tut."

"No, they wasn't interested in anything to do with taxes. All they talked about was official secrets and how everything in the Goldbury & Newman Bank was an official secret and I could be locked up and the key thrown away and nobody would know about it if I so much as whispered an official secret to anyone. I know you think I'm up to all sorts Superintendent, but even you can't think that I go round blabbing about official secrets. I wouldn't know one if it smacked me in the gob."

He didn't say nothing for a few seconds. "Are you spinning me one of your yarns again?"

"No, definitely not Superintendent. I showed you the card and, as I said, I don't know nothing about official secrets, or the Treasury come to that. How would I make it up? They asked me about the Bank and had I talked about any of its customers and I said no unless you count the Russian stuff—Nicky the Tsar that I told you about—but that was all a hundred years ago and nothing to do with anything now. They said everything about the Bank was secret, whether it was a hundred years ago or now. Then they just got up and left and I sat there thinking what was that all about? Now I'm beginning to think maybe it did have something to do with the Russian stuff after all, but I haven't the foggiest what."

Thacker gave me his big stare, the one that says, 'Whatever you're thinking, stop it now.' Then he said. "OK, you can go."

I was so surprised I said, "What, I can go?" before I had time to think. Thacker just got up and walked out—no "Watch your step"; no "I've got my eye on you"; nothing. Not like Thacker at all.

26

When the going gets tough the tough go boozing. That's my motto anyway. There's not many problems that don't seem much better after a few pints. The three of us was sat in the KB trying to work out what the fuck was happening. Deepak don't drink of course, so his pints was lime and soda. I did think of spiking them with a splash of vodka but that wouldn't have been fair. I do have my better side.

Things was making even less sense than they had before. Curting must have had something to do with Silver's death, even if we was all agreed that he didn't actually do the deed. Put enough pressure on that sort and they talk. Thacker could certainly put the pressure on, so why was he let go and who paid for his expensive brief?

Dany was always a bit of a pessimist. He likes to look on the dark side of things.

"I reckon you're right Spencer. There is definitely something funny going on. Someone is making sure that Curting doesn't talk. Thacker won't like it at all but there's nothing he can do about Curting, and, as I said to you before, he'll want to put someone else in the frame. Look at it from his point of view. How long has he got before he picks up his pension? A couple of years, maybe three. He's the last of the old style coppers. After him come the screen watchers and the box-tickers. We won't have coppering any more, we'll have the 'Police Service', which means not many police and not much service. He won't want to let a big murder go unsolved. It's been in all the papers. He'll want to go out with a big result, show them how it should be done. If he can't have Curting, he'll look for someone else. My guess is that whoever is shielding Curting won't be unhappy with that. Case closed; nothing to talk to our man about."

"And as you said Dany, the fall guy could be me."

"Afraid so Spence. Thacker wouldn't have too much trouble fitting you up."

"So what am I supposed to do about it?"

"Well I think you're going to have to try and point the finger somewhere else, turn detective so to speak, or at least try to muddy the waters. Who else do we think might have wanted Silver killed?"

Good question. The more I thought about Rachel Silver the more suspicious I was. She knew her husband was in Dogswell because she was with him in this very pub. She hadn't mentioned divorce and pretended it was all hunky-dory between her and him and she'd lied to Thacker about the phone call to Curting. You didn't have to have a suspicious mind to think something was going on. Dany was on it too.

"One possibility Spence, as we've already said, is that she was setting you up. As Thacker said to you, if she really just wanted to find her husband she'd have hired a top-flight private agency. From what Thacker said, he wanted a divorce only she was worried he would get half her money. Maybe he'd gone awol, maybe he hadn't, but she knew he was definitely still somewhere around Dogswell. So she gets you to find him. I bet she'd heard of your reputation and when you did find him she would have asked you to put a bit of pressure on, make him see reason from her point of view. Only he got killed. The question I'm asking myself is did she have a hand in it? We don't have any evidence that she did but we all know that the first question the coppers ask when someone is murdered is did their other half have anything to do with it? So she plays the grieving widow, lies about the phone call and the finger of suspicion is now pointing at you."

I was thinking along the same lines but there had to be more to it than that.

"OK Dany, I take your point. Maybe you're right and she would have wanted me to cut up a bit rough if I'd found him but somehow I don't think so. I don't think she's that sort. As for killing, definitely not. Far too risky and her sort wouldn't know where to start. On the other hand, was she telling the truth when she said Freddy Roswhathisname persuaded her that Silver's murder was just a random killing—wrong place at the wrong time and all that—and it would be best for all concerned if she kept shtum and didn't muddy the waters?"

Deepak had been sitting there saying nothing but then he decided to butt in.

"Look, I realise that murder isn't exactly my area of expertise but, how can I put it? You're not thinking analytically. I think maybe the techniques we use in constructing computer programs—using systems analysis to break the problem down into discrete modules and then assembling them and testing them until they work together—might be the way to go here."

Dany and me just looked at him. A computer program to catch murderers? That's a good one. Bye bye Scotland Yard.

"OK Deepak. If you think that's the way to go, why don't you put what we got into one of your computers and see what it comes up with?"

He threw up his hands. "No Spencer, you're being deliberately obtuse. I'm not talking about programs, I'm talking about the analytical method. Look, before we start asking who killed Silver, let's ask why, where and how—motive, opportunity and method—and examine each in turn. Of course it could just be a random killing, in which case all bets are off, but none of us really believes that do we?" He looked at us and we both shook our heads. "OK, then from what I can see there are at least four people or organisations that might have had a motive. The first, and most obvious is Rachel Silver. *Cherchez la femme* as they say. The second is the ENF; the third is the Bank and the fourth, although I admit this is very speculative, is some unnamed organ of the state worried that Silver might be in possession of some obscure and undefined official secret. Do we agree so far?"

We agreed, but as Dany pointed out, it was just a list. Where did it get us? Deepak started to tell us.

"As I said, use the analytical method. Let's take each in turn and then break each into modules. First Rachel Silver. She turns up in your office one day saying he's missing, maybe kidnapped. It definitely wasn't kidnapping and we don't actually know that he was really missing since she was with him in here a few days before. On the other hand, why hire you if she did know where he was? So let's assume he had decided to disappear. The questions then are why he did it and why she was so anxious to find him?"

I thought I could answer that one.

"He wanted a divorce so he fucked off. Maybe she wanted to make up or maybe she just wanted to make sure that he didn't get his hands on her money."

"OK, so let's assume that he did want a divorce. Why? After all, he had everything—beautiful wife, any amount of money, prospects of heading the Bank. What's not to like?"

"Probably the usual. He found someone else."

Deepak just laughed.

"Leave his wife and walk out on the Bank as well? Come off it Spencer. When was the last time you heard of a banker giving it all up for love? Anyway, didn't Rosquevoir tell you that the Bank snooped on its staff to check if they were having affairs and Silver wasn't?"

"Yeah, I'd forgotten about that."

"So unless he was lying it had to be something else, probably something she'd done."

"So are you saying that she had an affair and he found out. He wanted a divorce and she didn't?"

"That's possible I suppose but it doesn't really explain why he left the Bank and came to Dogswell. He could have called the lawyers in straight away and being the wronged party would be a big advantage in any proceedings. I think there has to be more to it. For a start, just wanting a divorce shouldn't be enough to get him killed. Does she strike you as the insanely jealous type?"

"No."

"Thought not. I think Silver was trying to get away from something else, not just his wife, but was he scared or going through some sort of mental breakdown or was he turning his back on everything he'd been up to now and looking for a new life? I don't think we've got enough to decide yet so let's leave the Silvers there for the moment and look at our second suspects, the ENF. What do we know about them?"

Where do you start with that bunch of cut-throats, dickheads and no-hopers?

"Some of them could definitely have done it. There's blokes in the ENF that would slit their mothers' throats for a few bob."

Dany agreed with me. He don't like them one bit, being black and all that. Deepak didn't seem so sure.

"We all agree that some of them are capable of it. The question is why? What's in it for them?"

Dany got his answer in first. "I thought it was obvious. Silver was giving money to that magazine, *Spotlight*."

Deepak didn't think much of that.

"I don't buy it. Lots of people give money to anti-fascist causes. I've done it myself. You don't expect to get killed for it. There's no record of the ENF doing anything like that. Besides, if the ENF had wanted to harm Silver for donating they'd have made it known so it would have been a deterrent to anyone else donating."

Dany wasn't put off. "Curting definitely had something to do with it. It's too much of a coincidence that he tried to phone Silver warning him off and he was around the night Silver got killed."

"True Dany, but then you and Spencer don't think Curting is capable of doing what looks like a professional job on his own. That would mean that somebody else must have done the actual deed. Then there's the question of how the ENF got to know about the *Spotlight* donation. Curting claimed the information came to their office through the post. Do we believe him Spencer?"

"Yeah, I think so. He doesn't have the nous to make it up."

"If he's telling the truth then it could only have come from *Spotlight* itself, the Bank or some outside agency monitoring either or both of them. I doubt that it was *Spotlight*, which leaves the Bank or the agency. "

"What, you think the spooks might have killed him?"

"I think we should be very careful about going down that road. It's the stuff of dreams for conspiracy nutters. On the other hand, it isn't outside the bounds of possibility. I found a rather intriguing piece on the *Daily Mirror* website. Take a look." He showed it to us on his iPad. The headline was 'MI6 dirty secrets: why do sex games appear to feature in so many spy deaths?'

> The sex game cover is a very useful mechanism in a murder. Not only does it provide a disguise for the actual means and method of death, it also trashes the reputation of the victim and blunts the energy of any subsequent investigation. And it appears to explain the astonishing number of spies, and other people who step into their murky world, who turn up dead

"That's very interesting Deepak. That guy Robert Haigh who wrote a book on royal money was supposed to have died in a sex game. Do you reckon he might have been killed?"

"Who can tell Spencer. As the *Mirror* says, that's the whole point of a sex game murder. It discredits the victim and blunts any investigation. However, with Haigh there's a royal connection. Don't you remember Al from *Spotlight* telling us that the security services identify with the Crown, not the people, and have often intervened to save royalty from embarrassment or worse. He warned us to be in his words 'circumspect' with anything to do with royalty."

"Yeah I remember but what has it got to do with Silver? He was found shot, not with nothing on and a rope round his neck."

"True Spencer. It might be that the spooks had nothing to do with it. On the other hand it might be that they felt the sex game tactic was in danger of being rumbled and they had to adopt a different strategy."

"OK, so maybe it could have been the spooks. What about the Bank?"

Dany chipped in too. He thought the Bank was more likely. Deepak seemed to agree.

"Let's go a step back. What have banks been in the news about lately?"

"One of your easy ones there Deepak. They're all at it. Hands in every till they can find. Should be strung up, most of them."

"Exactly. The Chancellor of the Exchequer would do well to take your advice Spencer. Everyone now regards big banks and bankers as criminals, tax dodgers and worse and when they go bust they have to be bailed out by the tax-payer. Their reputations are shot to bits. But what have you heard about Goldbury & Newman?"

"Nothing. In fact I'd never even heard of them until now."

"Quite so. It's a small, exclusive bank that has kept its head down and so far doesn't seem to have been tainted by the scandals affecting its big brothers. Which is just as well because who does it cater for?"

"Who? I don't know no names, apart from the Silvers, but posh people mainly I guess."

"Some of the very poshest. And what do the posherati want from a bank above all? Discretion. They don't want their bank in the limelight because they know that questions will then be asked about its clients and who knows where that will lead? Some of our great and good have plenty to hide."

I wasn't quite following this. Dany wasn't neither. "So what Deepak?"

"Maybe the Bank thought that Silver was doing something that might sully their spotless reputation."

"Like what?"

"Well, we've all thought that the stuff Silver had on his computer—George and Nicky, Constantinople, Trotsky, Lloyd George, Balfour etc etc—was just the harmless obsession of a history geek but suppose it was something more. Suppose he thought he had found evidence of events a hundred years ago that still have resonance today and might put the Bank in a bad light."

"Oh come on now Deepak. What are you saying? George and Nicky come back to haunt the Bank and frighten all their customers away?"

He laughed. "In a way, yes. I think what Silver is implying in his notes, though he never says so explicitly, is that many of the major events that shaped the twentieth century—the Russian revolutions, the entry of the USA into World War I and the outcome of the war, the Balfour Declaration, the creation of the state of Israel and the political destiny of the Middle East—were all intimately linked with the refusal of George V to offer asylum to the Tsar and his family."

Dany and me thought about that for a bit. I wouldn't know whether he was right or not. All I know about history is what I seen on telly—Henry the Eighth, Robin Hood and some weird stuff about knights and witches, though I don't think that one was true. Dany probably knows more history than me. He's got exams from school. You have to have them to be a copper, believe it or not, so he piped up.

"That's a big claim Deepak, but even if it's true, what's it got to do with the Bank?"

"That's a good question Dany and it puzzled me for a while so I thought I'd better do a bit of research myself. There's a book I would recommend you to read if you want to know a bit more. It's called The *Lost Fortune of the Tsars* by William Clarke. He attempted to find out what happened to all the riches the Tsar and his family were supposed to possess after he was forced to abdicate. Clarke was, of all things, a banker, but the book is a brilliant piece of investigative journalism. He was clearly something of an obsessive, like Silver, and he attempted to track down every last bit of evidence as to what happened to the Tsarist fortune.

"He wasn't the first person to try. For decades there were rumours that there were Tsarist millions lying in bank vaults in Europe and the USA, just waiting to be claimed. Several people claimed they were members of the Tsar's family who had survived the massacre. The most famous was Anna Anderson, who said she was Anastasia, the Tsar's youngest daughter. A lot of people believed her but in the end she was shown to be an impostor. The DNA evidence from the bones they found dumped down mineshafts near Ekaterinburg proved conclusively that the whole family were killed in 1918."

I thought I was beginning to get the drift. "So are you saying Deepak that Silver found out the Bank had been hiding some of the Tsar's money all these years?"

"I think it's a bit more complicated than that. Clarke did a pretty thorough job and came to the conclusion that there was no Tsarist money left in Western banks because all the existing deposits were withdrawn and transferred to Russia in 1914 on the Tsar's orders after the outbreak of the First World War. But there still remained themselves intriguing matter of the Secret Fund that Peter Bark mentioned and that the Tsar apparently controlled personally. We don't know what happened to it but I think we can begin to see what Silver thought might have happened."

"We can?"

"Yes. I think the key to it is Peter Bark. We already know that he had, to say the least, a remarkable career both in Russia and Britain and we wondered if he had some sort of hold on the British establishment. However there's nothing to suggest he was simply in it for the money. I think his seemingly charmed life once he got here may be more a case of a mixture of guilt and gratitude on the British side."

I had to think about that. Guilt and gratitude ain't exactly piled high around Dogswell. There's plenty that *are* guilty but not many feel it. Most of them yell blue murder and "stitch up" when they have their collars felt. Dany asked the obvious question. He always does.

"What have they got to feel guilty and grateful for Deepak?"

"What Silver seems to be implying is that he oiled some wheels or maybe even greased some palms. Let's step back a bit. You remember when we interrogated the Banks archivist, Milton Freeman and he mentioned the Amto account?"

I mostly remembered the little jerk wriggling and squirming as Jack Dapper gave him a hard time.

"Sort of. Didn't he say he hadn't no idea who Amto was?"

"He did. That's because Amto wasn't *a* person, it *was four* people. I think Amto is an acronym. It should really be all capitals—AMTO. It's made up of the first letters of the Tsar's four daughters—Anastasia, Maria, Tatiana and Olga."

Deepak can sometimes be too clever for his own good. That might have fitted but it didn't sound too convincing to me.

"That don't make sense Deepak. Nicky wasn't some shady businessman trying to hide his money, He was an emperor worth squillions, so why would he have an account in a funny name?"

"You might think that Spencer, but that's exactly what he had in another English bank. Clarke mentions that an account at an unnamed bank was code-named OTMA, Amto in reverse. As with his other accounts, the Tsar ordered the funds to be withdrawn once war broke out. Bark tried to talk him out of it, suggesting it might be insurance in case he had to go into exile. The Tsar wouldn't have it. Bark said it was the only time he had ever seen him lose his temper, so the money was sent back to Russia. It looks like the same thing happened with the Amto account, although it was never actually closed, just left dormant until 1917."

"OK. I just about buy that. So what happened in 1917?"

"I doubt if we'll ever know for sure but here's what I think might have happened. It was obvious to everyone in Russia except the Tsar and his wife that things were turning very nasty. The war was going disastrously and because the Tsar had appointed himself Commander in Chief he was getting most of the blame. He was away at the front most of the time and left Alexandra in St Petersburg where she was endlessly interfering in government policy, getting competent ministers sacked and lackeys appointed in their place. There were strikes and bread riots in Moscow and St Petersburg, The Duma, the Russian parliament, was turning increasingly against the Tsar. Many Russians were calling for him to abdicate. Bark would have seen all this and I think he decided it would only be a short time before the Tsar was forced out and then he and his family would be in a very precarious position. So, as a faithful civil servant with the best interests of his master at heart, he decided to reinstate the insurance policy that he had once urged to Tsar to keep and started transferring money into the Amto account, probably from the Secret Fund which he controlled. He could do so without anyone asking questions and probably without anyone else knowing."

"OK, even if I buy that too, the money might be in but we know from Milton the archivist that it went out. What happened to it?"

"Good question Spencer. This is inevitably supposition but we do know some facts. First, Bark was arrested immediately after the first, February, Revolution but then quickly released because the Provisional government needed his skills and knowledge to manage the state's finances. Second, Nicholas abdicated on 15th March by our calendar. By the 22nd of March, according to Sir George Buchanan, the British Ambassador to Russia, the British Government had said it was willing to allow Nicholas and his family to come to England. King George, as we know, had been initially very supportive of the idea but from the very first he was asking questions about where they were going to live and who was going to pay for their upkeep. He was a notorious skinflint as well as being a very stupid and unimaginative man. There's the book that every good republican should have on his bookshelf—*Money and Monarchy* by Robert Haigh, the late Robert Haigh, who died in mysterious circumstances as we now know. Read it and you'll see that George amassed himself a fortune by savings on the Civil List, the money the taxpayer gave him, while not paying any income tax. Even Queen Victoria paid it. At the same time he paid starvation wages to workers on his estates."

Once Deepak gets started he does go on and on. You got to stop him unless you want a load of lefty ear-bashing.

"Enough of the sob story Deepak. We all know you'd like nothing better than to plant the Red Flag on the ruins of Buckingham Palace."

"If only Spencer, if only. The point I am making is that George clearly didn't fancy footing the bill for the entire Imperial family and I don't suppose the government did either. The Amto funds would be very useful for his upkeep. "

"So where did the Amto money go?"

"We can't be sure without looking at the records. According to Milton the archivist there was no record of where the money went though he admitted that he hadn't looked in detail. I rather suspect that Reuben Silver did find out. We do know that Bark was personally acquainted with George. He carried messages between him and Nicholas during the war. We don't know who the signatories were on the account but who better to have as a signatory than George?

"Then we have Bark finally making it to England. He's invited to the Palace, asked to perform confidential tasks even though he's not actually British. That suggests something rather more than just guilty feelings. George was a cold fish. He cared more for his stamp collection than for his children. He wasn't given to expansive gestures like taking itinerant foreigners off the streets and showering them with goodies. I think there was a cash nexus here, as we leftists say. I think that once the situation turned nasty in Russia the money was transferred into an account that George knew about and maybe even controlled. That would make sense since he would be responsible for cousin Nicky once he got here or even if he had to live somewhere else. When Bark turned up in London George felt both guilty about his change of heart and worried that Bark might spill the beans. Johnny Foreigner, as we know, can't always be relied upon to know correct form, so better make him an honorary member of the British establishment asap.

"And then there's the curious case of Bark and the Bank of England. Again, he's welcomed with open arms and put in charge of various European Banks set up by the Bank. My guess is that the Bank also knew about the Amto account and wanted to keep Bark onside."

It's the way he tells them. Deepak could always cook up a good story even when he hadn't got much evidence. Dany and me sat there for a while trying to think of what was wrong with it. I was struggling a bit. Eventually Dany spoke up.

"It's all supposition Deepak. I couldn't see someone like the CPS going for it. I admit they're a bunch of lily-livered wankers but you know what I mean. And anyway, it doesn't answer the question we keep asking: what's it got to do with Silver getting killed?"

Deepak was getting into his stride. There wasn't no stopping him now.

"If I'm right the Amto money would have been transferred to another Goldbury and Newman account. Things would have to be kept very secret. Sending it to another bank would have risked disclosure. Then, when George changed his mind and Nicholas didn't come, there was a pile of money sitting in an account with nowhere to go. What to do with it? Could be embarrassing if the news leaked out, especially with the links to royalty. It's quite clear that even now the subject of George and Nicky is a very sensitive one for the Palace. As we know, nobody's allowed to see their records on the subject. I think Silver must have been quite close to finding out what actually happened. The Bank knew all about his researches because they had hacked his computer. If he went public with the accusation that the Bank was involved in a cover-up over the assassination of the Russian Imperial family the press would be all over it and Goldbury & Newman's reputation would be mud in the eyes of the establishment. They couldn't risk that."

Dany asked the obvious question.

"You think the Bank had him killed?"

"I don't think we can say that, but I do think Silver realised the Bank was on to him, which is why he left in a hurry. He was afraid of something and as it turned out he was right to be afraid. I can't see the Bank being directly involved in murder. There wouldn't be too many contract killers among their staff. Not their thing at all. We do know the Bank had links with the security services and we also know that Curting—and presumably the ENF—had some involvement in the murder, but what's the connection between them?".

It was then that I remembered the talk we had on Skype with *Spotlight*.

"Didn't the bloke from *Spotlight* say he thought MI5 or whatever pulled the strings with the ENF, a front he called it?"

Deepak gave me as look as if I'd said something clever.

"You're right Spencer, he did. I must admit I was pretty sceptical about all that conspiracy stuff. It's too easy to get paranoid, especially where spooks and royalty are concerned, but maybe, just maybe, there's something to it. We need to do a bit more digging. On that score I had a word with a friend of mine who's a journalist. I asked him if he knew anyone who might know some royal secrets and he suggested someone called Horace Stackpole. He used to be a royal correspondent in the glory days of Fleet Street. Worked on the *Mail* and the *Express* and then left to write a load of brown-nosing books on the royals. He's now something of a ridiculous old soak but my friend tells me that he does know a lot and if you buy him a drink he'll tell you anything. His usual haunt is the George and Dragon in Soho. You should find him there most days. Get there early was the advice."

"I suppose it might be worth a try but I can't really see an old bloke in his cups helping us out much. I bet he's all 'Yes Your Majesty' and 'You are very gracious Your Royal Highness.' We're not a lot clearer on which of our suspects done it, if any of them did, and meanwhile I've got Thacker on my back. He definitely thinks I'm mixed up in it."

"Yes, I think we need to be a bit more proactive and see if we can flush one of them out. The obvious one would be Rachel Silver. If she knows anything it shouldn't be too difficult to get her to talk. I think you should use that mixture of charm and menace which is your hallmark Spencer."

"You say the nicest things Deepak but what the fuck am I supposed to do?"

"I think you should contact her and tell her that you need to see her urgently. You can't talk over the phone. It has to be face to face. Don't say what it's about but make it clear that it's something serious."

"What do I say to her when we meet?"

"That depends on what we learn between now and then. I have a couple of tricks up my sleeve. Have you got her mobile number?"

"I have but why do you want it. Are you going to call her?"

He laughed at that. "No, I leave that to you Spencer. I'll tell you why after you see her."

27

Soho is going downhill because it's going upmarket. Nowhere in London will be properly seedy soon, except Dogswell of course. Dogswell as the new Soho. I can see it now. The George and Dragon was keeping its end up though, or down depending on which way you looked at it. Like a lot of pubs in Soho it was pretty tatty. They don't have to bother do they? The tourists come anyway and they can charge what they like for the drinks.

We got there early as advised, about ten thirty. Horace was there even earlier. We had a description but we'd have known who he was even without it. He was sitting in the corner, a roly-poly man with a bad comb-over, a big red nose and a little toothbrush moustache. He was wearing a check jacket that judging by the stains had enjoyed about as many meals as he had. I went up and introduced ourselves, saying that we'd heard all about him from a friend and wanted to have a chat with him about royalty.

"Dear boys, how very nice to meet you. Do sit down. Not before you've got yourself a drink of course. Pedro there behind the bar will tell you what I like."

What Horace liked was a Black Velvet with a whisky chaser, double of course. I got the drinks and brought them over. By the time I sat down he'd swigged half the Black Velvet.

"Cheers Horace. Great to see you too. They tell me you're a royal correspondent."

He went up like a rocket at that.

"*A* royal correspondent? *A* royal correspondent! Dear boy, I am *the* royal correspondent, the *doyen* of royal correspondents. You've heard of my books of course—*Throne of Splendour, This Blessed Crown, Seat of Majesty* and my particular favourite, *Long to Reign Over Us.*"

I could see Deepak nearly choking on his drink. "I haven't got through all of them yet Horace. Give me time, but I think I see where you're coming from."

He shook his head at that.

"Ah, *molto grazie* dear boy, *molto grazie,* but alas things have changed. I used to be on intimate terms, in the proper sense of the word, with everyone who mattered in the royal households. No press office minions for me. I went straight through to the private secretaries and they would tell me everything I wanted to know. They all knew that mum's the word with Horace Stackpole when they told me anything in confidence. The things I could have told my eager readers, but my lips were sealed. Alas, the days are gone when royal correspondents saw their calling as a profession, a vocation even. Now royal correspondents are all pretty women in flowery dresses, who only want to know when the next baby is due. Trivia, dear boy, trivia, that's all they are interested in. We old guard have been thrown on the scrap heap. Once all doors were open for me. Now I'm lucky to get an email about a minor royal opening a pudding factory in Droitwich or somewhere equally awful. And the publishers are the same. You would have thought that with my magnificent record they would be falling over themselves to publish my next *oeuvre,* which I have entitled *Pomp and Circumstances.* Not a bit of it. Turned me down, every one."

I thought I'd better commiserate.

"That's a shame Horace. I bet it's a cracker. Can't wait to read it."

"*Molto grazie,* dear boy, *molto, molto grazie,* but I fear you may never have that pleasure. The days when a new Horace Stackpole would have them queuing in Foyle's may be over but let me tell you this dear boy. They cast aside Horace Stackpole at their peril."

He picked up the glass and downed the other half of the Black Velvet. A little bit of foam added to the decoration on his jacket.

"That sounds as if you've got your dander up Horace. What can you do about it?"

The whisky chaser went down in one.

"What can I do? Spill the beans, dear boy, spill the beans." He tapped his head. "Inside the capacious Stackpole cranium is intimate knowledge of every royal skeleton of the last one hundred years. If I were to tell what I know it would blow the lid off the House of Windsor, Saxe-Coburg-Gotha as was. They could kiss goodbye to Buckingham Palace. They would be lucky to get a council house in Slough."

That sounded like what we wanted to hear. I know a thing or two about snouts and the first thing you need to know is what they run on. With Horace that was obvious.

You look as if you could do with a bit more refreshment Horace. Same again?"

"*Moltissime grazie* dear boy, *moltissime grazie*. Before you chanced upon my person I was practically dying of thirst. Sad to relate I am temporarily inconvenienced in matters financial. Those crooks and blackguards, my publishers, are attempting to withhold my rightful earnings. I have it on very good authority that *Long to Reign Over Us* swept all before it in the Majesty market, yet I have received scarcely a penny in royalties, scarcely a penny. A very stiff letter from my solicitors is even now winging its way to them. I expect funds to be forthcoming in the very near future, and on that joyous day I will of course be delighted to reciprocate your kind hospitality."

I sent Dany to get the drinks while I started on Horace. Just then an arty type come over. He must have been at least fifty but he was wearing a leather jacket, tight jeans and had a face that looked like a skull. "Ah Horace you old toper, you have company I see. Regaling them with a life spent tugging forelocks?"

Horace just shrugged it off. "Consultancy, Seymour dear boy, consultancy. These gentlemen, from a very reputable agency I might add, seek my wisdom and insight. I, of course, am only too happy to oblige."

Arty type sloped off. I asked Horace who he was.

"Seymour Dreadlock. Still calls himself an artist. He claims to have enjoyed the hurley-burley of the *chaise longue* with Francis Bacon, but I happen to know that dear Francis did no more than goose him a couple of times at the Colony Club and that was only in the hope of getting him to pay for something. I hear he now paints sentimental portraits of the favourite lapdogs of ageing dowagers and tries to persuade them to leave him a little *pourboire* in their wills."

For a moment I wondered what it would be like if he painted Fifi and Gazzer but we had other business.

"Now Horace, I was hoping you could help us out a bit, you being the world expert on the royals. We was looking into a few things that King George the Fifth did."

Dany put the drinks on the table and Horace took a quick swig. He then gave me a look.

"Before we go any further, all this is strictly *entre nous*." He tapped his nose a couple of times. "Nothing must get back to you know where."

"Of course not Horace. We promise we won't tell the Queen nothing."

He had to laugh at that. "Ah dear boy, you jest of course. I was not thinking of Her Majesty but of her most disloyal gutter press. Once we had the fourth estate, of which I was a proud member. We gave and received respect from those we wrote about. Now they will stop at nothing for a salacious titbit. Nothing we discuss here must reach the reptilian ears of what used to be called Fleet Street."

"Absolutely Horace old bean. What you see here are three wise monkeys. We don't hear nothing, we don't see nothing and we don't say nothing."

"Capital, dear boy, capital. Now where were we? Ah yes, the fifth of our Georges, not the most gifted of our monarchs in the cerebral stakes. He did at least learn to read and write, which is rather more than could be said for his elder brother, Albert Victor, or Eddy as we call him. Eddy preferred action to reading, the racier the better. He got himself into quite a few scrapes. Cleveland Street, you probably heard about that—rent boys provided for the cream of the aristocracy. Some even say he had a part in the Jack the Ripper murders—something about him fathering a child by one of the victims. Not sure I believe much of it. All hushed up in any case. These things always are. Then poor Eddy died and George had to pick up the baton and take on Eddy's betrothed, Princess Mary of Teck, as well. Queen Victoria insisted. Poor George had spent most of his life in the Navy up to then, so he was all at sea when he had to come home, get hitched and wait until he got the top job. Harold Nicholson in his so-called biography claimed that all he did for fifteen years was shoot animals and stick stamps in his albums. Damned impertinence. Nicholson was most unsound in my opinion. If you ever have the misfortune to come across a copy of his book I suggest you burn it and let a little light back into the world."

He was getting into his stride. Another couple of swigs and he was off again.

"George's biggest problem was of course his progeny. These things tend to skip a generation. His father, Edward the Seventh, as I'm sure you know, was a rake of absolutely prodigious proportions. Rogered half the aristocracy and only didn't get round to the other half because he ran out of puff. George's eldest son, David as we call him, was out of the same mould. You will have heard of his paramour, Wallis Simpson, the woman for whom he gave up the throne. Well I will let you into a secret. I am one of the very few who has actually seen the notorious China dossier."

He gave us a knowing look, only we didn't know what he was talking about.

"I can see from your faces that you are not quite up to speed on said document, produced by our secret sleuths in MI5. Before she met David, *la Simpson* spent time in Shanghai, where she was initiated into the wicked ways of the Orient, ways so wicked, let me tell you, that if you read the dossier your hair would stand on end—and not only your hair if you get my meaning. And while she was dangling the future King of England on a string she was also dallying with a certain Joachim von Ribbentrop, Hitler's sidekick, as well as a used car salesman from the West End."

"She had her bases covered there Horace. King or Hitler, whoever come up trumps. And if they both pegged out, she could always get a lift home."

"Quite so dear boy. The other sons were scarcely better. There was the runt of the litter, Bertie, George the Sixth as he became. He affected a stammer to hide the fact that he was so stupid. That's why they made him King. They made a film about it. I expect you've seen it. Then there was George, Duke of Kent, the only one with brains, but who was partial to certain intoxicating powders and was, how shall I put it, ambidextrous in affairs of the heart. He had a penchant for thespians. Noel Coward was a particular favourite I believe. Died in a plane crash during the war. All very mysterious. Lots of stories about it."

This was all very interesting but it wasn't what we had come for. We needed to ask him if he knew anything about George and Nicholas.

"OK Horace, let me put our cards on the table. We have a client whose husband was killed recently. Can't say who, client confidentiality and all that. What we do know is that he was obsessed with how George did the dirty on his cousin, Nicholas the Tsar of Russia, when he was due to come here after the revolution. First he was in favour of him coming then he was dead set against. Our client's husband seemed to think there was some sort of cover up of the real reasons why George changed his mind and we think that might have something to do with why he got killed. But all the evidence seems to be locked away or disappeared. We was hoping with your expert knowledge of royal matters that you could help us out, shed a little light on things, so to speak."

He leaned back and gave us a knowing look and a little smile that was made a bit bigger by the drink foam over his lip.

"You have come to the Oracle dear boy and the Oracle may help you find the answers you seek, but first it is customary to make a little offering to the Oracle." He looked down at his empty glasses.

"Yeah of course Horace. Same again."

Dany went to get them. Horace sat there saying nothing till he brought them back. He took a couple of sips and then started.

"This is a deep, deep question dear boy. Many a commentator has mused on George's abandoning a much loved cousin to his fate. The usual answer is that he was afraid of the reaction of the labouring classes. Absolute nonsense of course. The whole point of monarchs is that they are obliged to ignore the opinions of all classes, labouring or not. Otherwise what is the point of being a monarch? You might as well be a prime minister or something equally dreadful. You are quite right to suspect a cover up and I believe that I know exactly what was being covered up. Whoever didn't want the Tsar to come here had found out George's guilty secret and was threatening to reveal it." He quaffed half a glass, paused and then looked at us. "You will have heard the name Anthony Blunt?"

Deepak picked up on it first.

"You mean Blunt the spy, the man who looked after the Queen's pictures and had his knighthood taken away when he was exposed.?"

"Yes indeed. Poor Anthony, a dear, dear boy. I knew him well. He did get mixed up in some unfortunate business. He had two great loves, you see, Stalin and Poussin."

Stalin I did know about, but who or what I wanted to know was Poussin?

"Surely you have heard of Poussin, dear boy? He painted pictures of nymphs and shepherds doing all sorts of things to each other. French, of course."

"Next time I'm in an art gallery I must look him up Horace, but what has this bloke Blunt go to do with things?"

He sat back in his chair and stroked his moustache. A bit of foam came off on his finger so he gave his moustache another rub. He gave us a smirk.

"Prepare yourselves dear boys for what I am going to tell you. Anthony Blunt was the son of George the Fifth, on the wrong side of the blanket of course."

The three of us just laughed. We didn't know whether it was the Black Velvet or the whisky talking.

"Come off it Horace. Where did you get that from? Kings aren't supposed to play away, are they?"

"Dear boy, haven't you been listening? I think I have just told you that some of them do very little else. Let me elucidate. Blunt's father, the Reverend Stanley Blunt, was on the surface a moderately undistinguished clergyman with moderately low church leanings. He wasn't one of the 'smells and bells' brigade that still flourish not far from here, in the ancient liberties if you get my meaning. They're the ones who adopt the Scotsman's option, nothing under the kilt, and swing the censer so vigorously that their privates positively reek of incense. Adds piquancy to the fun and games after the service, so I'm told. No smells and bells though for the Reverend Stanley. Anthony's mother Hilda Master's people were something equally modest in the Indian Civil Service, but the pair were hardly the conventional denizens of the country parsonage. They named their first son, Wilfred, after his uncle, Wilfred Scawen Blunt, the poet who ran off with most celebrated prostitute in Paris. Hilda was best friends since childhood with Princess Mary of Teck, wife of George, and they enjoyed walks and teas together in Bournemouth and Bognor before George was King. The story goes that after several children Mary became rather tired of George's demands and Hilda sometimes had to step in. Unlike his father who flaunted his *amours*, George liked them prim and proper. A vicar's wife was just his cup of tea. When the heir to the throne calls, one's duty is to obey. Stanley and Hilda had their reward when George was King and appointed him chaplain of the British Embassy church in Paris, a sinecure if ever there was one and one that gave an *entrée* into the Parisian *demi monde*. Young Anthony learned a great deal in gay Paree, I can tell you. George always had a guilty conscience about the matter. His last words were 'Bugger Bognor', so now we know why."

We was all listening but we wasn't convinced, especially Deepak.

"If you don't mind me saying so, that's all tittle-tattle Horace. You can usually make any facts fit a story if you have a mind to. How do you know this and where's the proof?"

That got his dander up again. He blew the foam right off his moustache.

"How do I know? A little bird whispered in my ear one day. I cannot possibly say more. As for proof dear boy, just look at the faces. David, Bertie, George and Anthony—peas in a pod, dear boy, peas in a pod. Anthony was a bit lankier than the others. That's about the only difference. Look at what happened to the young Anthony. Swept up into the bosom of the Palace and put in charge of the Queen's pictures. He didn't even have to call the Queen ma'am. Only the family are allowed that. And he was the Queen Mum's particular favourite. He used to take tea with her. I believe he reminded her of her dear late husband. Of course, dear Anthony did like to take chances. He had a little fling with Prince George, another who liked to take things close to the edge."

What was he saying? It sounded like homosexual incest to me.

"Oh I don't think so, dear boy. It's only incest if it's with your sister or your mother. Otherwise it's plain old buggery. Was at my school, anyway. Anthony certainly led a charmed life. When he confessed to treachery in the sixties MI5 didn't dare to prosecute him. The Palace absolutely abhors a scandal among its own. It was only that dreadful woman Thatcher—the Queen couldn't stand her—who let the cat out of the bag. She was never forgiven for it. "

Deepak was quick to get in again. "That wasn't the only thing she won't be forgiven for. OK Horace, you've made it sound a bit more plausible but short of DNA testing we don't have what you would call proof. I doubt we'll ever get it. I bet he was cremated. If he was George's son they would want to hide the evidence forever."

I reckon Deepak had it about right. There could be some-thing to it but we would never know for certain. Great story though. Blunt was the Queen's uncle and a spy. Did he tell the Russians? Was there a file somewhere in Moscow with all the comings and goings at Buckingham Palace? That would have had them scratching their heads in the Kremlin. Horace didn't think so.

"I don't think he told them a thing, dear boy, not a thing. Have we heard a peep out of the Kremlin about it? No. Why not? The first rule of the Royal Family is that one doesn't talk about the Royal Family. That is how they have lasted so long. Never let daylight in on magic as someone once said. *Pas devant les enfants* and *les enfants* in this case are the Great British Public."

I wasn't buying all of that.

"Come off it Horace. As you said yourself, you can't open a tabloid without reading something saucy about the Royals."

"Things are changing a little, dear boy, I grant you. It is impossible to keep everything hidden from prying media eyes these days, but most of the time you only read what they want you to read. If someone in the Family does make a booboo then there are plenty of professional pooper-scoopers available to clean up the mess."

"Like who?"

"My lips are sealed on that one, dear boy. Best not to enquire further."

"Do you think they can keep up this magic thing?"

"I fear not, dear boy. Charles—Charles the Brief as we call him—exhibits some most distressing tendencies. He has opinions, something almost invariably fatal for a monarch, as his namesake Charles the First could testify. The Palace is in despair, but what can they do? I do fear for the future of the dynasty."

I thought we'd got about as much as we could out of Horace. He was beginning to get a bit squiffy. Not surprising, the amount he'd put away.

"OK Horace. Thanks a lot. You've been a star. We'll love you and leave you now."

He raised his hand in a wave.

"*Arrivederci* dear boys. A word of warning from the wise. Now you know what you know, watch your backs. There are dark forces at work."

"Is that right Horace? They're out to get us."

"They may well be. Remember the words of the Queen to Paul Burrell."

"Paul who?"

"Paul Burrell, butler to the late Princess Diana. He was up before the beak for taking some knick-knacks from her abode after she died, but the whole thing was thrown out when the Queen remembered that he had told her he had taken them for safe-keeping. Raised eyebrows all round, but nobody dared contradict Her Majesty. Afterwards she told him, 'Be careful. There are powers at work in this country of which we have no knowledge.' Nobody knows exactly what she meant but it sounded ominous. So I say again, watch your step."

"OK Horace, we'll be careful. Can we get you one for the road?"

"*Molto grazie*, dear boy, *molto grazie*. The road goes ever on."

28

The next day I got a ping from Deepak and went round to see what it was about. I found him looking at pictures of some old geezers on a screen.

"I had thought Horace Stackpole was a ridiculous old fraud peddling some even more ridiculous ideas, but now I think he might have been on to something. "

I said he must be joking. We all had a good laugh with Horace but the guy was living on planet booze-up. He was straight out of an old fashioned sitcom. I thought they didn't make them like him any more. Deepak pointed to the screen.

"Take a look at these."

"What am I looking at?"

"These are the four legitimate sons of George the Fifth and Anthony Blunt, Sir Anthony Blunt as he still was then. Which would you say was the odd one out?"

There was one balding, plump one that looked different so I picked him.

"No, that's Henry, Duke of Gloucester, George's third son. What do you think about the other four? Could they be brothers?"

I gave them a good look.

"Well they might be, I suppose. Some brothers look alike, others don't. I'm not sure that proves anything."

Deepak wasn't put off.

"Look at these two. They're both taken when they're about the same age, in their fifties. This one's the Duke of Windsor, Edward the Eighth as was, the other is Blunt. Look at the ears, the nose, the mouth, the hairline. They're very similar, remarkably so since they certainly had different mothers. Now look at this one."

Up come another oldish bloke with glasses.

"This is Anthony Blunt's brother, Wilfred. Who do you think Anthony resembles more?"

I took another good look and I had to admit he had a point. Anthony didn't look nothing like Wilfred and there was definitely a resemblance to George's sprogs.

"OK Deepak, you've made a case, but how could we prove it?"

"Good question Spencer. I checked and Blunt was cremated, so we can forget about DNA. But I did find one intriguing thing that might be a clue. Have you ever heard of a book called *Spycatcher*?"

I said I hadn't.

"It was written by a guy called Peter Wright. He had been a member of MI5 from the fifties to the seventies and on his own admission he and his fellow spooks had bugged and burgled their way across London in order to counter what they thought was Soviet espionage. He even tried to prove that Prime Minister Harold Wilson and the head of MI5, Roger Hollis, were Soviet spies. In the eighties he wrote *Spycatcher* about his exploits and there was a massive shitstorm when the securocrats got wind of it. Thatcher did her pieces and had it banned here. She even tried to get it banned in Australia. There was a famous legal case and the Aussies told her to get stuffed. It was never published here. I got my copy from America, where they don't have absurd restrictions on free speech. It's fascinating if you like that sort of thing. Wright was originally a technician and there's a lot on the technology of spying."

"Fascinating to you lot Deepak, I'm sure, but what's it got to do with Blunt?"

"I'm coming to that Spencer. Blunt was eventually unmasked in the sixties when an American called Michael Straight confessed to the FBI that Blunt had recruited him to work for the communists when they were both at Cambridge University. Blunt was part of that famous Cambridge spy ring that included Philby, Burgess and Maclean. Blunt was never arrested, let alone charged, even though he confessed, but he was questioned intensively for over a year and his main interrogator was

Peter Wright. I thought it might be worthwhile to have another read of what Wright said about Blunt, so I fished out my old copy and I came across a rather intriguing passage. Here it is."

> Before I began meeting Blunt I had to attend a briefing by Michael Adeane, the Queen's private Secretary. We met at the Palace.
>
> "The Queen," he said, "has been fully informed about Sir Anthony, and is quite content for him to be dealt with in any way which gets at the truth."
>
> There was only one caveat.
>
> "From time to time," said Adeane, you may find Blunt referring to an assignment he undertook on behalf of the Palace—a visit to Germany at the end of the war. Please do not pursue this matter. Strictly speaking, it is not relevant to considerations of national security."
>
> Adeane carefully ushered me to the door. I could not help reflecting on the difference between his delicate touch and the hysterical way MI5 had handled Blunt, terrified that he might defect or that the scandal might leak out. Although I spent hundreds of hours with Blunt I never did learn the secret of his mission to Germany. But then the Palace has had several centuries to learn the difficult art of scandal burying. MI5 have only been in the business since 1909.

That did look interesting so I asked Deepak if anyone knew what this mission to Germany was all about.

"Sami and I were on to it this morning. We've been hitting all the sources. Blunt was actually sent to Germany on secret missions for the Palace three times between 1945 and 1947. The second two were to recover pieces of jewellery and other trinkets that may, or may not, have belonged to the Royal Family. Adeane seemed to be referring to the first mission in August 1945. The official explanation, which was rather reluctantly admitted by the Palace, was that Blunt was supposed to collect letters between Queen Victoria and her daughter, also called

Victoria, who was married to the German Crown Prince. The letters were in a castle in Germany. The unofficial one is that he was also to retrieve some embarrassing correspondence between the Duke of Windsor and some top Nazis. Windsor and his wife, Wallis Simpson, were known to be friendly to Hitler before the war and there were persistent rumours that Hitler intended to reinstall him as king if the invasion of England succeeded. The official explanation does seem to be true, the unofficial may also be, but I don't see how either of them could be what Adeane was talking about."

"What do you mean?"

"If he just went to get back letters from Queen Victoria to her daughter why should Adeane say 'please do not pursue this matter'? What's the problem? The Palace admitted it anyway. The letters would be harmless and as far as MI5 was concerned there was nothing to pursue. On the other hand, an ex-king plotting with Hitler could hardly have more serious implications for national security. Adeane couldn't just airily dismiss it. I think he must have been talking about something else."

"And that something else could be who his Daddy was?"

"It could well be. I think Adeane feared that if MI5 started asking about this obviously sensitive assignment, and more particularly why Blunt had been chosen for it, he might crack and blurt out something that would be deeply embarrassing."

Deepak's problem is that he wouldn't put nothing past what he thinks is the establishment. I wasn't so sure. You can't keep that sort of thing secret forever.

"On the contrary Spencer, that's exactly what they can do, as Wright said. But let's just look at what we do know. It turns out that what Horace said about Blunt's parents rings true. They did name their first son Wilfred after his uncle, the poet Wilfred Scawen Blunt, who did have a scandalous reputation in Victorian times. He married the daughter of Lord Byron and had a string of mistresses including Winston Churchill's mother-in-law. He was an atheist, vehemently anti-imperialist and one of his most famous poems was called *Satan Absolved*. Not, you would have thought, the ideal role model for the son of a clergyman. Blunt's mother Hilda Masters and Princess Mary of Teck were childhood friends. Their mothers were very close, and the friendship continued throughout their life. Mary used to give Hilda some of her dresses when she had finished wearing them. There's even one allegation that it was George who handed out the dresses to women he favoured in return for sex, but I wouldn't give that too much credence. It comes from a book entitled *Hitler was a British Agent*.

"George may have had a rather stolid reputation in later life as being only interested in things like stamp collecting and shooting, but that wasn't true when he was younger. He and brother Eddy shared at least one mistress and there was a sensational trial in 1911 when a magazine called the *Liberator* was sued for criminal libel after it claimed that George had secretly married a Miss May Culme-Seymour, daughter of an Admiral, in Malta in 1890. The magazine lost but the Crown admitted that it was only repeating what 'thousands of reputable people had said for years'. Blunt's appointment as chaplain to the British Embassy in Paris, for which George seemed to have pulled a few strings, was also unusual. It was very much a plum post, normally given to a bishop. The Blunts were bought an enormous house in the centre of Paris with a ballroom big enough for 500 people and were given £1000 to redecorate it, a massive sum in those days. All in all a big step up for an obscure clergyman."

Deepak was definitely piling it on. I was almost starting to believe it.

"OK Deepak you could look at things your way, and Horace's way come to that, but I bet there's lots of others who can explain it all away."

"There certainly are Spencer but there is one thing that nobody has been able to convincingly able to explain away and that was how Blunt after he confessed in 1964 was able to remain in all his positions, meeting the Queen and attending all sorts of official functions as if nothing had happened, until he was finally exposed in 1979. He used to take tea with the Queen Mother. Maybe Horace was right when he said Blunt reminded her of her late husband. Just go on the Internet and you can see how intimately connected Blunt was to the British establishment. His knighthood was the Royal Victorian Order, the gift of the sovereign, the same as Peter Bark's. He was a distinguished academic at the Courtauld Institute, he was in charge of the royal picture collection and hobnobbed with the great and the good of the land. The usual excuse for not prosecuting him was that he was offered immunity for a full confession. MI5 and the British Government wanted to avoid embarrassment. Prosecution would reveal to Soviets what we knew, and so on. All nonsense. Lower class spies like John Vassall, an Admiralty clerk, and George Blake, a Dutch-Egyptian MI6 agent, were prosecuted even though both made full confessions. Blake got 42 years. At the very least, if Blunt was just your average upper-class spy like Philby, they should have moved him quietly to some obscure academic backwater, out of harm's way, but they didn't. I rather suspect that word got to Blunt that he could admit what he liked about his spying activities, but if he held his tongue about royal matters then nothing would happen to him and he could continue his life as normal. He obliged. As Peter Wright put it, 'the Palace has had several centuries to learn the difficult art of scandal burying.'"

Even if that was all true, there was one very big question. Who knew?

"A big question indeed Spencer. Did Blunt know all along? One biographer relates that he was very close to his mother but had almost no relationship with his father, Stanley, and never spoke about him. That might be indicative, although it's not altogether unusual behaviour with gay men. According to our sources, rumours about Blunt's parentage first surfaced about the time he was exposed, and probably came from the security services or someone close to them. The question then becomes when did they know and could it have been as early as 1917? "

"Well could it?"

"From what we have been able to find out, we think it could, although the evidence is only circumstantial. The security services were very active during the First World War and also employed a number of freelance operatives, mainly to keep an eye on suspicious foreign nationals who might be up to no good, but it's clear that they also came up with other titbits. One of them was Arthur Maundy Gregory, he of the sale of honours. Gregory worked very closely with Sir Basil Thomson who was Head of the Metropolitan Police Criminal Investigation Branch and the enforcer for the Secret Intelligence Service on counter espionage work. We know from *The Mask of Merlin* that Gregory told Thomson about Lloyd George having had had a brief liaison with Basil Zaharoff's wife. He seems to have had a talent for uncovering sexual peccadillos. He was also involved in the exposure of the black diaries of Sir Roger Casement."

What was all this about black diaries, I wanted to know.

"Casement was a British civil servant who had become a supporter of Irish revolutionaries and was secretly negotiating with the Germans to bring arms into Ireland. He was also gay, with a penchant for boys and young men, and he had written his activities up in his diaries. He was arrested and would probably have got away with a prison sentence but the contents of the diaries were circulated and sentiment turned against him. He was hanged in 1916."

"So are you saying that this Gregory knew about George's little bun in the oven?"

"We can't say that for sure, but if anybody could find it out it would be him. We do know from the sources we've looked at that Thomson paid him quite large sums of money without ever revealing what exactly he was paying for. We know that Gregory also worked for Zaharoff during the war and Zaharoff was close to Lloyd George, so it's at least plausible that the prime minister knew about anything Gregory found out."

"Plausible maybe, but it's no smoking gun though, is it Deepak?"

"Ok, but there's another thing that happened later that might be relevant. In 1921 Thomson was sacked, or rather he was told if he didn't retire voluntarily his pension would be docked and he would be dismissed. When he asked to see Lloyd George to find out why he was refused. Lloyd George later claimed that the reason for the dismissal was that Thomson was becoming obsessed with Bolshevik infiltration of the Labour Party and was producing all sorts of exaggerated and fanciful reports on the subject. The real reason, according to *The Mask of Merlin*, that he knew too much. He had found out, as we have seen, that Lloyd George had plotted with Zaharoff to undermine the Sykes-Picot agreement and give Constantinople to Greece. Lloyd George, who was almost alone in the Government in supporting the Greek invasion of Asia Minor, which was rapidly turning into a disaster, was afraid he was going to reveal it. They obviously feared that there was a lot more that he could reveal, so he was the victim of a classic set up. He was found in Hyde Park with a woman called, believe it or not, Thelma de Lava, who, it turned out, was a known prostitute. He was charged with gross indecency and fined £5. Little was heard from him after that. Even the official history of MI5 admitted that there might have been something fishy about the whole thing."

"OK Deepak, let's take stock. Let's say we buy the Blunt is a royal baby story and Lloyd George knows about it. Would that give him enough ammo to get George to change his mind about Nicky?"

"It would certainly concentrate his mind. There was a lot of republican sentiment around in 1917. It could only add to it. The other thing it does, if true, is explain the suddenness and vehemence of George's change of mind. Strikes and labour unrest had been around for decades. The British establishment were well used to them. They shouldn't have worried George unduly. Exposure in a sex scandal, a love child with the wife of a vicar, would be a different matter. He would be desperate to hush it up and if Lloyd George's price for silence was Nicky, then Nicky it would have to be."

29

Sometimes you have so many questions you don't know where to start. It was like that with Rachel Silver. Usually with these things it's straightforward. You ask who's doing the shagging and who's doing the divorcing and go from there. Somehow I thought it was going to be a bit more complicated than that. She was sitting there in her front room dressed as usual in her casual finery—light slacks, silk blouse and scarf and I was getting a faint whiff of that grand-a-drop perfume she used. She hadn't been too keen to see me. Tried to make excuses but I insisted, said there was something important we needed to talk about and it couldn't be done over the phone.

Like I said, where to start? Why had she told so many lies about not knowing where he was and about the phone calls? Did he, she or no one want a divorce? Did she know who killed her husband and why? Was she trying to set me up? I thought I'd start with something that would knock her back a bit.

"I showed that selfie that I took of you and me to a friend of mine, Jim Madgewick, the governor of the KB."

She looked blank.

"The governor of what?"

Maybe she thought the KB was some old British colony.

"The KB, the King William the Fourth. It's a pub in Dogswell. He said he recognised you."

I'll say this for her. Her expression hardly changed. Must be the breeding.

"I don't think so. I don't think I had ever been to Dogswell until I came to see you and I have certainly never been inside a pub there."

She was digging a hole for herself.

"That's funny. Jim's an ex-copper. He don't usually make mistakes about faces. Not only that, he says you was the blonde who was drinking in the pub with your husband before he got shot. I haven't said nothing to the police yet and I don't think Jim has. He don't like Thacker any more than I do, but if the word got out you might be in a bit of trouble."

Her face was a picture. All that front went up in a puff of smoke. It had obviously never occurred to her that she might get done and it put the wind right up her.

"That's ridiculous! I absolutely deny it. It wasn't me. They can't prove anything. Who could possible believe I had anything to do with my husband's murder? I mean it's just stupid, silly. It's just, just ..."

That's the way these thing tend to go. First they deny everything, then the penny slowly drops and they begin to realise they could be in the shit. I thought she was going to cry but she managed to stop herself. I didn't feel sorry for her.

"You haven't exactly been straight with me all along. In fact you've been telling me a pack of lies, haven't you? And I'm taking a lot of shit from Thacker because of your lies."

"No, no, please believe me."

"You lied about not knowing where your husband was. You were meeting him in the KB."

"No."

"You mean it wasn't you with him?"

She made a sound half way between a sigh and a sob.

"Yes, I confess I did meet him once. But then I couldn't contact him after that and I became worried."

"What was that meeting all about?"

She shook her head and didn't answer for a few seconds.

"OK, I suppose I ought to tell you. We were having a few problems. Reuben said he needed to get away for a few days, just to clear his head."

"He wanted a divorce?"

"No, no. Who said that?"

"Thacker."

"Oh that dreadful man! He insinuated the same thing to me. I denied everything. It's none of his business."

"He didn't believe you."

"Does he believe anyone?"

"Nope. He's not in the believing business. He thinks Reuben wanted a divorce and you were worried that he would come for your money so you hired me to frighten him off."

Her mouth fell open at that. If she wasn't shocked she was doing a good impression.

"That's absurd. Reuben couldn't touch any of my money. Daddy saw to that. Most of it is tied up in trusts and he made Reuben sign a pre-nup."

"A what?"

"A pre-nuptial agreement. If we were divorced Reuben would get nothing from me, not even the house. It was all in my name. I didn't want a pre-nup. I was full of love's young dream and I felt it suggested that I didn't completely trust Reuben, but Daddy was always practical in these matters."

"Another way of looking at it is Daddy thought young Reuben might be a bit of a fortune hunter and you went along with him."

She flared up at that.

"No, not at all. I respected my father. Much more than that, I worshipped him. You're not in banking. You don't know what a great man he was. Everybody in banking revered him. He revived Goldbury & Newman. He *was* Goldbury & Newman. It may surprise you to know that not long ago bankers were not particularly well paid. For years after the war nobody had any money. Everybody assumed that Goldbury & Newman's glory days were long over and its customers were slowly dying off. Daddy joined as a young man and quickly rose to be its head. He was among the first to realise that the numbers of the seriously wealthy were going to increase and he made sure that the Bank catered for their every need. The Bank became so profitable that the Royal London & Provincial made an offer that was impossible to refuse. He made a good many people connected with the Bank, including himself, a great deal of money. But money wasn't really the thing that motivated him. The Bank was his life. He had a fierce integrity and expected the same of every member of his staff. If I'm honest I have to admit that he could never quite let go, even after he retired. He did trust Freddy but he kept an eye on things to make sure his standards were up-held and he looked to me to make sure that continued after he was gone. Nothing or no one should be allowed to impugn the good name of the Bank and I am true to his memory. "

"And what would you do if you did see someone 'impugn-ing' the Bank, whatever that is?"

"Daddy left me clear instructions for what to do. I'm cer-tainly not going to go into them with you."

So she was a Daddy's girl. Daddy and hubby don't always mix well in my experience. I needed to find out a bit more about hubby.

"You didn't say why Reuben needed to get away."

She didn't like that.

"It's private between Reuben and I. Nothing to do with you"

"OK, don't tell me. Was it his idea or yours?"

"Don't you listen? It's none of your business."

"Right. Let me tell you what I think. He wants to go off 'to clear his head' as you put it, so chances are it was something that you said or did that made him want to go."

"Think what you like."

She was beginning to get annoyed, which was good.

"So let me tell you something else I think. You felt sorry about what you'd done. Maybe you wanted to make up. So you went to meet him in the KB. Only it looks like it didn't work. He didn't want to know. Must have been something bad that you did."

She gave me a right look.

"You don't give up, do you?"

"Yeah, I do sometimes. Some games just aren't worth the candle. But if Thacker gets to know about your little meet with Reuben then he won't give up until he gets to the bottom of it. Believe me, you don't want to go through that. Best be straight with me and then we'll see what we can do to get you out of this little mess."

This time she did give a couple of sobs and I saw the tears in her eyes. She slumped forward on the sofa for a good few sec-onds and then sat up.

"You wouldn't understand. You just wouldn't understand ..."

"Try me. I might not be as stupid as I look."

"Oh I don't think you're stupid, but no one would ever say you were sensitive."

What could I say? It ain't the first time I've been up on that charge.

"OK, maybe so, but let's put the facts on the table and we can see where we are."

She looked at me for quite a long time. I could see from her face that she was thinking about it, then changing her mind every few seconds. Eventually she did speak.

"Have you ever been married?"

"No"

"Why not?"

"Don't want to get divorced."

She laughed at that.

"That's absurd. Nobody goes into marriage expecting to get divorced. Sometimes it does happen, but lots of people stay married all their lives."

"Believe me, nobody would stay married to me for more than five minutes and I don't think I'd stick around long either. Divorce is far too messy, costs too much. Best stay out of it, that's my motto."

She paused again for a few moments.

"Have you ever been in love?"

What a fucking question. Here she was, husband dead and every chance of being deep in the shit, and she was asking me about my love life. There's no telling what goes on in some people's minds.

"What's that got to do with anything?"

"I'm sorry. I shouldn't have thrown the question back at you." She sighed and I could see her eyes tearing up again. "When I was young like most girls I had the romantic idea of being swept of my feet by Prince Charming and living happily ever after. I forgot all about those things of course once I grew up and I had, let's say, a fairly energetic love life. I had affairs, some great fun, others not so good, and even imagined I was in love a couple of times. Then I met Reuben and all those clichés about love suddenly rang true. Not in a soppy, sentimental way but as a seismic shock, a mind and body shaking ecstasy. Have you ever touched somebody and felt every element of your being, flesh and psyche, quiver with desire? Have you ever set eyes on someone and been almost paralysed by the emotions that surge like electricity through you? It takes you over, It consumes you. You can think of nothing else. You're no longer just you. You seem to be part of something bigger, a duality on a higher plane.

"It wasn't just a visceral attraction. It was who and what he was. True he was the usual things—good-looking, charming, witty, kind. He also represented for me—how can I put this?—the Jewish other. My family has been in this country since the eighteenth century. We're established, wealthy. My uncle is a lord. We're as English as any Jews can be. Reuben's family on the other hand came from the dark European heart of Jewry, from a *shtetl* somewhere in Eastern Poland. Even he didn't know exactly where. His father escaped to this country on almost the last boat before the war. Reuben put me within touching distance of my deep past—the culture, the literature, music, Yiddish, the klezmer, the joys of family, all those things, as well as the haunted, precarious, bags always packed, existence of most Jews. It was—and I'm ashamed to admit this—thrilling. Looking back now, how could I, from my safe, English existence, have identified with them and taken a perverse pleasure in imagining their lives, knowing what was to become of them? I suppose there's something in all of us that fantasises about being a victim—from a safe distance."

I wasn't sure I was getting all that but there was one question I definitely wanted to ask.

"So you was madly in love with him. What went wrong?"

By now she couldn't really hold back the tears. They was smudging her very expensive make up.

"I suppose I could call it passion fatigue. You can't keep up that intensity. It's impossible. I suppose most couples adapt, settle down to some cosy, domestic equilibrium. We couldn't.

Once you've tasted those fruits nothing else will do. I think Reuben realised it first. They say love makes you blind but it didn't make me so blind that I couldn't see what was happening. We were slipping away from each other and there was nothing we could do about it. The more we resisted the more inevitable it became. Do you know what it feels like to see the person you have loved most in the world—the person you will ever love most in the world—drift slowly out of reach and be helpless to prevent it? This may sound dreadful, but I came to resent him for what was happening. Every time I think of Reuben lines from a Paddy Kavanagh poem, *Raglan Road,* come to me."

> O I loved too much
> And by such, by such,
> Is happiness thrown away.'"

She started sobbing. My usual way when women cry is to put an arm round them but I wasn't sure she'd appreciate it, so I let her go on. After a couple of minutes she stopped.

"I'm sorry. I'm not usually like this. What must you think of me?" She pulled out a mirror from her handbag and looked at herself. "Oh God! Excuse me for just a minute."

When she come back she was all made up again. Maybe I was a bit the wiser why her husband wanted to get out but that didn't explain much.

"OK. I get it. You was breaking up but that don't explain why you lied to Thacker about the phone call and put me in the shit."

"I've already said how sorry I am about that. I just didn't realise it would affect you. As I said, Freddy Rosquevoir told me that the police believed it was just a random robbery and that it was best for all concerned if the Bank was kept out of it. I just went along with him. He can be very persuasive."

Freddy was obviously a bit of an idol in her eyes. I thought it might be time to bring him down a peg or two.

"Did you know the Bank was spying on Reuben?"

Her mouth dropped open. For a few seconds she tried to speak but nothing come out.

"What do you mean, spying?"

"They bugged his computer."

"How do you know."

"Deepak, my computer guy, found a bit of software on his hard drive that records all his passwords and stuff. They could see everything on it."

"Are you sure it was the Bank."

"Couldn't have been anyone else. Deepak's certain."

"That's appalling. Why would they want to do it? Reuben was a director. He was trusted and respected by everyone in the Bank."

"Somebody didn't trust him. Any idea who or why?"

"None at all. I'm not standing for this. I'm going to ring Freddy. I'm sure he'll be as appalled as I am to hear what's been going on."

I wasn't sure about that. I thought that maybe the thing Freddy would be appalled about was that she found out.

"I don't think that's a good idea just yet. Have you told Freddy we've got the drive? If you haven't then he might get a bit shirty, us poking about in his Bank and all. Maybe we should think about why they might have bugged him first.."

"Maybe you're right. I hadn't told Freddy because, as you say, I didn't think he'd appreciate it. What was on the drive?"

"Nothing much, apart for all that old Russian stuff that I told you about, all encrypted. It took ages for us to get it out."

"But that's all nonsense, and old nonsense at that."

"We, mostly Deepak, don't think it is." Then I told her about our theories about the Amto account, Bark, George and Nicky, Lloyd George, Constantinople and the rest. I think I got most of it straight but it's so fucking complicated I couldn't be sure.

"Are you seriously saying that my husband was killed because he found out about a cover-up that happened a hundred years ago?"

"We're not saying that exactly, but we reckon it might have something to do with it." Then I told her about my visit from the spooks and the ENF shenanigans. Even so, she didn't seem that convinced.

"That all sounds very fanciful. Such things don't happen here. I'll tell you what I will do. I am going to talk to Freddy. I won't tell him about the hard drive. I think you're right about that, but I will say that you have come to me with a story that someone at the Bank was spying on Reuben and that you won't tell me how you found out. I'm sure, as I said, that he will be appalled at the idea and make every effort to find out if it was true. And I will ask him to talk to you personally. I'm sure he will be able to explain things."

She looked at me as if that sorted everything out. Different fucking world.

30

After I left Rachel Silver's I gave Dany a call and we went over to Deepak's. He was sitting in front of one of his computers as usual. I told him what Rachel Silver had said. He wasn't that impressed.

"She keeps changing her story and from what you say she's a good actor. She can keep a straight face or lay on the tears as and when. I'm beginning to think our Mrs Silver may not be quite the innocent grieving widow she looks."

Dany thought so too.

"I still think she might be setting you up Spence. From what you said she was very much Daddy's girl and Daddy wouldn't want anything nasty to happen to his precious bank. Her husband coming up with all this stuff about how the bank helped George do the dirty on Nicky, true or not, is going to get right up her nose. She might decide it was time to say goodbye to hubby."

"That's a stretch Dany. For a start she says she didn't know what he was up to. That's why he didn't do it at home."

Dany wasn't having it.

"I don't buy that Spence. You said that she told you that they rowed about it. She thought he was being unpatriotic or something. I bet she knew exactly what he was doing. In fact I bet they discussed it. She would have wanted to make sure he wasn't doing anything to harm her beloved bank."

"Come off it Dany. Just because she had a row with her husband about something that happened a hundred years ago doesn't mean she wants him gone. What are you saying, that she had him killed and set me up for it? How would she do that? You think she has contract killers on speed dial?"

Deepak thought that Dany might be on to something.

"Nothing so vulgar as contract killers Spencer, but she would have contacts. We know that the security services take a close interest in some of the Bank's clients, for obvious reasons. Her father must have been well aware of it and now he's gone to wherever bankers go when they close their account she is, as she says herself, his representative on earth. She told you herself that Daddy made sure that she knew where to go if she thought there was a problem."

"So why didn't she just tell Freddy and they could hush things up like they always do?"

"That's a possibility but I think she did more. We've now had a good look at the key logger. It's not your average malware and it's not just a key logger either. It's a very professional bit of be-spoke code and would have been expensive to produce. It's attached to an operating system file and it's almost undetect-able. It was more by luck than anything else that we found it. I don't see a bank having any reason to commission it, especially because we think it can transmit data through the Bank's own security firewall. Somebody outside the Bank was keeping tabs on him. And not just on him. We can't be absolutely sure be-cause the code is very complex and whoever wrote it didn't want it to be read, but we think that once it was on one com-puter it is capable of spreading itself over the Bank's entire sys-tem. Whoever commissioned it could keep tabs on everybody—total surveillance. It would be very difficult to get rid of, even if they realise it is there, and they probably don't."

It looked like the finger was pointing at Rachel but I reck-oned we needed some hard evidence, not just supposition. Deepak thought he knew a way.

"Have you heard of SS7 Spencer?"

"Is that something to do with the Nazis?"

He laughed. "No, although on reflections they would have found it very useful. SS7 stands for Signal System 7, It makes sure that when you make a mobile call you contact the right person. You probably think that when you make a call there's a direct connection between you and the person you are calling, a bit like a walkie-talkie."

"I hadn't really thought about it but I'd have guessed it was something like that."

"Well it's nothing like that. When you make a call your phone contacts the nearest base station. They are everywhere round here. You can see their masts on the tops of buildings. The base station takes your request and then passes it over to the SS7 Core Network which routes the call and then passes it on to the base station nearest the person you are calling. The SS7 system also does lots of other stuff like the billing, call forwarding and sorting out roaming when you are calling another country."

"So what has this to do with the price of fish Deepak?"

"SS7 networks are completely separate from the base stations. They are run by the mobile operators. You can't get into them with your phone but you can get in if you know how. And once you are in you can do all sorts of things."

"OK, so how do you get in?"

"You don't need to know Spencer and I am certainly not going to tell you, but let's say security isn't what it should be on telephone systems. I think we should set up a man-in-the-middle hack on Rachel Silver's mobile."

"What the fuck's that?"

"Inside SS7 is a set of protocols called CAMEL, which stands for Customised Applications for Mobile Networks Enhanced Logic, but you really don't need to know that either. It allows calls to be rerouted. Any number that she calls can be rerouted to a number we control through one of our computers and then routed out to the number she is actually calling. Similarly any call to her phone can be rerouted to our number and then through to her. All her calls are recorded without her knowing."

Fuck me, that was clever. I knew Deepak was ace with anything to do with computers but I didn't think he could tap any phone just like that. He said he would sort it out. We was to come back in the morning to see what turned up.

...

"So what have we heard?"

"Not a lot yet. Mostly domestic stuff. A call to her hairdressers, a restaurant reservation and a few calls from friends, all women, mostly either trying to cheer her up or complaining about their husbands. One was complaining about her husband and her boyfriend—eeny, meeny, miney, mo, she didn't know which way to go. There was one call though that I think was interesting. Listen to this."

- Freddy, it's me.
- Darling, I'm rather tied up at the moment. Can I call you back?
- Please, you must Freddy. I've just seen Spencer Weintraub. He's been saying some awful things about the Bank, which I'm sure are not true, but I need to talk to you.
- Oh darling you mustn't believe a word he says. He's probably trying to get more money out of you. I have to go now but I will call you back.

Dany was the first to chirp up. "Fancy him thinking you were in it for the money Spence."

Har, har. I'm surrounded by fucking comedians.

"Look. I like a fee as much as the next bloke but there's a lot more to it than that. Let's think about this call. He called her 'Darling'. Now I call anything with tits darling but their sort ain't normally so free with the darlings. Something's going on there."

"Maybe they're having an affair" said Deepak.

"Maybe, but then it's an old established bank, old family money, a bit incestuous. Maybe they do all call each other darling. And then again, he's telling her not to believe anything I say even though he doesn't know what it is. I think we need to hear a bit more before we can be sure."

There wasn't no point in sitting around staring at a computer screen waiting for something to happen so we went off to the KB. Dany and I sank a pint or two while Deepak sipped at something veggie. Deepak had some sort of app on his phone that told him when something come in on his hacking system. Every so often it would give a bleep. Deepak would look at the number that come up and say he didn't think it was anything.

Then after a couple of hours it bleeped again. This time Deepak said Freddy had phoned back so we all went back to his place. We sat back and listened.

- Hello darling, it's me. Sorry it took so long. Very tricky client. Arab. Wants to buy himself a mansion in Knightsbridge but doesn't want anyone else to know, especially *chez lui*. Something going on there that he wouldn't tell me about. I think we've sorted him out. Now what seems to be troubling you?

- Oh Freddy, I'm so worried. Spencer Weintraub came to see me today and he's been saying such awful things about the Bank and about me as well. He virtually threatened me.

- Threatened you darling? With what?

- Well he knows that I met Reuben after he left in some pub in Dogswell.

- How on earth does he know that?

- I let him take a photograph of me. He said he wanted it for his records or something. I shouldn't have believed him. He doesn't look the record keeping sort to me. Anyway he showed it to the landlord of the pub who recognised me.

- Meeting Reuben in public was a little unwise of you darling. Why did you do it?

- I just thought we could perhaps sort things out face to face. It was he who suggested where to meet. He wouldn't tell me where he was staying. He said he wanted somewhere neutral.

- I wouldn't worry about it darling. No real harm done. So you met your husband in a pub. Hardly a capital crime.

- Yes, but Weintraub says that if that awful Thacker person, you know, the Superintendent in charge of the investigation, gets to hear of it then he'll think that I had something to do with Reuben's murder.

- Oh, don't you worry about Thacker darling. I've dropped a word in an influential ear in Scotland Yard and I'm sure he won't be troubling you.

- I'm not so sure Freddy. Weintraub says that Thacker is a law unto himself. He takes no notice of his superiors and doesn't give up until he gets to the bottom of things. I'm very worried Freddy, but there's another thing that I'm even more worried about.

- I'm sure it's nothing darling. Tell me what it is and I'm sure I can put your mind at rest.

- What he said was that he knew someone at the Bank was spying on Reuben though his computer ... Freddy, are you still there?

- Still here darling. I hardly know what to say. I'm as astounded as you are. How could he know?

- Apparently he is in touch with some computer boffins—hackers, I think they're called—and they've got to know about it. Don't ask me how Freddy. I know nothing about these things.

- I think he's bluffing. Either that or he has got hold of entirely the wrong end of the stick. All our computers are on a network and we have an IT chap in charge as our systems administrator. Files are going back and forth across the network the whole time as I understand it, but that's hardly spying.

- I don't think that was what he was talking about. He says he knows there were files on Reuben's computer that were confidential and someone broke in to them. ... This isn't a very good line. Still there Freddy?

- Yes darling, just thinking. What files are we talking about?

- Oh, I think you know Freddy. We've talked about it before. They were all to do with Reuben's obsession about George the Fifth and Tsar Nicholas again. According to Weintraub, Reuben was now roping in Lloyd George, the Balfour declaration, Constantinople and Uncle Tom Cobley and all. Complete nonsense of course. The thing that did disturb me was that he also says that Reuben discovered that money from a secret Russian account at the Bank that was supposed to have paid for the Tsar to come to England had gone somewhere else. A Russian chap called Bark was supposed to be behind it all but it all became too complicated for me and I didn't really understand it. You didn't mention this before. Is it true?"

- That sound utterly implausible to me darling. I'm not surprised you couldn't follow it. Besides I just don't think it would be possible for anyone to get into our system. We take computer security very seriously. We have to, given what we are and who we serve. We have the strictest control over access to our system. I'll have a word with out head of IT but I'm pretty sure I know what his response will be.

- But it's not entirely unbelievable that it could have been someone inside the Bank is it? You do keep tabs on your employees, don't you?

- Well, yes. We need to make sure they're not doing anything illegal—embezzling, money laundering, that sort of thing. Reuben certainly wasn't doing anything like that.

- And you keep tabs on their private life as well.

- Only to make sure that they don't embarrass or compromise the Bank. You know all this darling.

- Heaven forefend that the Bank should be embarrassed. We both know he was becoming a little unstable. Would that be embarrassing?

- It might have been darling, but I don't think it was ever going to come to that.

- Was that why he was killed Freddy?

- Oh darling, don't be absurd! It was just a random murder. Poor Reuben was in the wrong place at the wrong time. The Police have told us that.

- So why haven't they caught anyone? They've now let their only suspect go.

- They will, they will. I've been assured at the very highest level in Scotland Yard that they are giving it every priority. They are very confident of getting their man.

- I wish I shared your confidence Freddy. What else would be embarrassing? If Reuben knew about us?

- What! Are you saying he did?

- He accused me of having an affair with you. That's why he left.

- I can't see how he would know. Did he have any evidence? Maybe he was just lashing out. People make the wildest accusations sometimes. You said yourself that he was prone to jealous spasms.
- He wouldn't say. I denied everything of course, but he wouldn't be convinced.
- Darling, why didn't you tell me this before?
- I was going to and then everything blew up. I haven't had time to think properly since.
- Oh you poor darling. Well after this is all over I want to make it up to you. I want us to be together.
- O Freddy … Don't you think it's a bit soon to be talking like that. I've just buried my husband. I need some time to myself, to think about what I'm going to do. Besides, you're married, in case you hadn't noticed.
- Not for much longer darling. I'm going to ask Diana for a divorce.
- Please Freddy, don't do anything rash. Think how it will look.
- What do you mean 'look'?
- If you get a divorce and we become a couple then the police might suspect that we had something to do with Reuben's death. Weintraub hinted that he suspected something might be going on between us. Passion is after all the classic motive for murder. Everyone knows that.
- Now darling you're letting your imagination get the better of you. I've already told you that the police will not be a problem and you mustn't worry about what Weintraub has been saying. He knows nothing and can prove even less. Really, why on earth did you get mixed up with him in the first place? He's been nothing but trouble.
- You know why Freddy. Reuben had disappeared and I needed to find him before he did something silly.
- But why Weintraub? There are plenty of reputable agencies for that sort of thing.
- I knew Reuben was somewhere around there and I thought someone local would find him more easily.
- Even so, surely you could have found someone better?

- This is going to sound silly but I chose him because I thought he was ... Jewish.
- What! Why on earth would that make a difference?
- Comfort, something familiar, someone who might understand. Oh. I can't really explain. I just wasn't thinking. I was frantic with worry. And it turned out that he isn't Jewish. Weintraub isn't his real name.
- Really? What is?
- Reginald Nutbeam.
- Good God! Well your Mister Nutbeam could be in a spot of bother. The police think he may be mixed up in Reuben's murder.
- Oh no! Why do they think that?
- Apparently he knows this chap Curting who they arrested and have had to let go for the time being. They think Weintraub may have been planning to extort money from Reuben if he found him by offering not to tell you where he was. Playing both sides as it were. Do you think that's possible.
- I really don't know. I know Weintraub is rather rough trade but I always thought I could deal with him. Now from what you are saying I can't be sure.
- I know all this has been a terrible strain darling but you must try to take things a bit easier. It will all be over soon and then we can look forward to the future.
- Oh Freddy, you're such a tower of strength. I want so much to believe you. Would you do one thing for me? Talk to Weintraub. Whatever he might have thought of doing I do think we need to keep him on our side. We don't want him going round making all sorts of allegations. I'm sure you are the one person that can convince him that all his suspicions about me and the Bank are completely baseless.
- Of course darling. I'll have him eating out of my hand in no time.
- I'm sure you will Freddy. I would expect nothing less. Bye for now.

Either she was just a poor innocent or she deserved an Oscar for playing everybody for a fool. I knew which way I'd bet. She must have known that the spooks would spy on her husband at the Bank and they wouldn't let on where they got their information from so she could pretend to Freddy that she knew nothing at all until I told her. She was definitely pulling the strings. He thought he had her but it was the other way round. I could see it from her point of view. Lots of women coming out of a heavy situation look for a bit of relaxation—they want something hassle-free, maybe they feel a bit horny, and they look around to see what's handy. Freddy would have been very handy, just her type, but she didn't seem to be keen on making it permanent. She was right that doing it too soon might look suspicious, but there was something in her voice that told me that there might be more to it than that. I asked Dany what he thought, him being into psychology.

"A classic case of 'no fool like an old fool' Spence. Not that Freddy is that old, but the more powerful, the more self-confident a man is, the more vulnerable he is to the lightning bolt of love, a *coup de foudre* as the French say—and yes, as you're going to ask, I got that from one of my textbooks. And if you want a bit more advice on psychological matters, a thing that has been puzzling me is why Silver encrypted his puzzles. What was the point? I think he knew he was being watched and he wanted to tell the watchers that he knew. The first set of notes, about George and Nicky were encrypted but weren't in a puzzle. It must have been after that when he realised he might have been hacked. The only two people who knew about his work were his wife and Freddy and I think it was about then that he realised they were having an affair. He could have walked away then but he was clearly an obsessive. He stuck two fingers up to the watchers and gave them a bit more to think about."

Deepak and I looked at each other. That degree was coming in useful.

"Ok Dany, I buy that but do you think they worked out what the puzzles meant?"

"Bound to have done Spence. There are some very bright people working for the spooks. I met a couple once on a case we had. If we could do it they would have no problem."

"So I bet they told Freddy but he didn't tell her. They was both keeping things from each other while they was shagging. Only now she knows it for sure. That won't make her best pleased with Freddy. All that guff about not understanding what I told her was on her husband's hard disk is crap. She understood only too well that, if it got out, her Daddy's precious bank's name would be mud."

Dany agreed and then went off on another of his psychology trips.

"The real puzzle is why did Reuben keep going with it. OK, so it started out as in interesting exercise in historical research, with maybe a book at the end of it. But sooner or later he must have realised that it was getting right up his wife's nose. Then he decided to hide what he was doing from her by keeping his notes at work and encrypting them to keep prying bank eyes from seeing them. Then he somehow realised he was being hacked. He put two and two together and figured out that his wife and Freddy were behind the hacking and were probably having an affair. But still he kept on and created his little puzzles. It was as if he was telling them that he knew they were watching. He was clearly something of an obsessive. I think finally it dawned on him what he had done. He had wrecked his marriage and his career for the sake of a historical goose chase."

"I think it was more than that Dany. He realised he was in serious shit. His wife, his boss, the spooks, the ENF. There was a lot of people on his case. No wonder he finally ran away. The question is whether he was just trying to get away from wife and work or whether it was something else. Remember what Horace Stackpole said about what the Queen had told Princess Di's butler: 'There are forces at work in this country.' Maybe he ran because he thought they was out to get him. And as it happened, they was. The only question is who they was. "

Deepak then brought up something else.

"I came across something interesting on Silver's disk this morning. It wasn't encrypted. It was just an anonymous image file in a folder with some correspondence and reports. I hadn't bothered to open at it before. Take a look."

We was looking at a bloke in olden style dress with long black hair. Above him was the word POUSSIN in big letters. I asked Deepak what it was.

"It's a book cover. Look who the author is."

Down at the bottom it read 'Anthony Blunt'.

"I wonder what that was about. Do you reckon he was on to the George and Blunt story Deepak?"

"Who knows Spencer but I think we're beginning to see our way through this maze."

We talked about if for over an hour and by then we reckoned we had it more or less sorted.

31

Freddy called the next morning and asked if I would like to come over that afternoon. He don't waste time. I went over to Deepak's to see if there had been any more action on Rachel Silver's phone. The first thing I asked him was if he could hack her phone how did he know someone wasn't doing the same to him? He said he was pretty certain nobody was. First, he hardly ever used a phone and if he did he only used pay as you go mobiles and he had some software on his phone called SnoopSnitch that checked if anyone was hacking him. It was written by some German hackers according to Deepak. He says they're very hot on phone security.

It turned out that Rachel Silver's mobile had been switched off more or less since she last talked to Freddy, which explained why it had gone straight to voicemail when I tried her a couple of times. I wanted to have a chat with her, drop an even bigger hint that I knew what was going on with her and Freddy and see what she said. It was no go again on her mobile so I called her landline. The housekeeper answered. She's foreign, fuck knows from where.

"Allo. Silver residence"

"Can I speak to Mrs Silver?"

"She no here."

"Well can you tell me when she will be back?"

"She no come back. Gone away."

"What do you mean 'gone away'? Where's she gone?"

"Gone to airport."

"What, to catch a plane?"

"Yes of course. Why go to airport if no catch plane?"

"OK, so where was the plane going?"

"She no say. America maybe. Maybe somewhere else."

"Well if you don't know where she is how can I contact her?"

"You write solicitor."

"OK, so who is this solicitor?"

"She say I no tell who solicitor."

"How can I write to him if I don't know who he is?"

"You write her here. Post Office send to solicitor. Maybe he write back."

Brick wall and head bashing was the words that come to mind with her. It looked like Rachel Silver had done a bit of a runner. Did Freddy know and was he in on it?

I took Dany along with me as a looker. A looker don't say nothing. He just sits there and looks, without much of an expression on his face. It puts the other side off his stroke. He can never quite work out what the looker is there for.

We was escorted through security and up to Freddy's office by a flunkey in black jacket and striped trousers who looked at us like we was something the cat brought in. Freddy was his usual, all smiles and public school charm.

"Very good to see you again Spencer, and this is?" He held out his hand to Dany.

"Dany Bullimore my associate. He's been working with me on the Silver assignment."

"Very nice to meet you Dany. Now Spencer I know you're a Chivas Regal man. What would you like to drink Dany?"

Dany don't know any more about whisky than he knows about brain surgery. He thought for a few seconds and then pointed to one of the bottles on the sideboard.

"Ah, the Glenlivet. A single malt man I see. A very fine whisky of course but I think I might have something even more to your taste—a 17 year-old Balvenie. I guarantee you will not have tasted finer."

He poured out the drinks and we sat down. Dany and me was on one sofa and he was on the other, with a low table in between.

"Now gentlemen, I think we all know why we are here. Rachel, Mrs Silver, asked me to have a chat with you because she was afraid you might be under some misapprehension about recent, very sad events. I feel sure I can clear up any misunderstanding, so feel free to ask me any question you like."

I know we was a long way from Dogswell but my instinct is always to get in first and see what happens. Nothing ventured, as they say.

"You know she's left the country?"

"You're very well informed. Yes, she let me know this morning."

Let him know eh? Looked like he wasn't in on her decision. I thought I'd keep going.

"We know that you was having an affair with her."

Just for a second it looked like the mask would slip a bit, but he got it back on again quick.

"What makes you say that? Did she say so?"

"Not as such, but let's say I've got a nose for these things. I get a lot of it in my line of work."

He smiled at that. "I expect you do Spencer. Let's put it this way. If one is accused of having an affair with someone as beautiful and desirable as Rachel many might think it would be churlish to deny it."

I hadn't heard awayday shagging put quite like that before, but there you are. Different folks, different strokes.

"But you said having an affair with a workmate's wife was a no no last time we talked."

He smiled a bit more. "I said having an affair with a *client's* wife was a sackable offence because it could cause us embarrassment and cost us money. Among colleagues it would depend. In my case I exercise what used to be called *droit de seigneur*. I am the chairman of this Bank and so I can have an affair with any wife of a colleague who takes my fancy."

Wasn't he the lucky one. Nice work if you can get it.

"Don't the husbands kick up a fuss about it?"

"Some do, but they quickly think better of it. You need to remember Spencer the nature of banking. What we look for in a banker is a combination of first rate greed and second rate mind, although I don't think I flatter myself when I exempt myself from that requirement. The man at the top needs different qualities. To be fair I would have exempted Reuben Silver as well. He had a good mind and some honourable intentions, which is why he would never have lasted as a banker, good though he was. As for the others, where else would they go? They are paid far more than they deserve for what they do. They have their money and their houses and their expensive holidays – and usually their mistresses. What more could they want? A wife's affair is a small price to pay for all that."

"Is that so Freddy? I think there's more to it. I think you do it to keep them in order, show them who's boss. Toe the line or I shag the wife."

"*You* might say that Spencer."

"And you couldn't possibly comment I suppose. What about your wife? How does she take it?"

"Diana knows there is no such thing as a free lunch."

If she doesn't know now she'll know soon when she gets slapped round the face with the divorce papers.

"And the other wives just love it do they, when you make your move?"

He laughed at that. "I'm sure you're as aware as I am of the erotic charge of money and power. Most of our directors are on their second marriages with much younger women, trophy wives if you like, whose motives are, shall we say, not always of the purest. When someone who is even richer and more power-ful than their husband pays them attention, few of them care to resist."

"So Rachel Silver couldn't resist you?"

He looked away for a couple of seconds.

"Rachel was, is, different, as I think you know."

"Well yes. Her Dad ran this bank once and she has plenty of money of her own."

"That wasn't what I meant."

"You meant you was in love with her?"

"That wasn't what I meant either."

I'll say this for Freddy, he could keep up the front better that anyone I'd ever met, Time to push it a bit further. Give him a hint of what we knew.

"I think it was. I think you had plans for you and her only she had different plans. She'd had enough of Reuben and didn't mind a bit on the side with you but she wasn't looking for nothing permanent. So now she's gone off we don't know where and nobody knows when she's coming back."

He was beginning to get a bit rattled.

"I think this particular discussion has gone far enough Spencer. I understood that you were here to discuss other matters."

So we was and now he'd been put off his stroke a bit we could get on with it.

"Why was you spying on Reuben Silver?"

He shook his head like I'd said something completely our of order.

"We weren't spying on him. What on earth makes you think that?"

"You was bugging his computer."

I was taking a bit of a punt there, betting that neither Rachel or Jack Dapper had told him about the disk we nicked. I was pretty sure Jack hadn't said nothing. He would have been in trouble if he had and besides, he hated them. Wasn't so sure about her.

"That's complete nonsense. Rachel mentioned what you had told her and I discussed it with our head of IT. There was no 'spying' on Reuben as you claim."

"So you say, but Reuben had encrypted files on his computer that he hadn't told anyone about only you found out and put some spying software on his computer so that you could keep and eye on what he was up to. "

"This is fantasy Spencer. Wherever did you get that idea?"

"Believe me, it's not Freddy"

I think that shook him. For just a second or two he stared at me, saying nothing. Then that toff training kicked in. He wasn't easily put off his stroke.

"I'm told by our head of IT that our security is second to none. I'll mention what you said to him but I think I know what his response will be. Since you claim to be so knowledgeable, these secret files that you say Reuben had on his computer. Do you happen to know what they were about?"

"It was all that stuff we talked about before, stuff about King George the Fifth and Tsar Nicholas and a load of other characters from a hundred year ago."

I was expecting him to ask me how I knew but he didn't seem surprised. Instead he looked up and rolled his eyes.

"Ah, Reuben's obsession with conspiracies. I think he was secretly in love with the idea that someone or something is always out to get us. He and I discussed these things several times. Reuben's obsession—and it was an obsession—with the fate of the Tsar came from his family's history. Once your people really have been the victim of conspiracy and oppression then you tend to see all history in the same light. Reuben thought that the Tsar coming to England might have been another Sarajevo moment."

That stumped me. "A what?"

It's the idea that small actions can sometimes have huge consequences. A run of the mill assassination in an obscure Balkan town, Sarajevo, was the spark that ignited the First World War and smashed the old world order. Out went kings and emperors, in came revolution. I suppose the modern analogy is chaos theory. You have probably heard that expression of how a butterfly flapping its wings in Brazil could cause a hurricane in Texas."

"As a matter of fact I haven't, but what's butterflies got to do with the Tsar coming to England?"

"Reuben thought that the Tsar in England, away from the clutches of the Provisional Government, might have spurred a monarchist revival. Then no Russian Revolution, no Balfour Declaration, no Americans in the War. Who knows, the Germans might have won. That was Reuben's theory. Supposition upon supposition of course, as all counter-factuals are, but not entirely implausible. What think you Spencer?"

"If you say so. How would I know? But aren't you leaving something out?"

He gave me a bit of a look, like he was surprised.

"Am I? Good Lord. I thought there was quite enough in there already."

"I'm talking about what your bank was up to when all that was going on."

"What do you mean up to? We certainly weren't waging war in Flanders."

"No, I'm talking about the Russian money in your bank, the Amto account and this bloke Peter Bark."

Now he definitely was surprised. Even he couldn't hide it.

"You *are* well informed Spencer. I won't ask you how you came by it because I know you wouldn't tell me, but congratulations anyway. I may have underestimated you. So you know about the enigmatic Peter Bark—Sir Peter Bark as I think we should call him. After all few men deserve an honour more. I have to confess that I had never heard of him until Reuben told me about him. Reuben was fascinated by him. What an extraordinary career. Confidant of the Tsar, engaged at the highest level of financial discussions during the war, escapes from revolutionary Russia to start a new life here and becomes a confidant of the King and a stalwart of the Bank of England. What I wouldn't give to have a chat with him about his experiences."

"Well maybe if he does get in touch you could ask him about the Amto money."

He laughed and then shook his head.

"Ah, the Amto account. It was Reuben who discovered its existence. It would have been better for all of us if he hadn't. You know what Amto means of course. It's the initial letters of the Tsar's daughters—Anastasia, Maria, Tatiana and Olga. As I mentioned to you, Reuben told me some time ago that he was thinking of writing a book about what happened to the fortunes of all those royal dynasties that disappeared at the end of the First World War. Reuben was a diligent researcher. He told me once that he had had ambitions to become an academic and he kept me abreast of anything he found interesting in our archives, including the Amto account."

"What did you think when he told you about it?"

"Well, nothing much initially. It was just an old, dead account. We have thousands of those. I thought it would be an interesting titbit for his book, nothing more."

"So what made you change your mind?"

"It wasn't so much my mind that was changed as Reuben's. He descended into full conspiracy mode. According to him, the money in the account in 1917 was supposed to be used for one purpose but then was diverted elsewhere and a number of very prominent people were involved in its diversion. It all sounded perfectly preposterous to me. Reuben admitted that he did not have real proof of what he was alleging, but there was just enough in his allegations that I felt I needed to make a few discreet inquiries."

"What did you find out?"

"I can't tell you."

Freddy, Freddy, I was thinking to myself. You don't mind telling me what a world champion legover merchant you are, but you can't tell me about something that happened a hundred years ago.

"Why not?"

"Because, Spencer, of the shroud of secrecy that surrounds these matters in this country. It is a secrecy that has no limit in time. Something that happened a hundred years ago is just as much a secret as if it happened yesterday. In my opinion it's absurd, but there you are. I don't make the rules."

"So it's to do with royalty?"

"As I said, I can't tell you."

"OK, I'll take that as a yes. Why don't I tell you what we think happened—or are you not allowed to hear it neither?"

He had to smile at that. "Go ahead. I'm all ears."

"OK, so by 1917 things was looking bad in Russia. They was losing the war, the people didn't have nothing to eat and there was riots in the streets. Peter Bark, who was in charge of all Russia's money, thought that Nicky the Tsar might be for the chop and so he pushed a tidy sum, probably from a secret fund that they had, into the Amto account in your bank. It would be there waiting for Nicky if things got too hot and he and his family had to do a runner from Russia. He did get the chop and King George, who was Nicky's cousin and his wife Alicky's cousin as well, wanted all the family to be together and invited them here. The Government said yes and they was all set to come. Now here is where it gets very iffy. George suddenly changed his mind. He didn't want Nicky to come at any price and nobody really knew why—not then or now.

"We think Reuben worked out why George changed his mind. It was down to Lloyd George who was prime minister at the time. He had a lot on his plate. He had a war to run that wasn't going too well and he was looking round for a bit of help. He had this idea that the Jews ran most of the world and they was very big in Russia and America, so he thought giving them Palestine would bring them onside. He was trying to rope the Yanks in as well, with a bit of Jewish help. He also had some shady deal with Boris—not Karloff, the other one. Boris wanted the Greeks to have Constantinople after the war and Lloyd George said he would fix it, but the British Government had already told Nicky that the Russians could have it."

Freddy was almost laughing.

"This is complete tosh, Spencer, and a touch anti-semitic. Are you are going to throw *The Protocols of the Elders of Zion* in as well?"

"The what Freddy?"

He shrugged.

"Never mind, carry on."

"Lloyd George thought Nicky coming to England could have put the kibosh on a whole lot of things, especially if Nicky started spouting on about Constantinople and how he wasn't too keen on the Jews—bit like that Sarajevo moment you was talking about. So Lloyd George, who saw King George every week, had to put him straight. Some think that he told him that the workers wouldn't like it and maybe they would revolt like in Russia and string him up. Wouldn't have happened but George wasn't exactly the brightest button in the box so he might have bought it. But we think there was other reasons too

"Really, and what might they be?"

"Well, for a start, have you ever heard of Anthony Blunt?"

"Do you mean the notorious, no longer Sir, Anthony Blunt, the spy in the Queen's household?"

"That's the one. We reckon that Lloyd George might have found out that he was the sprog of King George by way of the wife of a vicar."

He didn't know what to say to that. He looked at me as if I'd gone fucking mad.

"Spencer, Spencer, what have you been taking? Whatever gave you that idea?"

"I can't tell you where it come from Freddy, but we've looked into it and we reckon there could be something to it. The other reason why we think he changed his mind is what happened to the money sitting in your Amto account. The first question you have to ask yourself is who knew about it? Apart from your lot, the one who must have known was George. He would have told Lloyd George who would have sniffed an opportunity. He would have pointed out to George that the money was doing no good sitting in the Bank. Better get it out and do something useful with it. And Lloyd George, being a wily old bird, would be thinking to himself that he could always remind George of their little secret when he wanted to make a lord of some dodgy character who had just given him a big bung, which was quite often, so they say.

"Now the other person who knew about the account of course was Bark. He seemed to disappear after the Commies got in in Russia and they must have thought they'd heard the last of him, but a couple of years later he pops up in London: 'Here I am boys. What can you do for me?' George must have wet himself, so he had to keep Bark sweet. Nothing was too good for 'Sir Peter' and the Bank of England was roped in to give him a job. To give him his due, Bark kept his part of the bargain and kept his mouth shut. Maybe he was an honest man. That would've made a change. So what think you about that, Freddy?"

Freddy smiled again. "Most ingenious Spencer—an elephant of speculation balancing on a pinhead of fact. It makes Reuben's theory look like an exercise in Einsteinian rigour. As conspiracy theories go, it is one of the more amusing ones I've heard, but you can't expect me to take it seriously."

"You bankers should know all about conspiracies. Look at the way you stitched up the public—trousered squillions for doing fuck all and then left all the shit for us to clear up."

Nothing shook Freddy in his suaveness. He just nodded and smiled sweetly.

"We are just a small private bank Spencer, so I don't think we can really be held responsible for the great crash, but I take your general point."

"You don't say. The banks shafted the country."

"The banks behaved appallingly and have not suffered as a result. That was no accident. Have you heard the parable of the frog and the scorpion?"

"Don't think I have Freddy. What are you talking about now?"

"One day a scorpion asked a frog to carry him on his back across a river. The frog refused because he thought the scorpion might sting him. 'Why would I do that?' said the scorpion. 'If I did we would both die.' So the frog agreed but half way across the scorpion did sting him. 'Why?' asked the dying frog. 'It's in my nature.' said the scorpion. 'It's what I do.' Banks act recklessly in the pursuit of riches and cause financial crises. It's in their nature. The only difference with the scorpion is that they require the rest of society to provide them with a life raft so that they can continue in their habits. It's what banks do. They would be fools to do otherwise."

"Whatever you say Freddy. I'm sure you've got everything sorted. Your lot always have. But what I really want to know is who killed Reuben Silver? This business is giving me a lot of grief. Thacker will pin it on me if he can't get anyone else so I have got to give him someone else and I was hoping you might help me out."

He gave me a look that I might have thought was sympathetic, if I didn't know better.

"Ah yes, guilt and innocence. I treat those two impostors just the same Spencer."

"What's that supposed to mean? Someone pulled the trigger. Let's get down to brass tacks Freddy. Someone shot Silver. That we know for certain. Thacker's suspect number one is Steve Curting. Thacker fingered him for it only he had to let him go. Did he do it? We don't think so. He wouldn't have the nerve nor the nous to do it proper. But he could have had something to do with it."

"So for once you agree with Superintendent Thacker?"

"He ain't always wrong. The ENF found out that Reuben had bunged a few grand to *Spotlight* so Curting was told to put the frightners on him. We know that for certain because Curting admitted it, thanks to a doggie friend of ours."

"And how did the ENF find out about Reuben's donation?"

"Now that is a bit of a mystery. According to Curting, and we think for once he might not be lying, it come in the post."

"Interesting. So who do you think sent this mysterious missive?"

"The way we see it there's three suspects. Number one is the spooks, the security services, who seem to get to know all sorts of things, fuck knows how. I do hear as well that they pull the strings of the ENF. Number two is Rachel Silver and number three is your lot at the Bank."

He had to laugh at that. Surprised innocence is one of Freddy's expressions. He probably has a lot more.

"Even for your soaring imagination Spencer that is a leap too far. Who on earth in the Bank would want to endanger one of our most senior people and what could possibly be their motive? "

"Who? You for a start. In my book there's only two reasons why people do things they wouldn't normally do—sex and money. When I'm asked to look for someone who don't want to be found, one of them is usually the reason. I reckon the same would be true of murder. So I ask myself where's the sex or money in it for the ENF to have done it? Can't see it. I believe Curting. They just wanted to frighten him. Besides they wouldn't be up to shooting a top banker. Too risky. What about the spooks? Not their style. They're supposed to be above that sort of thing. I'm told they prefer a quiet word or maybe a fake sex suicide. As for Rachel, she's got more money than she'll ever need and could have sex with anyone she wants. So that just leaves you Freddy—and in your case it's the double whammy, sex and money."

That seemed to cause him even more amusement.

"Really? What exactly do you mean by double whammy?"

"Reuben was going a bit rogue. He was threatening to talk about those things that you say you can't talk about. Wouldn't have gone down well with whoever it is that you can't talk about or all your posh customers. Could have been very embarrassing. On top of that, you was having an affair with his wife."

"Whatever there may be between Rachel and me is irrelevant. As for it being embarrassing for the Bank, I don't see a problem. Our clients value our services and they are unlikely to get as good elsewhere."

He was flannelling. He knew it and I knew it.

"Don't give me that Freddy. Murdered banker, beautiful wife and head of bank in love triangle, royal dirty tricks, tsarist gold—the tabloids would be all over it. You wouldn't be able to get off the front pages. You would have to give yourself a P45 and your posh customers would be getting out in droves. And what about your darling Rachel? She's told me a few fibs and she hasn't exactly been straight with you—leading you up the garden path and then running out on you when you was all set on making her yours."

For a moment I thought I'd got to him with that one.

"More nonsense Spencer."

Now was the time to rub it in.

"She's left you right in it Freddy. She realised that what her husband was up to was going to do her Daddy's bank no good. She was Daddy's girl and she wasn't having it, but he realised that she was suspicious and started hiding things from her. She needed to know exactly what he was doing at the bank and the way to find out is to have a fling with the top man."

I could see from his eyes he was beginning to get a bit rattled so I decided to push it further.

"At the start you was both in it together. She knew you was besotted with her. What she really wanted was the pillow talk. You could tell her how you was keeping an eye on what Reuben was up to and she would keep you dangling by letting you think she was going to give him his cards. You told her about the encrypted files on his computer. She tipped off the spooks and they gave you that bit of software. What they didn't tell you is that software doesn't just tell your lot what's going on it tells them too. They pulled a fast one. Our tech guy reckons it will be over all your system by now and all your little secrets, those little dodges and wheezes that you use to let rich people keep even more of their money than they're supposed to, will be winging their way to you know who. They've now got you and your bank by the curlies."

He stared at me. He didn't know enough to deny it and I could see that he was more than half convinced that it was true so I kept going.

"But then Reuben realised that he was being watched and he found out about you and her. That's when things got very messy. At first he just stuck two fingers up and put puzzles on his computer for you to work out. Then for some reason he got scared and done a runner. And that's when you realised that things might get awkward and you had better do something about it."

I could see from his face that he couldn't be sure what I knew and how I could know it.

"You're letting your imagination run away with you Spencer, piling fantasy on absurdity. How exactly do you think I managed to perform this deed? Let me remind you that on the night in question I was at a banquet in the Guildhall attended by more than two hundred very distinguished guests, including the Chancellor of the Exchequer."

You had to admire the style. I wish I could come up with an alibi like that sometimes.

"Of course you were Freddy. Your lot don't do alibis by half, do they? But you know the right sort of people--your old army chums. You would just have to tell them what was going on— Reuben mouthing all sorts of wild accusations, embarrassing the Royal Family, getting up the noses of the great and the good and causing you and your bank all sorts of grief. They wouldn't stand for that in the Regiment, would they? The chap was clearly what you lot call a bounder and he was Jewish as well. That wouldn't have done him no good neither. What did you say about them? 'Finest body of men in the land. Devoted to the honour of the Regiment and to Queen and Country.' And then there was that bit about having to get your hands dirty for the greater good. 'Leave it to us Freddy old boy.' they would say to you, 'We know what to do.' "

He looked at me for several seconds and then started smiling again.

"I'm lost in admiration for your powers of imagination Spencer. You really are wasting your talent. You should be writing fiction, crime novels. I think you would be a best seller."

I was getting a bit tired of him always trying to piss on me from a great height.

"It's what a bloke from the *Spotlight* magazine told us, your lot are part of the Deep State. You think you own this country and the rest of us can go fuck ourselves if we disagree. But you can't duck and dive forever Freddy. The fingers are pointing at you. Who else had the motive, the money and the means? I'm no Sherlock Holmes so if I can figure it out others will do the same. Rachel definitely did. Why do you think she skipped the country? She wanted Reuben out of the way but she didn't want him dead. You went too far and she didn't want to be around when any shit hit the fan. And knowing her there'll be another man – or two – in the picture. Her sort always like to have an insurance policy."

I always like to get a low blow in. Fair fights are for dummies. Still, he might have been a bit groggy but he definitely wasn't out. The old public school training was still keeping him up but it was beginning to crack.

"I take strong exception to your remarks about Rachel Spencer and I really do not want to hear any more from you about her. As for your self appointed role as Grand Inquisitor, no one else will take the slightest bit of notice."

I had a feeling he might be right but I thought I'd push it anyway.

"I wouldn't bet on it Freddy. Thacker for one don't give up easy."

"Ah yes, the estimable Superintendent Thacker, that dogged pursuer of the local miscreants. I understood he was convinced that he had his man but didn't have enough evidence."

The Curting business had been bugging us but now it all made sense.

"I have to hand it to you Freddy, the stroke you pulled with Curting was very smart. You tipped the ENF off about Reubens's bung to *Spotlight* and reckoned that they would do something about it. I bet they found out where he was staying as well. That would have put them in the frame when Reuben got shot, but on the other hand putting Curting in the dock would have been very risky. No knowing what might come out. You wouldn't want Rachel and you, the Bank and whoever splashed all over the tabloids. So a smart brief, which he couldn't never have afforded, and probably a few words in the right ears, and hey presto our Mr Curting is free as a bird. Of course the mud would stick to Curting a bit. Everyone will think it was just a common or garden robbery that went wrong. Nothing worth talking about. Forgotten in a week. Sweet."

He shook his head and let out a sound half way between a sniff and a snort..

"Come now Spencer, what do you expect me to say? 'It's a fair cop? Bring out the handcuffs?' Hardly. Even if all you said was true do not imagine that anyone is going to believe you. You have no evidence and even if you did there are some things in this state that cannot be challenged – that cannot be allowed to be challenged. Besides, truth is not a commodity much in demand these days. Haven't you heard that we live in a post-truth world. Veracity is for losers, so they say. Everyone believes what they want to believe, what chimes with their prejudices, and I'm afraid the prejudices of those who handle these things rather trump yours."

That was probably true but on the other hand he's stopped denying everything.

"I'll take that as an admission Freddy."

"Take it as you like Spencer, but there is one other we could add to the list of suspects. You were looking for Reuben and you knew Curting. The police have already hinted to me that they thought you might have been involved in what they called a 'shake down' by threatening to expose Reuben if he did not pay you. Violence is not exactly unknown in your neck of the woods. For some I believe it is the preferred method of negotiation."

I thought something like that might be coming.

"I don't think so Freddy. You don't want me in the dock. I'd be like Curting on steroids. It would all come out. And don't go giving your army mates any ideas about giving me the same treatment as Reuben. We've made sure that if anything happened to me everyone would know why."

"That sounds suspiciously like blackmail to me Spencer."

"No, not at all. Believe it or not Freddy, I don't do that sort of thing. Too much of a hassle. I don't want nothing to do with the law. It's just a lottery. You say you treat guilt and innocence just the same. I say they're just a matter of luck and I've got better things to do than risk it. So let's leave it at that. Call it a score draw."

He half-smiled and nodded.

"An interesting point of view Spencer. Perhaps I could add just one more. Maybe, just maybe, it was Reuben who summoned up his own demons. A sense of foreboding, so Jewish, never quite left him. He could never really believe that any good fortune would last. Somewhere in his darkest imaginings he thought that someone or something would rob him of it. His curiosity turned to obsession and obsession is akin to madness. And in that madness he imagined that he awoke things that had long been dormant. The ghosts of George and Nicholas, of

Lloyd George and Zaharoff, of Bark and Balfour and all the others came to haunt him. It seems that those ghosts had a long reach."

There he went again.

"That'll stand up in court, won't it Freddy."

He shrugged,

"Good luck with unmasking the culprit Spencer."

We walked out of the Bank and down the steps outside. It was a nice day. The sun was shining and we didn't say nothing for a little while. Then Dany, who had had to keep his mouth shut the whole time, finally spoke up.

"What was all that about Spence?"

"Fucked if I know Dany. Fucked if I know."